FROZEN FLAMES

A REKINDLED HOCKEY ROMANCE

ELITE EAGLES SERIES
BOOK 1

VH NICOLSON

·VH NICOLSON·

Published by: Kristina Fair Publishing Ltd

Editing by Sarah Baker, The Word Emporium.

Cover image: © Photographer: Wander Aguiar. Model: Matteo.

For my family

AUTHOR'S NOTES

Please note this book comes with a content warning. This book is intended for over 18s.

My books all come with the guarantee of a happily ever after but sometimes the journey to get there can be a hard fought one. The main focus of my books is love, romance and happiness.

Also, there is lots of humor too. Please keep that in mind.

However, just in case you aren't sure, and if you are a sensitive reader then please proceed with caution, here's a content warning list.

Triggers: Infertility, sudden death of a parent, loss, marriage separation, marriage in crisis, reference to divorce, attempted extortion, mental trauma from not being able to conceive.

For Content Warnings & Tropes of All My Books, Please Scan the QR Code at the Top of The Author's Note Page.

Happy reading... let's go...

PROLOGUE

Lily – Present Day

Dragging my pointer finger up the brushed steel handrail of the staircase, I pull it away and rub my fingertips together, letting out an amused chuckle as it confirms what I already know; our home is immaculate.

There isn't a speck of dust to be seen, nor a piece of furniture out of place in the fixer-upper house Ash and I renovated ten years ago and is now the place we call home.

Although it doesn't feel like home.

During hockey season, Ash is rarely ever home for longer than a few days at a time, so for seven months of the year I spend a lot of time by myself.

Alone.

Having a demanding job as head coach of the Edmonton Eagles, Ash spends a lot of his time at work, talking about work or locked in his office at work and at home watching game tapes, reviewing player technique and positioning. Slowing down videos, analyzing every minute detail, his dedication to the game is what makes him one of the best coaches in the NHL.

Coaching the team he loves has become more than a full-time job, though; much like mine, his job consumes him. While Ash throws himself into the hockey team, I've directed all my energy into growing my business, Tiger Lily Events.

The hard work has paid off and my business has grown exponentially, employing over fifty people who support me to manage, market, plan, and execute creative and memorable events. I love nothing better than watching a vision come to life. We go above and beyond to create unique experiences for our customers at Tiger Lily and I can't imagine myself doing anything else. However, the happiness my job brings me isn't enough to fill the huge Ash-shaped hole in my life.

Reaching the top of the glass stairs, I'm acutely aware of how much colder my feet have become. It's as if the cool glass against my soles is preparing me for getting into an equally cold bed. By myself.

Ash's flight should have already landed and I'm expecting him home soon, although he hasn't called yet.

One foot in front of the other, my feet slap gently against the white marble hallway tiles that look like smooth cake fondant. Giant patches of moonlight fall through the skylight windows, making the night shadows dance across the floor.

I stop for a moment and peer over the top of the glass balcony to admire my palatial surroundings. I can't deny how beautiful our house is. Long gone are the days I spent living in my cramped one-bedroom apartment, working two jobs where I used to walk or use the light rail transit to travel, because I couldn't afford a car.

Between us, Ash and I now have six cars, a housekeeper, people to mow the lawn, and a pool boy. I even have someone who color coordinates our closets, making it easier for us to pull outfits together, and get meal plans and fresh food delivered weekly to ensure we eat healthy.

I scoff at how ridiculous my life has become.

Knowing I've frozen more meals for Ash than he's eaten of late, confusion causes my brow to dip as I try to recall the last time we sat down to eat an evening meal together. Struggling to remember, I come up short.

I'm sure my girlfriends don't have time to think about how many days and nights their hockey husbands spend away from home, or ever get lonely because they all have families. Ash and I are the only couple who never had children. Because, despite how hard we tried or how much help we had, we couldn't.

Having a family was something we always dreamed about when we were younger, yet we no longer even bring it up anymore.

I would have loved to have a child. Just one happy, bouncing baby. A part of me and a part of Ash. That's all I ever wanted.

I still do.

A little more happiness dies inside of me because it's something I have been giving a lot of thought to lately. At thirty-eight, I'm certain my ovaries have already given up their dream of fulfilling their purpose; to create life.

I know I have.

After years of trying to conceive naturally and three failed rounds of IVF, we called it a day, promising to revisit it again when things were less stressful. As time passed, Ash moved from playing hockey to coaching and the pain of all those failed attempts meant it was something we discussed less and less. The truth is, it was rough on my body; the injections, hormones, the disappointment of seeing the single line on the pregnancy test every month—they were all emotionally taxing, and I felt completely isolated from my friends, who all conceived with ease.

With no one to speak to, or who understood the sadness and loss I felt of a future I always dreamed about, I struggled with episodes of fear and anxiety. Instead of talking to a therapist, I chose to throw myself into my career, as did Ash. We turned away from each other and did everything we could to hide our pain.

A lump the size of a melon forms in my throat and lingers for a minute too long, knowing that it may be too late to consider raising a family of our own. Ignoring my anguish, I move in the direction of the master bedroom and I can't help but reflect on how different things used to be.

When we first started dating, and in the first few years of our marriage, Ash and I were inseparable, sharing everything. We never wanted to be separated but when we were, the love, understanding, loyalty, and respect we had for one another was deeper than the ocean because we both allowed one another to chase our own goals, never sacrificing each other's dreams of becoming successful.

After retiring from playing professional hockey, Ash became the assistant coach for the Eagles four years ago. One year later, he was promoted to head coach. We were both so excited about his new position, but we knew coaching would mean even more time and effort than playing had involved. Conversations about starting a family fell to the wayside, replaced with everything that came from being head coach. Even though we both knew what to expect, it was a lot and his workload has only grown with the team's success... with his success as a coach.

I'm annoyed at myself for allowing things to change so drastically between us; no longer living, but existing.

All I seem to do is work. All Ash appears to do is work harder than when he was a player. It's not just training and time on the ice; team selection, training plans, video analysis, media interviews; the list goes on and on. And don't get me started on how many calls he receives from the players daily. Some days, I swear he's more like their father than their coach.

The thought brings a bitter taste to my mouth because he has a family... his team. While I am here, on my own.

We are both so busy being, well, busy.

Our lives are passing us by, and I can't help but feel that if we don't start making changes now, we may be making the biggest mistakes of our lives.

The only upside is that we both love what we do. We have so much passion and drive to be successful. However, living separate lives, we no longer seem to get much downtime to enjoy and celebrate our achievements together.

While he's out there coaching the team he loves, I'm working late to avoid coming home to an empty house.

My schedule has become incredibly predictable.

If I'm not visiting venues, organizing destination weddings, extravagant birthday parties, or yet another gender reveal party, which I find hugely painful and fake smile through every single one, I'm eating lunch at my desk on my lonesome, while counting down the days for Ash to return home from yet another away game.

Since winning the Stanley Cup three times in a row, which is incredible and one of Ash's proudest moments in his career, his schedule has become even more demanding.

Between flying to and from hockey games, making media appearances for the team at charity sport tournaments, and visits to the hospice for sick children, he never stops. Most recently, he was asked to coach a bunch of kids from the local group home who were desperate to start a team but didn't have the funds or expertise to do so.

Of course, Ash being Ash and with that big, kind heart of his, immediately said yes, giving up any spare time to help them form a team, raise money for their uniforms, and mentor them in the best way Ash knows how; with kindness, dedication, and drive.

I feel guilty because while I know he's supporting the future generation of hockey players, I miss him.

When he played when we first married, I traveled to some of his games, but when my business took off, I stopped flying to whatever city he was playing in, unable to drop everything for a few days just for him.

Thinking back on it, I was trying to fill my time to avoid facing the reality of being unable to conceive. If I could turn back time, I would give younger me a good shake. She built up walls and hid her emotions and now I'm here, dealing with the repercussions.

Every day, I'm repeating the same behavior, because while I'm busy at work, I don't have to think about how empty my life has become.

I'm not sure how much longer we can go on living like this; together, yet so far apart.

And my friends, they all appear to be happy.

But me?

The only time I feel happy is when I know Ash is on his way home. I still get that butterfly feeling in anticipation of seeing him again.

I love him with every bone in my body, and I know he loves me too.

Without a shadow of a doubt, I know this, because he tells me every day via voice messages or texts. He calls me in between meetings and interviews and right after every game. If I tell him I saw a cute purse in the mall, he'll call the store and have it delivered to me. If I complain about neck or back tension, he'll book me a massage. If my car is making a noise, he'll have someone from the garage on the driveway within half an hour to inspect it.

My husband is incredibly kind, caring, and the most loyal man I know.

He's the perfect man.

If only he was around more.

The enormity of my circumstances blindsides me, a pain squeezing my heart with a huge feeling of emptiness.

Not sure how I manage to put one foot in front of the other, and with a heart so heavy it sometimes feels I'm pushing a boulder up a hill, I step into our bedroom. The thick woolen carpet pushes between my toes in the room that's meant for a husband and wife.

My text alert from my phone breaks the stifling silence. Smiling, my heart fills with excitement knowing it will be Ash telling me he's landed in Edmonton from Calgary and should be home soon following their afternoon Battle of Alberta game against the Blazers. Rushing over to my nightstand, I lift my phone I left on charge earlier, only to be met with a tidal wave of disappointment.

Like a dead weight, I drop my ass onto the edge of the bed. That sinking feeling in my stomach I always get when his plans change, anchoring me down, as if pulling me under and dragging me further away from him.

ASH:

Our flight's delayed. x

Again?

ME:

Okay. What time will you be home? xoxo

ASH:

They think we are getting a take-off slot at nine thirty, which means I will be home around eleven thirty depending on baggage claim and bus drop off. My car is at the arena. I'm so sorry, baby :(

I check the time on my phone screen; nine o'clock.

ME:

Okay. I'm going to bed as I have an early start tomorrow. xoxo

ASH:

Wish I was there. x

Looking up from my phone, I catch a glimpse of myself in the mirror, and a mixture of pain that he's not back when I hoped he would be and embarrassment for dressing sexy for him tonight when he's not touched me in weeks, stare back at me.

I rise to my feet and untie my white silk dressing gown, revealing the new coconut white lace bodysuit I bought this afternoon. I thought maybe, tonight, well, maybe, we could break our dry spell we've been going through. It's been weeks since we have had sex; something we used to do a lot of. Before I change my mind, I turn and snap a quick photo to send to him. It shows off the beautiful lace detailing on the back and string thong bottoms.

ME:

This could have been all yours tonight. ;)

I hit send, then instantly regret it.

Biting my bottom lip anxiously, I zoom in on the photo around my thigh area and feel humiliation wash over me. "Shit. I look terrible," I hiss to myself, examining my saggy thighs and untoned stomach.

Unable to help myself, I check out my figure in the mirror.

I cup my no longer perky boobs, pushing them up to where they used to sit. "I need a boob lift," I mutter to myself.

My boobs look more like strangers than friends these days. I swear my cleavage is bigger than it used to be, and when I lie on my back, the girls face east and west as if they've argued with one another.

I smooth my hand down over my pooch belly and turn to the side to see how far it sticks out. Pinching more than an inch or two, I pucker my lips in annoyance, making a promise to myself to hit our home gym tomorrow.

Although remembering I have a slammed schedule for the next four weeks, I know I will break that promise in an instant.

It's no wonder Ash hasn't touched me in months. I begin doubting if it's our busy schedules that are preventing us from having sex or that he maybe just doesn't find me all that attractive anymore.

I make the decision to delete the photo I sent him, to be met with a read notification on our text conversation, informing me that Ash has already opened it.

"Shoot," I push out through my clenched jaw.

I jump in shock when the ringer of my phone sounds, but instantly smile when I see Ash's name.

I fall onto the bed and accept the call, pulling my silk rope around me to keep me warm. "Hey, you," I say nervously, my voice shaky, still slightly embarrassed about sending him the photo.

"Baby." His voice is low as he groans down the phone. "You look fucking beautiful."

"I have cellulite on my thighs."

"No, you don't."

"And I look tired. I have saddlebags under my eyes." And wrinkles.

"Nice as they are, I wasn't looking at your eyes. I was checking out that fine ass of yours. And you still look the same as the day we met." He pauses. "Hang on." His voice becomes muffled and scratchy shuffles are all I can hear down the speaker, as if he's moving somewhere to have our conversation in private.

"You there, baby?" His voice is clearer.

"Always here, Ash." I spend my life waiting for you.

"Your ass is fucking spankable."

Nervous laughter bubbles in my chest like a cauldron as I run the end of the silk cord through my fingers. I rarely sext Ash, but maybe it's something I should do more often.

"I might like it if you were to spank me." My words come out breathy and low, as heat pools between my thighs. "But it's been so long since we had sex."

Ash exhales a loud sigh that sounds heavy with disappointment. "Too long, baby. Far too long."

"We never see each other anymore, Ash. I miss you." I find myself longing for change. Something's got to give.

"I miss you too. This job is taking up more of my time

than I ever thought it would." He lets out a frustrated groan. "My life has become crazy since we won the cup for the third time, and since I won coach of the year. The press is never off my back."

Winning the Stanley Cup three times in a row hasn't been achieved since the nineteen eighties. The media have been fascinated with the Eagles record breaking success. They believe it's all down to Ash's extraordinary coaching skills and everyone wants a slice of him, trying to discover what makes Ash's techniques with his team so magic.

"It's okay," I lie. "We're both busier now than we've ever been." We're both at fault.

Frustration evident in his voice, he protests, "It's not okay. I miss you so fucking much. When was the last time we sat and had dinner together?" Asking me what I was wondering earlier gives me hope that he knows our schedules are dictating our lives.

"Maybe we should start being more conscious about what we accept invitations for." Being busy is a choice. "We should be choosing each other rather than work and book a vacation." It's become a terrible habit, and we haven't had a vacation in three years

Silence stretches between us and then he finally says, "You know I love you, right? More than ever, I love you." Sadness is heavy in his tone.

My eyes cloud with tears, and I clamp my lips together to conceal a sob because it's what I want to hear.

"Lily, please tell me you know I love you," he pleads, and when I take another minute to compose myself, he asks again. "Lily, please?"

"I do." I don't know why I'm so upset. "I love you, too." I've loved him since the day I met him. Sixteen years ago, when I was just twenty-two, I knew he was the one.

"We'll book a vacation as soon as I'm back. I'll make not being around tonight up to you. I promise," he assures me.

"Can't wait." I can't help the doubt slip into my thoughts. We've been making the same promise to each other for years and we still haven't booked a vacation.

He changes the mood of our call in an instant, his tone turning raw and sensual. "I want you to suck my cock while you wear that sexy lingerie."

I moan. "I'd like that." It turns me on, turning him on. I find it empowering, knowing I am the one in control.

"Good girl. Now take that bodysuit off and save it for me for tomorrow night. And save yourself for me too, do you hear me?" Ash loves nothing better than keeping me on edge, teasing me, insisting my orgasms are meant for him and him only. He gets off on my pleasure. "Shit," he curses. "I just remembered I said yes to us having dinner with Bree and Troy tomorrow night. The whole gang has been invited."

Like a bucket of iced water is tipped over my head, I'm brought back to reality.

We're a mess; we've become yes people.

Their dinner parties go on for hours and I know we'll roll into bed in the wee small hours of the morning, having consumed far too much wine and be too tired to be capable of having sex.

"There will be other nights," I say with disappointment and a feeling of emptiness as I pinch the bridge of my nose.

"We can cancel," he offers, sounding unsure if we should take a rain check.

I throw my legs over the side of the bed and jump up to my feet. "It's fine," I reply, tapping the speakerphone icon, allowing me to lay my phone on the bed while I slip off my robe and lingerie. "Like I said, there will be other nights." I try to sound cheerful to cover my disappointment.

"I'm the luckiest man in the world."

When I try to speak, I can't bring myself to joke back and tell him I'm the luckiest girl in the world because I don't feel like I am. I'm the loneliest.

But it wasn't always like this...

PART 1

THE PAST

Where it all began...

CHAPTER ONE

Lily – Age 22

I wiggle in my uncomfortable wooden seat and open a new document on my laptop.

"Welcome to this year's Archaeology Conference." The man standing on the stage, who I assume is the speaker for the day, scans his beady eyes around the tiered, enormous auditorium. He continues to talk and I think I hear him introduce himself, but I don't really catch the rest of what he says as I zone out.

A cold sweat flashes across my already hot, flustered skin as I scramble around in my wine-colored leather tote bag in search of my email confirming my course enrollment.

Finally, finding it jammed between my cosmetics bag and my notebook, I pull it out, ripping it in half unintentionally. "Could today get any worse?" I mutter under my breath.

Piecing the two halves together like a jigsaw puzzle, I try to work out where I *should* be. It's not an Archaeology Conference, that's for sure.

Skim reading the words in the email, I realize I should

be in lecture hall 8 *not* 3, which I am currently sitting in. *Shoot.*

Folding the two separate pieces carefully in half, desperately trying not to disturb the guy sitting next to me, I shut the lid of my laptop quietly and shove it inside my bag. Slipping it up over my shoulder, hoping not to be seen, I keep my head down as I slide out of the end seat to make my escape and tiptoe to the exit closest to me.

The man on stage's voice sounds louder than before when he barks, "Oh, I'm sorry, was it something I said, Ms.?" Only two steps away from the exit, I stop in my tracks and turn to face him. Knowing the entire auditorium is staring at me, I feel my face turn the same color as my leather bag.

"Murphy. Lily Murphy, sir," I almost whisper, forcing myself to keep my eyes trained on him for fear of seeing just how many people now know my name.

This is not exactly how I pictured my first event as a representative from High Octane Events going. Instead of arriving in a calm and organized manner at the Making Team Building Fun event I am supposed to be attending today, observing, and learning as much as I can because I will eventually be hosting these workshops myself, I'm a sweaty, discombobulated, mess who is badly in need of a refreshing shower. A shower I didn't have time for this morning.

I worked later than usual last night at the second job I work in the evenings to make ends meet. Dead beat, fully clothed, I fell asleep on top of my bed and I forgot to set my alarm, meaning I had to skip having a shower this morning, throw on some clothes, and then call a cab. Rush hour traffic was terrible, making me even later, which led to my current situation.

At this point, humiliated and standing in the wrong conference hall, I'm thinking it was a wrong decision to change my life plan.

I had no plans to return home to Canada or move to Edmonton.

But when my mom died, I turned down the once in a lifetime position as events assistant with Ivy Events in New York. It was a bittersweet pill to swallow. But my family needs me.

That's why I am here. To be closer to them, specifically my dad.

Having lost my mom only eight weeks ago, me, my sister, and Dad all need each other right now. Living thousands of miles away, where it would take a nine-hour flight to get home, didn't feel right, and moving to Edmonton made sense. Even if it wasn't what I wanted, it was necessary.

Fresh out of Columbia University in New York, of course, my dad wanted me to continue my role of Events Assistant with Kristina Harris, the most highly respected events planner in Manhattan, but once he realized I had already handed in my resignation and made my decision to return to Canada, he backed down.

Knowing how much I had always wanted to study and work in New York, he admitted he felt bad, but hey, I secured a great job in Edmonton, and it's a pretty cool role. It may not be as exciting as planning weddings for New York's elite, but the people are nice, my team is great fun, and everyone is super knowledgeable. I'm also adding another skill to my resume by working in corporate events. Something I've never done before.

Moving back has stirred up so many emotions. Mainly guilt. For not returning home more often. For not inviting my mom to come visit me to watch the infamous Christmas parade, and for not taking that girls' trip to Hawaii we always talked about.

I have so many regrets, but I made a promise to myself I wouldn't make the same mistakes with my dad.

Returning to Canada feels right. Now that I am here, I am reminded of how beautiful and cosmopolitan the city is. With different music, food, and cultural festivals taking place every month, and the vast landscapes and wildlife. I never thought I would hear myself say this, but I kind of missed it and it feels nice being home.

The view from the hill I climbed yesterday reinforced how incredibly breathtaking the wild landscape is. I'm certain on a clear day I will be able to see my tiny hometown of Spruce Plain only fifty kilometers away. The view is everything.

Standing at the lectern, the gentleman on stage asks me, "Well, Lily Murphy, is there a fire?"

Warmth grows hotter in my cheeks and neck. "I'm in the wrong auditorium," I tell him as I side eye the room quickly, then regret it. There must be at least three hundred people looking at me. *Wow, this is a really big hall.*

And who knew there were that many archeologists in Canada?

The cream wool scarf I'm wearing feels uncomfortably scratchy, and hot. Boiling in fact. It's similar to one that my mom always wore in winter when I was a little girl and although it's not the same, it still makes me feel closer to her. I give it a quick rub to bring me some much-needed comfort.

"So where should you be exactly, Ms. Murphy?" The host pushes his thin gold-rimmed spectacles up his nose, making me feel like I'm back in fourth grade.

"Making Team Building Fun. Hall eight," I inform him.

His eyebrows rise in amusement. "Wrong room and wrong floor. Maybe you should consider a visit to the optometrist, Ms. Murphy," he replies sarcastically, making everyone chuckle.

Great, just great.

"Noted." I nod in agreement, not wanting to annoy him any further. "I'm sorry I disrupted the seminar." My voice is soft and polite as I back away and head in the direction of the door.

He resumes his introduction to the day in his monotone delivery.

Phew, thank goodness I'm not an archeologist. His droning voice might cause me to become extinct; he'd bore me to death.

In haste, I turn the brass handle and then fling the door open, desperate to get out of there. It takes me by surprise when it hits something solid, like a wall of bricks.

A loud *humf* followed by a muffled *motherfucker* instantly sends me into panic mode. *Oh shit, I must have hit someone.*

I step out into the corridor and slam the door closed behind me, to reveal a bent at the waist figure who is clutching their face with their hand.

It's a guy. And he's huge, which means he's probably security, or a bouncer, or plays football or something equally as bodybuilder like and I just smashed his nose to pieces.

Oh no.

CHAPTER TWO

Lily

I gasp in horror and rush to him. "Oh, my goodness. I'm so sorry. Are you okay?" I reach out to touch his shoulder; his big broad shoulder. This guy is massive. "I was in the wrong seminar hall, and in a hurry. I'm not having a good day. I'm on the wrong floor, and I'm not even sure if I should be here," I ramble, and can't stop. "I should be in New York, but my mom died, so I'm now living in Edmonton, and I'm lost." In so many ways, without my beautiful mom. "...and, and..." Oh no. I feel like I might cry. Again.

I can't cry. Not now, and I've shed too many tears these past eight weeks.

No, no, no.

I inhale air through my nose, desperately trying to stall the unshed tears.

Dropping my bag to the floor, I cover my face with my hands and tilt my head back to hide the wave of grief. It's something I can't control. I'm not sure I ever will be able to.

Dabbing the pads of my fingers into the corners of my

eyes to catch any tears before they fall, I quickly compose myself, remembering what my dad told me. *How you feel today won't feel the same as yesterday, or tomorrow, or the next day after that, but with time, your heart will feel lighter, the sun will shine brighter and when it does, know that she's shining down on you.*

Despite how positive my dad's words are, I know he's trying to keep it together for me and my sister. I see the pain in his eyes, making him look older than I remember.

I suck in a deep breath and bow my head, and that's when I notice droplets of blood scattered across the polished gray floor.

"You're bleeding," I squeal, unwrapping my cream scarf from around my neck. "Here, please use this." I offer him my keepsake accessory, to use as if it were an old rag to stop the bleeding.

Head down, he mutters from behind his hands, "What the hell were you doing? These doors open out into the corridor, not in. You stupid..." He stops mid-sentence when he lifts his head and looks at me.

Like a bolt of lightning, his piercing blue gaze hits me first. It hot-wires something deep in my chest, sparking a quick pulsing sensation that's new and welcomed. His dark hair hits me next. It's cut short around the sides and is a bit longer on top. He's gorgeous. And dark. Intense.

His eyes crinkle around the edges as he narrows them, seemingly amused at my inspection of him and checking me out in return. He opens his mouth to say something, but stops himself, remaining silent.

Protecting his nose with one hand, a black backpack slips off his other shoulder and hits the floor with a loud *thud* as he stands to his full height of around six-foot-three, forcing me to crane my neck to look up at him from my five-foot-four frame. I've never felt so small standing next to someone.

Mesmerized, I offer him my scarf again. "Take this to stop the bleeding," I say timidly.

He takes it from me with his clean hand and lifts it toward his nose. Never breaking eye contact with me, he holds it under his bloody nostrils with his gigantic bear-sized hand and then says the most unexpected words. "Smells good." He doesn't use it to catch the blood that's slowly running down his top lip and into his mouth, as I had expected him to. Instead, he holds it close to his chest as if I just handed him a heartfelt gift.

I can't tear my attention away from him. He's gorgeous.

"I'm sorry." My tone is soft and remorseful. "I've ruined your day and I'm not having a good day, either." *Why did I say that?*

"You said." His left eye twitches as if he's deep in thought.

My brain isn't functioning properly and all I can think of replying is, "Right."

Another small stream of blood from his nose causes me to scrunch my face as a jelly-like feeling spreads through my legs as I notice how red, swollen, and painful it looks. *Damn, that must hurt.* "Do you think it's broken?" I ask, my curiosity getting the better of me as I move in closer to get a better look.

Barely an inch between us, beneath his finely tailored black dress jacket that looks like it was made for him, his large chest swells against the black tee shirt underneath it, his nostrils flaring as if he doesn't like me invading his personal space.

"I've had worse," he replies gruffly.

When I look up at him, he's peering down at me,

allowing me the opportunity to check him out further; tight square jaw, full lips, piercing blue eyes, and hot damn, does he have the longest eyelashes I've ever seen.

Why are men always blessed with the holy grail of lashes? It's not fair.

"Something I can help you with?" His lips twitch and it's not a smile. I'm not sure if grizzly bear man knows how to. He doesn't appear to have any laughter lines, unlike mine that run long and deep. Although in the last eight weeks, I haven't had much to smile or laugh about. I think I may have forgotten how to do both.

Shaking my head, a nervous stutter leaves my mouth. "Yeah, you have, um, nice eyelashes." I want to tell him his whole face is nice. He has the type of features I could look at all day and never get tired of. "Do you use some sort of lash growth serum, or are those natural?"

He grunts in response to my stupidity. "Shit, that's sore." He moans, and I assume he's experiencing shooting pains across his face when he clenches his jaw together and winces.

Exploring the bridge of his nose with the hand that's covered in blood, he says, "I need to clean up." He gazes down at me with a serious look.

Flustered by his never-ending perusal of me that heats my skin and I feel deep within my soul, I look around for a bathroom in my unfamiliar surroundings. I spot one on the other side of the corridor. "Come with me. I'll help. It's the least I can do." I expect him to argue, but when I pick up my bag and then his, he just follows me like a lost puppy. I groan at the weight of his bag. How he manages to carry it around when it feels heavier than a giant boulder is anyone's guess. Although, from the look of him, he probably lifts more at the gym than I weigh.

Once inside the restrooms, he cleans his hands under the water. Then I order him to sit on the edge of sinks. I find a packet of soft tissues in my bag and dampen a couple under some warm water to clean him up. He shuffles down for me so I can reach his face, never uttering a word, watching me with fascination.

Standing between his legs, he winces when I softly press the tissue to his skin. "I'm sorry. But at least it's stopped bleeding now." I try to sound cheerful, even though I can see the bruising begin to shine beneath the skin under his eyes and across the bridge of his nose. I feel terrible for hurting him. I'm the person who opens windows to let the flies out and I have never killed a spider.

"It's fine. It's not broken." His reassuring, rough tone sends shivers down my spine.

"You're not a doctor. You don't know it's not broken," I rebuke him for his self-diagnosis.

"I do. It's been broken twice before. It's not broken this time."

Maybe I was right, and he does play football. I'm certain they wear metal face protectors, though.

Or is he a bouncer like I first thought? Or perhaps he's one of those guys who picks a fight with anyone. His broodiness feels like he could be. The intensity of it bubbles beneath the surface of his skin. It's palpable. Unsettling, yet so intriguing.

He's spiked my curiosity. The need to unpeel his layers suddenly becomes a burning desire.

We are so different. He's like King Kong and I'm that tiny bride he clutches in his hand; he could easily devour me. Although that doesn't sound so bad. However, I'm pretty sure I'm safe. Grizzly bear dude would never be interested in little me.

And yet, he's still here, looking at me as if he wants to say something, but doesn't.

I have to force myself not to lean in and kiss him when I clean the blood off his upper lip. They are incredibly kissable looking.

I gave up on men during my freshman year at college and I've only ever kissed boys, but this guy, he's a man. A muscular wall of masculinity. From his intoxicating, spicy, rich smell to the size of his hands, he's all man. The last time I kissed a boy, because that's what he was, he squeezed my boob so hard I'm positive he thought he was kneading bread, earning him a swift shove, and I never spoke to him again. By the looks of this guy and his huge hands, I bet he knows exactly how to use them.

His inner thigh brushes my outer one as he shuffles from side to side as if he's trying to get comfortable.

I fit perfectly between his legs.

I wonder what he would feel like between mine.

Oh no, those thoughts will never do.

"You're blushing," he murmurs, breaking my sinful thoughts.

"I'm just hot."

Not missing a beat, he replies, "You're not wrong about that." His crystal blue eyes stare into my brown ones and a shimmer of something unusual, a feeling I've never felt before, sends warmth between my thighs straight through my core.

I jest with him to deflect how much he's piqued my interest. "Is that the line you use on all the ladies? I bet it works every time." I snicker because it almost worked with me. If he asked me to strip naked for him, I probably would. *I want to.*

What is happening to me? And why now with him? I

don't need a man in my life. I have a new job, two to be precise, and I'm in Edmonton to work my ass off, get the promotions I want, and pay off my college loans. Oh, and save for a home. And start up my own wedding planning business.

I have big dreams I want to achieve.

I don't need any distractions.

And this has never happened before. These sexual thoughts.

It's official. I'm losing it. I think I'm on the brink of mental burnout. That's the only reason I'd be having these thoughts about a total stranger. My sister did say that's what would happen if I didn't slow down.

Not responding to my last question, he remains quiet while I finish cleaning him up. I lean in closer again, accidentally pushing my hips against his and that's when I feel how thick and long his cock is.

An audible gasp leaves me. Mid-wipe, I freeze, then my hand falls to my side.

I've never been this close to someone so big and so hard. I've never felt a man's cock. Ever. I've never wanted to before.

But I've officially changed my mind. I want to feel his.

Now.

We stare at one another. He's gorgeous. The sexiest guy I've ever seen. I'm deeply attracted to him and really want him to kiss me. The handful of guys I've kissed previously feel like they were practice, but this guy feels like *game on*.

And all the guys from college who were into me were never my type, although I don't quite know what my type is since I've never had a boyfriend. But they were jocks, with huge egos, preferring to take selfies of themselves rather than the girl on their arm, or who slept around and wore it like a badge of honor. No thanks. Not for me, and that's why at the age of twenty-two, I'm still a virgin. I've been saving myself for *the one.* Well, that's what I keep telling myself, but the truth is, I've never liked anyone enough that I would go all the way with. Unlike my best friend from college, Zoey, who had an endless stream of boys in and out of her bed.

Zoey loved to lay it on thick, telling me I was missing out and that it was *just* sex. How amazing and different orgasms felt with a guy compared to getting off with my sex toy friend she named *Buzzworth.*

I miss Zoey so much already. I'm envious of the career she's continuing to pursue in New York as a marketing assistant at one of the largest women's magazines in the world, *Majestic.* Although I don't miss bumping into random guys she'd brought home for the night.

I couldn't think of anything worse.

Sex for me is more than sex. It's about connection and giving part of yourself away. I want it to be special. It has to feel *right* with a guy.

It never has before.

Rooted to the spot, and for some reason, right now, in a restroom, on the wrong floor of a conference facility, in a country I didn't plan to return to, only knowing one person in the city, my manager from the coffeehouse, this, right here where I am standing, with *him,* feels... right.

Lifting one hand, he pushes a loose tendril of hair that's fallen across my eye. He then tips my chin up so I'm looking straight at him. "You lost your mom?" His unexpected question catches me off guard.

I sink my teeth into my bottom lip as tears well in the corners of my eyes, making them sting.

Nodding slowly, a tear escapes and rolls down my

cheek. "Eight weeks ago. She had a heart attack." My bottom lip trembles. The pain is unbearable some days.

Grizzly bear guy wipes it away with his calloused thumb. "It gets better."

"It hurts." In a moment of vulnerability, I share my innermost feelings with this stranger.

"I know," he replies as if he has first-hand knowledge and when I search his face for an answer, he says, "My dad. Two years ago."

"It sucks." More tears run down my face.

"With time, it becomes more manageable. I promise." Compassion bounces off him and I feel grateful that he understands.

"Grief is such a strange thing." I still can't believe she's gone.

He inclines his head in agreement, then lists the cycle of emotions I have been feeling since mom passed. "Pain, anger, love, forgiveness, blame, reminiscing, laughing, back to pain." He seems like a man of few words, making every word he does say meaningful. His thumb is still resting on my face. I silently pray it leaves an imprint on my skin so I can remember this moment forever.

"I can't remember the last time I laughed," I confess, then blurt out, "And you don't look like you laugh very much either." He comes across as being quite a serious guy and he's not smiled once yet. Feeling uncomfortable and inappropriate for saying that to someone I don't know, I curse to myself, and as his hand falls away from my face, I take a step back. "I'm sorry. I shouldn't have said that."

He licks his thick thumb he used to wipe away my tears. And in that moment, the air sparkles between us. My nipples pucker beneath the fabric of my soft lace bra, imagining his tongue licking places I shouldn't be, and my deprived pussy clenches in response.

Well, that's new.

"How do I taste?" I did *not* mean to ask that.

He pulls his mouth to the side, and I think it's a glimmer of a smile. Maybe that's his version of one. He's a stranger to me, so I can't be sure. Whatever lies beneath that hard exterior he wears like a shield, I want to find out more. Discover everything.

"You taste like my best decision." He licks his lips, his eyes becoming hooded as he drops his gaze to my mouth. "And like you're mine." He sounds feral.

His reply causes a weird noise to escape from the back of my throat, my skin warming under his stare.

"Ha, good one." I do some sort of weird clap, finger snap, and point thing with my hands and throw the blood-stained tissue into the waste paper basket, missing it completely.

Get it together, Lily. Be cool.

I smooth down my black pencil skirt and try to remember why I am here; fun team building.

"I should get going." I clear my throat and grab the handles of my tote bag. "I'm so sorry about your nose." He rises to his feet, and even with two-inch heels on, I suddenly feel like *Thumbelina* again. "If you have any medical bills, please let me know and I will pay for them, yeah?" At this rate, I am never paying off my college loans, even with the job at the coffeehouse I started working at in the evenings last week. It pays well, and it's across the street from the arena used for sporting events and concerts, so the tips are incredible.

"It's fine." He stands wide and shoves his hands into the

pockets of his black dress pants, then proceeds to shamelessly readjust his cock.

"Okay, I need to go," I squeak, the octave of my voice now three times higher than normal.

I turn and almost face-plant the bathroom door. *How embarrassing.*

Glancing back over my shoulder, his attention is still fixed on me, amusement glinting in his eyes. A little beam of sun shines through the restroom windows, bathing him in bright white rays. He looks like he's glowing.

Wow.

I throw a stupid girly finger wave, making me look like I'm flirting with him, but I'm not, am I? Oh shit, I can't deny it. I am.

Pulling the door open to leave, he shouts after me, "Hey, what's your name?"

"Lily," I call back and just before the door slams shut, I hear him repeating my name as if he's committing it to memory.

One thing's for sure. I won't forget his face.

The gorgeous one I may have ruined.

And I hope he doesn't forget mine.

Then I realized that I didn't even ask his name.

Goddamnit, I'm a knucklehead.

Rushing along the corridor, I take the stairs, climbing up the cooler atmosphere of the concrete and iron stairwell. Feeling chilly, I reach up to tighten my scarf to keep me warm.

Then I remember; he still has it.

CHAPTER THREE

Lily – Three Weeks Later

I push the door of Ice Hot Coffeehouse open and run through a path of space between the chairs, shouting my apologies for how late I am. "Sorry, I got lost." Out of breath, I'm wheezing while pulling my arms out of my white woolen coat.

"Again?" Kourtney shouts back, giggling.

"I need a map." I hang my coat over the hook in the staff room and sling my bag over the top of it before unzipping my dress. Wiggling out of the tight fabric, leaving it in a blue puddle on the floor. I pull my jeans out of my locker and haphazardly toe off my navy pumps, before I push my legs into the tight denim.

"I'm so hot," I pant, bouncing up and down on the spot to pull them up. "I rush around all the time. Why am I not a size zero?" I mutter, sucking in my stomach, struggling to fasten the top button, then close the zipper.

Fanning my face with my hand to cool me down before pulling my coffeehouse tee shirt over my head, I push my feet into my already-tied white sneakers simultaneously and

I am ready to start my shift in record time. I've become a goddess at multitasking.

I throw my head back, inhaling the nutty roasted coffee scent, and eye the ceiling, taking a moment to catch my breath. Between working full time at High Octane Events, trying to figure out the maze of streets of Edmonton, and working evenings at Ice Hot, I can't remember the last time I had a meal while sitting at a table.

Shoving food into my mouth while doing three things at once appears to have become a normal occurrence.

Grabbing my maroon apron, I tie the taped ribbons of it at the base of my spine, grab my dress off the floor, fold it before carefully placing it on a chair so I can wear it another day and then head out to start my shift at the coffeehouse.

I love it here. It doesn't feel like work. It's fun. We laugh a lot and Kourtney, who owns the place, has already become my closest friend; my only friend here in Edmonton. We eat together, we've been out for cocktails a couple of times, not that I am as much of a party girl as Kourtney is, but it was fun and she invited me to go out with her and a few of her friends to the opening of a new nightclub on Saturday night. She has VIP tickets, as apparently, she knows the guy who owns the club. I only agreed to go because she made a good argument about how I needed to make more friends, network, and get to know who's who in the city.

She's right and I swear she would make a better defense lawyer than a coffeehouse owner.

There are lots of other reasons I want to go too, but it has absolutely nothing to do with trying to find a broken-nosed brute of a man with an attitude bigger than the Empire State Building. Nope, nothing to do with that at all. But, you never know, if he is there, then I could perhaps speak to him, couldn't I? Just to find out how his nose is healing, of course.

That's a big fat lie. I want to see him again. But I haven't seen him anywhere. It's as if I dreamed him up.

Kourtney squirts whipped topping onto a mug full of steaming hot chocolate, then sprinkles a handful of mini marshmallows on top of the white mountain peak of sweetness. "One hot chocolate with the works." Beaming a smile, she slides it across the counter to her customer, then turns to address me. "I thought you were finally getting the hang of the city."

"I went left instead of right." I sigh. Well, I think I did. Every boulevard, junction, and intersection looks the same to me. I wish they could color code streets like I do with my work planner. It would make everything so much simpler and easier to navigate.

"You are forgetting I've lived in New York for years, Kourtney. I'm the little country girl from Spruce Plain, and I only ever came to the city with my parents when I was younger, and they did all the navigating." I never paid much attention.

Wiping the brushed stainless-steel counter, she laughs at me again. "You have no sense of direction."

I really don't. "Don't ever ask me to read a map if we ever attempt a road trip together," I warn, looking at the carnage of milk spills on the drainer of the complicated coffee machine I've yet to fully master, and shake jugs needing to be washed. There must have been a ton of takeout customers before I arrived because there are hardly any customers sitting in.

"Received and understood." She salutes me in understanding. "Once you've cleaned all of that." She points in the direction of the dishes. "Could you please make me a large, half whole milk, half no fat, no foam latte with a shot of vanilla please?"

"Wow, that's specific," I mutter.

I let out a low chuckle when she says, "He can be specific about anything."

I cast a glance around the softly lit space in a search party for Mr. Specific.

"Oh, he's in the bathroom. You won't miss him when he comes out."

"I'll keep my eyes peeled." Smirking, I turn my back on the seating area and get to work clearing up. I like order and tidiness, and I most definitely can't work like this.

Within a few minutes, everything is sparkling, and the barista machine looks shiny and new again, so I make the first of at least one hundred drinks before my shift ends at nine tonight. I scan the order on the screen above my head and read it back, "Large, half whole milk, half no fat, no foam latte, shot of vanilla." Easy.

Once it's made, I check the name on the order on the screen, then place the coffee on the counter and call out. "Ash."

My eyes search the small handful of customers, and that's when I see him; grizzly bear bruised nose guy.

I didn't dream him up after all.

He's real.

CHAPTER FOUR

Lily

Looking surprised to see me, his brows shoot up, his face softening as he rises to his feet. Time stops as he walks in my direction, pushing his hands through his short, dark brown hair.

He towers over me and I'm forced to tilt my head back when he stops on the other side of the counter.

"Hey." I examine his nose, relieved that it looks better. "You look great."

A slow grin quirks his mouth.

Holy freaking hell, he's gorgeous when he smiles. "I mean, your..." Clearing my throat to pull myself together, I continue, "Your nose. It looks great. Better." There's only a little yellow bruising on the innermost corners of his eyes left.

"Not broken."

I throw my hand to my chest. "I'm so relieved. I really did think I had broken it, and I haven't seen you around to check in with you." Edmonton is a big place. What a dumb thing to say.

"Have you been looking for me?" Stance widening, his chest broadens.

I feel the urge to tell him how much I wanted to see him again, but I don't. Instead, I reply, "Yeah, to see if I needed to pay your medical bills."

"Not necessary."

"Cool." I sound like a dork and not a grown woman who can manage her household bills and hold down two jobs.

He points to the hot mug of coffee on top of the counter. "That's mine."

I jump into action. "Oh, you're Ash?" I move it closer to him. "Here."

"Thank you, Lily."

I push my lips into my mouth containing the scream that's threatening to leave my lungs. He remembered my name; I want to shout out loud and tell everyone that he remembers who I am.

I tilt my head to the side, watching him stride slowly back to his table. The way his jeans struggle to contain his thick thighs and muscular body is almost hypnotizing. *Wow, that is a nice ass.*

I'm jealous of that denim.

"Nice, huh?" Kourtney whispers in my ear, breaking my obvious staring fest.

I drop my head and begin fiddling with the tip jar and random items on top of the counter, tidying nothing and everything. "If you say so," I hesitate to answer.

"So, he knows your name?"

"Mmm, hmm." I continue to pretend to be busy. "I met him the other day, but I didn't know his name until he collected his coffee." I spin around to face her.

"You don't know who that is, Lily?" Eyes wide, her shocked face tells me that I should.

Who is he? Tell me now, Kourtney.

Bemused, she rolls her eyes. "He's like the hottest guy on ice. He plays center for the Eagles."

Huh. He plays hockey, not football, like I assumed.

Kourtney keeps reeling off everything she knows about him. "Twenty-two years old, hockey player. Doesn't date. Well, according to the rumors. Drafted to the NHL when he was eighteen. Nickname is The Bear, for obvious reasons, and he's always wanted to play for his hometown here in Edmonton." She raises a finger in the air as if she remembered something else. "And is a man of few words, and he's only ever been in here twice before."

I'm so shocked. "Wow, you really know a lot about this guy."

"I know everything about the entire team. I'm a big fan and in case you haven't noticed, my coffeehouse is directly across the street from the arena they play their games in. Please tell me you recognized Ed Crosby when you served him the other night?"

I shake my head. "I didn't," I mutter.

She rolls her eyes. "I give up. He's a hockey legend. The season starts soon and we'll be flooded with fans and players. It's good to know who is who and make them feel special. And that guy." Jolting her head in his direction. "He is not just any guy, Lily. He's Ash Johansson. He's an NHL superstar. One of the greatest of all time."

"Never heard of him." My father is a hockey fan, but I've never paid much attention to the game. It never interested me before, however, I may have changed my opinion; hockey just got interesting and has my full attention.

Kourtney keeps on sharing, "I've heard he's not a fan of puck bunnies and he—"

I butt in, confused. “Puck bunnies?”

Her mouth drops open. “How do you get through the day, Lily Murphy?”

Color rushes into my cheeks. I love fashion and interior design. I read gossip blogs and entertainment magazines about movies and pop stars, keep an eye on the latest trends, and love music. It’s my job to know what’s happening in the world, but sports, I don’t follow at all. If I find myself at the gym more than once a year, it’s a miracle, and I skip anything in the news about athletes because I don’t know who they are.

Kourtney fills in the blanks for me. “Puck bunnies are hockey fan girls. More specifically they like to sleep with the players. The more famous they are, the better.” She drops her voice. “They even rate the players on various blogging sites, and they keep tabs on the players' whereabouts by posting where they hang out.” She moves closer to my ear and whispers, “The players call them puck sluts.”

I screw my face up. “Ewww. That’s vile.”

Kourtney glances in Ash’s direction. “He may not be into puck bunnies, but he sure is into you, eh?” She’s less than subtle with her observation.

I steal a glance and right enough, he’s looking my way and I feel warmth flame my cheeks.

“So, how do you know him?” She leans in closer.

I rub my brow nervously. “I sort of gave him the remnants of those black eyes he’s wearing.” He must have looked like a panda for weeks.

She breaks out into spontaneous laughter. “Only you could meet the most gorgeous guy on the ice and try to spoil those good looks.”

"I didn't do it on purpose," I retort, instantly feeling stupid.

She wags her head in disbelief, adding, "And you didn't know who he was? Unbelievable." She chuckles softly when I nod. "That's why I love you so much already, Lily. You really are rather unique."

Looking over at him again, his hands are cupped around his mug, watching Kourtney and me chatting. Tipping his head at me in recognition, I lift a finger off the counter, acknowledging the grizzly bear guy I now know to be called Ash Johansson.

Ash.

I love his name.

"Incoming." Kourtney's voice is low in warning as the bell over the door of the coffeehouse rings. "Speaking of puck bunnies."

I jolt and follow the wild cackle of girlish laughter that's ruined the calm atmosphere of the coffeehouse.

Four beautiful, nope, not beautiful, stunning girls confidently stride in Ash's direction as if they know him and own the place.

Wow, those girls sure do know how to look after themselves. Not a hair out of place and so much thigh gap I could park a truck between them. I suddenly feel self-conscious and slick the strands of hair that have fallen out of my ponytail back into the elasticated band.

"Is there a beauty school close by? Where did they learn to apply makeup like that?" I ask Kourtney as we continue to watch on with fascination.

She scoffs, "You are prettier than all of them combined."

Biting the side of my mouth, I know she's just saying that to make me feel better, but I thank her anyway. I'm not great at receiving compliments.

In harmony, the four girls all say sweetly, "Hey Ash."

Before they can even pull out the chairs around the table where he is sitting, he's on his feet and packing his belongings into a blue and yellow kit bag.

"Oh, are you not staying?" Batting her eyelashes at him, one of the blond-haired puck bunnies asks.

"I was just leaving," he replies gruffly, looking thoroughly annoyed.

"But you haven't finished your coffee," another one of the girls coos, flicking her blond hair over her shoulder. They are all carbon copies of one another; they could be quadruplets.

He slips the strap of his bag over his shoulder, "I have somewhere to be." Clamping his jaw, his lips draw into a thin line and he leaves them without a goodbye.

It takes me a moment to figure out he's walking this way. In a panic, I pretend to be busy.

"Lily." His deep voice vibrates through his chest, and I swear I feel its ripple effect drifting over my skin.

I look up and grin nervously, wiping the already sparkling clean work surface with the dish towel, and manage a small, "Yeah?"

"What time do you finish?"

"Nine."

"I'll see you then."

"Okay," on auto-response, I reply.

But, wait, what?

And then the soft ding of the bell rings, indicating he's gone and I'm still standing here staring off into the space where he was standing, wondering what the hell just happened.

"Well, what do you know? Ash Johansson, the most aloof man in hockey, has a thing for Lily Murphy."

Kourtney throws her head back, laughing. "He just ignored them all." She pauses in astonishment. "For you."

Holy hell balls, he did.

My heart flutters fast in my chest as if it's trying to get my attention.

The feeling of being watched causes me to glance over at the girls perched around the table, and that's when I find four sets of death stares burning right through me. If looks could kill, I'd be reeling from the pain and begging for them to stop.

"Oh, dear. They do not look happy," Kourtney whispers under her breath.

I pull a fake smile so wide it hurts my face and wave over at them. "Make friends with the mean girls," I instruct Kourtney through the side of my mouth, and she joins in, waving.

Robotically, the four blond replicas stand in unison, and with their noses in the air, they glide out of the door without a second glance.

"Holy freaking shit," Kourtney squeals as the door closes.

My shoulders drop an inch. "I know. Those girls are intense."

She waves her hand through the air, dismissing my focus on them. "Forget them, Lily. I meant Ash 'The Bear' Johansson. He's meeting you here after your shift."

Oh shit, he's coming back.

I turn to focus on the mirror on the back wall to check myself out. Flushed face and smudged mascara under my eyes. "I look hideous."

"You look beautiful." Kourtney comes up behind me and lays her hands on my shoulders.

"I didn't wash my hair today." I smooth my fingers over it.

"I have some dry shampoo in my bag. Slick on a bit of lip gloss and hey, presto." Her face softens. "You don't need anything else. You, Lily Murphy, are gorgeous."

My eyes widen. "I'm not good with guys." The palms of my hands feel sweaty.

Wrinkles line her brow in confusion.

I close my eyes and whisper, "I'm nervous."

"Lily, he wants to see you after work. That's all."

"Are you sure?" I'm so inexperienced and he looks like he knows the way around a woman's body.

Still holding onto my shoulders, she turns me around to face her. "Yes. But what are you so worried about? You're twenty-two, beautiful. You've dated guys, right?" Her eyes are full of curiosity and tenderness.

"I've never had a boyfriend and I've never... you know?" I dart my eyes around the coffeehouse, making sure I won't be heard. "I'm a virgin." I draw my lips into my mouth, my embarrassment quickly turns to humiliation.

Eventually, a gigantic smile shapes her lips. "I'm so proud of you for saving yourself." She pulls me into a tight hug and then whispers in my ear. "If Ash Johansson pops your cherry, I guarantee he will rock your world, girly. And I want to hear all about it."

I push her off me playfully. "Oh, my God. I wish I hadn't told you now." It's not information I go around sharing. Although I don't know what the hell I am stressing about. It's not as if anything is going to happen. It's wishful thinking on my part, and yet I'm stunned by how much I want it to happen. I have dreamed about him, even touched myself thinking about him. He makes me ache in places I've never ached before and all from our brief encounter a few weeks ago. He thrills me and every time he looks at me, my heart pounds in my chest, making it feel like a car hitting a rumble strip.

Throwing me a cheeky wink before she moves back behind the serving counter, she looks over her shoulder. "Maybe he's a bear in the bedroom too."

"Will you stop?" I cry playfully.

"Oh, Ash, don't stop, please don't stop." She mocks a fake orgasm in a high-pitched voice, and I make a dash for the staff room to hide my embarrassment, wanting nothing to do with the attention she's sparking from the customers.

Slamming the door behind me, I lean against it and bring my hand up to my mouth to stifle my giggle.

I pull out my phone from my locker and plonk myself down on the wobbly chair, click open the web browser and quickly type his name into the search bar, grateful I can look him up before I see him again.

The search brings up hundreds of videos of him in training, during drills, interviews, stats, articles. Current headlines. It's all there in black and white.

Johansson named number one player to get excited about this season.

Edmonton Eagles center, Ash Johansson, wins prestigious award as top player in NHL.

Older headlines record when he was drafted to the Eagles.

Ash 'The Bear' Johansson to make debut with Edmonton Eagles.

Ash Johansson to follow in his father's footsteps.

Excitement builds as Ash Johansson arrives at Edmonton Eagles.

Ash Johansson is exactly what Kourtney said he is; a star.

I click on several photos. He doesn't smile much for the press. A wicked laugh bubbles in my chest as I desperately try to think of ways to make him smile more.

I still can't believe it; Ash Johansson is meeting me after work.

Sliding the wooden chair back, I push myself to my feet and catch a glimpse of myself in the small mirror on the staff room wall. Plain Lily, who likes nothing better than color coding her notebooks, making handmade celebration cards, organizing events, hiking at the weekends, and collecting old vinyl records rather than perfecting her makeup, reducing the size of her thigh gap, or visiting the salon every six weeks like clockwork... and that's when realization hits; he still has my scarf.

He's probably not interested in me after all. He just wants to return it to me.

Now that makes more sense.

"Never mind." I shrug, pushing the chair back under the small table in the staff room, and straightening out my apron.

I've had my fair share of interest from guys in the past and never wanted it, but somehow, the attention I thought Ash was showing me gave me hope. It's as if I craved it.

I didn't want to admit it, but I secretly thought he might have been *the one.*

And that thought leaves me more disappointed than I've ever felt.

Perhaps I'm destined to stay a virgin forever.

CHAPTER FIVE

Ash

Long gone is the mild October sun, the evening cooler now as the moon makes its appearance. Standing outside the coffeehouse waiting for Lily to appear, I tip back and forth from heel to toe, over and over. It feels like the longest stretch of time, even though it's only been five minutes.

Adrenaline from practice always makes me feel irritable and unable to stay still. I stuff my hands into the pockets of my jeans to stop me swinging them about. I'm nervous. I don't get nervous.

She makes me nervous.

Lily.

The tiny tornado of clumsy chaos with the biggest dimples that set my heart racing.

I'm glad she was in the wrong seminar the other week at the conference center, stopping me in my tracks and almost breaking my nose. It was a beautifully disastrous moment of fate. Painful as fuck, but totally worth it.

I'm convinced I wasn't just there to undertake a

leadership management course Coach signed me up for. I'm certain I was there to find *her*.

But I didn't see her again. And trust me, I've been looking.

And then, I found her out of the blue, in the Ice Hot Coffeehouse when I decided to grab a coffee before practice. I don't usually like eating or drinking before drills, because it makes me feel like my stomach's a laundry machine. However, I haven't been getting much sleep lately, lying awake at night worrying about the season starting, so I desperately needed a caffeine pick me up.

My dad was a huge believer in working your ass off to get what you want, and while I believe that too, I also believe in accidental encounters; much like the one between Lily, me, and that harder than hell wooden door.

Arching my neck back, I eye the indigo-blue sky, dropping my shoulders an inch or two to relieve the tension in my muscles.

The pressure of making this year a success is getting to me. Not just this year, but every year I play for the team. I'm already exhausted just thinking about my demanding game schedule that's about to hit me. I'm not alone; the rest of the team feels the same way, which helps a little, I suppose. As a team, we're determined, driven, and buzzing to get started. We'll unite and be the best we can be.

When I called my mom last night to do our weekly check-in, I admitted how I was feeling. I was skeptical when she reassured me that Dad felt the same way at the beginning of every season, because he always looked so composed and confident; completely sure of himself. She promised me that I could have it all. I could juggle practice, stay in touch with family, keep fit, and maintain a social life, and then she pointed out that I need to stop stressing and cut myself some slack. She was sincere in the delivery of her advice, and I know it's because she worries about me.

"The fans and team love you, Ash. You won the Stanley Cup last year." Her comforting words drifted down the phone. *"Try to have some fun, sweetheart. You've got this."*

It's on days like today, when my body and brain are tired, that I wish my dad was still here to talk to.

He was the greatest NHL player to have ever played, scoring the most goals, assists, and points in league history. My father was a legend, competing in the Winter Olympics, winning gold medals, the respect of his fellow teammates, and sports awards by the bucket load. On and off the ice, my father was a great man. They raised the bar when they made him; donating to charities, pushing to have every game televised, and raising the profile of all the players on his team by landing interviews with the nation's top celebrity broadcasters. He put ice hockey, and the Eagles, on the map.

Playing for the same team as my dad is what I have dreamed about since I was four years old. My dad was my hero and had me in skates as soon as I could walk.

Now he's gone.

At least he got to see me graduate high school and be drafted to the Eagles. He was so proud of me when he watched me play my first game with them, wearing his team colors.

A punch of grief hits me low in my gut.

Two years in since he slipped away in his sleep from a brain aneurysm, and the pain remains. Some days, deep sadness, shock, and numbness makes me physically unable to eat or sleep. I know my mom didn't need to say it, but she knows that it's not just my busy schedule and practice that are causing me to lose the much-needed shuteye; it's grief.

Although at least I get four hours of sleep a night now, unlike the one or two hours I did when he first died.

With time, it is getting easier, and I mostly have good days rather than bad, which Mom says is a positive step.

And she's never wrong about anything, so I hope she's right about this.

I pull the collar of my jacket up around my neck to keep the cold out as the tinkle of the bell above the door of the coffeehouse breaks the silence of the quiet sidewalk.

With all the grace of an angel, the indoor light behind her creates a soft yellow halo around her as she steps out into the dark of night. I swear she floats toward me wearing the brightest smart ass little grin and an immaculate, wide collared, white woolen coat with oversize black buttons.

Sweet and innocent in all the best possible ways, she steals the breath from my lungs when she says, "I can't believe you came."

Fuck yeah, I came. I couldn't wait to see her again.

She's the only woman I've been attracted to in the last two years, and I'm desperate to find out everything about her and why my body reacts to her in a way that's foreign to me.

"I'm a man of my word." I move toward my truck and point at it. "Get in, I'll drive you home." I don't mean to sound so gruff. "Sorry." I turn back around and soften my tone. "I would like to take you home." I try again.

Rooted to the spot, she calls out to me "I usually walk home with Kourtney and her boyfriend."

At that exact moment, her work buddy, the same girl from earlier, steps out the doorway as if she's been waiting to intervene. "See you tomorrow, Lily. Text me when you get home." She winks then walks off hand in hand with her boyfriend.

Unlocking the door to my truck, I turn to the side, opening the passenger door for her. "Please," I ask, sounding needy.

From the corner of my eye, my muscles uncoil when she takes a tentative step toward my truck, then another and another, until she's standing in the open space between the truck and the door.

Looking up at my Ford F-150, she looks petrified. "I'll need a ladder to get—" Her words turn into a squeal when I grab her waist and lift her onto the black leather passenger seat.

Her head whips to the side, and she stares at me as I stand in the open door. She looks angry and flustered, but I'm seriously turned on knowing that she's as light as air and will weigh next to nothing when she's sitting on my face.

Calm down, Ash.

"Did you just lift me into your truck as if I'm a child?" she shrills.

The fire she has within her makes me more attracted to her, and I break out into spontaneous laughter. I slam the door closed before she has time to change her mind and hop out. Jogging around the front of my truck, I pull the handle of the driver's door open, then jump in to find her staring at me.

"So, you *can* laugh?" She folds her arms across her body in shock. Or maybe it's anger. I can't work it out.

Turning the keys in the ignition, I pull my seat belt over my shoulder and lock it into place. "You're cute when you're annoyed." I side eye her, not knowing how she'll react to my playful words.

"I am not annoyed. I am... just... you... you are so infuriating." Her jaw is tight as she begins her rambled attack. "If you could just give me back my scarf, then I'll be off. I can walk home. I know that's the only reason you came back. I know someone like *you* would never date someone like *me* anyway. But I'm cool with that."

She doesn't sound cool, and she has no idea how much I like her or how wrong she is.

And still, she keeps on rambling. "Although, what I lack in the looks department, I make up for in book smartness, because *I am* smart. I went to Columbia University. I even had offers from Brown and Harvard, you know."

What the fuck does she mean? Lack in looks? She's incredibly beautiful. "And what I lack in height I make up for that in brain cells too, oh, and thick hair. I have good cheekbones." She runs her fingers along them. "I am a fantastic swimmer. I can't ice skate, though, so don't ask me to do that, or it will be like watching Bambi on ice." I think she just set me a challenge.

"I was jumping ahead of myself, thinking that you were remotely interested in a shortstop like me, but I'm not the proud owner of a thigh gap, so that rules me out. How do girls get that gap between their thighs anyway? Is it leg lifts or squats? Both?" She scrunches her face as if she's trying to figure it out, but I have no idea what the fuck is happening right now.

Her voice squeaky and shrill, she keeps running her mouth. "Although Kourtney said that apparently, you don't date, so I guess I'm safe, but how is that even possible? Have you seen you?" Confusion written all over her face, she shakes her head as if trying to process how true that is. "You look like your body is made from carved marble or something."

Humored, I raise my eyebrows in surprise; she's been checking me out.

"Is that what puck bunnies are into?" She waves her

finger up and down my body. "I suppose I can see the appeal. I mean, you are nice to look at." Then she scoffs, as if what her friend Kourtney said was impossible. "Don't date, my ass. You must pick up girls like this all the time. I mean, why you thought I would be your next accomplishment, I have no idea." She proceeds to drop her voice to mimic mine. "*I'll pick you up at nine. Get in the truck.* I mean, who even says that? I don't need to be picked up, or saved like some damsel in distress who can't get herself home after work. Do girls drop their panties on demand for you when you go all bossy like that?" She points her finger at me, and I force myself not to laugh again for fear of setting her off on another tangent, because fuck me, she is funny as hell.

On a roll she keeps spewing words out, words I don't think she means to say, but man do I love them. "And for the record, I would never drop my panties for you. No way, bucko."

Bucko? Yeah, it's official, she's cute.

Unable to stop herself, she's panting as if out of breath. "I am saving myself for the right guy. A guy who treats me right. Doesn't lift me into his truck, hoping to get his wicked way with me. Uh-uh. I want someone who treats me like a lady and smiles without being forced to. Did you use up all of your smile and laughter quota for the month today? One smile, one laugh, done." She slices the air with her hand.

Now that does make me smile again because she makes me want to. She's different from other girls, not caring if she offends me, or concerned with who I am, or wanting to jump into bed with me just because I'm a hockey player.

Saving herself? Does she mean...?

Then she makes a surprising admission. "And I will not give my virginity away to someone as brutish, rude, and quite frankly downright cavemanish as you. You manhandled me into this truck with hands that have probably touched every puck bunny that throws themselves at you. I've only just learned what a puck bunny is today." Repulsed by her findings, she sticks her tongue out and fake gags, then adds, "That's disgusting. Do they have no shame? I bet you make them sign some sort of secrecy act contract thingy to stop them from telling everyone they slept with you, or does that give them bragging rights? Or do you pay them to keep quiet?" Her eyes blow wide in horror. "Oh, my God. That's like prosti—"

"Fuck it," I mumble and before she's even finished her last word, I've turned my truck off, unclipped my seatbelt, leaned across the center console, grabbed her face with both hands and I'm crashing my lips to hers.

CHAPTER SIX

Ash

A soft squeak of protest bursts from her throat, her mouth tight at the unexpectedness of my actions. But within seconds, she relaxes, and when I push the seam of her lips open and invade her mouth with my tongue, she lets out a satisfied moan. A loud thud of something heavy sounds out and I can only assume she let go of her bag when she hooks her hand around the back of my neck, pulling us closer together. Tongues exploring one another, she tastes like chocolate and cinnamon.

Addictive.

I want more.

Threading my fingers in the hair at the base of her neck, I pull her hair band out, freeing her long blond locks, and I kiss her deeper.

With the need to hold her close, I place my hands under her armpits and lift her over the center console. Our mouths never lose contact as I position her on my lap, and she then straddles me.

Running my hands up her jean covered thighs, up

under her jacket, I move them to her tiny waist over her thin work shirt and I'm shocked at how good she feels beneath my hands.

She's perfect.

Wriggling in my lap, she brushes against my hard cock, pulling a low rumble of pleasure from my chest. "Lily," I rasp between our desperate mouth-fucking.

Her hands drift down to my chest then back up to my neck, as if exploring my body as well, and I welcome her warm, soft touch; I want her hands on me always.

I pull her hips closer to line her pussy up with my aching cock that's already leaking with precum and rock her back and forth.

Both panting with need, our excited pleasure is swallowed down by the other.

Grabbing her hair, I tilt her head back and kiss down the apple scented skin of her neck, then lick and suck the spot behind her ear that I know she will love.

She continues to rub her hips against mine, chasing her release and driving me toward mine, but I don't want to do this here. Even though I'm parked under a tree, in the dark, and every window is tinted, apart from the windscreen, this is not the type of guy I am. And I sure as hell now know, after her whirlwind of verbal gymnastics, that Lily isn't that type of girl either.

Virgin.

"We should stop." My whisper is affectionate, and I hate myself for putting a halt to how good this feels.

"I don't want to." Her hungry words fill the cab of my truck.

I pull out of our kiss, regretting breaking contact, so I kiss her softly again. "You'll hate me if we don't," I mumble against her lips as I fill my hands with her ass, rubbing her against me again, harder this time. "You feel so fucking good, baby." I find it difficult to stop.

"Ash." She sighs with need, and I love how good my name sounds out of her pretty little mouth, and as I picture her screaming it as I fill her with my cock, more precum drips from my slit.

I can't.

She's a virgin and I have no right to stake my claim. We've only just met.

Only something carnal within me wants it to be me.

Needs it to be.

The thought of another man touching her makes me want to hit something, and that is most unlike me.

The need to protect this unicorn of a woman who entered my life like a flurry of glitter in a snow globe consumes me; she's got me trapped in a whirlwind, and I'm more than happy for her to carry me off in it.

She tastes like happiness and rainbows. I want to keep on kissing her, overcome with the need to imprint myself on her so she doesn't think of anyone but me. Be the one she dreams about, wants to spend her time with, and be the first one she thinks about in the morning. I want all of her firsts.

Stopping her from rocking her hips, she lets out a frustrated groan before I kiss her one last time and let my head fall back against the headrest as I take a moment to look at her. Those deep dimples and big brown eyes of hers will be my downfall and I just know I'm going to fall so hard, so deep, and there is not a single fucking thing I can do about it. "You're so beautiful."

With only the low street lighting from outside shining through the windows, even the moonlight can't hide her cheeks filling with color.

I reach up and run my pointer finger down the length of

her nose, into the dip of her philtrum, and then trace the outline of her full top lip that's now pink and swollen from our kissing.

I think I should set the record straight on some of her assumptions about me. "I don't date or sleep with puck bunnies. Never have." Leaning in, our eyes level. "I dated a few girls in high school. Nobody special though. And I have only ever slept with one woman. She was older than me." I pause to let that information settle. Expecting her to respond, she doesn't. "I met her when I was drafted to the NHL. I was eighteen. She was a fitness instructor, and we hooked up for about two years." Like all aspects of my life, our relationship was kept private. She taught me how to please a woman, how to give pleasure, and how to receive it. I can't deny it was the best sex education an uncontrollably horny teenage boy could ask for, but I don't mention any of this to Lily. "I haven't slept with anyone else since then." I made dating sacrifices to protect my reputation. It's been two years with no sex.

We broke up before my dad died. Which is probably just as well as my responsibilities changed. I've been working and making sure Mom and Erika, my sister, are well cared for.

Plus, I don't trust easily. Some of the guys on the team have had their fair share of kiss-and-tell stories in the tabloids; none of which are pleasant or puts them in a good light.

And yet, somehow, I get the sense that Lily feels different, and I can trust her.

Hell, she had no idea who I was until tonight.

I open up some more. "Before my dad died, I used to laugh. A lot. But if it makes you feel better, I've laughed and smiled more with you than I have in a very long time. You make everything feel better." I don't know what the fuck is happening between us.

Her fingers slowly stroke my chest over my tee shirt, as if she's soothing me.

I close my eyes and say the most important thing I will all night. "I wanted to pick you up to make sure you got home safely." It's dark and not safe for her to be out walking, even if it is with friends. It shocks me how much I already care for her. "And I never saw you as the one needing to be saved. It's me that needs saving… from myself, mostly." I let that information settle between us, open my eyes, and look deep into hers. "I think you're the one who can do that."

I love hockey with every fiber of my being, but lately, I've been feeling like I need more. All I do is watch game tape replays, condition training, practice, and play hockey and while I love what I do, I've always craved more. Maybe Lily is my more.

Her curved lips turn into a full-blown smile. "For a man who doesn't say very much, you sure know how to leave an impression."

"You left an impression on me." I point at my face.

"The impression of your face was left on the door," she jests, chuckling at her own joke, and I smirk at how she seems to like finding humor in the smallest of things.

Tilting my head to the side, out of curiosity, I ask, "You're a virgin?"

She buries her face in her hands and muffles, "I can't believe I told you that."

I reach up to remove her hands, hiding what she thinks is a shameful confession, and make sure she hears every word I say next. "I think it's beautiful that you're saving yourself. Your body is yours. You get to decide what you do with it. Please don't ever feel embarrassed by your decision."

She bites her bottom lip before she says, "Thank you."

In all honesty, I want to be *the one* and the only man she ever lets touch her body. The idea stokes the fire growing within me.

"You kissed me," she says, as if not believing it. "I've never been kissed like that before."

I don't tell her that, despite my sore and bleeding nose, I've wanted to kiss her from the moment I laid eyes on her.

I nod. "I should have asked your permission, but I figured it would be the only way to get you to stop talking."

She cringes at herself and then repeats what I said earlier as if making sure she heard me right. "You wanted to take me home?"

"I did." I give her thighs a squeeze.

"You didn't want to meet me to return my scarf?" Her expression grows serious.

I move in for another kiss, unable to resist tasting her again. "I wanted to see you, Lily." My lips brush hers. Chests touching my heart hammers against hers. "I'm holding your scarf against its will."

Her lips confidently cover mine, our tongues dancing together, and her velvet soft mouth becomes demanding. She then breaks our kiss and asks, "Do I need to raise a ransom to get it back?" Her tone holds a note of mockery, and she doesn't give me a chance to answer before she smothers me with her lips again and mumbles against them, gasping, "You're a really good kisser."

Sucking her tongue into my mouth, I wrap my arms around her waist and hold her firmly against my body as I lose myself in her touch, taste, and addictive fragrance.

Dropping kisses down her neck, she moans in pleasure when I lick, then suck her sweet spot behind her ear.

"You're so hard," she whispers breathlessly.

I thrust my hips upwards, pushing her center against my cock. My mouth finding her earlobe, I gently bite it, then whisper, "You feel that? That's what you do to me."

Open mouthed, panting, she moans again, grinding herself down on me. "I meant your body, Ash," she scolds me. "But that too." She giggles sweetly and I want to make that the sound of my ringtone.

I lose count of our kisses as we both lose control, our bodies burning for one another.

Kissing has always been okay, I guess, but it's never been fueled by the levels of passion and heat I feel between us. Frantically grabbing the back of my neck, she whimpers loudly as she rubs herself against my cock. I stop her from doing it again, otherwise, I'll come in my boxers. "We can't do this here." I've said this before. "You are very distracting." And fucking delicious. No way am I treating her like sex is all I want with her. Because the truth is, I want to see where this thing between us goes.

There is also the worry that the press is never far behind me either. They are always on the prowl, waiting to pounce and find me in compromising positions. It's been four years and they are yet to do so, but that just seems to make them more desperate.

I keep my nose clean. I'm the least controversial member of the team, donating to charities, visiting group homes and the children's hospice. I continue to carry the torch of my father's immaculate legacy.

My father was a stickler for loyalty and, just like him, I refuse to be photographed with puck bunnies for fear of being associated with them or accused of dating them.

I keep my private life, just that, private.

But the press is hungrier than a pack of starving lions.

Like now, for instance, they'd have a field day. We need to move soon or my truck will be spotted and it will be game over before we've begun.

Chests heaving, I pant against her mouth. "I want to take you out on a date." I tease her lips, wanting to lick every part of her. "This Saturday, after our first pre-season game."

Her bold eyes rake over mine as if she's already thinking about what we can do together afterward, which quickly turns to disappointment. I can feel it bouncing off her. Flinching, she shifts uneasily in my lap.

Unable to work out what's wrong, I ask her, "What's up?"

"I promised I would go to a club with Kourtney this Saturday."

Disheartened, but determined, I suggest, "Next Saturday then?"

Sucking her lips into her mouth, she bobs her head up and down, her eyes glinting with excitement. "I'd like that," she responds with a shy smile.

I love hockey, love the game, love the buzz, the fans. It's been my life for as long as I can remember, and I am usually pumped up for a game, but right now I am wishing it was already next Saturday and the night of our date.

I can't wait until then.

And then an idea hits me causing me to grin wide.

"Another smile." Lily fakes a shocked, exaggerated gasp. "What's that one for?"

"You'll see." I smack a quick kiss on her lips. "Let's get you home. It's late."

She clumsily climbs back over to the passenger seat, and I already miss her warmth. "Do you have early morning practice?" Her voice is strained as she maneuvers herself around the tight space. "Phew, I'm in." She's already reaching round to put her seat belt on.

"I do." My muscles have already begun to ache after Coach's grueling session tonight. I know I'll feel worse in the morning.

Surprising me, Lily then says, "Can we finish off what we started next Saturday? It felt nice."

My heart races at supersonic speed. Fucking hell, she wants me. "If that's what would make you happy." I try to keep my voice controlled and casual.

"Oh, I think it would make me very, *very* happy." She rests her elbow on top of the armrest, places her chin in her hand, and looks at me with those big brown orbs.

Yup, Lily... I realize I don't know her surname. "What's your last name?"

"Murphy."

It's official. Lily Murphy, all cute dimples and smart mouth, is most definitely going to be my undoing.

I'm fucking done for.

Arriving outside her apartment, I tell her to stay seated as I jump out of my truck, then run around to her side to open the door and help her out.

I offer her my hand, grab her bag, and as soon as her feet hit the ground, I realize just how much shorter she is than me.

Taking her bag from my grasp, she pushes the straps over her shoulder, tucks her thumb under the leather handle to keep it in place, and then looks up at the red bricked apartment block. "This is me." Nervously she shifts on the balls of her feet as she stares at three women who are gathered on the concrete stairs, smoking cigarettes. The trio stares in our direction and a low murmur of questions travels through the air. *Wow, who is that she's with? Is he that ice hockey player? What's he doing here?*

Ignoring them while silently praying they don't tip off the press, I focus my attention on Lily. "What's your apartment number?" I close the space between us, forcing her to look up at me.

"Apartment 4B." Her voice is almost inaudible.

"I'll pick you up next Saturday at eight." I lie, knowing I will see her much sooner but want to surprise her. Cupping her face, I bend down and plant a soft kiss on her lips. "See you then." My hands drop to my sides.

Her true beauty shines through when she smiles, making her face light up. "Perfect."

Does she mean the kiss or the date? Maybe both.

I lean against my truck and watch her every move. Head held high, she runs up the stone steps and joyfully says *hello* to the women staring at her, and with one last glance over her shoulder, she throws me a flirty wave, then runs her finger over her lips as if remembering how our kiss felt.

I bob my head in recognition and give her a cheeky wink.

I can't wait until next Saturday to see her again.

She can kiss that idea goodbye.

CHAPTER SEVEN

Lily

Turning around behind the counter at the coffeehouse, I'm completely caught off guard and startled by a dark figure towering over me, causing me to let out a high-pitched shriek.

Ash.

Black baseball cap pulled low over his eyes, black padded jacket and dark eyes greet me.

Speechless, for a beat, we stare at each other.

Mimicking what he did in his truck the other night, he draws a line with his pointer finger down my nose then traces the outline of my top lip with the softest of touches making a shot of joy pump the blood in my veins a little faster.

"Customers aren't allowed behind the counter," I whisper, not sure what to say as my heart flaps about in my chest like a moth against a window.

"Shhhh." He places his forefinger against his lips; the ones I kissed last night and could happily kiss for the rest of my life. "You never saw me," he murmurs as he hands me a white envelope and makes a swift exit.

In a daze, I watch him out the window, running across the street toward the arena.

"He's got it bad, girl." Kourtney's voice breaks the spell he appears to have cast over me. "What did he give you?"

I look down at the stark white envelope I had almost forgotten about and grin ear to ear when I read my name which has been spelled using cut outs from magazines. When my gaze falls on the tiger lily flower at the end of the letter Y, I run my fingertips over it.

"You are killing me, Lily. For God's sake, will you open the damn thing?"

Unable to contain myself, I rip open the sealed envelope and pull out a folded piece of paper that looks like a genuine ransom letter that you see in the movies and I giggle when I read it out loud.

"I have your scarf. If you want to see it again, be at the main arena entrance at 9.15 p.m. Should you fail to turn up, the scarf gets it."

"I HAVE YOUR SCARF. IF YOU WANT TO SEE IT AGAIN, BE AT THE MAIN ARENA ENTRANCE AT 9.15 P.M. SHOULD YOU FAIL TO TURN UP, THE SCARF GETS IT."

"Well, what do you know? Ash 'The Bear' Johansson has a sense of humor after all and he's cute with it." Kourtney bumps her shoulder with mine, while I'm frozen to the spot, swooning with a goofy look on my face over his silly, yet super romantic, letter.

I check the oversized coffee cup shaped clock above the barista machine and nibble my lip nervously. Eight forty-five. Thirty minutes until I need to be at the arena.

It's as if he knew that if he gave me too much time to overthink his invitation, I would start flapping like a baby bird that's flown the nest for the first time.

"Go now." Kourtney turns me around, grabs my shoulders from behind, and frog marches me in the direction of the staff room. "I'll pay you until nine, like always."

"I can't let you do that."

Waving her hand through the air, dismissing my comment, she says, "It's only fifteen minutes." She rolls her eyes and then clutches her heart. "And who am I to stand in the way of true love?"

"Love?" I shrill. That's a bit of a stretch from one night of kissing, which I would appreciate more of. Only I was unsure if he really did like me after dropping me off at my apartment the other night. He didn't even ask me for my phone number.

"It could be." Her mouth curves into a devilish grin. "Never say never."

"Kourtney," I say wistfully, with a grateful undertone. "Thank you for letting me leave early."

"It's cool. You work damn hard, day and night, Lily. Time to have some fun." She claps her hands together with excitement. Her whole face lights up like a full moon when she smiles. "Grab your things and go."

I bite my bottom lip between my teeth. "I'm nervous."

"That's a great sign. It means it's important to you and you like him." She pushes me through the staff room door.

"I do." I barely know him, but I like everything I've seen, and kissed, so far.

Kourtney turns to head back into the coffeehouse, but before she leaves she says, "Great. Now go fuck his brains out and knock his skates off." With a loud laugh, she slams the door shut, leaving me staring at an employee health and safety sign on the back of it.

"I'm so screwed." Nerves flutter low in my belly.

I lift the ransom letter that's clutched in my hand and read it again.

I can't stop the smile spreading across my lips.

Before I give it a second thought, I've changed back into my dress I wore for my day job at High Octane Events today, slipped my high heels on, grabbed my stuff and I'm running in the direction of the main arena entrance.

If exciting surprises are Ash's love language, I want him to keep surprising me every day.

CHAPTER EIGHT

Ash

Creeping up behind Lily, she lets out a gasp of shock when I whisper in her ear, "Now Ms. Murphy, follow my instructions, and your scarf won't come to any harm."

"Okay, Mr. Serial Scarf-napper." She chuckles, but I can hear she's nervous when her voice cracks on her last word.

I slip her bag off her shoulder and take it from her. "Turn around slowly and follow me."

"This is ridiculous," she mutters under her breath, and I have to stop myself from agreeing with her. It is ridiculous, but also a date I never want her to forget.

Approaching the main door, it opens for us, just as I had planned with Sam from security.

I wink as I pass and slip him a tip as a thank you for granting me access to the rink tonight, something we aren't supposed to ask for. The installation team has been working hard preparing the ice for the new season which starts on Saturday. But I know Sam. He knew my father, and he's worked here for twenty years. He's more like a family friend than a work colleague. And this is the one and only time I have ever asked for a favor.

Lily's high heels click against the entrance floor as she follows me.

Curiosity gets the better of her. "Why are you carrying my bag?"

"In case you have a hidden camera in it. This could be a set up." I stop in my tracks and spin to face her. "Are you wearing a wire?" Getting into character, I narrow my eyes suspiciously.

She's so beautiful and I'm struck by how much power she has over me; I'm so attracted to her. It's almost overwhelming. The need to grab her and kiss her until she's moaning my name has consumed me since last night.

Having never seriously dated, or wanted to before, she has me imagining her walking into this arena to watch all the games as *my girl*. Celebrating my wins alongside my mom and sister, and spending Sundays with her, lazing on the sofa, watching shitty movies while my body recovers.

I dislike people encroaching on my personal space, so this is a huge shift in mindset for me. I can't understand why I am so drawn to Lily. I've never wanted to invite a woman back to my apartment before. However, I want her in my space; I want to see her every day. It's only been twenty-four hours since I saw her last. It's been far too long. It's almost been painful.

Looking up at me, she bats her eyelashes innocently, then whispers, "Would you like to do a full body check to make sure I'm not wearing a wire?" She steps back and unties her cream wool coat, then holds both sides wide open, exposing a baby pink dress that kisses her curves and fits in all the right places.

Shit, I should have told her to keep the jeans on she was wearing at the coffeehouse for what I have planned.

"How did you magic up a dress in thirty minutes?" I ask, confused, dropping my gaze to the heels she wasn't wearing earlier, either. My imagination runs wild as I picture them wrapped around my ears while I fuck her in that sexy little dress.

Chewing the side of her mouth, she replies, "I work two jobs." Her shyness is endearing.

"Two?" I hold up two fingers, double checking I heard her correctly.

She nods her head slowly. "I'm an events assistant for a company called High Octane Events." Playing with the woolen waist tie of her coat, she continues, "And in the evenings, I work at the coffeehouse. I have student loans, I want to pay them off quicker and I want a house to call my own so, I'm saving for a deposit." She keeps on sharing. "And I have a dream of owning my own wedding planner business one day."

She's book smart and dedicated and I love how independent she is. It shouldn't be, but it's sexy to know she strives for more and will do anything to achieve her goals. Deep down, I know she would understand my drive and ambition. We'd be the perfect team.

I knew it from the day we met. The energy I feel between us, the alignment of us banging into one another, and how we both have determination to achieve our dreams.

I find her independence irresistible.

"Hard work always pays off," I say knowingly. "If that's what you want, I have a feeling you won't let anyone stand in your way," I add, making her face light up.

"Thanks." She lets go of the ends of her coat tie she's

been holding out and grins at me. Her mouth is so wide it turns my heart into a thumping rhythm of erratic beats.

"I admire you for going after what you want. Having goals and ambition is sexy," I tell her. Staring at her, I can't wait another minute to touch her. Closing the space between us, my mouth is on hers in seconds.

Unlike last night, our kiss is slow and tender, and I love how she grabs the edges of my jacket collar to pull me closer.

I move my kisses down the side of her neck. "I have a surprise for you."

"My scarf?" moaning quietly, she asks.

I suck and kiss on the sweet spot behind her ear. "Better than a scarf."

"A pashmina?"

I pull back and look at her. "What the hell is a pashymera?" My brows pinch together in confusion, making her giggle.

"It's a scarf made from fine cashmere."

I roll my eyes. "Why can't they just call it a cashmere scarf instead of a pashymera."

"Pashmina," she corrects me, laughing louder this time. It echoes around the enormous, empty space. "And I don't know why." She lays her hand out for me to take. "Show me this surprise then, Mr. Serial Scarf-napper."

Like a good little puppy, I take her hand and do as she asks.

She's got me in a choke hold already.

CHAPTER NINE

Lily

"I can't skate." My hoarse, whispered panic slices through the silence of the space as I look around the empty rink that's lit up like the Fourth of July.

"Everyone can skate." He ignores my mini freak out.

I haven't skated for years. I was never any good at it when I was younger, choosing to sit on the sidelines and watch my friends. "Eh, no, not everyone. I sit in the can't skate camp. And I have a dress on." I look down at my pretty work dress and point to it like he hasn't seen my outfit and wasn't eye fucking me out in the hallway when I pulled open my coat and asked if he wanted to do a full body inspection.

Brazen hussy.

"Are you sure you're Canadian?" He eyes me suspiciously but doesn't give me any time to defend my heritage when he says, "If you want your scarf back, you have to put those skates on and go get it." He points to my cream scarf that's tied in a bow on the back of one of the wooden chairs in the middle of the ice. I inwardly do a little happy dance as I check out the table and two chairs along with a hamper, two fluted glasses, and a large green bottle of wine. Or maybe it's champagne, I can't tell from here.

How romantic.

But skating? I wasn't lying when I told him I'm like Bambi on ice. I'm the least coordinated person I know. Even dancing in time to music is a struggle.

At war with my inner emotions; the desire to go out there and spend a date on the ice overrides my fear of skating. "Oooo, you drive a hard bargain, Mr. Johansson." I'm praying I don't fall on my ass and end up looking like a fool.

Sitting on the bench around the edge of the arena, he chuckles to himself as he pulls on a pair of skates that were lying on the floor next to another much smaller pair that I assume are meant for me.

"Did you guess my shoe size?"

"Nope. I asked Kourtney."

"You asked Kourtney?" I ask, surprised.

"Yes."

"Right." He seems to have gone to a lot of effort. This man melts my heart. "Can I skate in a dress?" I have serious doubts about this whole thing and don't feel one bit brave as visions of me falling and smashing my head against the ice swirl around my brain.

Finished tying his laces, Ash picks up the other set of skates, then stands up on his blades, and, as if he couldn't get any taller, he does. "Woah, you are very big." I sound foolish, looking up at him as if he's a skyscraper.

He smirks. "Park your fine ass down and I will put these on for you." He pulls out a pair of thick white socks from the inside of the skates.

"Oh, thank God, I was just thinking how

uncomfortable my feet would be in those." Ash gets to work, slipping off my heels and pushing on each skate as I look around the arena, specifically the ice that looks like a sea of mirror glazed white chocolate. "Is it quite slippery out there? Do you ever fall? Is it cold? Have you ever broken anything? I have bills to pay. Please don't let that happen to me." My muscles tense, drawing my shoulders to my ears.

I look at him for reassurance to discover he's sitting back on his haunches staring back at me with a serious look on his face. "I would never let anything happen to you."

His protectiveness makes me feel safe, and I swear my heart is dancing in my chest with joy.

"Thank you." I let out a sigh of relief. "And you won't laugh at me if I fall?"

"I won't let you fall."

Does he mean in the rink or for him?

The silence stretches between us like an elastic band for a beat too long.

I blink and shake my head to break the spell cast over us momentarily and look down. That's when I discover he's finished putting the skates on. I roll the virgin white skates back on their heels, tipping the toes skywards. The laces are so tight. *Wow, that is uncomfortable. How does he wear these for a living?*

On bent knees, he shuffles closer and slides his hand up my calf, over the thin denier of my tights, and then moves his gigantic hand to my knee.

My body responds to him in a way I can't explain. I felt it last night in his truck. It wants to please him; *I* want to please him.

And I want him to touch me in places I've never allowed anyone to touch.

His hand rests on my knee, his fingertips gently massage my skin as he moves gingerly upward.

"Okay?" He asks for permission to continue.

I reply by letting my legs fall wider and edging my dress higher. His eyes never leave mine as his hand drifts slowly up, the calloused skin on his palms snags my silk tights.

"I can be gentle." He drags a finger upward, barely ghosting my thigh, making me shiver. "Or I can be rough." He pushes his bear sized hands under my dress, cupping my hips in his palms as he moves in closer, making me gasp in response. My ass teetering on the edge of the bench, my center perfectly aligned with his crotch, he moves his hips, rubbing me against him.

He's hard. Rock solid.

My entire body awakens, hungry for his touch, more, him; I'll take everything and anything he wants to give me.

His lips brush mine, teasing me with his words. "I can be whatever you want, Lily. But know this. When, not if, but *when* you ask me to take that virginity of yours, you'll be begging me. Then and only then will I take it."

His hands squeeze my hip and move to my ass. He drops one hand down between us and runs his finger over the fabric of my tights and panties between my pussy lips. "Have you ever been touched here before?"

My body aches in response, and I drop my head and moan into the curve of his neck, "No."

"You're so pure. Untouched." The tone of his voice is strained and full of longing.

"I want you to touch me." A hum of desperation slips from my lips, every cell of my body desperate for him to take me and show me what he has to offer.

"You are fucking soaked, Tiger." He's right, my panties

are dripping wet from the apprehension and possibility of what's to come.

I rub my hips against his hand, chasing the friction I need to get myself off.

Unexpectedly, his head disappears between my open legs. He mouths my fabric covered pussy, sucking and licking it, devouring me. He has me moaning with need.

"I can't wait to taste you." He drags his nose up my body to my nipple and bites it through my dress, then roughly nips at my neck. "You drive me fucking wild, Tiger." He's almost growling, grunting when he grinds my pussy against his jean covered dick again. "I will be the only man that will ever be inside of you. I'm gonna fill you with my cock." He licks my neck. "And fuck you so good, you'll never crave anyone else but me."

"Oh, God." Panting, I clasp the back of his jacket, feeling like I could come right now. And wanting to shout 'yes, please' to everything he's offering.

"Not God, Tiger. Ash." He nibbles my neck, then licks the shell of my ear. "Say my name," he demands in a low and dangerous tone, his hot breath making every hair on my body stand on end.

"Ash," I moan.

"Louder."

"Ash." My needy voice echoes around the vast space.

"Good girl." His lips are on mine in milliseconds. He works my mouth. Hard. Sucking my tongue and kissing me like a man possessed. The scruff of his short beard tickling and rubbing my lips and I know I'll have stubble rash tomorrow. The remnants of our kissing session last night have been cleverly concealed by my makeup today.

No man has ever held the power to make me want to rip my clothes off, and I don't care that it's cold in the arena. I'd quite happily freeze my nipples off if it meant Ash was touching them. "I want you," I admit.

"Soon." He cups my sex with his entire hand and the ache between my thighs pounds as if it has its own heartbeat. "This pussy is mine."

"Yours." Agreeing with him, I lay my hand over his, pushing my hips harder against him.

He smirks against my lips and when I open my eyes, he's staring at me. "Mine."

And all I can do is bob my head in agreement because it's what I want.

I buck my hips, causing him to inhale a sharp breath between his teeth. "You're a needy little thing, aren't you?"

It would be stupid of me to deny it. "Only for you."

"Soon," he says again. A low rumble of what sounds like reluctance leaves his chest when he moves his hand and leans back on his heels.

I can't wait for soon.

And when exactly is *soon*? Tonight, tomorrow, next week, when?

He has me in a spin, my mind reeling with questions as he expertly jumps onto his blades, sending a cool gust of wind in my direction, making my spine bristle.

His hand swallows mine when he pulls me to my feet as if I am a featherweight. I wobble like a baby walking unassisted for the first time.

Unsure of my footing, I push my hand out to the side that he isn't holding to balance myself.

"Shift your weight from your heels to your toes." He instantly flicks the switch from sexy to all about business. "Bend your knees slightly and try to keep your back straight."

That's a lot of things to remember.

"I've got you." He moves with me, walking slowly to the opening leading onto the rink, as I try to get the hang of walking, never mind actually skating.

I try a couple of quicker steps. "Oh, it's easier if I walk faster." I push my shoulders back as a sense of newfound confidence comes to me.

I look up, and he smirks knowingly.

"Don't let the skates lead you, you lead the skates, Lily." Ash steps onto the ice and expertly spins around to face me.

I hold on to the edge of the opening on either side of me. "You arranged a date on the ice?" I can barely contain how giddy I feel. "The scarf was a decoy just so you could lure me here, wasn't it?"

His eyes crinkle around the edges as he fights to contain a smile.

"I wanted to see you again. I couldn't wait until next Saturday."

I shake my head. "Me either." Nibbling on my bottom lip, now knowing he feels the same way, I shoot my shot. "Can I have your phone number?" I'm not waiting for opportunities to pass me by. I'm going after what I want.

And what I want is him.

"Leaving here tonight without exchanging numbers was not an option, Tiger."

"Tiger?" I question.

Lifting his hand to my face, he cups my cheek and looks deep into my eyes. "You may be pure as untouched snow, but you're hardly a white lily, are you? You have fire in your belly, drive, and ambition. You aren't afraid to speak your mind. You remind me of a tiger lily; vibrant and striking. You're a crazy ball of energy." He pauses. "And I like the fact that you couldn't give a fuck about who I am."

Stunned by his words, joy sparkles in my chest. "Those

are really beautiful things to say." I feel like I'm glowing. "I had no idea who you were until twenty-four hours ago." I'm embarrassed to admit that.

"Ouch." He closes his eyes and shakes his head as if I dented his pride, but when he opens them again, they are dancing with humor. "Way to kill a guy's ego." His thumb continues to brush the skin of my cheek, the familiarity between us planting roots and growing faster than a cosmos flower.

"I googled you and I'm up to speed with everything about your career." And absolutely nothing about his personal life; it's a mystery. The only photos of him online are those with crowds of fans, organized meet and greets, charity events, and from what I managed to digest in a short time, he's never been involved in scandals on or off the ice. I lay my hand over his that's resting on my cheek, lean into it, and say, "And your dad's."

"He was a great man."

"So are you." I discovered that he donates generously to the children's hospice on the outskirts of town and visits monthly. It made me like him more. If I'd had his number, I would have called him up to tell him how incredibly generous and kind he was.

He gulps loudly. "I think you're pretty great."

The same energy in the atmosphere I felt last night sparks between us, and it's as if the world ceases to exist.

"Something is happening between us. What is it?" I ask, leaning closer to him, the magnetic attraction between us too strong to pull away; I don't want to.

"Something," he replies with a wondrous, almost humorous tone.

"Something," I repeat, searching his eyes for any hint of doubt. However, it's not there.

The mutual attraction between us is real. I feel it. He does too.

I look over his shoulder at the wooden table set and woven hamper that looks like it's spilling over with edible goodies on top of the table in the middle of the rink.

He clears his throat as if he's trying to make his voice work. "This is a first for me."

I feel a little giddy and know he's telling the truth, but I can't help but ask him anyway. "Yeah?"

He bobs his head. "I don't date."

"You said last night." I rest my arms on top of his shoulders casually when he drops his hand from my face.

"Since being drafted to the NHL, I find it difficult to trust people."

"Because you never know if their intentions are genuine or if they only want to be your friend or date you because of your celebrity status?" I can't imagine how difficult it must be for someone as introverted as Ash appears to be. Privacy for him seems to be his one non-negotiable.

He scoffs. "I've never seen myself as a celebrity."

"There are thousands of news articles about you on the internet. If you were to search my name, you'd only find my social media pages, and those are pretty dull." I tell him the truth. "You're a famous hockey player," I state, then admit, "Super sexy, panty dropping handsome hockey player." His cheeks fill with color. "Completely untouchable. You're an enigma to women." I wiggle my eyebrows. "Some of the forums I read mentioned a huge reward for the puck bunny that manages to bed you." I chuckle because it's just so gross.

"What?" He screws his face up. "That's vile. Is that true?" Astonished, he shakes his head in disbelief.

"There are several bunny bounties out there on you.

One to kiss you, one to go out on a date with you, and then there is one to bed you. Maybe I should sign up. I'm already winning." Unable to keep a straight face, a burst of giggles leaves my chest. "And I do need that deposit for a new house."

"You wouldn't dare?" His eyes pop out of his head as he cups my face with both hands again and looks me dead in the eyes.

I move his hand over my heart and hold his palm tight to my chest.

Knowing how much he appreciates his anonymity, I make a vow to him. "I promise you can trust me with your privacy. But you have to promise me that in return, I can trust you with my heart."

With confidence and calmness, his face full of strength, he replies, "I promise you that you can trust me with your heart, your soul, your body. Everything."

Blissfully happy, a smile shapes my lips. "Everything," I repeat.

"You can trust me, Lily. But you have to know that if we are doing this, me and you, we may not get the option to keep us a secret for very long."

I think about how big a deal this is and know the press will hound us, and heaven knows what the puck bunnies will say and think about me. However, knowing how much I like him already, I am willing to give us a shot.

"I don't care. I really like you, Ash, and all I ask is that we agree to do everything on our terms. Not the hockey press team you probably have or the tabloids. We decide."

Satisfaction etches his face, as he says, "You are some kind of wonderful, Tiger. Are you sure you're ready to face the fans and the speculation?"

"I am," I reply.

He adds, "All I know is that for the first time I don't care about the press knowing if I have a girlfriend and that we are together. I want to spend more time with you. Whatever that looks like, however, whenever. Let them talk."

A warm glow of happiness flows through me as he talks about us as if we're official and already dating.

I look over his shoulder at the romantic set up in the middle of the ice again. "Is that champagne?" I'm excited and want to see what he's organized over there for our sweet evening date on the ice.

He nods his head shyly.

"Are you sure you don't date? This is super swoony of you, Mr. Johansson."

He avoids eye contact with me. "I asked my mom for some advice," he confesses. "I told you I don't date. I am way out of my depth here with you."

Now that is cute. "You did great."

"I did?" He looks bashful when he bites his bottom lip nervously.

"Yes."

"It's time to get your scarf back then, Tiger. She's missing you."

I laugh and reach down to weave our fingers together. "Okay. Show me how this skating thing is done."

I mean, what's the worst that could happen?

CHAPTER TEN

Ash

"I'm sorry I face planted your crotch." Slapping her hand against the tabletop, Lily bursts into another fit of giggles. Which, I've realized once she starts, she can't stop and anything visual with comedic value sets her off time and time again.

"How are the knees feeling?" I ask with genuine concern. She went down with an almighty thud.

As we moved across the ice, she was just beginning to get the hang of her balance when she twitched, leaned too far forward, and as I spun to catch her, I was too late. Her knees clattered against the ice and she head butted my cock, which was slightly alarming, but instead of crying like I thought she might, she rolled onto her back in the middle of the ice, spread herself out like a starfish, and broke out into hysterical laughter.

In every possible way, she's a surprise.

And nice.

Fun to be around.

And she talks enough for the pair of us.

Wiping the tears of laughter from under her eyes, Lily examines her knees. "They're fine." She gives her skin a gentle rub. "A bit bruised though." She waves off my concern.

"They will hurt tomorrow. Ice on them tonight to reduce the swelling."

Lifting her glass of champagne to her lips, she takes a sip of the golden liquid then says, "More champagne will help."

"Alcohol to numb the pain."

"Exactly." Her lips curve upward against the rim of her glass.

I bend sideways to pick up the box hidden under the tablecloth, then place it in front of her.

"What's this?" Sliding her fluted glass across the table, she stares at the white gift box.

"Open it and see."

Excitedly, she lifts the lid to reveal what's inside and lets out a shocked gasp. "Tickets to the first pre-season game on Saturday?"

I nod. They are like rocking horse shit; you can't get them anywhere.

Holding them up, she fans them out. "Three?"

"One for you, your sister, and your dad."

She looks at me, confused, her brows hunched together. "How did you know I had a sister?"

"I asked Kourtney that too. You'll be sitting in my family seats alongside my mom and sister." My mom and sister always sit in the front row of the area dedicated to my father. It's the only request my mom made when he passed. She bought several seats on the proviso that they would be allocated for our family only. Although, from time to time, she raffles them off for charity. "And I've booked The Fair

Donald Plaza Hotel for your sister and dad for Saturday night."

Motionless, she stares at me, then drops her gaze to the tickets. "This is hundreds of dollars' worth of gifts." She looks up again as if disorientated. "My dad is a huge hockey fan." Her voice is barely a whisper.

"Kourtney mentioned it." I can't work out if she's annoyed or happy and I'm seriously wondering if I messed up.

"He'll pee his pants." Her mood suddenly buoyant, a small grin widens.

Thank fuck.

Her hand moves to the box again and she gasps. "What's this?" She pulls out a yellow and blue hockey jersey.

This is where I'm certain I overstepped and I hold my breath as she turns it around.

"Johansson. Eleven," she says, then peeks around the side of the jersey and smiles.

She scrunches the fabric in her tiny fists and holds it to her chest. "You want me to come to your game on Saturday, wearing your team jersey with your number on the back, and sit beside your family with mine?" She stares at me.

"Yeah." Having never asked a girl to one of my games before, I flap the neckline of my tee shirt to cool me down. I'm suddenly feeling very hot and nervous. Sitting down for the past half hour, getting to know each other better, and eating the snacks I prepared for us, my body temperature had started to drop however, within a heartbeat, it's burning hotter than the sun.

I really am shit at this dating nonsense.

"I'm supposed to be going out with Kourtney on Saturday night to the opening of her friend's nightclub."

Kourtney said she would worry about that, explaining that Lily hates letting people down. "It's an early game. You can still go out afterward. Kourtney invited your sister to the nightclub opening too."

"But what about my dad? I can't leave him in the city alone." Her mouth twists unpleasantly at the thought.

"My mom and sister are taking him out for a meal after the game." I reach out to take her hand and reassure her.

She lays the shirt I gifted her down on the table. "So, they know they are coming to the game?"

"I had Kourtney pull your emergency contact details for your dad off your staff record. I wanted to surprise you. I hope you don't mind." Yeah, that may have been a bit far-reaching of me. And her dad actually hung up on me the first time I called, assuming I was playing a prank. I called back, asking if I could video call and confirm I was actually Ash Johansson from the Edmonton Eagles.

To say he looked a little shocked when my face filled the screen, would be an understatement.

"It's all arranged?" She asks, sounding surprised.

"Too much?" I question, feeling unsure of myself.

Shaking her head, her gaze shifts between the tickets, the shirt, and then me. "It's perfect."

Well, thank Jesus-fucking-Christ for that. My shoulders drop with relief and I let out a huge sigh.

Laying her hands out in front of her, she asks, "Help me up. I'm too far away from you, but I don't want to fall and look like an idiot again." She cringes as she must mentally recall her fall from earlier.

Wobbling on her blades, I help her move. With her legs together, she repositions herself on my lap and cradles my face with her dainty hands. She's cold, and that's my sign for us to get out of here soon before we both freeze our asses off.

I lay my hand on her soft backside as she wiggles about on my leg before she says, "You know, for a guy who doesn't date, you sure do know how to impress a girl. Thank you."

"You have my mom to thank for all of this."

"So, you're a momma's boy, huh?" she teases.

"Since my dad passed away, yeah." My sister, Mom, and me, we're tight and as I've gotten older, and I've become more of a... how did Lily put it... *celebrity*, I appreciate them even more and we now share everything.

"Well, Ash Johansson, I accept your invitation and I will be at your game on Saturday." Her nose scrunched. "Even if that means I am meeting your family for the first time." Biting her bottom lip, she adds, "Feels kinda... Official." She makes odd shapes with her mouth and drags out her last word.

"What did I tell you earlier?" I squeeze her thigh.

She makes a list of the things I have shared with her tonight during our dinner date on ice. "You are twenty-two, the same age as me, which is slightly depressing, as I work two mediocre jobs while you are a pro athlete and live in a fancy apartment in one of the nicest areas in Edmonton. You like horror movies, which I don't but love hiking, just like me. Oh, you collect retro games machines, and, you really enjoy working out, which I find weird." Her eyes question me as if asking if she got everything right, which she did.

"You missed something," I tell her.

"Did I?" Confusion wrinkles her forehead.

"You left out the part when I told you that you are mine and you agreed."

"Did, I? Are you sure?" Her mouth pulls to the side as

she triggers her mischievous switch again. I love how much she fucks with me.

I've been known to give off some serious fuck off and don't mess with me vibes. Something my teammates tell me I do often. They think I could bottle and sell my own brand of atmosphere. Lily doesn't give a shit and slices through it with just one smart-ass question.

"You're officially mine." When I want something, I go after it, and I want her. I can't get her out of my head. All I want to do is spend time orbiting her chaos and I can see myself having a future with her.

This is unlike anything I have ever felt before.

It feels great and I refuse to push that away.

She makes me want to smile, and that doesn't happen very often either.

Forget my own brand of atmosphere. Lily has a unique one of her own; it's addictive and all consuming.

And I want to be consumed by her innocence, joy, and the energetic cheerfulness she exudes when I'm around her because everything feels better when she's nearby.

She takes her ransomed scarf from around her neck that she's been wearing since we sat and loops it around mine to pull me to her.

Our lips a micrometer apart, they hover over one another like a hummingbird circling a flower. "I'm yours," she finally says, then she leaves me dizzy, and wanting more with an incredibly passionate kiss, making it hard to believe that she's a virgin.

Fuck.

She's a virgin.

How do I keep forgetting that?

Struggling to catch her breath, she stops kissing me and murmurs, "I trust you."

And I read between the lines, she trusts me to take her virginity, and while I would love nothing better, she has to be ready.

And right now, I know she's not.

She barely knows me, but I will do everything in my power to open up and let her see a part of me that no one else gets.

This is a huge deal for both of us, and I want to prove to her that this isn't a random hookup.

This is it for me.

She is it for me.

Lily Murphy, the woman who hit me with the force of a hurricane disguised as a wooden door.

The little cloud of happy chaos who giggles, talks, and smiles more than should statistically be possible.

Yup, Lily Murphy, I don't know who you are or what you've done to me, but you've got me.

Bring on Saturday, then everyone will know she's mine.

CHAPTER ELEVEN

Lily

"This is awesome, the best seats in the house." My sister, Gemma, claps with excitement as she chats away to my dad around the front row seats. My dad is equally excited, if not more, while I feel sick to my stomach as if a swarm of grasshoppers is bouncing around in my gut.

I could barely say two words to Ash's mom, Judy, and his sister, Erika, when they introduced themselves.

Overwhelmed is an understatement, and the game hasn't even started yet.

The place is buzzing; the atmosphere jumping with expectation and electric energy. From the noise of the crowd, the blinding spotlights, and the vibration of the music, to the eye stares from the fans and the whispers around us. So many whispers. They all keep asking who I am.

It's all extremely *wow*.

It's the only word I can think of.

"You're quiet. Everything okay?" Judy rests her hand on my arm.

"Yeah." I look over my shoulder to be met with at least a hundred sets of eyes on me. Whipping my head back around to face the rink, I do my best to avoid the glares from a line of puck bunnies seated five rows behind us. I recognize at least three of the girls from the coffeehouse.

"It's quite intense." I gulp, talking to nobody in particular. "And crowded." I bite my now non-existent thumbnail I've devoured since we sat down.

Judy slowly removes it from my mouth. "He wouldn't have asked you here if he didn't think you could handle those girls. Or any of this." Twisting herself to half face me, she takes both of my hands in hers. She has an air of authority around her that demands my full attention, which I give her. "He's never asked a girl to sit with us before."

"You're special." Erika points her oversized foam finger over Judy's shoulder. "The chosen one." She beams at me, and it's so goddamn genuine I know she's telling the truth.

"Zip it, Erika."

I laugh when Judy gives her seventeen-year-old daughter a snipped telling off and Erika rolls her eyes at the same as she stuffs a mustard and ketchup covered hotdog into her mouth with her free hand.

Ash's family is nice. And normal. Which I wasn't expecting.

His family has led a life in the limelight. They are extremely wealthy; I know because I looked them up. Ash's father was the GOAT; the greatest hockey player of all time, and yet, Erika and Judy were talking about how expensive the hotdogs were this season, and how much the season tickets had risen in price. They aren't cheapskates with their money, they're just normal, appreciating the value of something, which I find humbling.

"Ash has been different since his dad passed away."

Judy lets out a concerned sigh. "When he's not at practice, working out, or playing hockey, he hides himself away in his apartment. You being here tonight is progress. You're good for him."

"I'm not so sure about that." We've only been getting to know each other for a few days, although he did text me several times today, checking in with me, asking if I missed him yet and if I was still coming tonight.

He's a secret stress head if ever I saw one. He sounded playful in his messages, but I could tell he was worrying.

"Eh, yes you are. He's texted me ten times today freaking out about you. Questioning if you'd show up tonight and if you could handle all this and the speculation that will come after. He's worried about you." I knew I was right about him; he's a closet worrier.

Judy casts a glance around the arena and points to the opposite end of the rink where dozens of paparazzi are positioned. "He's concerned about how the press will treat you." She gives my hand a squeeze, her warm eyes meeting mine. "How will you cope with some of the slightly overzealous fans. Those wretched bunnies." She tilts her head in their direction behind us. "Trust me. I have been where you are. Ash is just like his father; he worried about me too and did everything to protect me. He's doing what his father told him; don't be afraid to shine and remember to take chances." She gives me a knowing wink. "It's time for Ash to come out of his shell, or his apartment more like it. And I think you might just be the girl to help him do that."

My cheeks fill with air, and I let out a huge puff of breath. "No pressure then?" The force of a thousand cannonballs weighs heavy on my chest. "It's just all so sudden, you know?"

Judy pats my hand. "When Ash's father, Theo, and I met, we both just knew we were meant for one another. Theo asked me to marry him within three months of our first date."

"Three months?" I quiz, sounding shocked.

Lifting one shoulder to her ear, she shrugs off my disbelief. "We were meant to be."

"I felt the same way about your mom," Dad whispers in my ear. "We got married six months after our first date."

I recall how Mom loved sharing how romantic my dad was; arranging a picnic in her favorite spot in the park by the river she used to take me and my sister to as kids in Spruce Plain. It's where he proposed, and they visited every year on their wedding anniversary. They loved each other unconditionally, and I always admired the bond that held them together more firmly than superglue. I wish she were here tonight. She would have loved this. Her and Dad loved watching all the hockey together. How Dad is coping without her, I will never know. He's been so strong.

"You guys move fast," I chuckle. Three months and six. Can you even organize a wedding in that time?

I guess it's proof enough for me that fated love isn't just a rumor or based on science. It's true, it can hit as quickly and as powerfully as a thunderbolt.

There is no denying the instantaneous attraction between Ash and me. Even Kourtney said the chemistry between us was so intense you could literally see the sparks fly in the two short times she's seen us together.

"And you are overthinking, Lily." My dad gives me a peck on the cheek. "What did your mom used to tell me to do?"

"Chill out," I confirm. When my dad would come home

from a stressful day in court, she would make him sit down with a beer to take a moment and tell him to *chill out*. As a divorce lawyer, my dad often said he saw what losing someone you once loved did to people, both the best and the worst.

Not giving me any more time to freak out, my dad says, "Oh, here we go." He rubs his hands together as everyone around us cheers and whoops loudly, the arena falling into darkness. Neon yellow and blue lights illuminate the rink, while laser beams pierce the air, dancing in time to the thumping music that's louder than before.

I watch the spectacle and fanfare with fascination. The overhead giant screens light up and the crowd grows even louder when each player is introduced and skates onto the ice.

When Ash's name is announced, I go wild and throw my hands in the air, screaming his name and cheering for him. Skating past me, he winks and smiles, making my heart flip in my chest.

Wow, that man is gorgeous.

Music booming and having never watched the first game of the season before or a game from start to finish, I can't believe the amount of fun these guys have out on the ice before a game, playing up for the crowd, and entertaining them with tricks and interacting with the fans.

The music changes and the sound of "We Are the Champions" by Queen booms out from the sound system, sending the crowd into a frenzy, the rink now swimming in a sea of blue and yellow.

The lights dim and a mixture of jeers and boos begins as the opposition steps into the arena like a colony of ants. The lights turn up again and that's when I see him.

Ash separates himself from his team. Eyes glued to

mine, he makes a beeline for me and stops on the other side of the Perspex directly in front of our seats. He beckons me to him.

Low huddled whispers of speculation move around me as they try to figure out who I am.

Any minute now, they'll all know; I'm Ash Johansson's girl.

You're mine.

His words have been looping around my mind like a song stuck on repeat.

As if by magic, I'm on my feet, facing him through the plastic divide. He slips his protective helmet up, revealing himself, and I almost gasp at how gorgeous he looks.

Face flushed, excitement sparkling in his eyes, he's so handsome, it's almost hard to believe he would like plain little me.

"You good?" he mouths, his face flooded with concern.

I bounce my head enthusiastically. "I'm great," I shout through the Perspex, feeling better now I've seen him.

This feels right.

He gifts me with an enormous smile then holds his glove covered hand up against the plastic wall and I take that as I sign for me to place mine on the opposite side of the cool Perspex.

When I do, the crowd goes bananas, screaming and cheering his name, as a few two-note wolf whistles give us their approval.

I throw my head back and laugh at how insane being in the limelight is, but I feel lighter than a helium balloon in the wind as he shows me off to the world.

"Give 'em hell." I slam my hand against the plastic divide as if giving him a high five.

"I like your jersey," he mouths.

I look down and give the ends of my cream scarf a tug. "I brought my lucky charm," I call out, making him grin wider than the arena.

"You're my lucky charm." He points at me, shouting to be heard over the rowdy fans and the wall of plastic between us. "I'll see you after the game, yeah?" I only just make out what he says over the noise and I nod in response.

He blows me a kiss.

On quick feet he makes skating look effortless as he glides across the ice and when I turn to go back to my seat only a few steps away, I realize there are thousands of sets of intense eyes on me.

Sensing my nerves have reappeared, Erika puts her hand out for me to take to usher me back to my seat.

In full on Janice from *Friends* style, my sister squeals, "Oh. My. God."

Judy pats my jean covered thigh before she says, "Well, they certainly know who you belong to now."

Hell, yeah, they do.

"Ash is kinda an all or nothing guy," Erika says matter of factly.

"I never would have noticed," I joke, making our families to the left and right of me laugh.

Eyes shining, standing with other members of his team, Ash finds me in the crowd again and treats me to his trademark smirk.

Happiness blooms in my chest, and I bask in the new emotions he's woken up within me as I blow him a flirty kiss. He pretends to catch it, then holds it to his heart while mine melts in my chest at his gesture.

I can't stop my stomach and heart from fluttering.

Holy crap, I think I just became Ash Johansson's number one fan.

Then it hits me.

Mr. Sexually Experienced-With-An-Older-Woman wants me.

And I have no idea what the hell I am doing.

CHAPTER TWELVE

Ash

An odd wave of calm washes over me as I step onto the ice as the commentator calls my name and whizz around the rink, getting pumped up by the crowd's never-ending support and passion for the game.

Their efforts don't go unnoticed by me. I see the same sea of faces turning up, traveling to each and every game, standing by the team even when we lose a game, or two, sometimes three in a row. They are the ones that keep us going; the banners they make, the fan mail, and gifts we receive. It's heartwarming and they feel like family. Although there are some fans who can become a little obsessive and those are the ones we're pleasant to but take a wide berth.

Regardless, the pros outweigh the cons, and I know deep in my soul that I found my calling. This is where I'm meant to be.

Hockey runs through my veins like hot butter. It's warming, comforting, and feels like home.

This is where I belong.

Pregame warm up, I'm surrounded by my team as they stretch, practice maneuvers, and throw the puck around with the end of their sticks to help with their hand-eye coordination. And for the first time before a game, I'm not doing any of that because I feel nervous.

And I don't get nervous before a game. Excited? Yes. Nervous? Never. Focused? Always. Love for the game at an all-time high? That never waivers.

However, tonight, I'm a little distracted.

By her. When I should be zoned into the game.

I can't believe she actually came. Of course, she said she was coming, but still, I doubted if she would show.

"What the fuck are you grinning at?" I look to my right to find Brayden standing next to me as he punches my shoulder.

"And holy shit. It smiles," Troy exclaims, making a joke about my normally emotionless face, but somehow, since I met Lily, I can't stop smiling like a Cheshire cat.

"Fuck off." I pretend to inspect my stick butt end. I don't need to. Superstitious about who touches my stick, I tape my own and in a very specific way; three layers of grip tape, just like my dad.

He maintained each one represented the three most important people in his life. A layer for my mom, one for me, and the other for my sister. Although I know it's because it gave him greater stick handling and control over the puck. I guess mine now represents the three most important people in my life; my mom, my sister, and my dad.

I look over at Lily again. Maybe I should add a fourth; one for her.

"Is the hot little blond sitting next to your mom

responsible for this shocking turnaround?" Leon pipes up and they all look over at her.

Feeling the weight of my stare, she looks our way and blows me a kiss. Automatically, I catch it and hold it to my heart.

And I know for a fact the cameras will have caught that.

"Well, I guess that answers your question, Leon." All three of them burst out laughing as the crowd's cheers become louder.

They are excited for the first pre-season game and there is no doubt in my mind that we won't disappoint them tonight.

I wipe my brow and keep quiet as my friends bombard me with questions.

"Wow, she is beautiful. Where do you meet her?"

"How long have you been dating? What's her name?"

"Does she have a sister?"

I shake my head, rolling my eyes at their predictability and if I don't answer them, they will never leave me alone. "She works at the coffeehouse across the road as a second job. During the day, she's an events planner in the city. We met a few weeks ago. She was the one who gave me the black eyes."

"Well, shit," Brayden exclaims. "Are you into that sort of thing? The slapping, hitting thing during sex?"

"Kinky." Troy bobs his head as if liking the sound of that. *Weirdo.*

"Shut the fuck up, assholes." I continue, "It was an accident. She hit me with a door. Then I bumped into her again earlier this week. Her name is Lily. Originally from Spruce Plain, she's been studying and living in New York for the last four years. Her mom died and so she moved back to Edmonton to be closer to her family. We've had one date and yes, she does have a sister. She's sitting next to mine, which, for the record, Leon, Erika is still off limits this season." And every other season.

Leon protests, "She's eighteen this year. Legal." He holds his hand out, pointing to her and I know he's screwing with me, but it's still a big, fat, no.

"You can't protect her forever," Brayden sings mockingly over the fans shouting and whistling, the music subsiding, getting ready for the game to begin.

"Maybe not, but if I can protect her from Leon-the-man-whore, then I've won."

Placing his hands on his hips, Leon pretends to be mad. "I'll have you know I haven't slept with anyone in months."

"Not possible."

"Liar."

"Is that a fucking unicorn sitting in the crowd?" Brayden, Troy, and I all say in unison.

Leon lets out a disappointed sigh. "You guys have no faith in me." He looks away as we wait for his confession, which arrives quicker than I thought it would. "Okay, maybe I slept with one, or maybe two girls last week." Holding his hands up in surrender, he then adds, "They broke a very dry spell. Almost two months."

Two months, my ass. We all chuckle. None of us believe him.

"I see what you mean and I get the message. I'll stay away from Erika." He makes it sound like that's almost impossible. I'll slice his balls off and feed them to him if he doesn't stay away.

Troy playfully pulls me into a headlock, and they all slap my helmet.

"We are so proud of you. Ash finally has a girl. We all thought you were asexual." Troy hits my head harder this time. "When was the last time you fucked a girl? Was it that fitness instructor you used to have an arrangement with a couple of years ago that you slipped up and told me about?"

"Two years ago?" Leon shouts a little too loudly, sounding horrified. "Fuck, I can't last two weeks." I knew he was lying.

With similar height and build, it's not easy pushing Troy off me. "Fuck off, needle dick." I almost drop my stick, but grip it tighter to prevent it falling to the ground. That would be the worst thing to happen. My dad always swore it was a bad omen if you dropped your stick pregame. I've never dropped it before a game, so I don't know how true that is, but with Lily watching tonight, now is not the time to test his theory.

Brayden wraps his arm around my shoulder. "We are really proud of you, man. This is the most you've told us what's going on in your life since, you know?" He means since my dad died.

I drop my head. "Yeah." It's been a quiet two years around me.

"Does this mean we're getting our old Ash back?" he asks, sounding excited.

"Maybe." I feel different.

"Well, shit. That must be one helluva powerful pussy if you've only known her a week and had one date," Leon says.

I screw my face up. "If you fucking speak about her like that again, I will chop your dick off with a blunt knife. And it's not like that." I look over at her again and she's laughing and joking with my family as if she's known them her entire life. "I think she's the one."

The boys fall silent.

"Happy for you, Ash." Brayden squeezes my shoulder. "She looks great in your shirt."

She does. It would look better on my bedroom floor.

"So, when do we get to meet her?" Troy skates backward, hitting his puck back and forth across the ice with his stick, indicating for us to warm up properly. We move toward him and copy his actions. Coach has no problem with us discussing tactics on the ice during warm up, but he'll be mad at us if he catches us gossiping like office workers around the water cooler.

"Tonight, after the game," I confirm. Best to get it over and done with, or they will annoy me until they do.

"Great, can you introduce me to her sister?" Leon chimes in.

"No." My firm reply makes Troy and Brayden laugh again.

Assholes.

Coach calls us over to have our final pep talk.

I lift my foot and pivot around, my heart fluttering for my love of the game. The tension, apprehension, the anticipation of the win ahead.

Time to focus.

Time to do what I do best.

Game on.

Twenty seconds to go, we are even. I'll be damned if we don't win the first game of the season. Fuck overtime, I want to win this one.

Heart racing, eyes on the prize, I skate right, slipping past three Toronto players, intercepting their pass, and gaining control of the puck. Racing across the ice, I pass it to

Leon, who may be a self-confessed man-whore, but he's the best winger in the NHL.

At speed, and with the agility of a gazelle, in Toronto's zone, he controls the puck while skating toward the goal.

Ten seconds.

At the last minute, he switches direction, deking the opposition's defender, going left instead of right, and separating him from his opponent.

Excitement builds in me, knowing what comes next. The crowd grows louder with anticipation.

With the flick of his wrist, Leon takes his shot. The puck skims across the ice, and the goalie is too late to drop to his knees as it shoots straight through the five-hole; the sweet spot between the goalie's legs, hitting the back of the net. The fans go wild as the goal horn blasts through the arena speakers, and then the Klaxon calls full-time.

It's a miracle and a wicked start to the season.

The crowd is cheering, deafening us with their support and I look around the arena, punch the air in victory, and give out an almighty cheer as happiness rushes through my body. I cast my gaze around the ecstatic fans and commit to memory the electric feeling buzzing through my veins. I never want that feeling to end.

Adrenaline pumping, heart racing, sweat dripping into my eyes, I race toward Leon with the biggest smile across my lips. Along with every player, we pile on top of him in celebration, screaming and roaring as dopamine floods our brains, triggering that good reward feeling. I don't envy him being stuck at the bottom of that pile. It's painful as hell when that happens, but the best feeling knowing you helped to win the game. What a fucking rush.

The arena goes wild and we unpeel ourselves from

Leon, allowing him to bathe in the appreciation and love from the fans.

I take a moment to look over at Lily. Her hands are in the air and she's whooping, cheering, singing, and clapping along to our anthem.

Hell yeah.

We may have won our first pre-season game, but I think I won something much better.

Her.

Bring on the season.

CHAPTER THIRTEEN

Lily

"It was incredible," I swoon dreamily, shouting over the thumping music in the multicolored neon lit nightclub I'm now standing in, following a quick change into my sparkly black dress back at my apartment.

I took a cab ride into the city to meet up with my sister, along with Kourtney, and her boyfriend, Drew, for cocktails before we made our way to opening night of their friend's new club, Lyrical. It's a pretty cool place and I'm glad I came now, although the other part of me wishes Ash were here, so I could tell him how brilliant he was and celebrate with him.

Amused by my enthusiasm, Kourtney shakes her head in disbelief. "The girl who lived in New York for years, couldn't have given a fuck about hockey, now has a new obsession with the game. You are fickle, Lily Murphy."

"I can vouch for that," my sister jumps in.

"Oh, be quiet, Gemma." I dismiss her sarcastic tone. "He's so—"

"Dreamy," Drew interrupts, appearing behind

Kourtney and impersonating a woman's voice. Kourtney joins in. "My boyfriend's so dreamy." Her voice, now three times higher, makes Drew laugh out loud.

"I hate you two." I ignore them and move in time to the bassy music. Adrenaline continues to run white hot through my veins. I refuse to let anyone burst my happy bubble.

Unable to contain myself when the game started, I was on my feet, shouting Ash's name. I got swept away by the passion of the fans and when Ash scored a goal, I was whooping and screaming with so much euphoria, I made myself dizzy.

Pride blossoms in my chest. I wanted to stay with him after the game, offering to cancel tonight but when he mentioned an after-game press conference, shower, post workout on a stationary bike session to flush toxins or lactic acid from his body or something I didn't quite understand, I knew he had a jammed packed schedule. So, it made sense for me to go off and follow through with my original plans.

There is a lot more that goes on behind the scenes to being a hockey player than I imagined. It sounded hectic and demanding, but Ash seemed to take it all in his stride. Especially when his teammates all stared at us with curiosity in the area outside of the locker rooms. Not one of them uttered a word, but the shoulder taps and helmet slaps accompanied by toothy smiles and winks all confirmed what they were thinking; *it's about time.*

I take a sip of my almost empty cocktail glass then continue to tell them how enigmatic Ash was tonight, not caring if Kourtney and Drew think I'm a lust filled fool. "The way he moves on the ice is almost unreal." He must have rocket fueled propulsion canisters attached to his skates or something to make him move that fast because he's a big guy and yet he skims over the ice with skill, agility, and speed, switching directions without hesitation.

Holding my arms in the air, I sway to the music, feeling warm and fuzzy from the two drinks I've had. "Hockey is my new addiction," I shout over the music, not caring who hears me.

"Ash Johansson is your new addiction," Kourtney sings over the music before Gemma points downward and says, "And he's coming this way." We all look over the glass balcony we are standing against.

I gasp. "No way." My eyes pop out of my head as he, and the other members of The Eagles, some with their partners, snake through the crowd, as if they are Moses parting the Red Sea. They move in the direction of the elevator to the VIP area we have exclusive access to.

"I arranged it with Ollie." Kourtney winks at me.

I suppose having the entire Eagles team here on opening night is good for Ollie's new nightclub. I would have agreed to giving them VIP tickets too.

As if he can feel the weight of my stare, Ash looks up, rendering me momentarily speechless and all I can summon my body to do is pathetically finger wave as my heart skips in time to the pounding music.

Square jaw set with determination; he quickens his pace as he leads from the front.

I can't believe Ash is here, in this club, on his way to me.

When he disappears into the elevator, I turn to Kourtney and Gemma. "Do I look okay? Is my dress too short? Can you see my ass? How do my boobs look?" I grab the girls and reel off a dozen more questions. If I knew Ash was coming, I would have spent more time doing my makeup instead of applying it haphazardly in the taxi ride here.

A set of warm hands removes mine from my boobs. "Lily, you look great," Kourtney reassures me.

"You look hot." Drew threads his arm around Kourtney's waist. "Not as hot as Kourt, of course." He kisses her on the cheek.

"You are smokin'." My lovely friend fans herself with her hand.

"On fire," Gemma confirms their thoughts.

"So hot we might need to call the fire department," Kourtney continues, making me giggle.

I rake my fingers through my hair to fluff it out, then use my pointer finger under my eyes to wipe away any smudged mascara.

"Okay. I get the message. Thank you." I pull at the hem of my short dress, but the soft sparkly Lurex fabric jumps back up again.

There is no time to second guess my outfit when the elevator doors slide open and Ash steps out in all of his bulky gloriousness.

Wow.

Not paying attention to anyone else, he strides confidently over to me, and within seconds, his lips are on mine. Dazed and slightly taken aback, my hands remain at my sides before he wraps his arms around my waist and closes the gap between us. I hook my hand around the back of his neck, his skin warm against mine.

"I've wanted to do that all night." He sounds desperate when he eventually breaks our kiss.

I was tempted to kiss him earlier, but with both our families, specifically his mom and my dad, as well as his team standing around us, I was forced to resist the temptation.

Stepping back, without shame, he bites his bottom lip as he checks me out. "You look beautiful."

Looking down at my outfit, I say what I'm thinking. "I'm like a human disco ball." The club spotlights reflect off my black sparkly dress.

"You fit right in. Look at this place." Eyes twinkling, he threads his fingers through mine, his eyes scouring the club as if finding his bearings. "This place is—"

I finish his sentence. "Over the top."

"Over the top," he echoes in astonishment.

If I had designed this place, it would be more chic than shocking. "The fluorescent is a bit much."

"Three colors would have been enough."

"Two." Not a rainbow. It's blinding and a little tacky. He holds my hand and pulls me back to him.

His mouth moves against the shell of my ear. "So, you are an interior designer as well as an organizer of events?"

"I have a great eye for detail."

"Necessary if you want to be a wedding planner." I love that he listens and remembers my dream of owning my own business.

I stretch out my arms to loop them around his neck. "Creativity is a must."

"I'll remember that. Not good at coordinating your feet on ice but can coordinate bridesmaid dresses with bow ties. Noted." He drops his head and kisses along my collarbone while my fingers pull at the short strands of his hair.

"Get a room." A choir of hair-raising jeers blow up around us.

Nuzzling into my neck, he laughs, shaking his head. "My friends are idiots."

"I can't wait to meet them." That's a lie. I've only ever met one famous person; that being the guy who is currently squeezing my hand and was sucking on my neck less than a minute ago. Superstars in their own right, I'm nervous to be introduced to his teammates who, side by side, look wider than an ocean.

Ash pulls me by the hand toward the vast wall of expectant grinning faces. "Everyone, this is Lily." He yells to be heard over the dynamic dance tune the DJ plays.

"Hi, Lily," they all sing together mockingly with accompanying waves, then burst out laughing and I can't help but join in.

"Lily, meet my asshole team."

Having spoken to his mom earlier, I know he's joking because his teammates are like family to him; keeping a tight friendship circle is paramount to him. Those guys are on his short list of people he trusts. I feel honored to be on it too.

A grinning brunette steps forward, hooks her arm into mine and ushers me away from Ash in the direction of a room with a huge pink neon tube sign that says *Chill Out Room* on it. When I look over my shoulder in a panic, I needn't be worried because everyone is following us.

In the soundproofed room, the friendly woman says, "It's not so loud in here. I'm Bree, Troy's wife." I'm stunned by how beautiful she is. And sexy. Her gold figure hugging dress leaves little to the imagination. She has the biggest boobs I've ever seen.

"Wow. You are beautiful." I appreciate a beautiful woman when I see one.

"And mine." A blond guy grabs her around her waist and nuzzles into her neck. "Hey, I'm Troy." He holds his hand out for me to take and I shake it. "So, you're the woman who has finally persuaded our boy to come out with us?"

"Does that not happen at all?" I assumed he went out now and again, but kept a low profile.

"Never." Troy shakes his head. "You're obviously good for him."

"It's about time." I get a small peck on the cheek from a guy almost twice my size. "I'm Leon." He winks. "I need a drink." He's at the small bar along the back of the private space before I can say *hi* in return.

"And I'm Buster." Another guy shakes my hand.

Then another and another... Mitch, Joe, Brad, Ed... too many to remember. I need name badges.

"Welcome to the team, sweetie." A sexy female voice breaks through the testosterone filled greetings. "I'm Candy."

"Sweetest thing I ever tasted in my life." A firm ass slap is given by who I can only assume is her fiancé, given the size of the diamond on her ring finger, making her yelp and arch her back in a quick step forward.

"Behave yourself, Brayden." Candy giggles.

Brayden kisses her passionately, leaving her breathless. "Later, baby. You know you love a good ass spanking." He leaves her looking dazed, as if under a spell.

Wow, these guys are what can only be described as extra and they don't hold back on the personal displays of affection, which is something I could get used to.

"I think I just threw up in my mouth." An awkward looking woman standing beside me who looks like an exact cardboard cutout of Candy covers her mouth. "I'm Tessa, Candy's younger sister, by the way. She forced me to come out tonight." Tessa looks less than impressed with the company, her tone indifferent.

"I've come to save you." Ash's strong hands shape my waist and I'm maneuvered away, relieved that my sister, along with Kourtney and Drew, have followed us in here and are introducing themselves to everyone, already laughing and having fun.

Ash slides himself into the half-moon shaped seating booth and situates me on his lap.

"I got you a drink." He points to a glass on the table. "Your sister said you like Cosmopolitans."

"I love orange liquor."

He grins lazily while staring at my lips, which he tends to do quite often.

"Your teammates are nice." They make a refreshing change to the stereotypical finance guys Zoey would bring back to our apartment in New York.

"They are." Looking around, his eyes land on my sister, and says, "Gemma and Buster seem to be hitting it off."

Standing inches apart, she's twirling her curled lock around the end of her finger. Both of us watch the sparks fly between them when he leans in and whispers something in her ear, making her cheeks fill with color.

"How old is she?" Ash asks curiously.

"Older than me. She's twenty-four. She split up with her boyfriend a few months ago." That's not completely true, but it's not my story to tell. She was heartbroken when she discovered her long-term boyfriend had been cheating on her with her best friend, Kaylee. It was the worst timing when Mom died around the same time. It's when she needed them both the most, but they weren't there for her.

When I moved to New York, we drifted apart. Focusing on our majors and then our careers became our priority. We lost each other for a while, but I'm grateful we found each other again, even if it was Mom's death that reconnected us. I missed her and it was another reason that moving closer to home was the right decision.

Following the weeks after her devastating discovery, she was in a bad place for a while, needing to take a sabbatical from work.

Anyone looking would think she was fine now, but I know better. She's never truly recovered from finding Tony and Kaylee having sex in his bed. Their deceit left a dent in Gemma's self-confidence, deciding to become celibate for all eternity. Although the way she is flirting with Buster, three months is possibly what she considers a lifetime.

I don't care what or who she does if it means she finds happiness again.

Reaching for my drink, I mean to take a sip but down half of it. I really need to get over how nervous Ash makes me feel when I am around him.

His mom was spot on when she said he's an all or nothing guy; he's been all in with me from our first meeting at the conference center, recalling he said I tasted like his best decision and his.

I love how confident and up front he's been with me from the beginning. It's a rare trait, but I get the impression his confession is even rarer; knowing he doesn't go out or date, and holds his cards close to his chest. Only, he makes me feel special, opening up to me in a way that seems foreign to both him and I.

"Buster's a great guy. They all are." Ash gives my knee a squeeze, making me wince. "I'm so sorry. They look sore." Running his finger over my skin with care, his brow becomes wrinkled.

"They're a little tender." They've been aching all day. I now have what looks like a miniature land map of bright purple and blue bruising covering both my knees. I almost didn't wear a short dress tonight because they look hideous.

"No more skating for you then. I'm sorry."

I hold my pointer finger in the air as I make my declaration, as if I am a knight about to slay a dragon, "I will not be defeated. I will master the art of ice skating." I pause. "And you are going to teach me." I'm determined to learn. I can't be a hockey player's girlfriend who can't even skate. That's just ridiculous, and embarrassing.

"Yeah?" His eyes bug out in shock.

"Yes. I want to learn how to move at speed like you. You were incredible tonight."

"Did you have fun?" He sounds surprised.

"The best." My answer is genuine and breathy. "I'm addicted."

"To hockey?

"No, to you. I could watch you all day." My skin heats and I'm sure he's aware of the effect he has on me. "I'm your biggest fan."

Visibly touched, he runs his hand down his face, then rubs his beard. "Well, shit. That's the best fucking thing I've heard all year, Tiger."

And he's the best thing to have happened to me in, well, ever.

Everyone joins us around the table, and the drinks flow, as does the conversion. Time flies as I dance with the girls and have the most fun I have had since I returned to my roots.

From the minute I started dancing, Ash never took his eyes off me, and I may have moved more provocatively just for him. Known for not having the best sense of rhythm, I made a huge effort to try and stay in time with the music, and it was worth it. I knew what he was thinking when he clenched his jaw as I swayed my hips suggestively, to get a reaction.

My hard work paid off when he was on his feet minutes later, grinding himself against me and kissing my neck. Every time our bodies connect, the heat between us grows stronger. We're one spark away from starting a forest fire. Ash even told me so as he ushered me back to my seat, declaring his fear of fucking me on the dance floor in front of everyone.

Returning to our seats, I opt for soft drinks as I want to remember everything about tonight.

As soon as Ash informed Candy what I did for a living she's been asking me questions about how I could help her organize her upcoming wedding.

I already know we're going to be great friends.

I'm excited at the idea that this might be the start of setting the wheels in motion toward my dream of being my own boss.

Throughout our entire conversation, Ash's hand never left my thigh, kissing the skin of my shoulder from time to time as if he was reminding me he was there. As if I could forget. His touch sets my body on fire, and I am desperate to get him alone.

At some point, Ash lifted me onto his lap, refusing to let me move. Sitting there, I give my ass a wiggle and silently pray he feels the same way I do when I lean in close to his ear and whisper, "Wanna get out of here?"

As lovely as it is to be out meeting new people, I've noticed Ash is incredibly quiet around larger crowds. I want to spend some alone time with him, and I get the impression he prefers an environment where he can spend one on one time with me, too. Even Leon confirmed it when he introduced himself earlier. Ash doesn't socialize with his team after games.

Not needing to be asked twice, Ash is on his feet, grabbing my silver clutch bag and guiding me toward the exit while hugging my hips with his big hands as we say our goodbyes to people as we go.

Ash gives Buster firm instructions to make sure Gemma gets back to her hotel safely.

I give Gemma a tight squeeze and tell her to have fun.

"Oh, don't you worry about me." She looks over her shoulder at Buster. "Maybe it's time to break that dry spell," she says, making me chuckle, then looks back at me. "Have a great night, too." She beams, then winks. "I know I will be." Spinning away, she dances off in Buster's direction. "Have fun, Lily." Throwing her hands in the air, her words reassure me that she's perfectly fine with me going home. I know she's enjoying herself and probably off to have the best night she's had in months.

I grab Ash's hand as we step out of the quieter chill out room into the noisy VIP area of the nightclub that has become busier than before. As I do, a group of girls call out Ash's name and wave over at him.

"Fucking puck bunnies." I work out what Ash is saying under his breath. Well mannered, he waves at them with a sickly-sweet smile plastered across his face and leads me to the elevator.

"Great win tonight." One of them congratulates him and I look over my shoulder to try and work out who it was; God only knows because they all look the same.

"Not staying, Ash?" another of the girls calls out to him using a tone that sends shivers down my spine in the same way nails down a chalkboard do.

He hits the call button for the elevator and wraps his

arm firmly around my waist. "I'm going home with my girlfriend, Britney." Bowing his head, he kisses me full on the lips in front of them.

"Shit."

"Aw hell."

"I told you to make your move this year, Britney. Now you're too late," are just some of the quips that fly from the girls' mouths.

Leaning out of our kiss, I turn my head in their direction as Ash kisses down my neck and say loud enough for them to hear me, "You never stood a chance, Britney." My confident words makes me sound braver than I feel.

Ash chuckles against my neck, then finds my lips again. "You're right. You're the only one for me." He kisses me with such passion I almost forget we are in a public place and making a scene.

Light illuminates us both as the elevator doors slide open. He takes my hand, urgently pushes me against the back wall, and ravages me with his mouth and I can't do anything but let him do whatever the hell he wants to me. Sliding his hand up my thigh, I wrap my leg around his hip and look over his shoulder just as the metal doors are about to shut us in. Mouths agape in complete shock, the girls are gawking at us as if not believing what they are seeing.

To be honest, I can't believe what Ash is doing to me either.

If we were in a private place, I would be fucking him by now. I've been imagining what that might look like, only it's difficult to imagine when you've never experienced sex before.

He bursts out laughing as the door finally closes. "I can't control myself around you, Tiger. I've been careless tonight. I'm sorry."

"Don't be." I giggle along as well. "You gave those girls something to talk about."

"They annoy me and the guys all the time. That Britney is like a fucking vampire."

"Waiting to suck on the blood of hockey players." I gasp when he thrusts his pant covered hard cock against my center.

"More like their dicks, but whatever." Another hip thrust from him, and I can already feel an orgasm building in my core. I need to come; he's been teasing me since our first kiss.

"Ash," I hiss his name and open my eyes for a moment. "Shit." I pull his hand out from under my dress. "There's cameras in here."

Immediately, Ash drops back and spies the discreet camera on the roof of the elevator.

Composing myself, I fix my dress. "It must be hard being chased by girls all of the time."

"Much fucking harder being around you." Ash turns away to rearrange his cock. He grins, pulling the lapels of his navy sports coat that looks like it was custom made for him.

Quicker than Ash moves over the ice, we're out the elevator, through the club, and into the chilly night. Moments later, we're seated in Ash's chauffeur driven car he has on speed dial.

Giving the driver my address, we're then on our way to my apartment.

Oh God, what if he wants to have sex with me tonight?

What if I want to have sex with him tonight?

Am I ready for that?

Jesus, Murphy.

Why didn't I think this through?

CHAPTER FOURTEEN

Ash

When the glass between the driver's cockpit and rear seats slides closed, locking us in, I wait for Lily to make the next move.

I'm more than happy to call the shots, however, I would prefer for her to take the lead, given the fact I blindsided her with tickets to my game tonight, introducing myself to her family and plunging her into my world.

I hadn't planned to seduce her in the elevator in front of those puck bunnies, only something happens to me when I am around her. I can't hold back; I can't think straight. My body craves her in ways that make no sense.

The more time I spend with her, the more I know she's the one for me.

And I should have been more careful. From now on, I will be.

There is no way I am blowing my chances with this insanely beautiful woman, and I really hope the press doesn't fuck it up for me either. They have been less than kind to Candy, revealing how she met Brayden in a gentleman's club. It didn't matter that they met when Candy was serving behind the bar, fully clothed, I might add. They still tried to paint her as an exotic dancer, only after Brayden for his money, which couldn't be further from the truth. Candy, along with five of her friends, own a string of exclusive clubs throughout the city. Not that Candy has ever revealed that to the tabloids. She sat back and let them creatively put their spin on the truth, which I found brave and couldn't help but admire her for.

Tough skin is what you need in our field, and I pray Lily is prepared for the fall out of our very public rink side encounter earlier, which would have been caught on camera.

Only, I wanted her with me tonight. Something I have never asked of or wanted from a woman.

I couldn't be happier that she accepted my invitation and wanted to be there. Playing while she was there gave me a whole new zest for the game. A sense of vigor I always felt when my dad watched me play.

I can't ignore the truth; she's coaxing me out of a dark hole I've been buried in for far too long. When Dad died, a small part of me died along with him, as if someone had flicked the switch off. Since meeting Lily, she's shined light into those dark places, bringing me back to life in ways I never thought possible. Having her wear my jersey, not caring what the press thinks, going out with my team. Dating. I mean, I'm dating, for fuck's sake.

What happened to me this week?

Surprising me, taking everything in her stride, my heart almost burst in my chest when I spotted her on her feet, screaming my name while wearing my shirt.

I'm your biggest fan.

I thought I'd died and gone to heaven when those words slipped out of her tempting mouth back in the club.

She drums her fingers against the leather of the seat with one hand, chewing her thumbnail on the other, nervously.

Reaching for it, I pull her finger out of her mouth, cupping her chin in my hand, turning her to look at me.

"Everything okay?" I ask. This week has been the most fun I've had in years, tonight topping it for me. I hope she feels the same way too.

Intertwining our fingers, she moves our hands down and places them back on top of the seat. My fingertips brush the top of her hand. Her skin is so soft in comparison to mine.

"I'm great." Tilting her head back, she lets out a contented sigh. "I've had a great night. I don't want it to be over." She blinks, then says, "But you kind of make me feel nervous."

I give her a wide-eyed look of shock. "I. Make. You. Nervous." I swear it's the other way around.

Sucking her lips into her mouth, she nods.

"I'm dropping you off, Lily, then I'm going straight home," I reassure her. I won't take advantage of her. She has nothing to feel nervous about.

"That's what I am nervous about." She clears her throat. "I wondered, actually, wanted to ask you if you would like to come in for a coffee. I don't have any beer or I would offer you that instead." Twisting her lips, she nibbles the inside of her cheek, making her dimples appear.

"I don't drink during the season. Coffee is good." I accept her invitation with a hand squeeze, happy I finally get to see the inside of her apartment. I've been wondering what it looks like and it's cute she's anxious. "Did you think

I would say no?" I shake my head. "How could I refuse those dimples?"

A beaming expression puts a sparkle in her eyes, her shoulders dropping as if relieved.

I close the distance between us, and as if she's done so a million times before, she rests her cheek against my shoulder and snuggles in. "It's just, well, I don't invite guys back to my place, that's all. Not ever."

"I got the memo on that." Or more of a direct thought that fell out of her brain and out of her mouth.

Virgin.

'Has anyone ever touched you here?'... 'No, Ash.'

Holy fucking shit.

I'm a bad man for having impure thoughts about taking her innocence and claiming her as mine. Also, a deep satisfaction runs like molten lava through my veins in the knowledge that no man has ever touched her before.

Mine.

I've spent too much time thinking about it this week. It's become a fucking obsession. It feels unhealthy and very unlike me to become this besotted with someone I barely know.

She mumbles her next words. "Unlike my old roommate, Zoey, who invited every man in New York back to our place."

"Oh. Yeah?"

"The walls in our apartment were way too thin." She chuckles. "I may have picked up a few tips though." She surprises me with that response.

"Really?" I ask, not expecting what she says next.

"Yeah. Never ask someone to fuck you harder if he has a small penis and is already inside of you. That causes arguments and does things to a man's ego."

My shoulders shake, trying to hold in my laughter.

Lily adds, "And never *ever* tell the guy you are fucking that the guy from the night before was better than him and had more stamina."

"Well, shit, that is harsh."

"Yup," Lily sighs. "Men don't like that."

"Zoey sounds—" I can't think of a word without sounding judgmental.

"Frank. To the point of being rude." Lily says the words I couldn't bring myself to. "She needs lessons in etiquette. Although I don't think she cares." Sounding sorrowful, she sighs. "I do miss her, though. She was my best friend in New York. I don't have many of them here. Everyone I knew has either moved away from Spruce Plain or I've lost touch with them. Although I do have Kourtney. She's been amazing to me since I moved."

Kourtney and Drew are good people. "You'll make new friends. Just give it time. You and Candy hit it off tonight."

"Candy is lovely and beautiful. I think she liked me." Her voice lifts in excitement.

"Everyone likes you, Lily."

When she was up dancing, the guys commented on how well she fitted into our friendship circle. They also couldn't help mentioning the fact that she was gorgeous and completely out of my league.

I knew they were screwing with me, but I couldn't argue with that.

Placing my hand on the exposed skin of her thigh, she sighs and nuzzles further into me.

"I like the way you touch me, Ash."

"Yeah?" I look down to discover she's smiling.

"Feels good." Covering her hand with mine, she moves it between her legs and drags it higher, pushing her short dress up. "I liked it when you touched me here the other night at the arena," she whispers, pressing my fingers against her center.

"Lily," I warn, knowing she's had a few drinks.

Sensing my apprehension, she reassures me, "I've only had three drinks, Ash. I stopped drinking after the one you bought for me. I know what I want." Tilting her hips, she grinds herself on my fingers. "Touch me," she begs on a breathy moan, causing my dick to twitch in my pants.

My fingers have been desperate to touch her all night, but I can't allow the lust that's burning a hole in my brain to overrule my *doing the right thing* reasoning.

"Lily." I drop my voice further.

"Just touch me, Ash." Arching her neck back, her hot breath dusts my neck and, as if on autopilot, I press my fingers against her pussy lips.

"You sure?" I double check she wants this.

"Yes." Spreading her legs wide, she confirms her answer.

Fuck it.

"Straddle me," I say, now desperate to make her come and show her what she's been missing.

I help her climb onto my lap; her lips are on mine within seconds.

"Ash," she moans, rubbing herself against my rock-hard cock. It's always hard around her and I need to do something about that. But not now.

Eyes half closed, her chest rises and falls in anticipation.

"What do you want, Lily?"

"I want you to touch me." A soft whimper leaves her lungs.

"Where? Show me."

Taking my hand in hers, she guides me to her center.

"Here." She groans when I cup her pussy, giving her what she wants.

"How do you like it?"

Widening her eyes, suddenly completely alert, she stares at me as if I asked her a question about quantum physics. "I don't know." She looks away, as if embarrassed.

This girl.

"Lily, look at me."

She does.

"When you touch yourself, how do you like it? Slow or fast?"

Thinking for a beat, she eventually whispers her reply, "Slow and soft at first."

Moving my fingers, I stroke her lips, then rub her clit through her panties. "Like this?"

Nodding, she confirms what she likes.

"What else?"

Her cheeks pink up.

I tip her chin upward. "Don't be embarrassed to ask for what you want." I know exactly what she'll like, but she has to tell me. "Words, Lily. I need words."

"I think I would like my clit rubbed with your finger inside of me at the same time."

"Do you use a vibrator on yourself? Is that what you do when you're touching yourself?"

"Yes," she pants as I circle her clit, her panties now soaked through with her arousal.

"I'd like to watch you fucking yourself with it. Will you do that for me one day?"

Another lust filled breath leaves her mouth, sounding more like a moan than an actual word.

"I'd do anything for you." Her honesty makes my heart swell. "You're all I want and all I can think about."

Her answer fills me with confidence, a wild storm of lust rushing through my veins like a hurricane.

This woman is going to ruin me forever.

Or break my heart.

Or both.

I haven't decided yet.

With one hand on her hip and the other between her thighs, I pull her panties to the side and glide my finger over her clit through her lips and push my finger inside her soaked pussy.

Knowing I'm the only man she's ever let touch her or been inside of her before makes my cock weep.

"Oh God," she cries.

"We can't keep having this same conversation, Tiger. It's Ash."

She moans my name as I push my finger in a little deeper, her fingernails digging into my shoulders as her tight pussy resists my thick digit.

Moving her hips, she rocks back and forth, stretching herself so she's able to sink down further onto my finger. "More, Ash."

I push another finger inside of her and scissor my fingers, loosening her up.

My cock strains against my boxers, and it's leaking like a tap as precum wets the fabric.

I thumb her clit, moving my fingers in and out of her. "You're already so wet, Tiger. Give me that cream though, baby, I want more." I finger fuck her faster, as her breathing quickens. When I feel the telltale signs of her getting closer, I remove my fingers, and with a protest filled moan, she whimpers. I lift my fingers to my mouth and suck them clean. "You taste sweeter than honey and like mine, Tiger."

"Holy shit, that's hot," she mumbles as her hooded eyes

watch me. I take her by surprise when I push my fingers back inside of her.

The feeling of her tight walls around them is a welcomed preview of how she'll feel when I'm inside of her.

"I can't wait to fuck you, Tiger." Desperate to make her come, I push a little deeper.

"Oh, fuck," she cries when I stroke her walls in a beckoning motion, as if begging her to come.

Rubbing her bundle of nerves with my thumb while finger fucking her, she lets me know exactly what she wants as she bounces up and down with need. Her fingers digging deeper into my shoulders and her pace quickens.

"Harder." Grabbing my hand, she squeezes it, showing me what she wants. It's a fucking turn on knowing that she trusts me enough and isn't afraid to hold back.

"Ash." She cries my name again. "Oh... yes—"

The sound of my fingers thrusting in and out of her slick wet heat combined with her soft pitched moans are enough to make a grown man come in his boxers like a frat boy. That may still happen if she doesn't come now and continues to fuck my hand and rub herself against me.

Laying her forehead against mine, mouth open, desire evident all over her face, she looks me dead in the eyes.

"Be a good girl and come for me, Lily."

She nods her head as if asking for permission, "Yeah?"

"Now." I'm firm with my demand. I can be sweet for her all day, but knowing how she reacts to my words alone, I know there's a little freak between the sheets, just waiting to break free.

Pressing my thumb against her clit, harder this time, I give it a flick, then rub her until she's rising, her moans rhythmic and in time with her hips moving.

Then her eyes blow wide, her pussy walls clenching

around my fingers. Moving her hand that was placed over mine, she grabs my face. Lips touching, not kissing me, but open mouthed, in sheer ecstasy she comes, her thighs tightening, gripping me between hers.

And she's loud. Almost screaming my name when she comes.

Panting, trying to catch her breath, she stares at me, almost in disbelief at how good I made her feel.

"Such a good fucking girl, coming for me when I told you to." I praise.

Slower now, I continue to slide my fingers in and out of her, her pussy pulsating around them as I guide her down from her high.

Twitching when I finally remove them, a deep low groan leaves the back of her throat and I can tell she's a needy little thing and wants, no, needs more.

"You're really good at that." Sounding shy, she dips her eyes downward.

"And you look hotter than hell when you come. It's the sexiest thing I've ever seen. Now suck." I push my fingers, which are coated in her juices, through the seam of her lips. Her head rises in surprise. Eyes locked, she twirls her tongue around them without me having to ask her twice. Her warm wet mouth is unsure at first, but then she closes her eyes, pleasure written all over her face.

"Kiss me." I grin devilishly, removing them from her mouth. I lick her lips, tasting her juices there. I'm already addicted to her taste.

"You are fucking delicious."

She mumbles against my lips, "This is not what I imagined sex to be like."

My lips pressed against hers. "This isn't sex, baby.

You'll know when I've been inside of you. You'll feel every inch of me for days afterward."

Clasping my face with both hands, she says, "I want that."

"We have all the time in the world."

I can be slow and patient with her. I'm prepared to wait for her to be ready to have sex with me. In the meantime, though, I won't hold back from showing her what I like and how I have no inhibitions in the bedroom. And I will make no bones about letting her discover what she likes too. There is nothing hotter than a woman knowing and telling you what she wants and isn't ashamed to ask for it.

Lily reaches down between us and rubs my throbbing cock over my pants, making me groan. Clearly feeling brave, she whispers, "I would like to help you with that."

"Not yet." I want her to know I want more than just sex with her.

"Will you show me what you like?"

I close my eyes and groan in reverence, "Fuck, you might just be my perfect woman."

"I'm going to be the only woman that ever touches you again. I want to learn what you like and do everything to please you." Her hungry fingers continue to rub me, and I growl with pleasure. "I might be yours, Ash, but you are mine too."

Her innocence and vulnerability mixed with her spike in confidence makes my pulse leap with excitement.

"Well, fuck, that's the second best thing I've ever heard." The first being that she's my biggest fan.

The driver's voice startles us when it crackles through the intercom. "Mr. Johansson, we have arrived at your destination."

I chuckle at his formality. In four years, Victor has never called me Mr. Johansson.

I press the button to answer. "Thanks, Victor. I will only be here for an hour. Can you wait for me?"

"No," Lily calls out, holding my hand on the intercom button. "You can go home, Victor." She releases the button. "You are staying with me tonight."

My eyebrows shoot upward in surprise. "Really?"

She nods her head enthusiastically and presses the intercom button again. "No need to get out, Victor. We can see ourselves in, but you can pick Ash up tomorrow." She leaps off my lap, gets out of the car, and is running up the stairs at the front of her apartment before I can say *Goodbye, Victor*.

Yeah, I was right, she's a little freak alright.

CHAPTER FIFTEEN

Lily

Preparing two coffees, I realize how tiny my apartment is as I watch Ash sift through my vinyl record collection. His shoulders are so broad—the width of a bear—I'm guessing that's where he gets his nickname from. Although in my eyes, he's a gentle giant.

A perfect gentleman, he waited for me to invite him into my home. Of course, that's when everything changed, pushing me against the wall like an animal waiting to pounce as soon as the door closed behind us. The things that man can do with his tongue... and his fingers.

But then, like the gentleman he is, he stopped and told me to make coffee first.

Coffee first, then what?

More of what we did back in the car?

I hope so.

He's the first man to touch my pussy and the first man to bring me to orgasm; I'm willingly giving him all of my firsts and I want him to have them. My body is aching for more.

He knows exactly what he is doing, and I can't wait for him to do lots of very naughty things to me; also a first for me. His are the only hands and lips I have ever wanted to touch me. I'm excited for what's to come. Preferably me coming lots more, and then him coming inside me.

What if I am completely shit at all the sex stuff?

I will die of embarrassment if I can't satisfy him, and by the feel of him, there is *a lot* of man to satisfy.

"How many records do you have?" he asks over his shoulder, pulling another album out to have a look at as I have a mental freakout.

At my last count, "Over twelve hundred," I reply. They took up more moving boxes than the rest of my belongings when I shipped my stuff from New York.

"Holy shit, you have a 1973 edition of Pink Floyd's Dark Side of the Moon." He swivels around so fast I'm surprised he didn't give himself whiplash.

"I do."

Turning the album sleeve over in his hands, he checks out its condition. "It's immaculate. You must have paid way over the odds for it. It's a collector's item."

"Ten US dollars." I beam brighter than a jukebox. "My proudest moment was picking that up at a thrift store. It was sitting in a donation box amongst old trinkets, just waiting to be organized and priced up." When I offered the little lady volunteering behind the counter ten dollars for it, knowing it was worth at least one hundred times that, she was distracted trying to fix her broken till to even look up and accepted my offer on the spot.

"I'm taking you with me to the next arcade game auction." Back turned to me, he continues to shuffle through my extensive collection.

"Arcade game auction? What the hell is that?"

Moving out from my kitchen, I join him in the living area of my tiny apartment and rest the steaming cups of coffee on top of my nineteen seventies style walnut side table.

I stand shoulder to shoulder in front of my wall of records. Although it's more like my shoulder to his elbow because there is a huge height difference between us.

"I collect old retro arcade games. They only happen twice a year and I missed out on Pac Man and Ms. Pac Man at the last one. Someone outbid me."

"Can you not buy them online?" I narrow my eyes to help me read the minute text along the sides of the paper sleeves to find my favorite album, although the one I am looking for has a tiny black dot on the side of it to help me find my most loved ones.

"There is no guarantee that they work, or I can't see what condition they are in if I do that. I like them to be like new." I love how particular he is. That's cute.

I run my finger along the spines of another row of albums and ask, "How many do you have?"

"Nine so far."

"What's your favorite?"

"Well, that's easy." He rests his ass on the back of my sofa and folds his arms. "Space Invaders."

"I knew you'd say that." I find what I was looking for and pull the record out of its hiding place. "Gotcha."

I look up to find him staring at me. "How did you know I would say Space Invaders?" he asks.

I sway my head back and forth as if weighing up my options. "It was either that or Streetfighter." I lift the lid on the record player I spent months saving up for.

"You're good."

"I know." I knew it would be either one of those. "It's

what the boys in my class at school used to play at the arcade in town."

"What have you got there?" he asks when I slip the record out of its sleeve, carefully handling the edges and placing it on the turntable without my fingertips touching it. Any trace of oil from skin affects the sound quality, and this album is one my grandfather gave to me when I was just ten years old. It's one of my favorites.

"Soloman Burke."

"Really?" He sounds surprised.

Placing the needle on the record, it crackles when the first song begins. I kick off my black patent heels and give my achy toes a wiggle, then turn to face Ash. "I love any music, but this record is one I play a lot." I hold my finger in the air. "And this song is the best one on the album." I lift the needle off the record and swing it across, hovering over the spot I know off by heart, dropping it down into position to play "Cry to Me".

The bassy vibraphone beat floats through my speakers, the soulful voice of the singer fills the room, his low *doo wahs* begging your hips to move in time.

"*Dirty Dancing*?"

I'm surprised he knows. "It's my favorite movie. My mom loved that film. We would watch it at least once a month."

"My mom loves it too."

"Chick flick." Still sitting on the back of my sofa, I stand between his open legs. His hands find my waist and he pulls me closer to him.

"Memories to treasure forever."

He's right. I remember my mom's laughter, and how much fun we used to have trying to reenact the dance routines. "I will always have those."

"Let's make new ones." He removes his navy blazer and throws it over the arm of the sofa before he stands up. "Dance with me."

God, this man.

"I'm not very good."

"You shook your ass perfectly fine earlier in the club. You're a better mover than you give yourself credit for."

His words fill my confidence up to capacity and I hold out my hand for him to take. "Okay."

Squeezed tightly together, we sway side to side in time to the sexy, soulful song. My ear rested against his heart; it beats strong in his chest, as if in time with the music.

Dropping a kiss to my neck, he nibbles, then licks at my skin and moves to my mouth.

Our lazy kisses quickly turn passionate, and before I know it, I'm tugging him in the direction of my bedroom.

"We didn't drink the coffee." He grins through muffled words.

Rubbing the outline of his hard cock over his pants, I mumble, "Forget the coffee. I think there is something else I would like to put in my mouth."

"Fuck." His breath hitches, mingling with mine, as I rub him harder.

"Bedroom. Now."

CHAPTER SIXTEEN

Lily

My door ricochets off the wall as we burst into my bedroom. I flick on the light switch and push him down onto the bed, making him bounce on top of the mattress.

My desire to finally find out what his body looks like under those designer clothes of his and officially make him mine causes me to behave in a way I didn't know I was capable of.

Grateful I had the foresight to close the drapes earlier, I straddle his thick thighs, sit upright, and stare down at him. Before I change my mind, I grab the hem of my dress and pull it up over my head, leaving me exposed and almost naked, except for my panties because I didn't wear a bra under my backless dress tonight.

"Jesus Christ, Lily." Ash sits up and immediately sucks my nipple into his mouth, obviously feeling as desperate as me. Grazing it with his teeth, he tugs at my sensitive peak as his fingers work the other. "You are fucking beautiful."

Threading my fingers into his short hair on the back of

his neck, I pull him closer, urging him to suck harder. "Oh, that feels good."

With my other hand, my trembling hungry fingers dip to the waist of his pants, undoing his button before pulling down his zipper.

He pauses. "You don't have to do this, Lily."

"I want to," I confess, and bite my bottom lip suggestively. "I want to do *this*. With *you*." I'm so far out of my comfort zone, but I'm ready to explore whatever is happening between us.

"You sure? We can wait." Warmth fills my chest, knowing that he's being patient for me.

"I won't tell you again, Ash. I want you."

Cupping my face, his thumb skimming my cheek. "We'll go slow." Pausing to think, he then says, "Because we have forever to get to know one another."

"Forever?" I nervously ask, realizing it could be a slip of his tongue.

"Don't question what we both know is inevitable." His confidence in our connection boosts my joy.

Eyes locked, my brain fizzes with happiness. I nod, confirming I feel the same way, although I am still a little shocked that he's so sure about us. "But I don't want to go slow," I admit. "I want you to show me what you like."

He throws himself back on the bed and pushes his hands behind his head, looking relaxed. "Take off my pants," he commands, confidently.

I reposition myself on the bed before pulling his pants along with his boxers down his hips. I suck in a deep breath. *It's now or never.*

When I remove them completely, my eyes pop out of their sockets as I stare down at him. That is one thick and long, beautiful, glistening dick.

And how the hell will that ever fit inside of me?

It's huge.

Ash unbuttons the top of his shirt, lifts it up over his head, and drops it on the floor beside the bed. My eyes rake over the black washed out ink that paints his chest; the skin of his pecs branded with an elaborate eagle on one and a bear on the other.

My gaze moves down as I take in his strong thick thighs, and athletic washboard abs I could clean my clothes on, but my eyes linger on his cock. I can't stop staring at it.

"Panties off, Lily." Rousing me from my spell-like state, I suck in a breath and summon all of my confidence as I slide the lace fabric down my body and let them fall to the floor, grateful I managed to book a last-minute wax appointment this afternoon.

"Fucking beautiful." Ash curls his pointer finger, beckoning me to him, as he wraps his large hand around his cock, fisting himself slowly.

I crawl back up the bed between his widened legs and skim my hands up his thighs. The crackling sound of the music drift into my bedroom from the living area.

The thick head of his cock leaks with precum, and with each pump of his fist, more leaks from his slit. I'm mesmerized, watching with fascination as my fingernails dig into the muscular flesh of his thighs and wonder what he will taste like.

"Tell me what you want, Lily?"

I lick my lips. "I want to taste you," I whisper, my chest heaving with a cocktail of desire and anticipation.

"Wrap your hand around my cock." He continues to stroke himself and I lay my hand over his so he can show me what to do. "I like it slow." Together, we move our hands up and down his thick shaft. "Just like that," he mumbles, his cock becoming harder with every downward stroke.

"Let me try."

Releasing his grip, he lets me take over. When I touch him for the first time, he throws his head back into the pillow, closing his eyes while his hands curl into fists at his sides. Seeing the effect I have on him boosts my confidence. "Like this?" I ask as I begin to move my hand.

"A little tighter. Don't be scared to squeeze."

"Is that what you like?" I clench my fingers a little firmer and he groans in appreciation.

"Just like that. You're doing so good, Lily." His hips flex upward as if wanting me to go faster. "If you want to take me in your mouth, don't let me stop you."

Whispering, I reply, "I do."

The heat between my thighs is growing, the ache, a dull throb needing satisfying. After what Ash did to me in the car, I know how good it can feel and I want more.

"Have you ever?"

Blushing, I shake my head. I don't know what he will think about my inexperience. I've never done anything sexual with a guy. How embarrassing.

"Lily."

I look up at his handsome face.

Laying his hand back over mine that's gripping his dick, he says, "We will learn everything about each other this way. Together. I feel privileged that I'm your first everything. I have so much respect and admiration you saved yourself for someone special."

"You're my special someone."

He smiles. "Which makes this more meaningful."

He wasn't lying about him ruining me for any other man. He's already stolen my heart with his words alone.

I look down at our joined hands and lean forward. "I've been wondering what you taste like."

Removing his hand, Ash bends his legs at the knees to widen them, giving me better access. "Wet those pretty lips first."

I stroke him a couple more times as I lick my lips, then I drop my mouth to his cock, and lick his full length. "Jesus fuck," he cries.

I look up to find him watching me. "Okay?" Desperate to please him, I slip my lips over his head and rim his slit with my tongue. Precum leaks from him and the salty taste of him makes my mouth water for more.

"Fucking hell, Tiger." He clenches his eyes shut. "Better than okay."

I wrap my hands around his shaft, more firmly this time, moving them up and down his cock in tandem as I pull him into my mouth.

"Holy fucking shit. That's so good." He thrusts his hips upward. "Are you sure you haven't done this before?" he pants.

"I read Cosmo magazine," I mumble around his cock, making him burst out laughing.

"Fucking hell. Keeping reading those how-to articles because you are fucking good at this."

Am I?

My jaw aches from his size, although I love that he thinks I know what I am doing when really I'm using my hands to accommodate his girth and length.

I take that as permission to do what I've read, push him out of my mouth, and spit on him to make it extra wet. Keeping my tongue and lips soft and loose, I suck and take him fully into my mouth again. His crown hits the back of my throat, earning me a loud groan in return.

"Fuck, you have no gag reflex, do you?"

I shake my head as he pushes in a little further.

And when I grab his balls and roll them between my fingers, he fucks my mouth faster. He grabs my face with both hands and feeds me his cock to show me the pace he likes. His grip tightening around my jaw, and I don't think I have ever been so turned on; the slickness between my thighs, evidence of how aroused I am. I moan in pleasure, letting him hear how much I am enjoying this.

Pushing him out of my mouth, I lick his length again as I catch my breath. "You taste so good. I love how good you feel in my mouth."

"Fuck," he exclaims.

My lips hover over his cock, and I flick my tongue across his weeping head. I love surprising him. I read every blog, article, and forum I could today, researching how to be more confident in the bedroom and how to give the ultimate blowjob to blow his mind. I think I'm doing okay so far.

"Now fuck my mouth. Don't hold back." I'm almost purring when I lick down his shaft, then softly suck on his balls, one after the other. I pull him back into my mouth and then hollow my cheeks, flattening my tongue to the underside of his cock. As I move, he bucks his hips. Any restraint he was using earlier, gone.

His thumb moves back and forth slowly as he dusts my cheek and it's such a sharp contrast to the power behind his thrusts as he fucks my mouth.

It's not long before he's moaning louder, releasing my face and fisting the sheets between his fingers. "Lily," he cries out.

I groan, moving faster, giving him permission to come down my throat and he comes in a rush, his hot cum hitting my tongue. When I gaze up, he's throwing his head back as he spills into my mouth, roaring his release as he loses all control.

I swallow him down, loving the taste of his saltiness. It turns me on in a way I wasn't expecting. His hips jerk and his grip around the sheets loosens as he comes back down from his blissful high.

"Well, fuck." He sounds shocked. "I don't think I need to teach you anything." His low chuckle fills the room and I guide him out of my mouth and lick my lips. "Did I hurt you? Was that too deep?" His voice is thick with concern.

I drop a gentle kiss on his tip, making him flinch, then kiss his laddered abs. "Never."

"You enjoyed that, didn't you?"

"Loved it." I straddle his hips and move up his body. The music has stopped playing and I wish I could get up and play the other side. It set the mood and has now moved to the top spot of my top ten most favorite albums; it will always remind me of him.

"Dirty little Lily." He grins.

"*Your* dirty little Lily." I reach his face and press my body against his. Sealed together, chest to chest, I kiss him, letting him taste his pleasure on my lips.

"That was incredible," he mumbles, looking starry eyed.

"Really?" I say quietly, not knowing what comes next.

"Fucking insanely good." He pulls me closer to him, squeezing both of his arms around my waist. "The best."

"You can fuck my mouth any day of the week," I tell him.

"Every day." He bites my bottom lip.

Our tongues twist and twirl around one another. "Watching you turns me on," I admit, panting.

"Oh, yeah?" Lowering his hand between us, he runs his finger through my pussy lips. "You're so wet."

I am. Shamefully and painfully so.

He flips us over, making me squeal as I'm caught off guard.

He kisses a path of soft kisses down my body, over my stomach I've never liked, then along the untoned muscle of my thighs.

I tense, knowing his last sexual partner was a fitness instructor and while I'm all wobbly and squishy in places, he's solid and firm.

"You have a beautiful body, Lily. I love everything about it." He kisses the other thigh, then mouths my pussy and I begin to relax again.

Oh God, I may have died and gone to heaven. I swear I hear angels singing when his tongue finds my clit as pleasure weaves its way through my body.

I'm not prepared when he spits on my pussy, then pushes a finger into my core. It's so hot and unexpected that my back bows off the mattress. His tongue laps my clit while his finger is in deeper than before, creating a completely different sensation. I'm already on the verge of coming again.

The fire in my core burns hotter than Hades, as he builds pleasure in my body faster than my brain can keep up with. I grab onto the back of his head and push his face into my pussy to chase my release. Not caring how desperate I am, I want more; everything he can give me, I want. When I look down, he's looking right back at me.

He stops, then makes his demand. "Come for me." Covering my pussy with his mouth, he sucks my clit and I come. His finger stroking a spot so deep inside, it feels like a meteor shower bursting as pleasure, unlike anything I have ever felt before, scatters through me. Gasping, writhing, and jerking underneath him, he intertwines his fingers with mine and lets out a low and long moan of his own.

Warmth and pleasure rolls over my hot skin, my heart racing in my chest as I try to catch my breath.

Ash kisses my swollen clit when he removes his finger, making me giggle as it's so sensitive.

"Good?" he asks, dragging his tongue through my folds before he pushes his tongue inside of my pussy as if he can't get enough of me. "Fuck, you taste good." He sucks my opening and I cover my face with my hands from the intensity of his actions.

Who knew sex could be this good? I've been missing out for years. Although I could never see myself doing this with anyone else. "Ash," I gasp as he moves up my body, then kisses my mouth with passionate force.

Everything about us feels right. Even the taste of me on his lips feels good. And there is no ignoring his yet again hard cock that's resting on my hip.

"I want you." I reach down to touch him.

"Not yet, Lily." He grabs my hand to stop me.

"No?" I sound disappointed, although I'm sort of relieved. My pussy already feels sore from his fingers, and his cock is at least four times the thickness of those.

"Patience." He smiles against my lips, then moves to my side.

"We have forever." I turn to face him.

Reaching up, he runs his finger down my cheek. "Exactly." We stare at each other as if we are the only two people in the world and I'm amazed at how comfortable I am around him, even though I'm completely naked.

"I've had the best night, Ash." I can't quite believe everything that's happened tonight. Not just the making each other come, but the hockey game was so much fun, spending time with my family, and his, then the club. And it was wonderful meeting some of his teammates. My mouth lets out a loud, lazy yawn and I cover my lips with the back of my hand. "I'm so sorry. That was rude."

Eyelids drooping, he lets out a loud yawn, too.

"Tired?" I ask.

"Yawning is contagious." He's fighting sleep, his eyes almost closed. "I'm exhausted. A feisty tiger made me go out to a nightclub after a game tonight," he mutters. "It was totally worth it though."

Chuckling, I reluctantly jump out of the bed and pull on his dress shirt, then make him get under the covers. I run around my apartment, turning off the lights, unplugging my record player, and grabbing two glasses of water, smiling to myself as I pour the untouched coffee down the drain.

Returning to my room, being careful not to disturb him, placing the water on the nightstand, I tiptoe around the room. He's almost asleep when I hop back into bed and I take this opportunity to get a good look at him. My gaze lingers for a moment longer on his beautiful, tattooed covered chest as I remove my makeup. Like a magnet, I can't stop myself from reaching out and running the tip of my finger over the intricate ink. Small Roman numerals curve around the outer edge of the eagle neighboring his father's name. His memorial piece dedicated to the man who inspired him to be a hockey player and is his hero took me by surprise when he removed his shirt. His steel exterior camouflages his soft center and big squishy heart.

Pulling the covers up over us both, I snuggle in, stealing his warmth.

"Night, Tiger." He wraps his arms around me and drags me closer to him, my back to his front.

"Night, Bear." I use the nickname the fans call him.

Planting a soft kiss into my hair, he chuckles. I thread my fingers into his and he squeezes me tighter.

"The tiger and the bear," he mumbles, half asleep.

"Two very different beasts but they both eat people." I reach over, switch the sidelight off, and get comfortable.

Hot breath warms my neck. "I'm going to eat you out every day for the rest of my life."

I have no doubt about that. And yes, please. I'll take that to go.

"Now go to sleep, Tiger. We're meeting our families for brunch tomorrow."

Are we?

When the hell did he arrange that?

This man.

Within minutes, his breathing slows, and I know he's already asleep, his body relaxed and heavy with tiredness.

And for the first time since my mom died, I fall asleep for a solid eight hours inside a solid set of arms.

CHAPTER SEVENTEEN

LILY – TWO MONTHS LATER

"How do I look?" I step out of Ash's bedroom into the huge living space overlooking the city to show Kourtney my devastatingly jaw dropping, *he will definitely want to rip it off,* dress.

Sliding her champagne glass across the coffee table, she gasps, "Holy shit, you look beautiful. And sexy." She rises to her feet as if not believing what she's seeing. I can't deny this dress hugs all my curves in all the right places.

Tonight is the Eagles' Christmas party. Although I've attended all of Ash's games, this is the first official team social event I have been invited to. To say I am nervous is a huge understatement; I might be sick or wet myself, maybe both. I can't decide. My stomach is whirling around like a carnival ride.

I do a twirl in my strappy diamanté heels, showing off my red satin to the floor dress.

"The back is stunning." Walking over to me, she does a full three hundred and sixty degree walk to get a better look at the diamanté spaghetti straps at the back. "You look like a princess."

"I feel like a million dollars." I poke my leg out of the thigh-high split of my exquisite gown.

"You look like a future hockey wife."

I wave her off. "Yeah, yeah. Whatever." Ash and I have briefly talked about marriage, but never in detail. We both want to get married, and that's as far as we dipped into the subject. It was enough to keep our curiosity satisfied.

"You know that's what is going to happen. You two can't keep your hands off one another. The last time you were in the coffeehouse, he was all over you. When was that?" she asks.

I sift through my memory bank for an answer. "Two weeks ago?"

"Was that the last time I saw you? That's too long." She shakes her head. "I miss you working for me." Sticking her bottom lip out, she pouts, looking like a baby that's about to have a tantrum.

"I miss you too, but I miss the tips more," I tease.

"You miss me more, admit it."

I no longer work at the coffeehouse because not only did Candy, who I discovered is really called Candice, sign with me to plan her and Brayden's wedding, but once she told her friends who was organizing it and who I worked for previously in New York, I signed another three couples. Between working at High Octane, attending hockey games, date nights with Ash, and planning four huge high-profile weddings, I barely have the time to eat some days, although Ash is an amazing chef and always has a hot meal waiting for me to come home to when he doesn't have a game.

Home.

I'm practically living in his luxury apartment with floor

to ceiling windows and a bed almost the same size as my whole apartment, because as Ash says, *I live in the heart of the city; you work in the city. It's easier if you stay the night.*

So, for the last two months, I have made myself at home in his place. It's far nicer than my apartment, and of course, he has the biggest television to watch movies on and a dedicated game room filled with his rare retro arcade games. He's been teaching me how to play pool. I've even beaten him a couple of times, and I am only two spots behind him on Pac Man that I helped him win last month at the specialist auction. Ash thought it was down to me being his lucky charm and wearing my lucky cream scarf, when in fact, I may have whispered a little too loudly making sure everyone heard when I said that it didn't work and needed a full refurbishment costing thousands of dollars. It was just a teeny tiny white lie. Of course, there was nothing wrong with it. It worked, no one bid on it and he won it, snagging it for less than half the price they usually auction for.

To say that my life has continued to be normal would be a huge understatement. My female work colleagues are fascinated by our relationship and get super giddy and excited on the days he picks me up from work when he's not playing a hockey game or training.

The past two months have been a whirlwind, no, more like a tornado.

From the press going wild over our first public appearance together. Then Ash doing everything he could to ensure the tabloids don't hound me, feeding them little snippets of our relationship every now and then. He thinks it's the way to appease them and keep them at bay. So far, it seems to be working.

Then, of course, there are the special day trips he arranged for us either hiking or coffee dates in the park where we enjoyed the views. It's where we have chatted for hours, and watched the leaves changing color as the first frost hit. The fact we had to huddle together to keep warm was simply a bonus.

I'm almost able to do a full revolution of the ice rink skating by myself without falling over. Now that is progress. Ash has been so patient with me and the perfect gentleman in every way.

Sometimes he's too much of a gentleman. Because we still haven't...

"He won't be able to keep his hands to himself tonight. He'll be fucking you in the limo." Kourtney stands back to examine me again and claps, then rubs her hands together.

True to his word, Ash has taken the time to learn every inch of my body, allowing me to discover what I like and what I don't, showing me what he likes too. Over and over again. But...

"We still haven't, you know?" Pinching my eyes shut, I can't look at Kourtney when I confess that we haven't gone all the way yet. I'm still a freaking virgin and trust me, it's not from lack of trying but again, Ash being the painfully perfect guy he is, wanted me to be one hundred percent ready and sure.

Well, Ash Johansson, I am.

I couldn't be more ready. The connection we have is stronger than ever; tonight is the night.

Kourtney's silence feels louder than a bomb.

I pop one eye open to see if she's still here. Her mouth wide open, she closes it, then opens it again as if she's a guppy fish, then holds up her pointer finger. "Wait. You still haven't done the deed yet?"

"The deed?" I don't like sex being described this way. Sounds like something you would write on a to do list.

"Yeah, you know, the pump, jumping bones, ride the pony, bang, boink, bumping uglies, squatting the cucumber patch, pounding the punani—"

"Pounding the what?" I yell, disgusted, causing Kourtney to throw her head back with laughter. She sits back down on the sectional sofa in Ash's apartment that's big enough to fit at least twenty people and tucks her legs under her. "You have so much to learn."

"We've done everything else. Just not *it*." I flap my hand about dismissing her stupid words. I put my hands on my hips, annoyed with her for thinking I am sexually inexperienced. I am far from it. Ash has explored lots of different kinks with me; restraints, edging, blindfolds, voyeurism; which is my personal favorite, I love nothing more than watching Ash fuck himself with his hand while talking dirty to me and vice versa. It's the hottest thing, knowing how hard I can make him come with just a few words or while watching me play with myself; something I never thought I would be comfortable doing with anyone, but it all feels so natural with him.

Right.

Perfect.

"Oh, chill out, Lily. I'm messing with you." Expectation written all over her face, she asks, "Do you think tonight is the night, then?" She covers her mouth, trying to hide her glee, her eyes sparkling with mischief.

I bounce my head up and down excitedly. "I hope so." If he doesn't jump my bones tonight, I'm tying him to his bed and doing it anyway. That way, he won't have any choice.

Consent, Lily, consent.

"Okay, quick checklist." Kourtney sounds serious, her face deadpan. "Waxed?"

"Yes."

"Condom?"

"Yes, but I'm on the pill." I made an appointment with the doctor the week after we announced our relationship.

"You're prepared, good stuff, but see how you feel in the moment. You might decide you want to use one." Kourtney thinks for a beat. "Lube? You know, just because it's your first time."

"In the top drawer of the nightstand." I hook my thumb over my shoulder in the direction of Ash's bedroom. Although we won't need it, I get wet simply looking at him.

She lays her hands out flat on each side of her. "You're all set for the big event."

"What big event?" Ash's low sexy voice cuts through our girl talk as he steps out of his walk-in closet behind me, his heady cologne invading my nostrils.

Kourtney wolf whistles then says, "Looking sharp, Mr. Johansson."

I spin around slowly to look, my mouth instantly dry.

Wow.

Ash Johansson is sexy. Period.

However, Ash Johansson in a tuxedo is next level handsome.

He's in front of me, cradling my face with his rough hands and lightly kissing me into a drug-like state. "I don't want to mess up your lipstick. You look incredible." Moving his mouth to my ear, he whispers, "I hope you're not wearing any panties."

I lose all sense of my surroundings when I let out a soft moan.

"Oh, don't mind me." Kourtney clears her throat. "I was just here to do the hair and makeup and check if the dress was suitable." She scuffles about behind me as Ash chuckles.

I spin around on the balls of my feet quickly. "Thank you for—"

"Checking the list with you?"

I shake my finger at her. "Yes, that. Big help." We grin at each other knowingly and Kourtney heads for the door to leave.

"Have a great night, guys." She winks at me. "See you at my New Year's party." Waving over her shoulder, she's gone before I can say *Have a nice Christmas.*

"What big event was she talking about, Tiger?"

I feel my skin heating under his stare. I think he knows what we were talking about, but I lie. "Tonight. It's a big deal meeting your entire team and management. I promise to be on my best behavior."

"You can be my bad girl any day of the week." He lifts his phone off the kitchen island. "And it's cute how nervous you are, but you don't need to be. You know that, right?"

"I'll be fine once we're there." I give myself one last look in the mirror on the far side of the room. I love this dress. I do look like a future hockey wife.

Don't push it, Lily.

His words cut through my far-fetched wishes. "Let's go then. The sooner we get there, the sooner we can come home."

My brow tightens, wrinkling up at his words. "Do you not want to go?"

"Coach said attendance was mandatory. It's the last place I want to be tonight." He rolls his eyes, fast fingers typing the illuminated screen of his phone. I assume he's sending Victor a text, letting him know we are ready to go.

"Why?"

He looks up from his phone. "I would rather be home alone with you."

I smile goofily, "Yeah?"

"You fucking know it, Tiger." He looks me up and down, then licks his lips.

"Time to go." I almost skip to the door.

"You never confirmed if you were wearing any panties." He follows behind me like a lovesick puppy.

Over my shoulder, I bat my eyelashes. "Well, that's for you to find out."

Teeth clenched tight, his jaw tics. "Let's get this night over with. I need you back here, on my bed and completely naked."

"Home by midnight," I say sweetly. "I'll turn into a pumpkin otherwise."

"And I turn into an ogre. Make it eleven o'clock."

I grab my silver clutch bag off the console table and reach for the door handle, pretending to be upset. "But that means I bought this pretty red dress for nothing."

"Not for nothing, because I'm going to rip it off that beautiful body of yours and do despicable things to you later." He locks his apartment door behind us.

"Is that a promise?" Standing in front of the elevator, I ask sweetly.

"That's a guarantee."

Thanks, Santa.

Merry Christmas to me.

I press the elevator call button. "Eleven it is."

"Deal."

CHAPTER EIGHTEEN

Lily

Our clothes are scattered throughout Ash's apartment.

He wasn't joking. Home by eleven o'clock and we were naked in minutes.

It was an incredible night; dancing, chatting, food, and lots of laughter. We had an emergency situation when Candy bent over and ripped the seam of her tight dress, flashing her peachy ass to everyone. I almost wet myself laughing, as did she. Luckily, she had a silk scarf to wrap around her, which Bree and I styled beautifully into an oversized bow. All the guys promised they didn't see her ass, but if we did, then everybody did.

From the ice sculptures to the fireworks, it was perfect, but when Ash and I were dancing together, and I whispered that tonight was the night, we were out of the hotel ballroom within minutes.

Lying on top of the bed, with Ash positioned between my thighs, he pushes his finger inside of me. "So wet, Lily. You're always so ready for me."

The low lighting of the room makes the shadows of our

bodies dance across the walls. "I want you, Ash." Cupping my breast, he pinches my nipple as his lips move to kiss my neck and then my mouth, while he slides his finger in and out of my wet center.

"You've got me, but I need to make sure you can take me." He pushes in another finger to stretch me a little more, scissoring them to get me ready.

"Please. Fuck me, Ash," I cry out, begging him like he predicted I would when we first met.

"I'm not fucking you, Lily." His lips brush mine, then he traces his finger down my nose and across the top of my lip like he does every day.

My heart drops in my chest as he slams on the brake pedal before he's even pushed the accelerator. I turn and look away, rejection flooding through me. "Oh," I say deflated, my eyes stinging as tears form behind them.

Moving his lips to my ear, he whispers, "I'm going to make love to you, Lily." The heat from his breath fills my body with warmth, his words comforting me.

I roll my head back to the center, where I find him looking down at me with a lazy smile full of love.

Because that's what this is. Love.

Stretching over to the bedside table, I reach out to stop him. "I'm on the pill. We don't need a condom." He knows I'm clean, and he's tested regularly as part of his medical. "I want to feel you," I whisper, my voice barely audible.

He blinks once, and then twice, but no words pass between us until he finally growls, "Kiss me." He drops his mouth over mine, pouring love from him into my skin as our tongues twirl around one another.

Ash teases my entrance with the head of his cock, my legs widening to receive him. He moves closer, pushing in slightly, making me wince as I press my fingers into his skin, not believing that we are finally about to make love.

"Breathe and keep kissing me." He caresses my hip and lifts my leg, his hand cupping my ass as he slides in a little, his thickness stretching me painfully.

Whimpering, I keep kissing him when he slides out and then back in, much further this time, and it hurts, but not as much as I thought it would.

Moaning, his mouth on mine, he pants, "Fuck, you're so tight." Sliding in and out a few more times, he pushes in further with each gentle thrust.

Kissing my jaw, he moves to my neck. "Almost there, Lily. You're taking me so good."

"Ash," I cry out, my back arching off the mattress, when he pulls out fully and then slides himself all the way back in this time. Startled for a moment, a shot of pain shoots through me as I'm filled and stretched for the first time, taking my virginity, making me his.

My eyes clenched, I'm gasping, my heart racing as we cross a line we know we can never come back from. And I don't want to.

"There you go, baby. You okay?"

I open my eyes and I know he's concerned when he wrinkles his brow, worried that he's hurting me, which he is, but in a good way.

"Move, Ash," I urge.

He eases out of me, then slides back in again. The pinching sensation, which is less painful than before, is quickly replaced by pleasure. I'm lost in the moment, my body on fire from being touched like this for the first time... he consumes me, blanketing my skin, filling my body. I feel him everywhere and I'm not sure I'll ever get enough of this man.

"You are so tight, baby." He chuckles and I laugh too as a mix of nerves and relief washes over me.

I cradle his face, his beard much longer than it was when I first met him, because apparently, it's bad luck to shave it off during the Stanley Cup but Ash doesn't shave it for the entire season for fear of losing a game. "What's so funny?"

He stares into my eyes. "We're doing this," he says as if disbelieving how far we've come together.

"Yes, we are." Beaming up at him, I wrap my legs around his hips, taking him deeper, making his eyes roll into the back of his head and groan with pleasure as he really starts to move.

"Baby, you feel so good." He pushes my hands over my head, and laces our fingers together, rocking into me with firmer thrusts. I cry out eagerly when the head of his cock hits me deep in my core.

"Feels so good," I tell him.

"Yeah?" We move together, his hard body pinning me to the bed. I moan an incomprehensible response when another wave of pleasure hits me, and a rush of my wetness coats his cock.

"Fuck yeah. There you go."

Wanting more, my body is aching for him, his slow strokes not enough. "Faster, Ash."

Digging his knees into the mattress, he does as I ask, and my needy pussy takes everything he has to offer.

Tension searing between us we are a clash of hot kisses, panting, and hip thrusts as he pistons into me. My walls begin to ripple, and I moan again, the ecstasy escalating, the beginning of my orgasm flirting with me. This feels so different from everything we've done before. It's more intense, more intimate. I've never felt this close to another human being.

Continuing to buck his hips into mine, he lets go of my hands, pushes one arm underneath me, wrapping it around my waist, letting me know he's got me and cups my face with his free hand then kisses me so deep, I swear he's trying to climb inside me.

Thick veins bulge in his neck, his pulse thumping visibly hard, and I can tell he's trying to restrain himself.

"Don't hold back, Ash. Show me what you've got." I push my hips into his, to move in time with him over and over, begging for more; begging to be filled.

Groaning, his finger digs into my waist, and this is it, the point of no return. My body tuned into his. I'm so turned on. The pleasurable feeling escalating, the feeling I want to chase and catch right now. A feeling I have never felt before.

"Ash, I think I'm coming." It's a different sensation of pleasure I have felt before.

"Come," he says, panting. "Look at me." All gentleness gone, he hammers into me, the fire between us melting me and turning me into hot liquid gold. He nods his head. "Come for me."

He crashes his lips to mine while he fucks me so hard and so deep, I can't help but squeeze my inner walls around him. His balls slap off my ass, my clit rubbing against his pubic bone with every inward thrust.

I grab his ass to push him deeper into me. His thick head teases my G-spot and it feels utterly delicious as warmth bursts through my core, and I explode like a meteor hitting the earth's atmosphere. A noise leaves my chest that doesn't sound like me. Already addicted to the throbbing in my core, he takes me to the edge and beyond, coating his cock with my release.

"Aw, fuck," Ash cries.

Open mouthed he rests his lips against mine. "Lily," he calls out as holds himself deep inside me and shoots his load, filling me with his cum. The aftershocks cause him to flinch, jerking the last of his release as he continues to a leisurely slide back and forth.

Loosening his grip around my waist, he ghosts his hand up my body, tickling my ribs with his soft touch.

Our bodies pressed together, we kiss, completely satiated, every cell of my body singing with glee.

"Mmmmm," I hum loudly when he licks my neck, no longer feeling like a girl, but a woman. Ash Johansson's woman.

Leaning his forearms on either side of my head, his face flushed, our eyes locked, he says, "That was incredible."

I enjoy being in his arms, with him still inside of me, because everything we do, no matter how big or small, is incredible.

His face turns serious. "I didn't hurt you, did I?"

"You could never hurt me, Ash." I roll my head side to side on the pillow.

Drawing an invisible line down my nose, then across my top lip, he says, "You are so beautiful."

"I love it when you do that."

"Yeah?" His eyes crinkle around the edges when an easy smile shapes his lips.

I look deep into his blue gems, and I say what I have been wanting to say all week. "I love you." I'm not expecting him to say it back because it's probably too soon and maybe it's stupid of me to fall in love with the guy you lose your virginity to or the first guy you've ever dated, but

I feel it in my heart and deep within my soul. I just know it.

His smile changes into a full-wattage grin that's brighter than the sun. "You love me?"

"Uh-huh. You got a problem with that, big guy?" I tease because I know he's messing with me, otherwise, he wouldn't be smiling.

"Never." Happiness bounces off us both. "I love you, Lily."

Although I could feel it, I still wondered if I was imagining it.

He adds, "I've loved you since the day you hit me with a door."

A loud giggle shakes my chest. "You have not." I pinch his ass playfully and groan when I feel him inside of me, pleasure zipping through my over sensitive clit.

"Ouch. Okay, okay," he surrenders. "Maybe not, but definitely when I saw you in the coffeehouse. I knew then." He rubs the tip of his nose against mine. "Your dimples, the way you make great coffee." He's so silly. "Those big eyes I saw myself in, your runaway mouth." Yup, there is always that. I tend to ramble when I'm nervous.

"And of course, there's my lucky scarf," I add jokingly.

"It's *our* lucky scarf." He makes me wear it to every game. "Aside from that, I love spending time with you. I like preparing meals for you, grabbing lunch together." Pausing for a moment, he then says, "Picking you up from work is the best part of my day."

Ash is so sweet, a side of himself I've found that he saves for only a chosen few, me being one of them.

I could get used to being cocooned together like this. I tighten my legs around his hips and wrap my arms around his neck. "When you pick me up from work, it's the best part of my day, too." I start staring at the clock from around two in the afternoon every day. "Although I think my female colleagues quite like it when you pick me up as well."

He drops his head to my shoulder in embarrassment and muffles, "I think Edna has a thing for me."

My fingers lightly dance across the skin of his muscular back.

I think all the girls have a thing for him. "I know how much you like older women."

He lifts his head, his eyes popping out of their sockets. "It was one woman, and she was only five years older than me. Edna is sixty."

"About the right age for you, then." I find perverted pleasure joking around with him.

"I am twenty-two. That's not right," he protests, growing louder.

His reaction amuses me, and I know how much he enjoys our sparring as much as I do.

Looking down between us, he then says, "And my cock is still inside of you and you're talking about me with other women."

"You'll just have to punish me for my bad behavior."

"Be careful what you wish for, Ms. Murphy." A loud slap sounds across the room as he spanks my backside, making me moan with pleasure. He's learned that it's my weakness. "Shower. Now." I love it when he's bossy.

Sliding out of me slowly, he looks down between us again where we were joined and I recoil.

"Sore?" he asks.

"A little." He'll know if I lie and say otherwise. He knows me so well.

"You'll be tender tomorrow. I'll look after you."

I stare at him with longing. I know he will.

He sits back on his haunches, tilts his head to the side, and stares at my pussy, then at the faint pinkish blood painted on his cock; the proof of my virginity.

On stretched out arms, he moves back up my body, bracketing his with mine, his face full of determination and dominance. "Mine," he declares.

"Yours." I brush my thumb over his rough, thick beard. "Although I might not want to wait until tomorrow to do what we just did again."

He narrows his eyes. "Really?"

"It felt good."

Disbelieving, he sways his head side to side. "My little Tiger Lily wants to have more willy."

"You did not just say that?" Seeing the amusement in his eyes, I can't help but laugh.

His mouth twitches with humor before he points to his chest and raises his eyebrows. "Hey, you're the one that just said you wanted more dick."

"So, what are you going to do about that, big guy?" My bold words test him.

Momentarily tongue-tied, he startles me when he picks me up as if I weigh nothing, throws me over his shoulder, spanks my bare ass, and tells me all the things he's going to do to me as he walks us to the shower before making me dirty again.

Over and over.

CHAPTER NINETEEN

Lily – Four Months Later

"It's tradition. You have to do it," Candy drawls, checking her manicure as if bored with the entire concept.

"Is it though?" I look around the arena that's buzzing with excitement, the fans staring down at the line of hockey wives and girlfriends, or WAGS, as the tabloids label us.

Urgh. I hate that term and if I appear in one more magazine calling me that with yet another headline speculating over when Ash will pop the question, I will, well, I don't know what I will do, but I'm sure it would be something dramatic like, maybe, you know, post an announcement on my social media quashing those rumors. See, this is what I can't figure out, I'm so dull, and yet the press love Ash and me. It's weird. Weird when they photograph my outfits, then publish where you can buy them from, and also freaky as hell when the gossip columns write about what I had for lunch and how cute it was when I dropped mayo down my blouse while sitting in the park having lunch with Ash one day.

Apparently, I'm normal.

That's what they like about me.

Down to earth Lily, who fell on her ass while running in heels in the rain and burst out laughing. It was all caught on camera. How is that even news?

I'm dull. Very, very, dull.

Why don't they see that?

I bite my nail nervously.

I don't want to walk the red carpet toward where the boys are all lined up on the ice like soldiers on parade.

The Eagles sailed through this season but tonight they play against Montreal in the hope of winning the coveted Stanley Cup and become this year's NHL champions. Again.

I play with the ends of my cream scarf and while Ash is excited about tonight, all I can focus on is what feels like a colony of frogs jumping about in my stomach.

"Are you sure this is what they always do? I watched videos this afternoon and not one of them had their partners lining up to wish the players good luck pregame."

Candy rolls her eyes, "Okay, so maybe I lied. It's a new thing."

"Do I have to do this? I think I need to pee."

"Will you shut up?" Bree, Troy's wife, chimes in. "You're like this powerhouse wedding planner, and yet when it comes to this hockey stuff, you shy away from it like a wallflower."

Her truthful observation hits a cord. "Fine. I will *shut up*." She's always right. They've reassured me that it gets easier. I'm hoping that happens soon.

"Great, now let's do this." Bree points at Candy, who has already made her way through the opening leading onto the red carpet they have laid out for us over the ice. Which is just as well as Candy's heels are sharper than an icepick.

She might pierce the ice and disappear through it, never to be seen again.

"You should've worn a dress and heels," Bree says from behind me as I watch Candy shake her ass in her figure-hugging leather pants and hockey shirt with Brayden's name and number on it, casually waving to the crowd as they cheer us onto the ice. She's a natural at this.

Questioning my outfit, I look down at myself. "What's wrong with what I have on?" I thought I was genius to find blue skinny jeans the exact shade of royal blue as the Eagles to pair with my hockey shirt with Ash's number on it.

"Never mind," she stutters. "It's just, you might regret wearing jeans, that's all."

"What?" I snap over my shoulder. "What are you talking about? We practically have the same outfit on."

"Will you two stop bickering like a pair of jitterbugs. Now smile and wave." Candy shoots instructions at us over her shoulder. As a seasoned girlfriend and soon to be hockey wife of the infamous Brayden Scott, she's accustomed to the exposure and limelight that comes with the sport.

I do what she says, waving like I'm a queen and forcing a smile. God, this is a little overwhelming. Until I see him. He's there, standing at the end of the red carpet. He's smiling at me and I swear I melt on the spot like hot butter. I don't care about my clothes, or the fans or anything else for that matter, because the man I love and the man who has changed my life for the better, is here and he has this uncanny ability to settle all my nerves and concerns with the flash of his smile.

Hi, I mouth and wave in his direction. A few more steps and I'm standing directly in front of him.

"Hey, Tiger. You look beautiful."

He would say that even if I was wearing a garbage bag.

The best months of my life have passed me by in a flash. Like Ash's mom said, I helped him come out of his shell; going out with his teammates regularly, calling them to come over to his apartment for boys' nights, organizing team visits to the children's hospice wing to raise their spirits, even inviting the press along to shine a light and increase awareness of the great work they do, in the hope that more people would donate. He knew it would work, and in the short time I have known him, he's a changed man. Just ask his friends. They can't quite believe how much he smiles since we started dating.

Together we share everything, food, apartments, although he's hinted how much easier it would be if I gave notice on my lease and moved in with him. It's still early days, however, it does make sense. I did argue that if I do, I will contribute toward the bills and rent, but he dismissed me entirely and told me that I could pay him in other, more creative ways; blowjobs being one of them.

Of course, there's the other side of him that no one gets to see but me. The sweet side that's held me in his arms while I grieve my mom, calmed me down when I signed three wedding planning contracts all on the same day and freaked out, and has been there to work out my plan to finally leave my position at High Octane.

He's a great man. The best.

Overhead, the commentator introduces himself, preparing the crowd for tonight's proceedings and when I look to my left and right, I notice there is quite a bit of space around us, as if everyone has moved away. I turn from Ash and tune in to the commentary, looking up at the giant screens above us to discover my face on the screen.

The commentator's voice blares over the speakers.

"Attention please, can I ask if everyone could simmer down for a few minutes? We have an important announcement."

Unsure what the hell is happening, I patiently wait to see what unfolds.

The arena falls quiet, but I can hear gasps. Unsure what they are all seeing that I can't, I look left and right, but I find nothing.

The arena is now so quiet you can almost hear a pin drop. It's hard to imagine the fans can contain themselves. Their excitement always makes the arena feel like it's alive, like it has its own set of lungs and heartbeat.

The commentator then says, "Ash Johansson, it's over to you."

What?

I spin around to look up at him, but he's not there. He's lower, much lower. He's down on bended knee, holding an open ring box with a diamond engagement ring sitting inside of it.

"Are you—" *Oh, my God, he is.* My pulse zooms around my body at breakneck speed.

With an air of calm and self-confidence around him, he's not nervous at all because he already knows my answer.

"Will you be my forever?" Grinning up at me, he looks pleased with himself.

Like always, we love teasing one another and I playfully reply, "Oh, go on then." I nod my head then say a loud, "Yes."

The sound of cheering begins immediately, almost deafening us, filling the arena with higher levels of excitement than I've ever heard before.

He slips the ring on my finger, and I can't contain my gasp because I don't think I have ever seen such a beautiful cluster of diamonds; the center solitaire hugged tight by a halo of smaller ones.

"It looks like a flower."

"For my Lily." He leaps up, kisses me, then lifts me into the air. The noise and excitement rippling, the entire stadium vibrating with energy.

Spinning us around, I squeal, wrapping my legs around him, and grab his beard, that's so long now it's ridiculously scratchy. I look forward to him shaving it all off tonight after the game. It hides his gorgeous face and I miss it.

Kissing me breathless, I mumble against his lips lined with bristles. "I'll be your forever."

"And I'll be yours."

Organizing client weddings brings me so much joy, but planning my own will be incredible. "We have a wedding to plan," I say excitedly.

"I hear there's a new firecracker wedding planner in town. Tiger Lily Events or something."

"I may have heard of her."

"She's the best."

"I heard she works hard." I've spent too many late nights at my dining table and Ash's kitchen island working into the wee small hours; three more clients and I can finally hand in my resignation at High Octane.

"I hear she has a nice ass." He lowers his voice, not that anyone will hear our conversation over the roars from the fans.

"I hear her boyfriend is super-hot."

"Fiancé."

We smile goofily at each other.

"Right, put her down." Candy shouts over the rowdy cheers that are still going, and he carefully lowers me down onto the red carpet.

Bree grabs my hand to get a look at my ring. "It's beautiful," she gasps. "I'm so happy for you, Lily."

"I should have worn a dress." I roll my eyes, understanding what she meant now.

She grants me a huge, genuine smile, then throws her hands in the air. "I told you so. Instead, you wore jeans and his shirt and actually it couldn't have been more perfect. The tabloids and fans love that shit." Pulling me into a hug so fierce, I'm surprised she doesn't squeeze all the air out of my lungs. Candy joins us completing our triangle.

These girls feel like sisters to me; my soul sisters.

Candy says what I am thinking, "I love you girls. Welcome to the circus, Lily."

I love these girls too.

Over Candy's shoulder, I smile as I watch Ash's teammates shake his hand, pat him on the back, congratulating him.

Our eyes lock, my heart filling with unconditional love for this man.

My forever.

CHAPTER TWENTY

Ash – Five Years Later

I swirl the ice cubes around my empty glass, circling them distractedly as the familiar blond at the bar catches my attention.

We played against Florida tonight, but now the team is back at the hotel. I'm all worked up, adrenaline pumping through my veins, and I'm in need of something to take the edge off.

And there is only one woman in the entire universe who can do that.

And she's here.

"Are you even listening to me?" Troy punches the top of my arm.

"Nope." I can't take my eyes off the beautiful woman who has now crossed her legs and is flashing her tempting thighs at me, teasing me, inviting me to look, and I know she's doing it on purpose.

Because this is the game Lily and I play.

"Excuse me." I rise to my feet in a rush and push my phone into the pocket of my jeans.

"Fucking typical." I can almost hear Troy's eyes roll.

"Leon will be down soon."

Grinning, Troy looks over at the bar. "You're a bad man."

I twirl my wedding ring around my finger. "I am the worst."

"You really are," he says, chuckling.

I stroll over to the bar and sit down beside the woman who hasn't stopped looking at me since I walked in. I lift my chin to signal to the bartender.

"Evening." I turn in my seat. "Would you like a drink?"

"Yes, please," she smirks, twisting the stem of her empty glass between her fingers.

"A Cosmo for the lady." I order for her, knowing fine well that's her favorite.

Lifting her eyebrows, she seems surprised. "You know your cocktails."

"I might know a woman who likes them."

"A woman?" She drops her gaze to my wedding band, and I check to see if she's wearing the one that matches mine. She's taken it off, although there is a slight indent; evidence that she wears one. "Does that *woman* know you're buying a drink for another woman in a hotel bar in Florida?"

"I don't have a woman in my life," I lie.

Lines of concentration deepen on her forehead. "If you did, would she kick you in the balls if she knew what you were up to right now?"

I run my finger back and forth across my bottom lip. "Much worse. She'd chop them off and feed them to my fans." Because they love my wife more than me.

"Fans? What do you do?"

"I'm a hockey player."

Her mouth downturns, looking unimpressed, and I almost laugh when she says, "Fancy. I hate to burst your bubble, but who are you?"

I give a fake name. "William."

"William," she repeats as if she's trying it on for size. Lifting her glass to her lips, she takes a sip, then takes two huge glugs as if she's nervous. "I hate men who cheat." With a sly look, she side eyes me.

"So do I." I've never cheated on Lily. There is no other woman for me other than her.

"But you're wearing a wedding ring." Her mouth spreads into a thin-lipped, disapproving smile, her nostrils flaring with disgust.

"It's a piece of jewelry. It's not a wedding ring." Another lie to play the game.

"I hope that's true," she mutters dryly.

"Why do you ask? Are you interested in me?" I smirk.

"Why would you come over to speak to me if you didn't see me looking at you?" She turns to face me, uncrosses her legs, flashing me her lace panties, then crosses them again. "And I think you like what you see."

Fuck me.

In an instant, I'm hard. "Oh, I like what I see." My eyes drop to her red gloss covered lips when she licks them. "You are very beautiful." I've thought that since the day we met.

"Thank you." She accepts my compliment. "You're not so bad yourself, even if you are a hockey player."

"Not a fan of the game?" I scoff.

"Nah. I prefer baseball."

She makes me laugh out loud. She's such a tease.

Leaning forward, she runs her hands up my thigh. "But I could make an exception for you. If I asked you to come up to my room and spend the night with me, would you say yes?" She moves in closer, her hand millimeters from my throbbing cock, her lips almost on mine. "Would you like to find out what I taste like?"

I gulp, my needy slit now leaking with precum.

I want her. And I already know what she tastes like. Delicious.

Her mouth finds my ear, her voice dripping with sex. "I'd like to find out what you taste like."

I groan.

"Fuck me tonight. Forgive yourself tomorrow, William." The husky sound in her tone is my undoing. I can't take it anymore.

"Come with me." I grab her hand, stand up, and pull her behind me as I stride toward the elevator. She doesn't say another word and follows me obediently.

"Have fun," Troy's voice mocks from behind, his voice full of amusement.

Tapping my foot impatiently, the digital elevator counter counts down as I continue to hold her hand firmly.

When the doors open, I pull her inside and fix my gaze on her.

"Floor ten, William." She bites her bottom lip and I'm relieved no one else joins us as I hit the button. The doors shut and I'm pushing her against the wall, slamming my lips against hers, and sliding my hand up between her legs to find what she gave me a glimpse of at the bar.

Threading her fingers into the hair at the back of my neck, I kiss her breathless and she lets out a soft moan when I move her panties to the side then push a finger into her wet center. "You didn't tell me your name, sweetheart." I lick her lips, nipping at them a little, her signature apple scent makes me feel dizzy.

"It's Suki."

I lean back and screw my face up. "Suki?" I question her fake name.

"Suki Cockoff," she says with a straight face.

I burst out laughing just as the elevator dings indicating we are stopping to let someone on.

Panicking, I quickly pull away while *Suki* straightens her skirt. That's when I notice her mouth and chin are covered in red lipstick. I point at her to look in the mirrored walls, but she's too late to fix it. The doors slide open and on the other side stands Leon.

Fuck.

My eyes bug out as a big cheesy grin fills his face, knowing exactly what we've been up to. "Hey, Lily," he says casually, greeting my wife. Then considers getting in. "You know what? I'll get the next one."

Before the doors fully close, he shouts through the gap. "That shade of lipstick suits you, Ash."

I spin around and look at my reflection to discover my lips are stained with red lipstick too. "Shit." I try rubbing it off.

A giggle causes me to snap my head in *Suki's* direction. "Oh, you think this is funny, do you, *Suki*?"

"Hilarious." Lily tilts her head to the side, her eyes dropping to my crotch. "Well, that was fun." Breaking out of character, she beams at me.

I pin her against the wall and attack her mouth with mine.

"Ash," she moans.

"It's William." I press my cock against her hip to show her what she does to me.

"I'm not calling you William. You're my Ash." She sucks my tongue into her mouth, making my dick even harder. I fucking love it when she does that.

Once a month Lily flies out to meet me when we are playing an away game. It's when we act out our fantasies in a sexy game of role play. Tonight, was pretend not to know each other, which Lily picked, And I have to admit, it's not the role play that turns me on, it's her. It's always about her.

She turns me on so bad.

Last month she was a chambermaid who happened to be in my hotel room when I finished a game. She's always up for trying new things to keep the fire burning between us.

Although, this is becoming more and more difficult as Lily's business expands. She doesn't only plan weddings anymore; it's evolved into luxury events and all kinds of celebration parties, employing several planners and admin staff. I've never been so proud. How she manages work, remodeling our fixer-upper house, attending every home game, and flying to meet me in between, I will never know; she's a master in the arts of multi-tasking.

Without doubt, I couldn't do this job without her. She's my rock, my confidant, my lover, and my best friend.

I wasn't lying to her down in the bar. I *have* never and will never cheat on her.

We keep kissing all the way out of the elevator, along the corridor, and through the door of our hotel room, clawing, pawing, and attacking each other.

"And you are not calling me Suki all night," she protests, slamming the door shut and shoving me against the wall.

"I will call you anything I want."

With fast hands, she's unbuckling my belt, undoing my pants, and has my cock out of my boxers in seconds. I press down on her shoulders. "Now drop to your knees and suck my cock."

I bang my head against the wall when she pulls me into

her mouth and sucks hard. "Aw fuck." With both hands on the back of her head, she lets me fuck her mouth.

Pressing against my taint, she massages it expertly before she moves her finger backward, working my ass with skill. It's not something I thought I would ever enjoy, but with Lily, everything feels good. Cupping my balls with her other hand, she rolls them gently, then squeezes them just the way I like it.

When she's doing all three things at once, I can't hold back. "Aw, fuck, Tiger. I'm coming."

Knowing how much she loves making me come, her small moans and groans of pleasure are my undoing. I look down and she's watching me. My mouth drops open and I roar out my release. My balls draw up into my body, my ass throbbing as I shoot hot ropes of cum down the back of her throat and she swallows everything I give her.

I cup her cheek and smile down at her. "I love you, Lily Johansson."

She kisses the head of my cock before rising to her feet. Then, using her stage voice, she whispers, "I love you more today than yesterday, Ash."

I trace my finger down her nose and across her top lip.

"Promise me we will always be like this." Her hopeful eyes burn deep into my soul.

"I promise." I kiss her lips and she sighs contentedly.

"I want to have a baby, Ash. I'm ready to start a family."

Imagining Lily pregnant makes my dick spring to life again. "I think I can help you with that. Now get on the bed, Suki Cockoff. And put your wedding ring back on. Let's make a baby."

Giggling, she runs to do as she's told.

I will never let anything come between us, Lily Johansson, I promise.

PART 2

THE PRESENT

15 YEARS MARRIED

"What the hell happened to us?"

CHAPTER TWENTY-ONE

Ash – The Evening After the Prologue

Lily and I are at Bree and Troy's dinner party.

Something they host every couple of months, ensuring we keep in touch, and for those with kids, allow them to have 'adult time'.

How I wish that was the case for Lily and me.

As our marriage progressed, and once her business took off, her focus changed from building the business to starting a family. All she ever dreamed about was having a family of her own and all I ever wished for was to give her everything to make her happy. And yet I couldn't give her the one thing she dreamed of; a baby.

Something our friends are acutely aware of.

Unless Lily asks about their kids, they don't share.

Friends since we were all drafted to the NHL the same year, Bree and Troy along with Candy and Brayden, Buster and Leon who are yet to settle down, both bringing plus ones along tonight that I didn't catch the name of, have remained friends. Troy is now the Eagles Video and Coaching Analytics Coordinator, while Brayden is one of three of our assistant coaches. Buster got himself out of the game altogether and went on to become an author, writing crime books set in Edmonton. His latest book became a New York Times bestseller, and we couldn't be happier for him. Leon, on the other hand, is still a self-confessed man whore who, following his retirement from hockey, went on to become a player agent and owns a sports bar with Buster. We remain tight but don't get much downtime to see each other lately.

Completely focused on her business, I don't think Lily meets with Candy and Bree as often as she used to either. Which is a shame. They were always close.

The past few years have been hectic, and since we won the Stanley Cup again for the third year running this year has become even more stressful. Everyone wants to know how I do it, how the team does it, and what training, drills, coaching, and specialist training are we doing. What's our secret? The truth is, together, we just work. The magic formula is all of us. But everyone is watching. They want to see if we can do it again this season. Can we break the record no one has ever achieved before? And that weight of expectation is playing havoc with my sanity, sleep, and stress levels. I can feel it building, as if someone has wrapped their fist around my lungs, squeezing every last drop of air until I can't breathe. Some days I can't concentrate, on others my heart races so fast I can't regulate it.

Add to that, the mounting pressure it's putting on my marriage. It's reached peak levels and I've barely seen Lily.

I miss my friend, my lover, the only person I trust to share everything with. And yet, I haven't told her how unwell I have been feeling; the heart palpitations, headaches, insomnia. I swear I'm on the brink of having a mental breakdown.

All I do is run about, replay video tapes, and manage and organize the players. Media and press interviews never stop and I stupidly volunteered myself to coach the peewee team for the local group home. I am seriously considering telling them I can't do it anymore. But the boys are always so invested; they listen to me and the way they look at me like I made their whole day fills my heart with joy.

But it's all taking its toll.

I haven't been to the gym in weeks, which is unheard of.

And I'm late for everything.

I no longer have time to myself or to spend with Lily.

It's becoming a ridiculous problem.

Yesterday was a prime example of that and, while I did make it home from our delayed flight from Calgary, it was much later than I expected. And as usual, Lily was already fast asleep when I let myself into the house. And early morning training today meant I was up and out the door before she was even awake.

She looked so beautiful and peaceful, and tiny, lying in our gigantic bed; one she spends too many nights alone in.

I'm all too aware that something must change.

We both know it.

Our stressful jobs seem to have taken over, and like a perennial weed, I don't know how to excavate it from our lives or get it under control.

Tonight is the first evening we've spent together in over two, or is it three weeks? Fuck knows. But, however long it's been, it's too long.

I give Lily's thigh a squeeze under the dining table. "You're quiet tonight, everything alright?" She was silent in the car driving here, too and she's hardly eaten a thing.

Pulling her mouth into a tight line, elbow bent, her chin resting on her hand, she twists her neck and I know she's hiding something when she says, "I'm fine." The usual sparkle in her eyes is missing. She looks sad, making my guts twist like a snake recoiling in my stomach.

Following a strategic rewatch of last night's game with the entire team this afternoon, which made me late again, I only had minutes to spare to grab a shower and get changed for tonight. When I arrived back at the house, Lily was already waiting for me with a glass of wine in hand. Lost in deep thought, the house was eerily quiet as she stood, frozen to the spot, staring out of the bay window. I asked her the same question then too and her answer was the same; *I'm fine.*

"You know you can tell me anything?" I whisper so no one else can hear.

Nodding, she assures me. "We need to talk—" She starts to say but is interrupted by my phone ringing. "And there it is." She sighs, staring at the lit-up screen on the table with a withheld number. "That phone never stops." Grabbing her glass of red wine, she downs the last of it and pushes her seat back. "Excuse me."

I can't deny it; she's right. The role of being a hockey coach continues off the ice more often than I realized. The weight or expectation of winning games, upholding the Eagles' reputation, media interviews, and managing the often-unruly team on and off the ice means that I'm never not working.

My phone continues to scream at me and I reluctantly pick it off the table and excuse myself. Following in Lily's footsteps out of the dining room and into the entryway, I catch her disappearing behind the bathroom door.

Hitting the accept button on my screen, I lift my phone to my ear. "Hello?"

"Is this Ash Johansson?" An authoritative sounding male voice hits my eardrum.

This better not be a press call or I will lose my shit. No one has access to my private number. "Speaking. Who is this?" I reply, defensively.

"Sir, this is Sergeant Martin from Edmonton Police Service. We have a Wade Collins in custody."

I dip my head as the feeling of yet another headache threatens to throb through my temples. I rub the tight space between my brows. "What did he do this time?" I sigh.

"Brawling in Finch's Bar."

Fucking hell.

"Was there any press around?"

"Luckily for you, no." I can almost hear the humor in his voice.

Wade comes from a broken home and an equally unstable background and didn't exactly have the best start in life, which he seems to be unable to shake off. Lily thinks he's perfectly balanced; he has a chip on each shoulder. She's not wrong, and this isn't the first call I've had from the Edmonton Police Service. Wade is turning out to be a real fucking pain in my ass. "I'll come get him." My voice is defeated, reluctance thick in my throat.

"Much appreciated. See you soon, Mr. Johansson."

I hang up, shove my phone in my pocket, and walk over to the bathroom, lightly tapping on the door. "Lily, can you open up, please?"

"Give me a minute." Her sweet voice echoes from behind the door as the sound of the toilet flushes. A few clicks and she's unlocked it and let me in as she makes her way back to the washbasin.

I close the door behind me, lock us in, and move to stand behind her.

"What's up?" Lily runs her now soapy hands under the flowing water, then looks up at me in the mirror.

"I have to go. Wade's been arrested."

"Again?" She rolls her eyes while turning the faucet off and grabs the fluffy white towel to dry her wet hands. "That boy needs therapy. And a good mother."

She turns around, placing the towel on the edge of the basin, and leans against it. "So, you're leaving?"

"I promise I'll make it up to you."

Folding her arms in front of her, she looks down. "I'll come. I don't want to stay here without you. I spend most nights by myself, waiting around for you. I don't want to do that again tonight."

Lifting my hand that's tattooed with a giant lily, one of many I have branded into my skin to signify each year we've been married, I place my knuckle under her chin and lift it up so I can stare into her beautiful eyes. "I'm sorry." How many times will she accept my apology? It can't be many more.

"I miss you." Her eyes turn glassy. "I miss us."

She said the same thing last night on the phone.

I pull her into my arms, wrapping her in a giant big bear hug she loves so much. "Hey, no crying, baby. I miss us too." I kiss the top of her head, enjoying her closeness and the smell of her perfume she's worn since the day we met. It's comforting; she's always felt like home.

She snuggles into my shoulder, then unravels her crossed arms and wraps them around my waist. I hug her tighter, enjoying this precious time we haven't had much of lately.

"Do you still find me attractive?"

"What?" I exclaim and pull back to look at her. "Are you being serious?"

She looks at me, then looks away sheepishly. "It's just. It's..." She appears to struggle to find the right words. "We haven't had sex for a while." Her voice is quiet, barely a whisper.

"Is that honestly what you think? Jesus Christ, Lily." I pull her back into my arms. "I love you. With every beat of my heart, every breath I take, every minute of every day, I think about you."

"Love and sexual attraction are not the same thing." She sniffs and I pull out of our hug and cradle her face to discover tears running freely down her cheeks. She looks away. "I'm not as slim as I used to be. I'm no longer perky or young like those puck bunnies that follow you around, and—"

"Lily, look at me," I demand, angry at her for thinking these stupid thoughts, but even madder at myself for not showing her how much I love her and how sexy I think she is. She's the only woman I have ever felt a deep, undeniable, unique attraction to. "What did I tell you on the phone last night?" I ask her when she finally makes eye contact with me.

"I don't remember."

"You look fucking beautiful. You looked so sexy last night in that photo. If I could have jumped through the phone, I would have. You made me hard just looking at you in that sexy lingerie. And what else did I tell you?"

She shakes her head, and I hate seeing her upset.

"That you still look the same as the day we met."

She scoffs, as if not believing me.

"You do. I would never lie to you. I find you sexier now than the day we met. My attraction to you only grows, never lessens. When I'm not with you, all I do is wish I was. I hate traveling to away games, knowing I won't see you for days. I hate it when you travel for work and all I do is wish I could go with you. I love everything about you. That's never ever changed. Your smile, your laugh, your silly dancing you do around the house, although I would much prefer it if you did that naked more often," I try reassuring her. "I love coming home to you. Love your organizing and labeling of our pantry. I love the way you alphabetize your vinyl records and, most of all, I like spending days off together doing nothing."

"We haven't had many of them lately." Her hope filled eyes stare deep into my guilty conscience. "When did we start scheduling each other in? We'll be penciling in sex soon."

I drop my forehead to hers. "That might actually mean we're guaranteed to do it then." I try making a joke of it, but it doesn't sit well.

"I'm thinking of selling the business," she announces unexpectedly, and for a moment I can't think of what to say. My hands drop to my sides in shock.

"What? Why?" are the only two words I can form.

Her shoulders sag with relief as if she's glad to get it off her chest. "If I wasn't working, at least I could come with you to the home, as well as the away games again. There would be no destinations weddings or evening events to attend that get in the way of me seeing you. My business is taking over my life. I spend boring lunch breaks at my desk working alone. I go home when you're not here and I work at night. When I'm not in the office, all I seem to do is organize events or answer yet another bridezilla's demands. I arrive at the office before everyone else, because most of them have kids and I'm always the last one to leave because

I never have anyone to come home to. Candy and Bree both have children who seem to attend every peewee sports club and dance class known to mankind and I can't exactly tag along now, can I? That's just sad. And while they might not mind Brayden and Troy being away because they still have their children to keep them company..." Her words pick up speed, her chest moving in and out quickly. "I hate you being away all the time. I hate when I have to go away with work, and leave you behind." Swiping away her tears, she flicks them off her cheek. "I hate that we never have sex anymore. I hate doubting if you still find me attractive. And I hate that we never *ever* talk about having a family anymore."

She drops the bombshell we both know we've been avoiding.

After trying for years, with no success, we went through three rounds of IVF. It broke my heart watching hers break at the end of every cycle that didn't end with a pregnancy. The tears we shed together, the bruising she endured from the injections, nausea from the fertility drugs, and the toll it took on her mental health watching her friends fall pregnant when she didn't. It was too much for both of us.

The last failed cycle changed something within my happy Lily. Throwing herself into work, she said she didn't want to speak about it again.

It's like the elephant in the room that neither of us wants to acknowledge. And how can you have a baby if you never even try to make one? It's been weeks since we had sex. *What the hell happened to us?*

Stunned into silence, I can't think of anything to say because I know she's right.

"I don't think I was meant to be a mom." Covering her face with both hands, she sobs into them and my heart fucking stops at how gut wrenching she sounds, wondering how long she's been bottling this all up. "I'll be forty in two years. I'm too old to have a baby." Her voice is somber and I feel her fighting spirit dwindling.

Too oblivious, or scratch that, too self-centered to notice how much she's been hurting. I want to hit myself in the nuts with a sledgehammer; it would be less painful than hearing Lily cry. My ambition to be successful has clouded the single most important thing in my life. Her.

My possessive arms are around her, holding her tight as she cries into my shirt, drenching it in tears.

"I don't know what's wrong with me." Sobbing, she mumbles, "I don't feel like me lately. I feel so down and I never feel depressed. I can't concentrate at work sometimes; it feels like I have brain fog. You're never around to talk to." Just when I think she can't break my heart anymore, she does, smashing it into smithereens. "And I'm so lonely. I'm not just saying I miss you for the sake of it, Ash. I really mean it."

When her sister and father moved to Edmonton to be closer to us, Lily was so excited. Only since Gemma split up with her husband last year and went traveling, not having her sister, who was her best friend, around anymore has been hard for her. Then, of course, her dad found happiness and remarried Diana around the same time.

Driving the knife in deeper, all of our friends have kids and are always so busy. I can see why she's lonely. I may be surrounded by the hockey team and my friends who I work with, but I guess I feel the same way as Lily. Although, for me, I seem to be able to switch off that part of my brain when I go to work, allowing me to focus on my job and just get it done.

I rub her back gently, gliding over the fabric of the dress

to comfort her. "This is all my fault, Lily. I didn't know you felt this way." Or maybe I did, and I chose to ignore it. It's as if the joy has been sucked out of her. "I don't want you to feel like this anymore." I want to take all her despair away.

"Neither do I. I think I need to see a doctor. Maybe my thyroid is playing up or I need Vitamin D shots or something," she says, her voice hoarse and thick with sadness.

Or she needs a husband who comes home to her every night.

"Why don't you make an appointment, see what she says, then let's make an appointment with a fertility specialist?" I always wanted to start a family with her. We both shared the same dream. Only we've been too career focused and I am praying that we still have time.

"Maybe." She's non-committal with her reply, which worries me. I thought that's what she wanted. "Let's go and get Wade out of prison." When she looks up at me, a stabbing pain shoots through my heart. Her bloodshot eyes are lined in a pinkish-red tone and wetness soaks her cheeks, her nose flushed on the end.

"I'm calling one of the assistant coaches. They can sort it. I'm taking my wife home." She's far more important than Wade Collins.

"You don't have to do that. We can go together."

"No." My reply is firm. I pull my phone out of the back pocket of my navy chinos and text Edward. I would ask Brayden, but that's not fair on Candy, especially if she feels the same way as Lily. We all work too hard and haven't had a day off in three weeks.

I need to speak to management tomorrow and ask them to schedule in some compulsory days off for everyone, otherwise, I'm either going to have a heart attack with the amount of pressure I am under, or I'm at high risk of losing my wife. Maybe both.

Looking at herself in the mirror, Lily runs her fingers under her mascara-stained eyes and cheeks. "I can't let them see me like this." She looks at my reflection in the mirror. "And you have mascara all over your shirt. That's never coming out."

"I don't care." I brush the damp stain.

When Edward replies, informing me that he's on his way to get Wade, I switch my phone off for the night and push it back into my pocket. I am way too accessible. That needs to stop too.

Both facing the mirror, we stare at each other. "We'll tell them you're feeling unwell, and we have to go home because you have a painful tummy ache that's made you cry. No one ever needs to know. Okay?" I bracket my arms on either side of the washbasin, caging her in while I rest my chin on her shoulder. "Then we are going home, and I am going to kiss every inch of your beautiful body. Every curve, every freckle, every delicious part of you."

"I put my new lingerie on for you tonight." Her lips twitch with mischief and I groan, remembering the photo she sent me last night.

"I want you to take it all off. I don't want any of you covered up. I want to see you. All of you." Kissing her neck, I ghost my lips against the shell of her ear and watch her reaction in the mirror when I whisper, "Then I'm going to lick your pretty pussy until you're screaming my name, Tiger."

The skin on her neck flushes and her lips part slightly, knowing how good I can make her feel. "I think I'd like that." She swallows.

"Then I'm going to fill you with my cock and fuck you

so hard. And maybe then you'll realize just how much you turn me on." I'm rock solid just thinking about it.

I grind my hips into her ass, making her gasp. "Do you feel that? Feel what you do to me?" I grab her hand, pull it back, and rub it over my throbbing cock. "Still think I don't find you attractive?" She shakes her head. "Good. Now get your sexy backside out there and act like you have the sorest stomach. It's time to go, Mrs. Johansson." I back away to let Lily straighten herself up. "I will ask Brayden to take tomorrow's training session and you're taking tomorrow off because we are going to spend all day in bed and I'm going to worship your body."

"All day?" She giggles, as if not believing I still have the stamina.

I widen my eyes, "All day. What? You think this old man can't keep it up for that long anymore?" Although I don't know if I can, it's been a while since we did that.

"You'll have to prove me wrong, Mr. Johansson, and show me what you got," she says, smiling and sounding more like her cheerful self. Although I can't deny that I'm worried about her, and want her to make an appointment with the doctor as soon as possible.

Biting her lip, as if nervous, she says, "Although I do have clients tomorrow."

"Cancel them." Fuck the business for one day. I unlock the bathroom door.

"I might not be able to."

Organizing weddings and events for Canada's rich and famous sometimes has its pitfalls; most are Daddy's entitled little princesses, where money is no object and budget is a dirty word.

"Tell them no." I'm adamant we are spending quality time together.

"I don't think they understand the meaning of that word."

I reply with a heartless shrug, "You are taking tomorrow off."

"Okay."

"Now," I wrap my hand around the handle and twist it to open it. "Time to pretend. Sore stomach, remember?"

Before I open the door, she walks over and kisses me. "I love you, Ash."

"I will never stop loving you, Lily."

My love for her is eternal.

When we get back to our home, I will show her exactly what that looks like.

Then she'll remember.

CHAPTER TWENTY-TWO

Lily – Two Months Later

I'm numb.

I can't taste the hot chocolate I'm drinking.

Or the food I ate at dinner. Alone. Yet again.

Nothing's changed.

The day after the dinner party at Candy and Brayden's, everything went back to normal.

We couldn't even take one day off.

I was summoned to work that afternoon by a very outspoken bride-to-be who demanded she see me and refused to leave the office until she did. Ash was asked to go into work following a career-changing injury one of the players encountered. At the first hurdle of trying to reconnect, we failed.

Although he did make good on his promise, making love to me all night, showing me how much he adores me. He didn't lie about kissing every inch and freckle, either.

That was eight weeks ago and we've barely seen each other since. Like a lighthouse, we call out to one another but keep missing the signal.

Sitting out on the patio in the bitter night, I pull the blanket in close around me, not that it matters.

I don't feel the December cold.

I feel nothing.

But shame.

And deep loathing for myself for what I am about to do.

A loud bang from the front door alerts me to Ash returning from work. I tap my phone to check the time; ten o'clock.

Yet another sunrise and sunset without each other.

"Lily," he shouts, seeking me out. Eventually, he finds me sitting outside on the wicker dining set I spent hours selecting. Pointless now when I come to think of it. There's only been a handful of times I've sat out here.

"What the hell are you doing out here? It's freezing." He shudders, sitting on the seat across from me.

"I didn't want to sit in the house by myself." I'm done being alone. So done.

"I'm sorry I'm late."

He's always sorry. I'm always sorry. We are forever apologizing to each for being busy.

"It's fine." It's not.

"Are you flying somewhere tonight? I didn't see anything in the calendar?" He swipes at the screen of his phone, double checking he's not wrong about the suitcases lined up in the entryway.

"No," I answer flatly. "I'm moving out."

His head snaps up.

Silence.

Paralyzed, he does nothing but stare at me.

He knows. He knew it would come to this.

I fill him in on today's events. "I went to the doctors

today. I'm not depressed or blue or down or going crazy." I thought I was at one point. "She thinks I'm burnt out."

I've worked myself into a state of exhaustion.

He remains silent.

I was hoping Ash could come with me when I went to my appointment today, but yet again, he couldn't make it. Of course, it wasn't his fault, but something to do with a media interview being unable to be rescheduled.

My voice rises in frustration. It echoes around the vast expanse of our beautifully manicured and quite frankly pretentious backyard. "The doctor doesn't think there is anything wrong with me other than my body is stressed. The doctor suggested that I may be going through an early menopause or there could be something wrong with my thyroid." The two have similar side effects. Both outcomes aren't exactly sexy, are they?

"I had blood tests today." I'll know exactly what is wrong with me in twenty-four hours.

I finish my hot chocolate, ignoring the scorching liquid burning my tongue, and place the mug on the table in front of me. "We know this isn't working anymore, Ash, and I don't think I will ever be able to give you the family we hoped to have one day." I let out a resigned sigh. "Something I think I accepted a very long time ago anyway." A sharp pain stabs at my heart because I haven't accepted it. "I make unfair demands on you that you can't deliver on. I'm not like Candy and Bree, who put up and shut up and simply wait for their husbands to come home whenever the NHL allows them. I want more. I need more."

"You deserve more." Rising to his feet, his haunted eyes hit mine. "I made a promise to you that I would never let anything come between us."

And yet, hockey does.

"You are never here, Ash. I might as well be single."

Too shocked to say anything, his gaze burns with pain, his jaw twitching, his hurt eyes glistening as we take every breath together.

I move my legs out from under me and place them on the ground. "We can't keep pretending that this is what we both want anymore. I think we need some time and space apart." I can't think straight in this house.

"Don't do this, Lily." His voice breaking under the weight of it all; cracking like our marriage. A tear falls down his face and mine fall too.

When I go to speak, my chest hurts, my heart feeling as if it's being ripped from my chest and I hiccup from trying not to cry, but fail and do anyway. "Did you not hear what I just said? I can't give you a family. I can't be the woman you want me to be. I'm not a stay-at-home mom. I haven't been to a game in God knows how long. I'm a shitty wife, unlike Bree and Candy, who go to most of the home games." Perhaps I should have tried harder, although where the hell would I slot anymore into my days? "Have you seen our calendar? We have four days where we are both free over the next two months. That's not a marriage, Ash, and you know it."

"Don't leave me," he sputters, moving to me he fails to hold it together. "Please, Lily." Pain etched into his face, I can't look at him as we fall apart. The magic that made us who we were together is fading away as tears slide down our faces; the plans and hopes we had for a future, the ones that connected us, are no longer enough to keep us together.

I step back and hold my hand up, instructing him to stay where he is. "We live separate lives. Our lifestyles don't match anymore. From my destination weddings to your away games with the team, and all of your media appearances. I see you on the team's social feed, Ash. I see the glitz and glamor. The younger girls." I sound mean and jealous, spiteful even.

I feel old. I feel like I've lost my sparkle. While those puck bunnies are young with bright futures ahead of them. And fertile. I hate those girls. Britney, who always hung around when we first started dating, went on to become a member of their marketing team, and without fail, she's always hanging about like a rotten smell. Two nights ago, she was pictured with some of the team and of course, she stood to the side of Ash, her arm around his back while Ash had his arms in the air cheering. I don't think he realizes how clever she is. She's just waiting to step into my heels.

"I've never cheated on you." Angry now, he roars, tears flowing down his face, his nostrils wet from crying, fear oozing out of him like molten lava.

Dropping the blanket in the wicker chair, I push my feet into my shoes. My heart thumping in my chest, I know if I don't leave now, we'll both continue to drift even further apart than we are now.

"I think I just need some time away from this house." Away from the loneliness I feel coming home to it. I miss him being here. His face, his love, his warmth. I miss him coming into our bed every night. Away from him, I'll be even more lonely, but at least I won't feel the disappointment of being let down yet again.

"You're not leaving." He moves at speed and throws his arms around me. Tight. "You're not leaving," he repeats, his voice cracking and breathless. "You can't go. Please don't go, Lily." His hand on the back of my head, he holds me close, so close I can hear his heart sounding like it's bursting out of his chest.

I explode into a blubbering mess as uncontrollable tears spring from behind my eyes. Like a breaking dam, I can't stop them as I sob into his shoulder.

"If one of us isn't willing to give anything up, then how is this ever going to work?" I splutter and stutter between sobs. "Everything is against us."

"I can't lose you." Ash's fingers cup the back of my neck. "You're the only thing I got right."

I shake my head, disagreeing with him. He's wrong. Angry with myself, I push his shoulders to break free and wipe my nose with the back of my hand. "I'm the one thing you got wrong, Ash."

"Don't say that." His voice is raised and my heart speeds up because we never fight like this. Not ever.

"I'm not the one for you." My words slice my heart wide open, obliterating it.

"You are the *only* one for me." Bellowing, his voice travels far into the darkness of the night. "You are *the* one." He points at me, the thick veins in his neck protruding from his neck, his pulse pounding wildly. "Don't fucking do this." The rising redness in his skin moves from his neck up to his face.

I hang my head in shame, feeling lost and so goddamn lonely. I don't want him to be mad at me and I don't want to feel sad. "I just can't do this anymore, Ash. I need you and you're never around. We don't go to the theater anymore or hiking like we used to. We do nothing together as a couple. I work. You work." I pause. "But together we're not working."

Frantically, he lifts his phone off the table that he dropped with shock earlier. "I'll quit my job."

"You're under contract, so you know that's impossible. And you love your job." I lunge forward to grab his phone, trying to stop him from doing something irrational, but he holds it up high so I can't reach it.

He cups my face, emotion pouring from him. "I love you more. Tell me what you want from me."

I can't think of anything because honestly, I think I just need space. To think and get my head straight.

He turns his back on me and madly taps on his phone, then spins back around. "Done. I quit."

In shock, I plonk my ass back on the chair behind me. "No," I whisper. "That's not what I want. You will resent me for making you quit. I can't let you do that. You know the NHL is who you are."

He ignores me. "Next. A fertility specialist. Who's the best?"

"Ash," I plead, but he continues to ignore me, obsessed with searching for answers on his phone. I say his name again to get his attention.

"There is one in New York. We'll go tomorrow."

I rub my forehead as a headache threatens to make an appearance. "I won't go."

"Isn't that what you want?" Determined, eyes glazed, he holds his hands out to the side of him. "What else?" He sounds desperate as he tries to fix our mess of a marriage.

I stand and shout at him because he won't listen otherwise. "Listen to me. I will not go through IVF again. My body doesn't want to have a baby. We both know it and I don't have it in me to go through another cycle." Holding my stomach, the phantom pains of the injections from last time around still linger. "That's not what I want."

"Well, what the hell *do* you want?" Sounding defeated, his voice drops.

I cover my face with my hands. "I don't know." Bawling

noisily, I cry into them. "I just don't want to feel like I have no one to turn to anymore."

"You have me." His voice is thick with emotion.

Dropping my hands from my face, I look into his eyes, not caring that I have snot and hot tears running down my face. "I don't," I let out with a sad sigh. "It's late when you come in from work, and your job is so demanding that you're always exhausted. If I've had a shitty day, I keep that to myself so I don't add to your stress levels. When I get up, you're usually already gone. An empty glass in the sink is the only evidence that you've been here. I come home, you're not here. I watch television by myself with my laptop open and work so I can distract myself from the loneliness that fills this empty house. Our friends all have kids, so they are a big no-no for weeknights out and don't think I haven't noticed them leaving me out of their mom chats. I know that Candy is pregnant again, by the way, because one of the girls at work told me." Yeah, that hurt more than I thought it would.

"She didn't want to upset you." He lowers his voice, and I can't tolerate the pity in his eyes, so I look away.

"I *am* upset. She should have told me." Using the cuffs of my sweater, I wipe my eyes again and walk over to the table and chair set that's more like an ornament than furniture.

Laying my hands against the tabletop, I bow my head. "Do you know we've never sat around this together?" I shake my head back and forth, then look up over the landscaped backyard. "We've never sat on that bench around the edge of the pond since it was installed." I twist my neck to look at him. He still looks like the same guy I slammed into with a door and almost broke his nose. "You are still so handsome, Ash, and I will always love you. But it's been seven nights since we last had dinner together. Seven days of missing you. Weeks since we've had sex... because we're both so tired when we do spend the night together." We have no energy for each other at the end of our long days.

Shoulders sagging, we stare at each and he knows this is it. Make or break.

"I know your job is stressful and how much they rely on you, Ash. And you know they won't let you quit." He lets out a knowing sigh. "I won't let you either. Go and make history, Ash. That job is what you were made for. The guys, the fans, management, they all love you, and I never want to be the one to prevent you from taking your career to the next level." I read an article recently that the Boston Bears wanted to make him an offer. If they have, he hasn't told me. "Without me, you can go anywhere, accept any job."

Dropping into the seat behind him, he rests his elbows on his widespread knees, weaves his fingers together, and holds them against his chin. Thinking, he stares at me, his eyes red and bloodshot from crying. The pain in my heart stabs at me like a million shards of glass, knowing I'm the one who made him hurt.

The silence grows deadly.

"Say something," I whisper into the night.

He blinks once, then twice before he finally says, "Go."

"What?" I blink back, almost confused that he's giving in and not fighting for us. *Is that what I wanted?*

Out of character, jaw twitching, his eyes take on a manic look about them as he stares into my face. "I said, fucking *go*." Rising to his feet slowly, he points to the French doors of the kitchen. "This is what you want, isn't it? You want me to tell you to go? So, go. You've already packed, Lily." He runs his hands over his short hair. "You made your decision without me." He looks up at the house that's never felt warm or welcoming. "You know, we worked our asses off to rebuild this, to make it a home for us. I thought it was what we both wanted, but it seems like it wasn't. And never, for a second, did I ever wonder if I wasn't enough for you. Until now."

"Ash, that's not—" I hiccup, unable to stop crying.

"Just admit it. I can't give you a baby or an hour of my fucking time. Or even sit down with you to have an evening meal. We have more money than we know what to do with and yet we can't even figure out where we can slot in a vacation to spend it." Silent tears flow down his face and when he finally looks at me, he says, "You're lonely. I hear you now. I understand." Haphazardly, he wipes his wet cheeks with the palms of his hands. "Find whatever makes you happy, Lily." Head bowed; he shoves his hands into the pockets of his jeans. "I'll put your bags in your car," he mumbles. "But for the record. I miss you, too."

He walks through the kitchen doors and out of my life.

CHAPTER TWENTY-THREE

Lily

My legs buckle and I fall to the ground, my world crumbling beneath me, and I scream. My lungs burn with every emotion I've been bottling up for months. "No," I yell into the night. "This can't be it." A crumpled mess on the ground, I look into the sky for answers. "No," I whisper. I clench my eyes shut and hang my head in shame. I couldn't give him everything. He's got this all wrong. "I'm so sorry." Shoulders shaking, I weep with the greatest sadness I have ever felt. "I'm sorry." I failed him. Failed us.

Strong arms wrap themselves around me, flooding me in his familiar scent, and he scoops me off the ground. "I'm so sorry," is all I'm capable of saying.

He shouldn't be so kind. I caused all of this.

"It's okay." Calmly, he carries me into the house, bride across the threshold style, and up the stairs to our bedroom. "You can't drive like this. You're too upset. It's not safe, baby." I cling on to him, loving how close we are.

"I miss you." Sniffling, I nuzzle into his neck.

"I know." He pulls me closer to him. "I know," he repeats with a resigned sigh.

"It's not your fault, Ash." My nose is blocked from all the crying, making me sound like I have the flu.

He lowers me onto our bed on top of the comforter, his mouth pulls to one side. "Then why does it feel like it is?" Avoiding eye contact, he pulls the blanket sitting at the foot of the bed up over me. "You're as beautiful as the day I met you." Gently, he runs his finger down my nose and across my upper lip, then turns to leave. "Sleep here tonight. I'll leave."

Reaching out, I grab his hand tattooed with a lily. Even if we are over, he will forevermore be covered in reminders of me. "Stay with me," I beg, wanting him to stay because he's my person. The only man I have ever been with. Having spent too many nights apart over the years, I crave his comfort.

"I can't," he says, his sad tone tugging at my heartstrings. He pulls his hand out of mine and walks toward the door. "You broke my fucking heart."

A black shadow of gloom looms over me.

"I broke mine too," I whisper. "But please don't blame yourself, Ash. We both lost sight of each other. We're both responsible. I just think we need some time to regroup and think about what we want." And we need to make changes. Sitting up too quickly, my head throbs. I push my fingertips into my temples. "Let's talk, Ash. I should have talked to you."

I wish I had.

He stops in his tracks as if weighing up his options.

I rest my head back down on the pillow again and gaze at the ceiling.

How did we get here?

Where did we go wrong?

Is this what I want?

"Loving you was easy." His voice breaks through the silence, and I push myself upright again.

Facing away from me, his drooping broad shoulders drop lower as he continues to stare at the open doorway. "But losing you." He struggles to continue. "Losing you is harder and more painful than I could have imagined."

He takes a few more steps toward the door then grabs onto the doorjambs on either side, his knuckles whitening from fisting them so tight, as if needing something to hold him upright. "If you want space, then you've got it. Although, you've just told me I give you too much, and still you want more. I can't win." Defeated, his voice is so low I can barely make out his words. "I love you," he finally says. "You're all the reasons I believed in love." His voice breaks on the last few words and I can hear his pain. He sucks in an audible breath before he disappears.

I hear his footsteps sprinting down the stairs. The sounds of him crying echoing throughout the huge space before the front door slams shut, leaving me alone.

Again.

He gave me what I wanted.

I asked for this.

Leaving us both heartbroken.

Completely destroyed.

I scream his name into the emptiness, realizing what I have done.

The hate bomb I have for myself exploding in my chest.

Losing him is more painful than I ever imagined too. I hate this feeling.

And despise myself for causing all of this.

Lips quivering, I don't think I have any tears left in me,

but they fall and fall until they dry up. I must sit for hours in the dark just staring off into space.

Where did he go? I have no right to text him to ask him if he's okay.

He's not okay.

I'm not okay.

We're not okay.

I reach for my phone Ash must have placed on the nightstand for me and text the only person I trust.

ME:

I need you.

ME:

Please come home, Gemma.

I need my sister.

ME:

I think I messed up.

"I'm so sorry, Ash," I say into the empty room, curling myself into a ball, wishing my mom was still here.

CHAPTER TWENTY-FOUR

Ash

I take another sip of my beer and close one eye, trying to focus on the television playing replays of archived Eagles games.

"Fuck hockey," I mutter and down the last of my beer straight from the bottle.

"Another. In fact, make it whiskey," I call over to the bartender, who is cleaning glasses and eyeing me suspiciously. I slap a one-hundred-dollar bill on top of the bar. That'll change his mind.

"Make that five."

Bleary eyed, I follow the familiar voice and look to the left of me.

Brayden.

"Hey, man." A firm hand squeezes my right shoulder, and I twist my neck to see who it is.

Troy.

I want to be alone. "Go away."

"Well, aren't you a fucking ray of sunshine this evening?" Troy flops down on the bar stool next to me.

"And if you didn't want anyone to know your whereabouts, you shouldn't have sat pickling your liver inside the bar Buster and I own and where everyone knows you." Leon appears behind the bar alongside Buster.

Subconsciously, I think I wanted them to find me. However, Home & Away is the best sports bar in Edmonton and I wouldn't drink anywhere else.

Leon and Buster's bar manager fills five whiskey tumblers with the amber colored liquor and distributes them in front of us. "Thanks, Ricky." Troy grabs a glass.

"Traitor," I slur in Ricky's direction, knowing he was the one who most likely alerted Leon to my presence.

Brayden swivels round to face me and rests his elbow on the bar. "Management said they've been calling you all night."

"I switched my phone off. Fuck them." I down my whiskey in one and choke on the smoky, bitter taste.

Troy slaps my back while I cough and splutter uncontrollably. "Easy, Ash. You've never been able to handle your drink."

"Fuck off." I push his arm off me. "Leave me alone."

Alone.

How Lily feels.

Brayden jumps in, sounding worried and equally annoyed. "Do you mind explaining what's going on with you? First, I get a frantic call from Dustin screaming down the phone, telling me you've quit via a text message. If you were going to do it seriously, you could have at least emailed the Eagles' general manager with a formal letter of resignation. And second, Ricky calls me to tell me you're drinking yourself into a hole on a Thursday night. In my bar. So, what the fuck is going on, Ash?"

I can't bring myself to tell them.

I'm too ashamed to admit I failed my wife.

My absolute rock and the only woman who really knows me.

We've shared everything, including our tears tonight.

Resting my elbows on the bar, I drop my head into my hands and stare down at the floor.

I feel empty.

I lost her.

"Ash?" one of my friends pushes me for an answer.

Head bowed; unable to hold my tears in any longer, I let them fall. They splash to the floor, leaving mini puddles on the red tiles beneath me, making them look like shiny dots.

"Fuck. This is an emergency," I hear Buster saying, then calls time early, closing the bar and asking everyone to leave.

I can't look up as their patrons grumble and argue with my buddies as they herd them out of the door.

Resting my forehead on the bar, because my head feels too heavy to hold up, my body is full of nothing but sadness and regret.

"Cheers, Ricky. We'll clean up," I hear Leon tell him. There's a loud clank of what sounds like someone locking the door, leaving just me and my four friends in the empty bar.

"Are you dying?" Troy tries guessing what's wrong with me.

I feel like I am.

"Much worse." I lift my head and stare at the mirrored wall behind the bar. The skin on my face is blotchy from crying, my eyes red and sore looking. I wipe my running nose with the back of my hand and finally tell them. "Lily moved out."

Stunned silence, much louder than any words could express, tells me they knew this was coming.

I think we all knew this would happen, eventually.

I've let work consume me. Striving for success made me selfish.

I work longer and harder than anyone on the team.

None of that matters now. If I don't have her, I have nothing.

And I took her for granted.

Eventually, she had enough. My beautiful Lily is lonely, and that's the saddest fucking thing I've ever heard, knowing I wasn't there for her.

"Has she already gone?" Buster asks.

Dazed, I stare at my reflection, "She was too upset to drive tonight. I left her in the house." Pausing before I admit, "I put her bags in the car for her. I don't know why I helped her." I should have hidden her stuff.

What a fucking idiot I am.

"She won't be there tomorrow," I add. Or the next day, or the day after that, or the one after that either.

Then I tell them everything. About how lonely she is, how we never have any time or energy for one another. How late I work. I'm never there for her, and the fucking kicker, no family to even keep her company.

"I couldn't give her what she wanted," I mutter.

"You gave her everything, Ash. But she didn't want *things*." Brayden pauses before he says what I know is coming next. "She wanted you. All of you. Not just the leftovers after everyone else had their bite of you. I don't understand why you don't utilize your assistant coaches more. That's what we are there for. And you should be using the video coaches to review all the tapes, to catch the bits you don't. You are shit at delegating."

I've become a control freak.

Brayden grabs my face between his hands, making me

look at him and squeezing my cheeks. "Is she still at the house?"

"For tonight," I say between my squashed lips.

"You're an idiot." He releases his tight grip, then pulls his phone out of his jacket pocket.

"Gee, compassionate, Brayden. My world just imploded and you're calling me names? What the fuck?" My voice raised; he's properly got my back up. "And what else was I supposed to do? She's moving out. I couldn't stand and watch her leave." My heart's already broken. I couldn't take much more. "I had to get out of that fucking house."

Ignoring me, he taps on his phone, then holds it against his ear.

"Hey sweetie, can you call your mom and tell her to come over to take care of the kids? It's just for a couple of hours."

"You can't tell Candy." I try grabbing the phone away from his ear, but he bats my arm away while Buster grabs it and pushes it behind my back, locking it in place.

"Lily needs you. And Bree," he tells her.

Forced to grit my teeth together, I almost roar in pain when I struggle with Buster. *Fuck, that's painful. He's still so strong.*

The words I never thought I would ever hear Brayden say slip off his lips as he tells Candy what's happened tonight.

"Look after her. I love you, sweetie." He hangs up. "She's going to go over to the house as soon as her mom arrives."

"I've texted Bree. My mom was already at our house, so Bree is on her way over to yours now." Troy confirms.

"You shouldn't have done that." She'll hate them seeing

her so upset. It smashed my heart when I saw her slumped on the ground outside. My beautiful wife is broken.

"Gemma is out of town. You know how she hates bothering anyone. She only trusts her sister. So she won't confide in her father or your mom, so who else does she have? She needs someone. She needs Candy and Bree," Buster interjects. Being close friends with Gemma, he knows how tight Lily and her sister are.

He's right. But she needs me and I need her.

"I should go to her." I slide my barstool across the tiled floor, making it sound like it's screeching in pain, a mirror image of my heart.

"Don't. She needs her girlfriends. Let her calm down and give her the space she asked for."

I reluctantly sit back down.

"She knows about the baby." I side eye Brayden, my throat tightening at her admission that she doesn't want to try again.

How can we when we aren't together anymore, anyway?

Space won't make her change her mind about us. Her decision sounded final, and I know from watching other friends who separate. It's never just a separation. It always, *always*, leads to divorce.

I rub my heart over my shirt. Man, that hurts.

When I married her, I married for life. When I said my marriage vows, I meant them, every word.

"How did she find out about Candy's pregnancy?" Brayden asks.

"I don't know. Maybe Sloane at work." She knows Candy and their kids go to the same school.

"Candy called her at the office the other day because

she wanted to break the news to her personally but couldn't get a hold of her," he adds.

Too late. "Well, she already knows."

"I'll text Candy and let her know." Brayden's fingers move fast against the screen of his phone.

What a mess. Nothing like sending a pregnant woman over to console your upset wife who can't have children herself. Talk about rubbing salt into the wound.

"This is all my fault," I say quietly.

"It's not. You both have demanding jobs. You are both responsible for making time for one another, but you need to sort your schedule out, Ash. You work way too many hours and haven't had a vacation in years. You've turned into the team's agony aunt, you never stop for lunch, and you make yourself far too available. You do more than coach. You could do all of our jobs with your eyes closed."

I've turned into a workaholic.

My father would be disappointed in me for letting hockey come between me and my wife. My family even. Other than seeing Mom at games, which she still attends faithfully all season, I haven't visited her for months.

I've turned into a walking, talking work bore and if I don't take my foot off the pedal, I'm going to crash and burn. I already blew up my marriage.

Leon lays his hand on my shoulder. "I hate to break it to you, buddy, but maybe Lily leaving is the wake-up call you needed."

Losing my wife to teach me a lesson? It's a bit brutal, but could he be right?

"I can't lose her." I won't. I refuse to stand back and let that happen. Maybe I have already and I'm too late.

"I'll drink to that." Leon refills my glass. "So, what are

we going to do?" Leon's dark eyes dance with challenge and mischief.

I can see what he's getting at.

"Are you a champion, Ash *The Bear* Johansson?" he asks with fire and determination in his tone.

"Fuck, yeah I am." I slam my hand down on the bar.

Troy asks next, "Did you or did you not woo the pants off that girl from the minute you met her?"

"Fuck, yeah I did."

Buster takes his turn, getting into the spirit of our game. "Did you turn into a fucking soppy bastard when you asked her to marry you in front of thousands of fans?"

"Yes, and I'm not ashamed of that." I hold my hands in the air, cheering for myself. "Just call me Valen-*fucking*-tino." I already feel better.

The energy between us buzzes like electricity through a circuit.

Getting worked up, Brayden raises his voice. "Have you ever failed at anything, Ash Johansson?"

"Never." Suddenly feeling sober, my voice is full of confidence.

He asks another. "So why the fuck are you sitting in a bar on a Thursday, crying like a baby into your whiskey glass, when you should be—"

I cut him off. "I'm going to win her back," I say with newfound determination coursing through my veins, my heart pumping fast.

"Fuck yeah."

"Yeah, you are."

"Yes!"

"Here we go," they all say in unison.

"And we're going to help you." Troy raises his glass in the air.

We all pick up our glasses and I make a toast. "To winning Lily back."

"And never losing her again," Leon interjects. We all move our glasses in the air to chink them together in agreement.

"Wait." Buster holds his hand up, stopping us. "Here's to Ash winning Lily back, to never losing her again, and if he does, his friends get to chop off his dick and feed it to the bears in Jasper National Park."

"I'll fucking cheers to that," Troy chuckles.

Leon joins in. "A bear for a bear."

"Shut up." I hold my glass and lift my chin, telling them to seal the deal, and we all down them, coughing uncontrollably with the fumes.

"Fuck that's awful." I screw my face up and wipe my lips in disgust.

"I'd rather have lemonade." Troy vocalizes what we're all thinking because we've never been the type of guys to drink until we can't remember, which is ironic, given Buster and Leon now own a bar.

Brayden agrees, "So would I."

"We're a bunch of pussies." Like a naughty schoolboy, Leon giggles. "Taxi for five." He raises his hand in the air as if hailing a cab.

"So, what now?" I look around at my boys for help.

"We make a plan." Buster pulls out his phone.

Now the game really is on.

Come hell or high water, I'm getting my wife back.

CHAPTER TWENTY-FIVE

Lily

"Oh, Lily, darling." A feminine voice breaks through my daydream, or nightmare more like, and I know it's Candy. She could be one of those girls you phone for a sex chat. She has one of the sexiest voices I know.

Bree's sultry tone breaks through the silence. "We let ourselves in with Troy's key Ash gave him in case of emergencies. We heard what happened."

I'm glad they're here. This is an emergency.

The bed dips on either side of me as I count the sparkling crystals dangling from the chandelier above the bed.

"I miss my mom," I admit. It's been sixteen years since she passed away and the pain of her death has never disappeared. "And my sister." Gemma never replied to my text. She's too busy finding herself. Like *Elizabeth Gilbert*, she's probably meditating, eating nothing but cabbage soup, and having sex with monks or something equally life altering. Discovering herself. It's what I call running away. Gemma married Chris, who she thought was her soul mate, around five years ago.

She's never had much luck with men though, and yet again her husband broke her heart and had an affair with their next-door neighbor, Jack. None of us saw that coming. So, she packed up her stuff and left Canada six months ago. Utterly heartbroken and too ashamed to stay and face her ex-husband's deceit, she ran to Peru, of all places. Although it would be hard to stay around and avoid him, considering he moved in with Jack next door. But hey, life seems to be throwing shitstorms at the Murphy girls this year. Although I'm a Johansson now.

I do love being Lily Johansson. I always have.

"She'll be home in a couple of months," Candy says, lying down next to me on one side while Bree makes herself comfortable on the other.

"That's too long." I sigh, feeling hopeless.

Bree pats my hand. "You have me."

Candy takes my other hand in hers and turns onto her side. "And me."

And yet, sometimes I don't feel like I have them at all.

"I'm sorry I didn't tell you about the baby," Candy whispers, staring at the side of my face.

I roll my head to look at her and smile in the low light. "I'm really happy for you." I am. "I know you think your news would hurt me." Sometimes it does when I hear of yet another friend expecting another baby when I can't even have one. However, I'm honest when I say, "It doesn't hurt, but it makes me jealous." Envy is a terrible thing and a trait I never possessed before we started trying for a baby with no success. Although, I still can't accept what isn't possible, and it messes with my inner peace. I was advised to attend therapy sessions after our last cycle of failed IVF. I'm now wishing I had gone. "Congratulations, Candy. I bet Milly and Flynn are excited." Brayden and Candy made two very cute kids already. I'm positive this one will be just as adorable.

"They wanted a puppy," she explains, and I don't know where I find the energy to laugh, but I do.

"Let's hope the new baby is hairy then," Bree drawls, setting us all off.

I let out a huge breath and stare at the ceiling again. "I don't know what I'm doing."

"You're telling him you've had enough. That's what you are doing," Candy says, understanding the long hours our husbands work. "It's hard, I know. But at least I have the kids to keep me company when Brayden's away."

"Me too," Bree pipes up. "That doesn't mean to say that you're not welcome to come over. You should know that. You've stayed away from us for way too long."

I confess my thoughts. Might as well get it all out in one night. "I hate the fact that you girls don't talk about your kids around me. When, in fact, I love hearing when they move to the next level in dance class or when they have their violin recitals. I don't have the plague. I just can't have a baby. And that doesn't mean I'm not interested in what your kids have been up to." I pause. "It makes me feel closer to you guys."

Candy and Bree squeeze my hands.

"And Bree, I really liked it when I overheard you telling Candy your birthing story. It sounded amazing." Something I could only ever dream of, but a water birth sounded so much nicer than Candy's epidural labor, she told Bree about in return. "I overheard you both talking in the kitchen not long after you had Katie," I confess. "I wasn't eavesdropping." But I know they didn't have the conversation in front of me for fear of hurting my feelings.

"We're sorry." Bree sits up and looks down at me. "We never meant to make you feel like the odd one out."

"I know." Recently we've grown apart. Like me and Ash.

I feel like I'm being left out at sea to float all by myself with no paddle. Everyone around me is close, yet so far away.

Candy leans up on her elbow. "We thought we were doing the right thing."

"It's fine," I reply. It is. I understand their reasoning.

Struggling to pull my body up as it feels heavier than a lead balloon, I move myself up to the top of the bed and rest my back against the cream velvet headboard; the girls sit up on the mattress and cross their legs yoga style.

"I think I messed up." I fiddle with my fingers.

"We think you're fed up." Candy tries to make me feel better.

"I hurt him." And hurt me in the process. "I didn't mean to." Didn't want to. "I packed my bags."

"We know."

I look up at them. Knowing how private Ash is, he wouldn't have called his friends.

Bree kills my curiosity. "He was drinking in Home & Away."

Drinking?

Ash rarely drinks.

"Ricky called Brayden. Dustin called too. He was hopping mad." Candy cringes. "Ash quit his job via text message. Which Dustin didn't accept."

I can't believe he texted the Eagles' general manager. I thought he was kidding when he did that. Ash is the paramount of professionalism, that's so unlike him.

He was trying to do the right thing by me, but that's not what I wanted either.

Why is this so confusing?

I cover my face with my hands. "I feel terrible. I'm so confused." I space my fingers to peek through them. "I need to speak to him. Is he okay?" I tried calling him, but his phone went straight to voicemail. I've cried a river already. I feel like crying again, although I don't know if I have any more tears left inside of me and my eyes feel like they've been stung by a thousand cacti.

"You're both hurting." Comforting me, Bree rubs my knee.

Still covering my face, I hang my head in shame. "We were always so close and now we barely see each other. I don't know what happened to us."

I can see why Candy sold her shares in the clubs she was an owner of before she got married. They are now the largest chain of exclusive clubs, not just in the city but throughout Canada. There is no way she would have time in her schedule for that now.

She did what I didn't do; she prioritized her family over business.

I love my business, but it's taking over my life, just like Ash's job. That's what they have become, jobs, not careers.

Candy says, "Life happened to you. You're a successful businesswoman. You have one of the top businesses in the city. You're the best wedding planner in the country." Candy emphasizes her last three words. "You've remodeled this house while building your empire. You have multiple properties you rent out and manage yourself." Oh, yeah, I forgot about that. "And your husband is the head coach for one of the top performing teams in the NHL. He's not home very often. He has a demanding job. The press is never off his back and he is forever on call to those unruly players."

Ash always says his job is worse than herding a gaggle of geese. He's not wrong.

Bree adds, "I think you've done a great job holding everything together. You're a great wife."

"And friend," Candy says. "Oh." She wiggles about, then holds her swollen stomach. She was definitely hiding that bump at the dinner party eight weeks ago. She's much further along than I thought she was.

I lean forward and worriedly ask, "Are you okay?"

She rubs her tummy. "We have a wriggler, maybe a football player." Looking at me, she bites her lip, then tentatively asks, "Do you want to have a feel?"

My eyebrows shoot up in surprise. "Can I?"

She nods her head excitedly and I move onto my knees.

"Just there." Candy takes my hand and lays the palm flat against her bump. "Wait."

I look down at where I'm touching her stomach and can't imagine what that must feel like to grow a life inside of you. It's magic.

I jump when the baby kicks. "Oh, wow," I cry in surprise, and then another little kick makes me laugh. "Strong," I say in awe.

"Tell me about it." Candy rolls her eyes. "This one is trying to burst my kidneys."

I pull my hand away slowly. "Thank you." My voice breaks with emotion. "That's beautiful."

She cups my face affectionately while Bree's hand finds mine. "Have you ever considered fostering, adoption, or surrogacy?" Bree asks.

"I always wanted one of my own. Half Ash, half me." I'm honest with them. Adoption and fostering are more intensive and complicated than people think. And surrogacy is not an avenue I wanted to explore or even physically and emotionally put a surrogate through.

None of the options were what we wanted.

We sit in silence for a few minutes before Bree asks, "So, where were you going to go?"

"Ash's old apartment in the city." We made so many memories in that place. It's where we lived when we first got married. I still love it. "It's sitting empty." It's fully furnished and only rented out to hockey players we know from time to time. Mainly when they are transferring to the team and need somewhere to live until they find their own place. It still has some of Ash's old arcade games and the pool table in it, something we never got around to moving to the new house.

"Well then, let me drive you there. You aren't staying here tonight in this big old lonely house by yourself." Bree looks around. "It's beautiful, but what the hell made you move all this way outside of the city? It's so dark outside." She looks out the bedroom window, overlooking the yard, the bright moon shining off the pond.

"We liked the house and the yard." Now I'm not so sure if I still do. It *is* too far out of town. It's no wonder I am lonely. It sits by itself like a widowed giant, up the long drive with no other houses around it for miles.

Bree bounces off the bed. "Well, Mrs. Johansson. We will get you settled into your old apartment. You need a good night's sleep. And I think you just need some space to figure out what you want. This is just a blip."

"A glitch." Candy walks across to the door. "Wow, your carpet feels incredible." She wiggles her bare toes, pushing the wool between them, and Bree does the same. "Oh, wow," she moans. "Orgasmic carpet."

I laugh again, which I didn't think was possible. I have missed these girls.

Bree high fives Candy. "We made her laugh, kudos to us."

"I might cry again." There is a high chance of that happening when I close the door on this house tonight.

Candy loops her arm around my shoulder. "Grab your phone and keys and anything else. Bree will drive your car and you can come with me."

"Thank you." I look between the two of them.

"We've got you." Bree moves in for a three-way hug.

And right on cue, I start crying. "I'm sorry. I feel so sad. And lost. I broke his heart," I sob.

They hold me until I stop, reassuring me that everything will be alright, not once saying mean things about Ash or man hating on him. Because they know he's a great guy.

"Are you sure I'm doing the right thing?" I ask them both.

"Only you can answer that," Bree answers.

"I don't want to stay in the house." I look around my bedroom. And that, I suppose, answers my question.

Maybe they are right. Maybe this is just a glitch.

But how can we ever come back from this?

I can't figure it out.

Maybe we never will.

Because *I broke his heart.*

He'll hate me forever.

And I will hate myself for longer.

CHAPTER TWENTY-SIX

Lily

Waiting to greet me in the underground parking lot are my dad and his lovely new wife, Diana. Just as Candy parks up, Kourtney jumps out of her car to wait for me with them.

Candy lays her hand on my knee and gives it a squeeze. "You need people."

"I didn't want anyone to know." However, I feel relieved they are here. I need them more than I thought I did.

"Stop pushing people away, Lily. You can't do this on your own."

Candy opens her driver's door and wiggles herself and her cute baby bump out of her high jeep.

My dad is already by my door, opening it and helping me out. No words needed, he wraps me up in his love with one of his comforting hugs, making me cry again.

"I'm sorry," I weep.

"You don't need to be sorry for anything, Lils. I'm here now. Let it all go, sweetheart." He pats my back. "C'mon, let's get you inside."

Keeping his arm wrapped around my shoulder, he tucks me into his side as he walks us in the direction of the elevator to take us up to our old apartment.

Bree rolls my suitcases inside behind us, kisses me on the cheek, then exits the elevator.

"Are you not joining us?" Sniffing, I wipe my cheeks with the palm of my hand.

Candy waves at me affectionately. "Your dad, Diana, and Kourtney will look after you. We'll catch up tomorrow, yeah?"

"Okay." I'm too tired to argue with them.

"Thanks, Candy. Bree." My father gives them a curt nod as they wave goodbye and the doors close.

I'm settled into the apartment, a cup of chamomile tea in hand, which I think Diana must have brought with her because there is not a scrap of food in this place. Diana is such a caring and kind woman and perfect for my dad in every way. She filled an empty space that was missing from his heart and his life. I couldn't be happier for him. With no children of her own, she spoils both Gemma and me at Christmas and birthdays, and she ensures Dad keeps in touch with us regularly, even when they are away on yet another cruise. He'll be upset with me for not telling him I've been struggling.

Kourtney rests her head on my shoulder. "Why didn't you tell me how you were feeling, Lily? I feel bad for how much I talked your ear off last week when we were out for dinner and did nothing but moan about the problems I have with the new coffeehouse opening. I feel like a terrible friend. How did I not see this?"

Kourtney and I still meet every week for dinner, or lunch, whenever we can squeeze each other in with our busy work schedules. However, my marital issues are not something I like to talk about. With anyone. Especially while out in public.

"It's fine. I'm fine."

"You are not fine. This..." She motions to the apartment. "Is not fine. You and Ash are couple goals. What the hell happened?"

Diana and my dad sit down on the two armchairs on either side of us just as my phone rings loudly, cutting through the melancholy atmosphere around me.

I almost leap on top of it, hoping that it's Ash returning my calls, but it's not; it's Gemma.

Picking up her video call, her sympathetic sun-kissed face fills my screen, and my eyes instantly fill again with emotion. I can't stop crying.

Her mouth downturned, she leans in as if trying to hug me through the camera. "Hey Lils, I'm just off the phone with Candy and Bree."

Which means she knows I moved out.

Her voice soft and gentle, she asks, "How are you?"

I shake my head. "Not great." I suck my lips into my mouth. "I miss you."

"I miss you too, Lils. I'm thinking of coming home sooner than planned."

My heart fills with hope. "I would love that."

"You know we love you, right? And Ash."

"I know." The distress I feel tightens my throat.

"Do you want to tell us what happened?"

My dad and Diana join Kourtney and I on the long sofa, and surrounded by my good friend and loving family, I tell them how lonely I've been and how I've been feeling for the last year.

They let me talk as I get everything out in the open, assuring me they will support me no matter what.

And I know I'll be okay.

I always am.

But it doesn't feel like that right now.

CHAPTER TWENTY-SEVEN

Lily

I didn't want to come into work today.

Since the day I opened my business over fifteen years ago, there hasn't been a day I have not wanted to create a mood board for an upcoming wedding or reply to client emails.

I feel so uninspired.

How can I organize a wedding when my own marriage has fallen apart?

I'm a fraud.

I should go home.

But if I do, my team will definitely know something is wrong and I don't want to draw attention to myself.

If the press catches wind of our separation, all hell will break loose and the last thing Ash needs is more stress in his life. I'm hoping we can keep our marital status to ourselves until we sort *us* out. Honestly, I'm not even sure if there is anything left of *us* to fix.

The tabloids were extremely unkind to Buster when his fiancée called their wedding off three days before, blaming it all on him. The truth was, Claire, his future wife, was cheating on him with his brother, but tabloids don't care about the truth.

Brutal.

It was heartbreaking to watch that unfold.

While Buster carried on like a true champion, I don't know if I could personally deal with that level of judgment. On the surface, it looked like Buster took it all in his stride, but I know, after spending a couple of nights with Ash and him, he was hurting. Staying with us for a week while he looked for a new apartment and to keep him company, he let us see a different side of him. He's a great guy and someone I always thought would be perfect for Gemma. I'm positive something happened between them back when Ash and I first started dating, but neither of them ever mentioned it, so maybe I imagined it.

I fill my cheeks with air and blow out a long sigh, admiring the scripted gold lettered logo I designed that's debossed on the wall on the far side of the office, Tiger Lily Events.

Ironic, given the fact I organize events for everyone else while my own life is uneventful.

Reading the pet name, Ash gave me tugs at my heartstrings and I can't bring myself to look at it for any longer than a few seconds.

I rest my neck on the back of my office chair, then spin it around to look out of the window overlooking the park opposite my office.

It's a glorious day. The winter sun beaming through the trees, casting shadows over the fresh snow that fell overnight. I take a moment to gaze down at the people in the park, using it as a shortcut, trying to get out of the biting cold to get to their destination quicker.

In the summer, the park is usually filled with moms out running with their strollers, which I know for a fact I would never do, but I admire their enthusiasm.

It's also the place Ash would turn up unannounced and call me down to spend my lunchtime. When we first got married, it was where we spent hours enjoying the picnics he'd prepared for us on the grass. We'd laugh, talk about everything and nothing, and kiss each other without a care in the world. Young love. There is no better feeling. Everything was new, exciting, and felt like an adventure.

Now everything feels lackluster. We lost our shine, getting lost in the humdrum of life.

It's been four days since I left Ash.

I've tried calling him, but he refuses to pick up. Although he texts me every day with three words.

I love you.

Simple but significant.

And yet he still won't speak to me.

He's angry with me. He has to be. I moved out of our marital home.

Maybe he needs time before he speaks to me again.

I suppose it's what we both need. It's what I wanted.

Although he's most likely prepared a voodoo doll of me and is currently sticking needles into my eyes. I swear that's why they are painful. Of course, it has nothing to do with the amount of crying I have done over the last four days.

Not wanting to face the world, I stayed in bed all day yesterday. Something I have only ever done with Ash in that apartment.

It feels weird without him there.

Everything feels weird without him.

The divide between us is wider than an ocean.

And if he isn't picking up my calls anymore, how will we ever fix us?

It might be too late for that.

I pulled the pin and blew our world apart.

I doubt he will ever forgive me.

But I still love him. He's the love of my life.

So, what the hell was I thinking, leaving him?

I hope I did the right thing, *regrouping*, as Candy and Bree called it. I needed space and being in that huge house, I was drowning. Weirdly, I feel better not being there. I love our old apartment. It feels like home.

And while leaving him was a difficult decision to make, we had tried to reconnect, but it didn't work and life, yet again, got in the way. It was time to break the cycle we created ourselves.

We need this.

I know we do.

We need change, and while I hate to be the catalyst to make that happen, I hope Ash understands my reasons.

From behind me, the elevator pings, the doors sliding open as someone returns from their break. It's lunchtime, and, like every day, my staff went out to eat. They all love the little deli below the office block. They serve the most mouthwatering delicious rolls and soups. Oh, and their buttery pastries are to die for. If I ate there every day I would have to start going to the gym. And that sounds like hell.

While my staff are encouraged to leave their desks, I, on the other hand, chose, yet again, to stay in my office. Eating and talking to people seemed like a huge chore I couldn't handle. And I have no appetite for food. I've felt sick to my stomach since Thursday.

With today being Monday, I realize I've barely eaten anything in days.

Giggling from behind me alerts me to Janice's return, along with a deeper masculine voice that sets her off again.

A deep voice that has been seared into my soul.

Oh, my God.

I spin my chair around to see where it's coming from, unsure if I am hearing things.

But sure enough. He's here. Ash. And he's laughing and joking with my receptionist.

I hold on to the edge of my desk, close my eyes, and open them again.

Nope, I am not hallucinating.

He's here.

And he looks completely fine.

Happy even.

Not the wreck I imagined him to be or the same guy who left the house distraught the other evening.

There is no denying it, he's utterly drop dead freaking gorgeous.

If sex was a physical being, Ash Johansson would be it.

Glued to my seat, I can't move as my heart beats like a set of bongo drums against my rib cage, following his every move in my direction. Eyes glued to his black puffer jacket, with a simple white tee shirt underneath and black jeans that fit him in all the right places, I can't stop staring; he's only gotten sexier and more handsome with age, and holy shit, what was I thinking when I left him?

I'm the world's biggest fool.

A lonely fool, but nevertheless, a fool.

"Hey, beautiful." He confidently steps through my office doorway, flashing a perfect row of white teeth, filling my space with his own brand of testosterone that makes me want to rip off my clothes and jump his bones. "How's your day been?" He pulls off his black baseball cap and places it on the table, his eyes sparkling as the low winter sun shines through the window, making him look like he's glowing. The sunrays highlight the tiny silver hairs that have appeared in his beard over the last year. His scruff is more like salt and pepper now. I like older Ash. Like a fine wine, age suits him well. Very well. It's as if I'm seeing him through fresh eyes.

Why is he here?

Why is he not heartbroken and looking like a complete wreck like me? My hair is up in a slick bun because I haven't washed it today, and I have on whatever makeup was hiding in my desk; lip balm, red lipstick I used as blush, and mascara I'm certain has been in my office drawer long enough for it to give me an eye infection.

I'm speechless as he places a wicker picnic basket on top of my desk and begins moving my pens, notebooks, and files out of the way to make space for the dozens of food items I can see in the basket.

"Have you been busy?" he asks nonchalantly, as if we didn't experience the most traumatic event of our marriage last Thursday.

"What are you doing?" It's a question I should be asking myself. At this point, I don't know. I'm questioning all the decisions I made last week. My gaze follows his ink covered hands as he places the delicious looking food on my desk. Croissants filled with salmon and cream cheese, sushi, raspberry chocolates, freshly squeezed lemonade; all my favorite things.

"I'm having lunch with you," he replies matter-of-factly as if everything is completely normal between us. "Have you eaten lunch yet?"

"No." I look up at him and he's smiling down at me.

"You look beautiful today. Did I tell you that already?"

"No." I say that word again because, clearly, it's the only word I can say.

He winks. "Well, you do." He rubs his lily tattooed hands together and looks down at the exquisite buffet of food. "So, what would you like?" He slips off his jacket and throws it on the sofa behind him, then sits on the chair at the opposite side of my desk, placing the empty picnic basket on the floor. "I didn't know what you would prefer for lunch, so I just made everything." He waves his hand over the top of the food as if he's a magician while I stare at him.

His muscular, tattooed covered arms have always done something to me. They are such a turn on. I look from them, down at the delicious food, then back at his arms, then the food, and up at his amused face.

I want to ask him what he's doing here, but instead, I say, "Ash, I'm so sorry about last—"

He cuts me off. "Let's not talk about that now. Do you remember our first date?" he asks, face serious, focusing on the sandwiches in front of him, deciding which to have. He makes his selection, lifts it to his mouth, and takes a bite.

"Do you?" he asks again, mumbling around his food.

Looking more relaxed and carefree than I have seen him in years, he lifts his leg, rests his ankle on top of his other knee, and my eyes automatically land on his crotch. The fabric of his jeans tight around that area. Which is only natural; he's a big man after all.

When I look up, he's grinning at me. Cream cheese wedged between his teeth, he knows I was looking, and I blush when he arches an eyebrow and takes another bite of his sandwich.

He's more youthful today, and playful. Much like the Ash I fell in love with.

"I remember everything," I answer.

"What was the best part of that date?" Having poured two glasses of fresh lemonade, he slides one in my direction and takes a sip of his.

This feels surreal.

"The skating," I finally answer.

"Really? That's surprising. It took you a while to learn."

But I did it.

"You're a great skater now." He pauses. "I think I preferred my ransom note," he counters.

"Clever," I admit. It was such a unique idea.

"It got your attention." He demolishes the last of his sandwich. "Eat." He points at the croissant he's placed in front of me. "You haven't eaten for days, by the looks of it."

He tears open the packet of luxury hand cooked chips I love, spreading them out for us to share. "These potato chips are great. Have some."

"Ash?" I ask curiously, elongating the *A* in his name as I pick up my sandwich, instantly starving and feeling like I could eat a bear.

I'd quite happily eat Ash *The Bear* Johansson any day of the week.

Not now, Lily.

"Yeah?" He draws out the short word, mimicking me.

"What are you doing here?" I take a bite and almost moan at how delicious and buttery my croissant is. *God, that's good.* Groaning with welcomed pleasure, my stomach rumbles in response.

"We are having lunch together, Tiger. Just go with it." He pushes a chip into his mouth and crunches down on it loudly. "Want to know what I remember?"

Mouth full, I nod for him to tell me as I chew my flavorsome food.

Drumming his fingers against his thigh, he thinks for a minute before he says, "I remember that baby pink dress you wore and the cream wool coat you used to wear all the time with the buttons on it that made you look like a cute snowman."

I cover my mouth, fearful of sending flakes of pastry everywhere, and giggle.

"I remember you head butting my dick when you fell over," he adds.

I almost snort pastry out of my nose.

"First time you touched it," he whispers jokingly. "Branded in my memory forever." He grins, tapping his temple.

Then he drops his voice. "I remember thinking you were the prettiest girl I had ever seen. I still think that." Much softer, he continues, "And I remember thinking how I knew you were the one. My everything."

"Your Tiger Lily." It's what he called me on our first date and he's never stopped calling me by that nickname. I've always loved it.

He tilts his head to the side and smiles. "The perfect combo. The tiger and the bear."

We've always been great together.

"We still are," he says as if reading my mind.

Sitting, not saying anything, but just enjoying this precious time, we eat while staring at each other.

It feels nice.

Normal.

I pop a chocolate into my mouth and check the clock. "Shouldn't you be at work?" It's way past his lunch break.

Ash doesn't take time off, choosing to do what I do; eat on the run or at our desks.

"I took today off. This is just the beginning." Pushing himself to his feet, he tidies up the empty packets and leftovers, putting everything back inside the picnic basket.

Mid chew, I stop eating the raspberry chocolate in my mouth and blink up at him. "What?" I almost choke on my sweet treat. The last time he had a day off was Christmas Day last year, and that was almost a year ago.

"My priorities have changed," he adds.

"What about your training schedule, your job, your career?" I ask, aghast.

"Do you want one of these for later?" He holds out a homemade Nanaimo bar, knowing I could never say no to the chocolate, coconut, and custard dessert bar. They are my favorite. "My job will be there when I go back." He doesn't wait for me to reply and places the layered dessert bar on my desk.

"But—" I jump in to protest, but he doesn't let me.

"Lily. I was drafted to the NHL when I was eighteen. I went straight from being a player to an assistant coach to head coach. What you said the other night, about the NHL being who I am." He shakes his head. "I disagree. You are what makes me, me." He pauses for a beat before clearing his throat. "I haven't had a break in years, and I need one." He points at me. "So do you. But we'll talk about that another day."

Oh-kay.

He checks his watch. "I've taken up way too much of your time. Now, back to work." The opportunity for me to ask any questions slips away when he pushes his arms into his winter jacket, picks up the basket, and makes for the door. Nimble footed, he spins around before he leaves.

"Walk me to the elevator." He holds his hand out for me to take and it's only when I look up through the glass partition walls of my office, I notice all my staff are back from lunch.

On autopilot, I roll my chair out from under my desk and get up to walk to him.

He instantly takes my hand and kisses the back of it.

Too shocked to protest, holding hands, our fingers laced together, we walk through the office toward the elevator. All attention on us, the staff can't quite believe the infamous Ash Johansson is here. Of course, they all know I'm married to him. But he's a sporting legend, an enigma, and he never comes here, unless it's to pick me up, and on those instances, he sits outside to wait for me.

Janice, who has worked for me from the beginning, waves him off as we stand waiting for the elevator.

"Make sure she has a break this afternoon, Janice." He points at me. "And no working late either," he shouts over to her, causing everyone to look our way.

He releases my hand, cups my face, then kisses my lips. It's the softest, most gentle kiss that I feel all the way down to my toes.

"Are you okay at our old apartment? Do you need anything?" he murmurs, his face full of genuine concern.

I know he would have found out that I was staying there from Brayden and Troy, specifically Candy and Bree.

He has no right to be so kind to me. Not after what I did last week. "I need to get groceries." I suddenly appear to have my appetite back and there is zero food in the apartment.

"Is everything okay between you and Candy?" His hand is still cradling my face. He's being so attentive, more like the man I met all those years ago.

"She let me feel the baby kicking," I tell him, not

meaning to. Sadness sweeps across his face momentarily, but in a flash, it's gone again. "We're fine." Back to the way things always were between Bree, Candy, and me. They've kept in touch every day, calling and texting, making sure I am taking care of myself. They even dropped in on Saturday for lunch, although I didn't eat what they brought for me.

Then, of course, Dad appeared with Diana on Sunday morning on their way to church to drop off flowers to *cheer me up and brighten up the place.*

And between Gemma, the girls, Kourtney, then Diana, and Dad texting and calling every other hour, I'm not sure I would have had the time to eat even if I had been hungry.

"You're the strongest woman I know," he says seriously.

Some days I don't feel very strong, more like a boat made from blotting paper; floundering and sinking fast.

He kisses my lips again. In a daze, I kiss him back.

"I worry about you, Lily."

"I worry about you." I gaze into his eyes.

"I worry about us." His forehead lines with concern.

"Ash—"

"Not now." He presses his lips to my forehead.

He surprised me today; everything was unexpected and welcomed. I've loved spending time with him.

Only it wasn't enough.

I want more.

"Same time tomorrow, Tiger," he whispers, making my heart flutter like a dragonfly. Then he's inside the elevator, waving farewell and smiling at me as the doors slide shut.

What the hell just happened?

"Wow." Janice wolf whistles, making everyone laugh.

"We can see why you keep him hidden away," one of

the guys shouts and I know instantly it's Elliott. "I need a cold shower."

My heart a mix of confusion and flapping faster than a dragonfly, I turn around to find Elliot pretending to fan himself with his hand. "I'm not sure your boyfriend would like to know you've been drooling over my husband," I joke with him.

I beam. I must be glowing. I feel like I am.

He brought a picnic to my work.

I play it cool, feeling like I'm on cloud nine as I walk to my office. I then run the last few steps to my desk and lift my phone from my desk to text him.

ME:

Thank you for lunch.

He replies immediately.

ASH:

You are welcome, Tiger. See you tomorrow.

ME:

Were you being serious about that?

I thought he was joking.

ASH:

Deadly serious. As serious as I am about us.

ME:

We need to talk.

ASH:

We will. For now… just enjoy. But know this. I'm not letting you go and I'm not giving up on us. I made that mistake last week when I told you to go. That will never happen again.

My stomach does a weird flip that feels like a gymnast somersaulting inside of it.

ME:

Okay.

ASH:

Have a great day, Tiger. xo

Noticing he left his baseball cap behind, I pick it up and lift it to my nose, inhaling his scent.

I find the group chat I'm in with Candy and Bree and hit the video icon on the screen.

Candy picks up first, then Bree. Their gorgeous faces fill the screen of my phone.

"Why are you calling at this time of the day? Is everything okay?" Candy frowns, looking at me down the camera, obviously worried because I never call during work hours. Running across my office, I close my door and take a seat on the cream leather sofa.

"Ash came to the office today." I wait for their response.

"And?"

"Did you talk?"

They both ask at the same time.

"No," I answer.

"No?" Candy asks.

"He brought a picnic and then sat and had lunch with me."

Bree's mouth drops open while Candy says, "Holy swoon."

"It's like he was trying to recreate our first date or something." It dawns on me that it was exactly what he was trying to do.

"He says he's coming back tomorrow." I feel excited about seeing him again.

Today was amazing. I feel better than I have in days. Months even.

Bree leans into the camera, her eyes dancing with expectation and impatience. "Tell us everything."

Never being one to overshare, as soon as I'm done, I can't hold in how excited I am, and I call Gemma and Kourtney to tell them too.

CHAPTER TWENTY-EIGHT

Lily

I need a hot shower, a good meal, and several hours of uninterrupted sleep. This afternoon I made up for the lost time I spent staring at my computer all morning.

Ash's surprise appearance gave me the zest I needed to get through the rest of the day, which was much needed as I had a to do list as big as the Eiffel Tower to work through.

I finalized the décor lists for two upcoming weddings as well as several large-scale events coming up. One event being the Christmas party for Candy and Brayden, something they host every year for the entire Eagles team. This year they've requested all guests wear a Christmas themed costume, which reminds me, I need to go back to the house to pick up mine.

I have sore eyes, not only from crying for most of the weekend but from staring at my computer screen all afternoon. Ordering ten-foot-high garden baubles, Christmas trees made entirely of fake candy, and thousands upon thousands of fairy lights is enough to give anyone a headache, but it's all organized now.

Candy and Brayden's eyes lit up like a neon sign when I suggested erecting a giant gingerbread house in the garden for the kids. They loved the idea of popcorn machines, chocolate fountains, a cotton candy maker, and a mocktail bar to keep the children entertained as well.

They can even enter the enchanted garden full of treats and festive goodies including a find the Santa maze, where they will win a prize if they find him. Candy and Brayden's enormous backyard lends itself well to the plans I have, which is convenient as we are also erecting a party tent big enough to accommodate over two hundred guests. It's going to be huge, and I'm beside myself with excitement to start setting it up next week.

Smiling, I push my key in the door of our city apartment, immediately stopping in my tracks, confusion getting the better of me. The strong smell of rich food being cooked invades my nostrils, making my stomach rumble again. Something I have been ignoring all afternoon; the food at lunch wasn't enough to fill me up. It's groaning at me for more.

Through the gap in the door, three things hit me at once.

The side lights. Which are switched on, making the apartment look cozy and welcoming.

The music. Which sounds like my old *Dirty Dancing* record playing, the crackles from the needle giving the vinyl its unique richness.

And humming. From what sounds like a man, singing along to it.

Then something else hits me. Doubt.

In myself.

"Oh, shoot," I panic under my breath, pulling out my phone from my purse, quickly tapping open my calendar.

Swiping left and right, I click on today's date to check if I rented out the apartment and forgot to block it off.

Something I have never done before.

"Evening, Tiger." Ash's voice cuts through my moment of crisis.

Snapping my head up, he greets me with a huge smile. "Here, I'll take that." Lifting my purse off my bent forearm, he leans in, kisses me on the cheek, then slides the handle down and off my arm.

Dumbfounded as to what he's doing in the apartment, I watch him walk back into the open kitchen area, still wearing what he had on earlier, although he's now barefoot, and I know he's doing that on purpose because I have a thing for him walking around barefoot and in jeans. I don't know why it's so sexy, but it is.

Shirtless is also a bonus.

I'm still standing in the open doorway holding my phone and staring at him when he calls over his shoulder, "Dinner will be ready in an hour. I ran you a bath." He casually places my purse on the countertop as he passes, then turns his attention to the steamy hot pot on top of the stove to stir the food he's cooking. "I hope you're hungry. I made enough to feed the hockey team." He chuckles at his own joke, maneuvering around the kitchen smoothly from cabinet to drawer.

"Are you coming in?" he asks, uncorking the bottle of red wine resting on the counter that was not there this morning, then fills two glasses.

In a daze like dream, I walk over to the kitchen island and stand opposite him. Laying my hands flat on top of the white quartz marble, I ask, "What are you doing?"

"Making dinner." He lifts a glass full of deep red wine and passes it to me.

I push my phone into the pocket of my taupe-colored overcoat, then take a sip. The sweet black cherry and marzipan spiced alcohol makes me pucker my lips.

"45 Cellars?" I ask, already knowing the answer.

"Your favorite wine from your favorite local vineyard."

I swirl the red-black liquid around the glass. "Did you drive over an hour and back again to get this for me today?"

He nods. Taking a sip of his own, he looks blissfully happy as he surveys me over the lip of his glass. Blue eyes gleaming, I know that look. He's up to something.

"Okay." I look around at the apartment scattered with lit fragranced candles, which were clearly purchased by him. As well as the food.

"I let myself in with the spare key."

My eyes land back on him. "Right." I can't figure out what to say.

He points at the refrigerator. "I stocked up and bought groceries."

"Ash, we need to—" He doesn't let me finish.

"Your bath is getting cold." I look at the warm yellow lighting peeking through the bathroom doorway. "Take your wine with you." He picks up the sharp paring knife and slices the vegetables on top of the wooden butcher's block.

"Are you having dinner with me?" I ask hopefully.

He stops mid chop and looks up. "Only if you want me to."

"I do." I'd love that.

The knife cuts through the rest of the carrot, making a *whick* sound, a sexy lazy smile shaping his lips into an upward curve.

I've always loved his mouth. Truthfully, I've always loved every part of his body.

Running my finger over my bottom lip, I check I'm not drooling. My attraction to him has never died.

I motion my thumb in the direction of the bathroom and walk away quickly before I do or say something I might regret. My heels loudly *clack* against the hard-tiled flooring,

Feeling the heat of his gaze warming my back, I push the door open and gasp in shock, momentarily taken aback at the luxury I am about to dip into. Overflowing with bubbles, the bathroom is filled with dozens of tiny lit candles in glass jars, casting dancing shadows over the tiled walls. The smell of essential oils from them fills the air with a sweet, fresh scent, making me feel like I'm in a spa.

I lay my wineglass on the bath caddy tray that has a built-in space to hold it. Picking up one of the many lily flowers from the lip of the bath, I pull it to my nose. It's not real, but smells like lavender.

"It's soap." Ash appears in the doorway and leans against it. "The lilies. They are soap flowers."

"I've never seen anything like these before." I rub the soft, realistic petals infused with soap between my fingers. "They feel real."

"Enjoy. Dinner will be ready in an hour." Ash pulls the door toward him, sealing me inside my mini retreat.

This is wild and wonderful, but why is he here?

I scratch my head. The tight bun I've had all day has given me a tension headache and my scalp is screaming at me to unravel it. I pull out the elastic band and bobby pins before I fluff out my hair. I can almost hear my hair follicles singing with relief as I give them a rub.

Stripping out of my clothes, I fold everything neatly, place them on top of the laundry basket, and step into the bubble bath, letting the hot water relax my bones, my muscles unwinding as my body basks in this indulgent, calming soak in the tub.

I pull a petal off one of the lilies and submerge it in the water to activate the soap, coating my arms in the lavender perfume, and then I take a huge mouthful of wine. The alcohol provides a gentle buzz, relaxing me more and sending me into a state of bliss.

I hold up another of the petals. "Where did he get these from?" I ask myself. A shock of joy has my heart swooning.

Why is he being so nice to me? There is no revenge or hate toward me. He should be angry, cutting up my clothes and stuffing them into garbage bags, shouldn't he? Although that's not who Ash is. He's always been kind-hearted and caring, but I assumed we would have at least one shouting match after I left. It's what they do in the movies.

But it's been radio silence from him until today.

Ash is not one for rocking the boat. We have very rarely ever argued. We squabble from time to time but are talking to one another again within minutes. On those occasions, I think that's down to me being unaccustomed to him living in the house and disrupting my routine. And while Ash is tidy, my one big pet peeve is leaving wet towels on the bed and wearing boxers with holes in them. *Throw them out, Ash.* Oh, that's two, although I do have a third. Not washing the blender after he makes a protein shake in the morning when he's around. And why does he feel the need to swear excessively when he comes home from work? Being around a group of testosterone-filled men who throw *F*-bombs blindly all day limits Ash's vocabulary considerably. *Fuck* appeared to be the only word he knew when he stubbed his toe on the end of the bed several weeks ago. I found it hilarious when he fell onto the bed in pain, but using the F-word a dozen times was an overreaction, in my opinion.

And oops, that's four pet peeves. What can I say, I've gotten very used to living alone a lot of the time.

Because of Ash's good nature, we've never had a full-blown fight. And I'm discounting the time I completely lost my cool when he bought a Mario Kart twin driving arcade machine which cost him, sorry *us*, fifty thousand dollars. My flip out was totally justified; it was a ridiculous amount of money to spend on a game. Although Buster and Leon disagreed and bought one for the bar. I'm surrounded by grown, athletic men who act like children, find fun and laughter in everything, and have no intention of growing up.

I smile at that. Ash and I have a wonderful friendship circle.

It's such a shame we don't see them more often.

Which reminds me… I lean over to grab my phone out of the pocket of my coat, splashing water and bubbles all over the cream tiled floor and leaving dark watermarks on the fabric of my overcoat.

I snap a photo of my luxurious tub time, wiggling my toes to break through the bubbles, and set up a new group chat, adding Gemma who couldn't change her plane ticket to come home, Kourtney, Candy, and Bree, and send the photo.

CANDY:

Looks lush.

BREE:

Oh, I am having one of those later. That looks incredible.

ME:

Ash is here in the apartment. He ran me a bath and is cooking dinner.

KOURTNEY:

He's there now?

ME:

Yeah. He was here when I got home from work.

GEMMA:

He's up to something.

I'm pleasantly surprised when Gemma answers straightaway, as her phone reception is always terrible.

CANDY:

I'm interrogating Brayden when he gets home later.

BREE:

I'll ask Troy, too.

ME:

Is it not weird that he doesn't hate me? He hasn't said a nasty word or questioned what happened last week.

BREE:

Maybe a little.

KOURTNEY:

I agree, but I think it's lovely he's trying.

GEMMA:

And so romantic.

Which he was in the beginning. He's always been attentive and given me everything I wanted, as well as things I never dreamed of having. Only, I always craved time with him more than any amount of material things.

I take another sip of wine.

ME:

Can you ask Brayden and Troy about his job? He said he had taken time off, but I don't believe him. Can you find out what happened with management?

BREE:

Of course, I want to find out too.

Bree does love good gossip. She knows everything about everyone on the hockey team. Mainly to keep an eye on Britney, the old puck bunny who hung around the team when Ash and I were dating, because she doesn't trust her around any of the guys.

Her fascination with the team is borderline obsessive. She spends an unhealthy amount of time on social media talking about them. I understand social media is part of her position, however, she's already been given two warnings by personnel for releasing a press release earlier than planned, and for taking a candid photo of one of the players getting changed in the lockers, then posting it, asking fans if they should do a Christmas calendar. All without consent from the player or approval of the head of marketing. One more mistake and Ash thinks she's at risk of losing her position with the team.

I don't dislike many people, but that girl gives me bad vibes. I don't trust her.

KOURTNEY:

Enjoy your evening and let us know what happens.

BREE:

I want all the details.

I laugh to myself.

ME:

Thanks, girls xoxo

I finish my wine, then place my phone on the caddy tray, sliding it carefully down the lip of the tub then submerge myself into the water up to my chin. Tilting my head back to wet my hair, the muffled sound of the bathroom door handle clicks open, and Ash sticks his head through. "Do you need anything? More wine?" He points to my empty glass as I push my wet hair back off my forehead.

"I'm fine, thank you." I look up at him, moving into the room and resting his back against the wall. "How was work today?" he asks, as if everything is normal between us, which feels oddly comforting and nice.

"Candy and Brayden's Christmas party is going to be spectacular."

He nods in agreement. "They always are. It's you who plans them, after all. I wouldn't expect anything less."

"Thank you." Although he's seen me naked thousands of times, I suddenly feel self-conscious, realizing I'm completely nude beneath the water, the surface bubbles barely hiding my body.

"Is the water nice?"

"Amazing." I lift my hands and play with the bubbles between my fingers.

He drops to his knees at the side of the tub and lays his arms along the edge.

Eye level with me, he rests his chin in the crook of his folded arms. "Does it need topping off with hot water?"

"You tell me." My voice is breathy.

Eyes locked on one another; he dips his fingers below the surface to test it. "It's still warm." His tone is low and husky.

Feels hotter now that he's here.

His fingers move, making the water ripple around me.

His hand disappears, his fingertips finding my stomach. Drawing tiny circles across my body, he tickles me with his touch.

Skimming my inner thigh, passing the place I want him to touch, he traces over my hips and up my waist. I inhale sharply when he cups my breast, then pinches a nipple, rolling it between his finger and thumb.

Moving north, he continues, drawing his finger between my cleavage and up the side of my throat, leaving goosebumps in his wake, despite the warmth of the water.

Even submerged, I'm wet for him, the deep throb in my pelvis pulsing with a desperate ache.

His hand appears out of the water and scoops some of the bubbles from his fingertip onto my nose, making us both smile.

"Did I lose you, Lily?" His question is fragile and shaky.

I shake my head left to right slowly, answering no. Because he's not lost me. Not completely.

My heart aches for my beautiful man. At how confident he appears on the outside to everyone else, and yet when he's with me, he allows his barriers to come down, showing me his vulnerability.

"Are you still mine?" he asks doubtfully.

I tilt my head up in a nod of reply.

Sliding his arm around the rim of the bathtub, he moves toward me, cupping his hand around the back of my neck. Lips almost touching, he stares at me as he places his wet hand back under the water, tickling my skin again with his fingers as he moves south, down over my stomach, and between my thighs.

Eager for him to touch me, because it's been weeks

since we've been intimate, I tilt my hips, his fingers slipping between my pussy lips as he slides a finger inside of me.

I moan in need as the heel of his hand edges my clit and he applies more pressure as he works his finger in and out.

Breath for breath, blink for blink, we move simultaneously as my hips rock back and forth beneath the water.

Desperate for him to kiss me, I lift my hand and grab the back of his head, smooshing our faces together. I can't wait another second. He pushes his tongue into my mouth, and I lick it, enjoying his familiar taste and touch.

My skin, no longer accustomed to him, will get a beard rash from the prickly scruff. It's been weeks since we last kissed passionately.

But his touch eases all the hurt I have been feeling as he pushes another finger inside of me, his curved digits stroking me deep and slow while his thumb now rubs my clit in dizzying circles. The water softly splashes against the sides of the bath as I chase my release.

"Who do you belong to, Lily?"

"You," I moan, deepening our kiss, the fire between us no longer dying and cooling down. It's burning brighter and hotter than ever.

"Show me then." His mouth finds my ear. "Show me I'm the only man who knows your beautiful body."

I grab his hand between my legs, sandwiching it between my pussy and my tight grip, fucking it as my orgasm builds fast.

His hot and heavy breaths against my neck send shivers across my skin, my body humming with happiness as he licks, then bites the skin of my throat.

My head flung back, I cry out as my orgasm weaves a

path of intense release through my core, my inner walls clenching around his fingers as he holds them deep.

My body burning for him, I come.

In a moment of total surrender, the tension I've been feeling between us explodes into earth shattering pleasure. My climax rips through me, and a sound I don't recognize escapes from my throat as I find the release I need.

Ash frantically kisses me, swallowing my moans of joy. "You're beautiful when you come," he says between kisses.

Like a rag doll, my body feels jelly-like as my particles of pleasure float off, evaporating into the air.

I grab the neck of his tee shirt, scrunching it into a ball, soaking it through, devouring his mouth.

The sex we have has always been incredible. I want to feel him again. I want all of him. I want us to go back to the way things were.

The passion, the heat, the fire, it's been burning slowly away in the background. All that's left is dying embers, but tonight he took the lighter, sparked the fire, reigniting what's always been there.

Ding.

The timer from the oven goes off.

"Dinner's ready." He smiles against my lips.

My stomach rumbles at that exact moment.

"I think someone's hungry," he chuckles.

I release the fabric of his tee from my clenched fist. "I'm starving." For more than just food, but it's too soon. I lick my lips and stare at his. I know what he can do with that mouth, and I've missed our closeness and intimacy.

The rapport and kinship between us are what made us unique.

Us.

"I've been a fool, Lily. What was I doing, letting you slip through my fingers?"

Unsure if I should answer, I keep my mouth shut. We need to talk things through, although he's told me *not yet. Three times.* I guess I need to be patient. Something I've become good at. But we can't fix what's broken if he doesn't talk to me about how he is feeling and figure out how we move forward.

He rests his forehead against mine. "I'll serve dinner," he whispers, his voice heavy with regret, then he presses his lips to the tip of my nose. "I'll see you at the table, Mrs. Johansson. Dry preferably, you're soaking."

"Doesn't matter if I dry my body with a towel. I'm always wet for you in other places, Mr. Johansson," I lower my voice and say, against the shell of his ear.

He groans and drops his head on my shoulder. "Fuck, you make me so hard."

"Time for dinner," I sing sweetly, stand up, and step out of the bathtub, being careful not to slip.

Grabbing the towel, I look back at him over my shoulder as I leave him there, noticing how he's rearranging himself, adjusting his cock inside his jeans. I chuckle to myself at the pained expression clear on his face.

Feeling happier than I have in a long time, I skip to the bedroom. This is the most time we've spent together in months. And one thing is very clear.

I still love him.

CHAPTER TWENTY-NINE

Ash

I've been walking around with my head up my ass.

And it took her to leave me for me to finally pull it out and realize what I've been ignoring. What's been in front of me all along.

Too focused on my career, I lost sight of my priorities.

And while I am married to my job, Lily is my number one priority.

The only one I should have been concentrating on.

Becoming head coach has taken over my life, more so than when I was a player or an assistant coach. The long, untraditional hours, time away from home, working late; she had enough, and I don't blame her. I can't deny that so have I.

She woke me from my stupor. I just hope we still have time to save us because while she says she's still mine, it kills me to see the doubt flickering in her eyes.

Clearing everything away from our meal together, I stack the dishes into the dishwasher and wipe down the last of the kitchen surfaces. Lily chats mindlessly away as she scrolls through the television menu, trying to decide what to watch. It gives me hope; she seems quite relaxed around me, open to me planting myself unexpectedly into her day.

It's been years since we sat and watched a movie together, something we used to do regularly.

While my job is demanding, my life outside of work seems to consume me too. My friends were right, I am never off the clock. Between wrangling the team, ensuring they stay out of trouble, answering their endless emails, calls, and pulling Wade Collins out of police custody on the regular, as well as the constant stream of media interviews I seem to do now, it's had a detrimental effect on my marriage.

As heartbreaking as it was, she was right to pack her bags.

But this isn't the end of us.

It can't be. I refuse to let her walk out of my life again.

Operation Get Lily Back is underway. I just hope I can execute it in the way it played out in my head and I talked it through with my buddies.

My plan has to work.

After tomorrow's meeting with management to iron out a few gray areas, where I'm hoping they'll meet me at least halfway, then and only then can I move the plan forward.

If I go too fast or too slow, I could fuck it up with her.

And if I fuck this up, I will have lost her forever.

I'm nothing without Lily. She's my purpose. That's why there is no other option but to fight and save us.

"I don't know what to watch," Lily sighs, endlessly scrolling the menu.

"Why don't we start a series?" I suggest.

Turning around in her seat, she rests her arm on the back of the sofa. "That's a serious commitment," she replies, looking at me knowingly.

And what she really means, but doesn't say out loud is, can I commit to it? And do I have the time and will we still be together to finish it?

"Select one that has at least five seasons," I tell her. That should show her how dedicated I am.

Worry lines wrinkle her forehead before she says, "I left you last week, threatening to end our marriage forever. We shouted, but you didn't go crazy, smash my car up, or call me names, although you may have drawn devil horns on my head on our wedding photos for all I know."

"Yeah, I might have done that."

"You didn't?" She gasps.

I chuckle and shake my head while walking over to sit down beside her. "I didn't. That's not who I am, Lily."

"Who are you then? Because while I have loved spending time with you, and adored the bath and the picnic you prepared today, I'm not entirely sure what we're doing here. You're not mad. You're being too nice to me and it's kind of screwing with my head. I can't have you playing Casanova and then everything goes back to the way it was, Ash. I need more. We need to talk."

It's what she's been asking for, and I can't keep putting this off forever.

Tucking my leg underneath me, I turn to face her on the sofa. Her natural beauty, even after all these years, steals my breath. "I have a couple of things I need to sort out first. I promise you, I want to work everything out between us, but I need some time to do that."

"Like what? What do you have to sort?" She shoots questions at me, ones I can't answer truthfully. "You can't quit your job. I would feel responsible, and you are too talented to throw it all away. I won't allow you to do that.

We need to navigate ourselves first and sort the bigger things later."

It's the bigger stuff that's the problem. "Do you trust me?"

"I do." She rests her hand on my bent knee.

"Then trust me to do what I need to. Also, I can't tell you what I don't know myself yet. Just know that I'm trying." So fucking hard. "I'm trying to fix what I broke." I lay my hand on top of hers. "Please know I'm not mad at you. I'm mad at myself. You were right to leave. I think you needed to get out of the house to have space to think. Time to consider what you want. Because you may decide that I'm not the one for you anymore."

Tilting her head to the side, face crestfallen, her eyes well with tears. "Ash."

"It's okay," I realized last week she may decide to call time on us, ending our marriage completely. If I can't get my shit together, that might still be a possibility. I rub my thumb over her wedding ring. "I'm sorry. All I do is work, and sleep, well sometimes, I don't sleep at all some nights. And I've been having these chest pains," I admit. Something I have been hiding from her, and everyone. It feels like a relief to share how I have been feeling.

Obviously worried, she instantly jumps in. "Have you been to the doctors?"

"I'm okay. The doctor thinks it's being caused by the huge amount of pressure I'm under at work." The need to win is making me sick. "I'm stressed."

"Like me," she says, adding, "My blood tests came back normal. I don't have anything wrong with my thyroid and I'm not going through early menopause either, like she suspected."

"That's great news." It's the little slither of hope we needed. She's okay. Thank Christ for that.

Stress is such a strange thing. After reading the leaflet the doctor gave me, my heart palpitations, my irritability at work, my anger with the team, which can be triggered by the smallest of things, and my impatience all point to stress. And all I do is worry about the outcome of the season. There is no fun or enjoyment in my job anymore, nor is there any in my personal life. The only thing that keeps me anchored is Lily. If I lose her, my stress levels will hit an all-time high. I can't let that happen.

But even now, I don't have her; she's moved into our old apartment.

"We've separately been running ourselves into the ground." I did it because I loved my job and also because it's expected of me, now I'm questioning if this is what I want. And Lily throws herself into work because I'm not around.

It's unhealthy.

"If you are making changes, Ash, I need to make some, too. This isn't only your fault like you said last week. If I ever made you feel like that, I am sorry. But it's not."

"It's time for both of us to make changes." Or we will kill ourselves working. For what?

She looks down at my fingers that are fiddling with her wedding band. "We need to find us again. How do we do that?"

"Baby steps."

"Baby steps," she repeats.

"First, we are going to sit here. With my arm wrapped around your shoulder, and pretend we are on a first date at the movies." Satisfaction and joy flood her face when I say that. "And we are going to enjoy whatever we decide to watch and just *be*. Downtime, relax, and stuff our faces with the truck full of snacks I bought this afternoon."

"I still can't believe you went shopping for groceries." She sounds shocked as she laughs at how undomesticated I've become. It's been years since I did that. Paying people to prepare meals for us and have them delivered to the door, I've turned into an entitled, almost forty-year-old workaholic.

I find her amusement enchanting. "I did," I answer.

"I need proof. Did they have security cameras?"

"If they do, you'll see me dropping a large carton of milk, then helping the staff to clean it up." Lily covers her mouth to hide her laughter. I continue, "You'll also see me signing over thirty autographs and taking selfies with Eagles' fans in the parking lot." I froze my nuts off in the process.

"Oh, no." Lily covers her mouth, trying desperately to hide her amusement.

"It took me over an hour to get just a few things." I knew there was a reason we had them delivered.

Resting her head on my arm along the back of the chair, she smiles. "Thank you for doing that. I'm very grateful. Although, I've been unable to eat much until today."

We're lovesick. "Same."

I'd forgotten how much I loved sitting down, having a home cooked meal with Lily, and chatting about our day. Our routines have been shot to smithereens, choosing to stay at work and skip meals.

Unable to detach myself from my job, I've become addicted to it.

I blurred the lines, taking work home with me and letting it take over my life; I don't like who I have become.

All that is about to change.

It has to.

"So, what are we watching?" I ask.

"*Game of Thrones*," she replies, with a glint of humor in her eyes. "Eight seasons."

"Wow." I feign annoyance when secretly, I'm buzzing happily inside that I get to spend all that time with my beautiful wife.

"Seventy-three episodes. Do you have the stamina for that?"

"Oh, you know I have stamina. I think I proved that last time I kept you up all night." I'm ashamed of myself, knowing that was the last time we had sex, and it was weeks ago.

She examines her nails and screws her face up. "Meh, that was ages ago. You've aged since then."

Enjoying our verbal gymnastics, I downturn my mouth. "Ouch. Harsh." But it's true.

I pick the television remote off the sofa cushion. "Well then, we had better get started. Does she have sex with the dragons?"

"Oh my God, Ash." She throws her hands in the air and we both burst out laughing.

Yeah, this feels nice.

Everything's going to be okay.

Right?

CHAPTER THIRTY

Ash

"So, what happened next?" Brayden asks as we skate onto the ice to start today's practice and make our way to the middle of the rink.

"We fell asleep on the sofa watching *Game of Thrones* and woke up this morning wrapped up together." Best morning ever. "She got ready for work and I drove her to the office. Then I came straight here to grab a shower." I didn't rush here today like I usually do. I refuse to do that again. I've become the rabbit from *Alice in Wonderland;* anxious, letting the pressure from management dictate my life.

"And she was cool about you coming for lunch again today?" he asks enthusiastically.

Slowly skating, I check the whiteboard I'm holding and skim the training notes I've written on there. "Yeah." The deli below Lily's office is preparing lunch for me today, which I will grab on the way.

"Great, but remember, you can't force yourself on her; she needs to want this too."

"I think she does." She told me she was excited about having lunch with me, which I'm taking as a positive sign.

"What time is your meeting with management?" Brayden cuts in front of me, skating backward.

"Eleven."

"Have you memorized what you need to say?"

"Yes." I'm praying they agree to my proposal.

Although I have a better idea about what I want to do with my future and have a meeting with someone located in New Jersey. He might be the key to helping me have a more sustainable and healthier career in hockey.

"Whatever you decide, we'll support you." He punches my shoulder and then looks over it. "Does Jordan look like he's limping?" Brayden mutters under his breath, skating to my side again.

I stop in the middle of the ice, waiting for the team to join us and sure enough Jordan Miller, wingman, all-round top guy who never complains, looks like he is struggling with his right leg.

Observing his movement and facial expressions, I suspect he has a knee injury and is trying to mask it. "Jordy." I skate over to him and wrap my arm around his neck, ushering him away from his teammates.

Some of the guys don't mind it if you know they have an injury, while others, like Jordy, will do everything in their power to hide one for fear of making them look weak, even to their own teammates.

"You good?" I ask, pulling him in closer to my side, my ear in line with his.

"Top notch, Coach. Ready to go," he says confidently when I know he's struggling.

"Good to hear." I drop my voice. "Then why are you limping?"

He looks off to the right, as if embarrassed I caught him lying.

"If you train today, you could cause more damage. Or worse, something irreparable. Is it your knee?" The way he isn't putting pressure down on his foot tells me he can't fully extend his leg.

"Fuck." He pulls off his helmet, knowing I won't allow him to train today.

We move over to the boards and stand against them. Still facing away from everyone, I give him a minute to let the reality set in; he's not just missing training today, but possibly another two weeks of it, if not more.

The guys love me because I'm a great coach. Firm but fair. A player, first and foremost, I know the physical pressures these guys put their bodies through. It's grueling and hard hitting to the point of insanity, and not everybody can handle the intense training and game schedule.

It's left a lasting impact on my body and I groan like an eighty-year-old man getting out of bed most mornings. My hips and knees are shot to pieces.

"I turned to the side too quickly in training and twisted my knee yesterday," he confesses, without me having to push him.

I pat him on the back. "Which means you either have a ligament or cartilage issue." Both common injuries for hockey players. "I want you to change out of your gear and then go see the training team. We need scans of your knee today. I'll call ahead to let Tim know you're on your way up." Tim is the head physical therapist. One of the best in the country, and I know he'll have scans and a full email report to me by the end of today. Although I won't be there when that lands, I plan to leave early and spend more time with Lily tonight.

"If I catch you lying again, though, Jordan, you'll be missing more than just a handful of games. You're no good to us injured. Got it?"

"Coach." He acknowledges the meaning behind my words. I don't have to tell him that he's easily replaceable.

The world of hockey is savage.

"From the look of you, I think you'll need therapy, physical treatment, and a session with the counselor is available if needed. When you get back on the ice, I want one hundred percent of you on it. But if we see your mental health start to decline or a slip in confidence, and you haven't taken me up on the offer, then there'll be hell to pay. Understood?"

I care about my players both physically and mentally. Hitting the ice at the speed they do can be difficult if they don't do the mental work to build their self-confidence. When their minds are strong, it makes their physical bodies even stronger.

"Understood. Thank you, Coach."

"We'll talk tomorrow after we get your scan back." Dismissing him, he nods, skating away from me and I glide across the ice toward my next challenge of the day; drills.

And as soon as this is over, it's a meeting with management. My thoughts drift to what I'm going to say when raised voices steal my attention.

"What the fuck did you just say about my mom?" Wade smashes his helmet down on the ice and launches himself at Zane Edwards, our goalie, and I'm skating at full speed toward them breaking them up in a flash, my hip screaming at me to stop.

Fuck my life.

I'm too old for this shit.

CHAPTER THIRTY-ONE

Ash

"You want the next three months off and on your return, you want to either scale down your hours or become the youth hockey development officer for the Eagles?" Dustin MacKinnon, the general manager, tries to remain calm, but I can see the pulse beating fast in his neck, his fingers drumming against the top of his desk, giving his thin patience with me away.

"That's correct." I hold firm.

"Why?"

"I have heart palpitations. I can't sleep. The pressure of the job is too much for me this year." I'm not ashamed to admit that now. If I lose my job, I'm certain I will find another one because I get offers constantly, but if I lose Lily, well, that's a different story altogether. There is only one of her. "And, as you'll see in my doctor's report, he diagnosed me with stress disorder. If I'm not careful, I'm at risk of complete burnout." The doctor even mentioned the risk of a stroke or heart attack. Yeah, that's not happening.

"We've never had a request like this before."

"Your last three head coaches moved on after only a season in the role because it was too much for them." They all coach minor divisions and college hockey now. "And one of them had a heart attack. I'm thirty-eight, Dustin. I never take a day off." My life is passing me by.

"You did yesterday," he cuts in, sounding bitter about allowing me one day off.

"The first in years, and I haven't had a vacation in years either." He knows how hard I work.

"You all get allocated the same amount of vacation time," he reminds me as if I didn't know that.

"And on those days, Dustin, I still do interviews on the radio or fly to television appearances. Do you know how many calls I answer a day from the players? And emails I reply to? The texts? It's like babysitting a bunch of frat boys." The players are unpredictable and think with their dicks. The number of times I've had a panicked call about yet another girl, one of them has gotten pregnant. I swear to fuck none of them got sex education in school. Except maybe Jordan. He's quiet and reminds me of myself at that age.

I continue, "You demand more from me than most. I spend hours watching playbacks." More than all three assistant coaches combined, which I have only just discovered. "I don't sleep, can't sleep. My mind and body are never off the job. I've been down to the police department five times in three months to talk them out of charging Wade Collins for assault. I've become the advice columnist for the team. And the real reason for me asking to change my role or scale down my hours is because Lily left me." I'm out of breath as I get out everything I wanted to say, and maybe some information I didn't. I swore I would protect Wade from management. If I'm not here, I won't be around to do that, and ultimately, they'll discover what's been happening with him, so I may as well tell the truth.

Leaning forward, he brackets his fingers and rests them against his mouth. He remains quiet for much longer than I'm comfortable with. "Lily left you?" He cuts through the silence.

"I haven't told anyone." It's too embarrassing. "She moved into our old apartment."

"Are you still living at the house?"

"No." I couldn't handle staying there without her. "I'm living in the apartment above Home & Away." It was sitting empty and made sense. I asked Leon and Buster to keep my whereabouts under wraps for now, but I am seriously thinking about selling the house. Lily is right. It's too big. Empty. It's another thing we need to talk about.

"Did you text me about quitting the night she left?"

I nod.

He sits back in his chair and lets out a long sigh. "Ash, you think I didn't know something was wrong? Nobody quits their job via text, especially not you. Did you think I believed you when you sat here the following day and told me everything was fine, and you sent it by mistake?" The concern in his voice for my well-being makes me feel guilty for not telling him the truth sooner. "I knew something was wrong, but it's not my place to pry. I know how private you are, Ash, but as your boss, you should have been honest with me. You can trust me."

"I can, it's just—"

"Difficult."

"Very." I take a moment before I say, "I want to save my marriage. I need time off to do that."

"So you want to do a less demanding role?"

"And to do less hours."

"As you know, you're under contract, which is up for renegotiation at the end of this season. But how will continuing to be head coach work? You only attend home games? What about the pressure that will put the other coaches under? That's not an option, Ash and the youth hockey development officer's position has already been filled."

Any hope of me staying with the Eagles in the capacity I want dwindles.

Then he adds, "But I'm willing to grant you a career break."

The tension across my shoulders releases at the unexpectedness of his response.

"However, there will be conditions."

"Okay." I thought he might have some.

"Two months off. No pay."

Money isn't an issue. We have millions in the bank. Lily and I have always been sensible with our investments and savings. "Okay."

"I want you to use this break to decide whether you want to carry on your career with the Eagles."

"Oh."

"It's all or nothing, Ash. No in-between. You're a dynamic head coach, the best in the NHL, in my opinion. You're young, relatable, the guys love you, and you've won us the Stanley Cup three years in a row." It's unheard of in the modern era and hasn't happened in decades.

"I didn't win the Cup; the team won." It's the truth.

He wags his finger at me. "Yeah, but without you..." Shaking his head, he adds, "You're special, Ash. The best."

Hell, now I feel guilty about making my demands.

He lets his offer settle, then he makes sure I understand. "Work out the rest of this week. Give the guys a few days to get used to the idea of you being off. We don't need to give them a reason why. We'll tell them it's personal, which we will do in a press release as well. The deal is, two months off, no pay, and if you do come back, you will resume your full-time position as head coach. And if you decide it isn't for you anymore, then we go our separate ways." Dustin rubs his chin.

He's right, I'm an all or nothing guy.

Shit. This seems final. "I've been part of the team since I was eighteen."

"I know."

"This is my family." I'm almost too scared to agree.

"Ash, your wife is your family."

"She's my everything."

"Then take the deal. Sort your marriage out and don't be an old fool like me with an ex-wife who hates me for choosing hockey over birthday parties, and a daughter I barely know. Trust me, dating at my age is complete shit. Online dating sucks balls." He makes me chuckle. Dustin is at least fifteen years older than me, and I have no plans on being single ever again.

"I never knew you were married or had a daughter."

"Because I never saw them and vice versa, Ash. This place rules my life and has become my life. I have nothing to go home to."

Yeah, that has made my decision easy. I don't want that. "I'll take the deal." It's time for a change.

"Great. Well, not great, but I think you made the right decision."

"Do you have someone in mind to replace me?" Don't say Brayden, I inwardly pray or Candy will kill me.

He replies quickly. "Not Brayden or Candy will serve us your nuts on a silver platter at her Christmas party." He knew that wasn't an option. "I need to make a few calls and have a meeting with the scouting team tomorrow. We'll do the paperwork and press release sign off at lunchtime today for release on Sunday afternoon."

Sunday morning for release sounds perfect. The focus won't be on me on Saturday night's game. Although I hope they keep Britney away from it, even at the age of thirty-four, she's incredibly immature and I don't trust her not to leak anything to the press.

The constant crazed look in her eyes makes me feel uneasy.

"Sounds like you have everything under control." I feel like I just made the biggest mistake and yet the best one of my life all at the same time. It's a mix of emotions I'm not sure how to react to.

"Can you come back at lunch and we'll both sign off on the press release together?" Dustin asks.

Shit, I had plans with Lily for lunch today, which I will have to cancel.

I need to speak to her. Or maybe I should wait and tell her my news on Saturday night?

Rising to my full height, Dustin stands on the other side of his desk. I reach over to shake his hand. "Thank you, Dustin. I appreciate this."

"Do great things, Ash." He winks. I think he already knows I won't be coming back. Sandwiching my hand between both of his, he adds, "And win that game on Saturday night. Go out with a bang, ma boy."

Emotion the size of a bowling ball gets stuck in my throat. "Thanks." My short word cracks.

"And don't lose her."

"I don't plan on it."

"Your father would be immensely proud of you, Ash. You're a credit to him."

It's been eighteen years since he passed away and I still miss him. I hope he'd understand why I am taking a career break and be proud of me for putting my family first.

"I appreciate that, Dustin. Thank you."

Turning to leave, I gather myself to tell Brayden my news. It's what I wanted, no, needed, and yet I feel like I just severed a part of me that's been with me since I was four years old. I feel slightly untethered and need Lily to ground me.

Stepping out of Dustin's office, I know deep down in my heart I'm making the right decision.

Although it could be the beginning of the end.

Or the beginning of something better.

I quickly text Lily.

ME:

Sorry, baby, I have to take a rain check on today's lunch date.

She responds immediately.

LILY:

You can't even commit to me for two days in a row, Ash.

Fuck, she's right.

ME:

I'm sorry, I promise I will make it up to you. I had something important come up.

LILY:

More important than our marriage?

If only she knew I'm doing this to try to save our marriage. I hit her name and call her.

"Pick up, pick up, pick up. C'mon, Lily." But she doesn't and goes to her voicemail.

"Fuck." My voice echoes through the long empty office corridors of the Eagles training facility.

I push my hand to my heart as stress pains shoot through my chest again. They come and go like the shifting tides of the ocean.

Or it could be from the pain of it being broken last week.

Either way.

It hurts.

What if I do all this and lose her anyway?

That thought is the most terrifying of all.

CHAPTER THIRTY-TWO

Lily

Following lunch at my desk, alone, yet again, I've been stuck in meetings all afternoon. While it was considerate of Ash to have the lunch he missed delivered to my office, it would have been better if he had been the side order that came with it instead of a salad.

Last night was wonderful. We spent all evening on the sofa bingeing *Game of Thrones,* while eating most of the snacks Ash bought. Waking up in each other's arms was a complete surprise this morning. I enjoyed his warmth, our familiarity, the closeness of us. It felt like before.

He either has the resistance of one of those unbreakable rubber exercise bands I've seen Gemma use when she's *strengthening her thigh muscles*, or he's taking things slow. Mending us mentally and emotionally before bringing us together intimately.

A lazy and yet heavy make out session was more than enough to put a spring back in my step this morning. We kissed each other breathless, which was such a huge turn on. No words needed, a mutual understanding between us that comes from so many years together. When he didn't take anything further, and neither did I, it confirmed we still have so much love and respect for one another.

I know he cherishes me, making sure I ate before work this morning, dropping me off at the main entrance of the office, and seeing me out of his truck. He carefully held onto me, ensuring I didn't fall in the slippery snow. He's invested in us, and I know he wants to make it work.

But that goddamn coaching job gets in the way of everything.

While the hockey team may consider themselves to be like one big happy family, that hockey family comes before everything. Even your marriage, apparently.

I breathe out my disappointment, wishing he could have been here for lunch, as I stomp out of the conference room and through the office.

Head down, staring at my phone, I check to see if I have any messages from Ash.

Nothing.

Lifting my head, I slow my pace and gasp in shock at what I can see through the glass walls of my office.

It's filled with dozens and dozens of orange tiger lilies, making it look as if the space is on fire.

I spin around and look at Janice from across the open plan space, then point back to my office. "Are those?"

"From Ash." She smiles, looking starry eyed.

I snap my head back to look at the flame-colored flowers and slowly step through the threshold. An earthy, sweet, and spicy fragrance overwhelms my nostrils.

"Wow." I gaze around the room.

"There are fifteen bouquets. A dozen in each." Janice says through the doorway.

"Fifteen?" Astonished, my voice cracks.

She nods her head.

"Tiger lilies aren't even in season. He must have had these flown in for you or he knows some important people to find them."

I gasp, rubbing the bright orange petals dotted in crimson spots between my fingers. "No way."

"There's a card." Janice points to the bouquet sitting on my desk. "You are one lucky lady." She closes the door with a huge smile shaping her lips.

I feel giddy as I lift the card out from between the trumpet shaped flowers.

Emotion bubbles in my throat when I read the words he's penned.

Fifteen years of marriage = fifteen years of loving you.
Although I have loved you for much longer.
And I will love you for a lifetime.
Don't give up on us, Tiger.
Forever yours, Ash xoxo

My phone is by my ear in an instant.

"Hey, Tiger." Ash picks up on the first ring.

"Hi." I clear my throat, taken aback at his sentimental gesture. "Thank you for my flowers. I love them."

"Yeah?" His question is cheerful and I can almost hear him smiling down the phone.

"They are beautiful." Sitting behind my desk, I can't stop admiring them.

"Just like you," he says without hesitation.

He's told me I am beautiful hundreds, if not thousands,

of times before, but today I feel his words. Today I am feeling everything.

"I love you, Ash. I have never stopped and *will* never stop loving you." I pause for a beat. "I want us to work."

He lets out a long breath as if he's relieved. "You have no idea how good it is to hear you say that. It's the only thing I want and I'm sorry about lunch. I promise I am trying to fix my insane work schedule, or I wouldn't have canceled otherwise."

"Okay." I believe him.

"I've taken the next two months off work with no pay."

I rise to my feet at the speed of a shooting star. "You did what?" I shout a little too loud at the unexpectedness of his news, and like a mob of meerkats on high alert, every one of my employees looks my way as if a predator entered the room.

I give my forehead a rub to ease the tension. He can't leave his job.

"It's what needs to happen," he says, firmly.

"We should have discussed this together first," I shrill, feeling panicked.

Blooming with confidence, he says, "It's done. I've already decided."

"Without me?"

"It's because *of* you."

I take a moment to gather my thoughts. "Ash," I say eventually. "I can't let you quit because of me."

"I don't see it that way. I'm not quitting hockey. I'm saving our marriage."

Well, when he puts it like that.

I place my hand on my hip and look out over the snow-covered park. "Is that what you want to do? Are you sure?"

"Yes." His answer is simple and to the point.

Then I make my own confession, which I wasn't going to tell him about until the deal was signed. "I also have plans to reduce my workload."

"You do?" he asks hopefully.

"I want to save us, Ash. More than anything."

"So, we're doing this?" he asks, sounding excited.

"Yeah." My phone pressed to my ear, I lean against the floor to ceiling window.

"I love you, Lily Johansson. I will love you until my last breath."

As if hearing it for the first time, I giggle at how romantic that sounds. He's making this grown woman feel young at heart again.

"I can't believe you bought me all of these flowers." I look around my office. "How will I get them back to the apartment?" I'm not ready to move back to our house.

"I'll have someone pick them up to take you and them home." Interesting that both of us have always thought of the apartment as home. It is much cozier and homelier than the big house ever felt. He adds, "I would come and do that myself, but I have the press release to sign off by the end of the day about my leave of absence. That's why I couldn't make lunch, Lily. They wanted me to meet the marketing team to discuss it over lunch. I asked for some revisions. It'll be done by six o'clock."

I can imagine what the fallout will be from the fans. They won't like it because they adore Ash. "When will it be published?" I ask, feeling concerned for him and his team.

"Sunday. We have a game on Saturday, and I don't want my announcement to cast a shadow or be the focus of it."

"The fans will want answers." Knowing Ash, his statement will be brief and to the point.

"They aren't getting any. It's vague, stating that I am taking time off for personal reasons. That's it."

I smile, knowing him so well.

He continues, "My main job, as your husband, is to look after you. And us. I refuse to let this job come between us anymore."

He couldn't be any more delicious if he tried. "You're kinda hot when you're this protective."

"Oh, yeah?"

"Yeah." My reflection in the window captures how wide I am smiling. "I liked this morning. The way you kissed me was so sexy."

"You made me hard."

"I know." I felt it. "You made my stomach flutter."

"Mine too."

"Do men get that?" I ask, genuinely wanting to know.

"No, I just said that to sound super romantic. It was actually my dick tingling."

Pressing a hand to my mouth, I half laugh and snort.

He then redeems himself by saying, "I love the way you taste, the way you smell, the way you feel. I love everything about you, Lily. I always have."

"I may have just let you off the hook for your no-show at lunchtime after saying those lovely things about me."

"How about I make it up to you and I take you out for dinner tonight? Caspers?" He suggests, knowing how much I love that place.

"I have plans for dinner."

"With who?" he asks, sounding sharp.

"Dominic Holmes."

"Dom? What the fuck are you—" he barks.

"Are you jealous?" I consider teasing him a little longer

before setting the record straight, but I struggle to contain my laughter.

"You made that sound like a date. You're screwing with me?"

"I am," I admit. "It's business. Come with me. It would be good for you to hear what he has to say." That man gives me the creeps. "He sent over a proposal to buy shares in Tiger Lily Event that suck, big time, and I asked him to make me a better offer."

I hope he turns up tonight with a more acceptable one and one that works in my favor and not his.

Although if he doesn't, I'm also okay with that. Part of me doesn't want to give it all up. I do love my job. If only there was a better solution, where I can still have my cake and eat it.

"Are you for real? I didn't think you were serious when you said you were thinking of selling the business." Ash sounds shocked at my news. "This is not something I think you should do, Lily. I will be there." I know he will. There is not a chance in hell he will let me go for dinner alone with Dominic. "He might very well be Canada's top entrepreneur, Lily, but that man is Lothario in the flesh."

He is a ruthless businessman and apparently a scoundrel when it comes to dating women, often several at a time. "It's business, Ash. That's all." I try reassuring him, knowing perfectly well that he's not known for being a nice guy in his personal life. He made me a cheeky offer following a brief conversation I had with him about how I wanted to stop working so hard. That was over a month ago at a business owner's lunch and I had forgotten all about it. But he's piqued my curiosity.

I don't know if I believe the rumors about him in his

personal life. My brand name is immaculate and the last thing I would ever want is having his name tied with my business if they are true. I must ask Janice before our dinner tonight, as she seems to know everything about everyone in the city.

"I'll be there. I don't have a suit at the apartment, so I'll have to go to the house first." I take a mental note he didn't call the house home again. Neither do I. "I'll pick you up from the apartment."

"Like a date?"

"With Mr. Seducer as a third wheel, not likely," he mutters dryly.

"Then afterward?"

"Afterward what?"

"Then afterward, we could, maybe, you know? Play?" My voice is breathy and low as I make a brave suggestion.

"As in..." He trails off, but he knows what I mean.

"I'll let you think of something, Ash." I give him control of the reins. We haven't role played for years and if we want to make this work, then it's time to put the heat back into the smoldering embers. We need that flicker of adventure to get that fire burning ferociously between us again.

"It's not too soon?"

"I want you, Ash." I let him know I'm ready. I can't wait another day. I thought it was too early, but it's not. We need this.

"Let me show you how grateful I am tonight. I'm proud of you for making the first big change in our lives." I need to make changes and step up too. "This is a huge move, Ash, but you've shown me how much you want to make us work. I thought we'd lost each other, and I was mad at you for canceling lunch." He had perfectly reasonable reasons.

I should stop jumping to conclusions from now on.

He's trying.

Taking time off from his job is a big deal for Ash, showing me he is going above and beyond for us. He's making sacrifices to prioritize our marriage.

He hasn't suggested we have sex either, proving to me he's genuinely invested in us reconciling; choosing to spend time with me watching television shows over using sex to fix us.

While sex was always incredible, it's not the only thing that's broken. We need to work on everything together; communication, workload, including what we do in the bedroom.

I love how available he made himself this evening, wanting to take me out to dinner. He's invested in us.

"I may have an idea or two," he finally responds to my role play request, the timber in his voice deep and rich.

"Our reservation is at eight."

"For three people?"

"I'll call the restaurant and change the booking."

"I'll see you soon. Be ready, Tiger." He's referring to post dinner activities, not my actual pickup time.

"Can't wait." Nerves swirl low in my belly.

"Love you."

"Love you more."

"That's impossible."

CHAPTER THIRTY-THREE

Ash

Watching Dominic Holmes in action is like watching a sneaky octopus camouflage itself to evade becoming prey.

He's slimy and has no fucking backbone like one too.

In contrast, with all the grace of a swan, I watch my phenomenal wife take it all in her stride.

"So, let me get this straight." She looks at the proposal he brought with him and summarizes what's in it. "You want to buy sixty percent of my business, meaning I will have no influence over the bigger decisions. You want us to merge with an event company I have never heard of, and who you bought last year for a song, because they were struggling, which tells me you want to use Tiger Lily Events to float the business. I would need to do a full reference check on them if that is the case." Tiger Lily Events is a reputable company. I know she won't do that.

Pride grows in my chest as she reels off another three issues she has with the proposal and then she surprises me when she says, "And lastly, you've been rude to my husband not once, not twice, but several times during our meal. The deal is off." She closes the folder and lays it down on the table.

I swear I was about to punch him in the face if he mentioned he was a Lynx fan again. They've won fuck all in ten years.

She stands and I follow. "Now if you will excuse me, my husband and I have plans."

Hell, yeah, we do.

Unable to look Lily in the eye, speechless, Dominic remains seated while running his finger back and forth across his bottom lip.

Lily saw straight through him, and her staff would hate him.

"It's a relief *not* doing business with you, Dominic."

Before we leave, I add, "Since you know so much about the Lynxes, maybe you should have their management call me, Dominic. They need all the help they can get this season."

He looks up at me, then quickly drops his gaze. Nostrils flaring, his jaw clenched so tight it's causing the skin of his neck to turn red. "I'll pay for dinner," I inform him, placing my hand on the small of Lily's back, signaling for us to leave.

"Have a good night." Lily waves goodbye.

I know our night is about to get increasingly better.

"What are we going to do now?" Staring through the windshield of my new Chevrolet Corvette, Lily sounds distressed. I love how she said *we*.

Lily has always included me when it comes to making decisions about her business.

"I don't think you should give up control."

"No?" She snaps her head in my direction as we cruise along the street.

"Do you want to keep it?"

She bites her bottom lip. "I think so, but what can I do to ease my workload?"

I've got a plan for this, too. I've been giving it a lot of thought. "First of all, you can't manage everyone yourself, which you do." I expect her to disagree, but she doesn't. "I suggest you hire four new team leaders and split your staff into teams, making people more balanced and manageable. Hire two managers above the team leaders, buffering them from you. That way, the only people who report to you directly are the managers, not everyone, as it is now." Like me, she's too available. "Same for finance and marketing. You need a manager; they can't all be assistants reporting to you to ask everything."

"Okay, go on."

"I know you love event planning, but I think you need to delegate and oversee the plans rather than design them and then physically turn up at venues and events to implement them. If you took on a more strategic role to focus on finance, growth, and marketing, there would be more time in your schedule for vacations, appointments, spa days, maybe a day off to watch television, read a book, or go hiking."

"I haven't been for a hike in months." She sounds melancholy.

"Self-care isn't just about spa days and having a bath, although that's okay too. But I think if you took on a more executive director role, not an event planner role in the business, you would find the time to do things you want to, and we could spend time together too. Maybe Hawaii?"

"I've always wanted to go to Maui."

When I look over at her, her eyes are lit up like a jukebox. "I know." And yet, I've never taken her. I'm a douche canoe.

"You can hire interns too." I check the rearview mirror, hit my blinker, and turn onto Jasper Avenue.

"That's something we've never done."

"It will increase your workforce but allow your senior employees to delegate administrative tasks so they can focus on the important, bigger ones." I make several more suggestions, all to help Lily ease her workload and gain more control of her life.

She summarizes my suggestions. "More senior staff, split up the teams, delegation, interns, and I could employ an assistant. Hire a manager specifically for destination weddings. I don't want to do them anymore." She beams. "And promote Janice to replace me and hire a new receptionist as well as an assistant for her. We have money in the budget for it."

"Do it."

"This feels good. Progress." She sighs contentedly.

"This feels incredible." I lay my hand on her knee, referring to spending time with her and not about the business, although that's awesome too.

"We're going to be okay, aren't we, Ash?" she asks, sounding apprehensive.

Pulling into the valet area at the ICE hotel, the swankiest one in the city, I place the car in park, unfasten my seat belt, and turn to face her. "No matter what it takes, we are in this together."

"I don't know what I would do without you. I should have stayed last week. To talk."

"I'm glad you didn't, Lily. You gave me the kick in the ass I needed." It was fucking horrible, but the wake-up call I deserved. "I will never let you walk out of my life again."

"Never."

We lean into each other at the same time. Her eyes full of expectation and apprehension, I press my lips against hers and kiss any remnants of doubt she has away.

Grabbing my tie, she pulls me closer and moans my name as our kiss turns passionate.

"Time to play." I lick her sweet lips.

Looking over my shoulder, frowning, she asks, "Are we staying here tonight?"

"Only if you want to."

She answers by unlocking the car door and pushing it open.

"I packed a bag for you. I've already checked in and your bag is there." I shout to her through the gap in the door. Popping her head back into the car, she lays her hand out and I place the keycard for the room into it. "Presidential suite."

"What? Oh my God, Ash, it's a weeknight."

She's worth every cent. "We don't often have a spending spree?"

Pointing at my new car, she raises her eyebrows. "I have to disagree."

"Whatever, Mrs. Know It All." I laugh.

"I love the color."

It's orange for my Tiger Lily.

I can tell she's excited, her voice full of sunny cheer. A sharp contrast to the snow lined sidewalks outside. "Forget the car. What are we playing?" she asks.

"You'll see." I wink, my cock twitching in my boxers just thinking about it. "I'll be up in ten minutes."

Eyes gleaming, she slams the car door, and runs into the warm safety of the hotel.

I hope she loves what I have planned.

CHAPTER THIRTY-FOUR

Lily

Having been years since Ash and I did this, nerves tickle my lower belly, and I have serious doubts about the outfit Ash laid out on the bed for me as I put it on. I feel like I am bulging out of it in all the wrong places, and it's been over three years since I wore this.

A knock at the door indicates it's playtime.

Unladylike, I wobble on my heels, adjusting my suspender thigh straps that are digging into my skin. Oh God, he's going to think I look like the marshmallow man and not the sexy police officer I'm supposed to be.

I take one last look at myself in the mirror and pull the high shine collar of my navy mesh sheer bodysuit down, giving me a better cleavage. Aligning the mock buckle on the belt in the middle, I adjust the fake police badge over my left nipple and play with the handcuffs I'm wearing as if they are bracelets.

That will have to do. A nervous giggle leaves my chest.

"Pull yourself together, Lily." I inhale a deep breath before opening the door and put on my game face.

Ash barges in, making me stumble backwards in my high shoes, and holy freaking shit. He's wearing all black, except for a Halloween costume mask I've never seen before. Criss cross LED lights form the eyes and more lights make it look as though his mouth has been sewn shut.

I'm simultaneously scared and turned on.

He slams the door closed and then switches off the hotel suite lights, making his mask glow even brighter, looking increasingly menacing.

My heart is beating faster than a racehorse in my chest as I walk backward into the darkened room. His head tilts to the side, but he remains quiet, and for a moment, I'm rendered speechless.

"Would you like to play?" he asks, his voice slightly muffled behind the mask, but the tone does something to me, making heat pool between my thighs.

"That depends." My voice cracks.

C'mon, woman. Get it together.

"On?" He tilts his head the other way.

"If you've been a good boy." My ass hits the window as I reach the other side of the room, and I let out a small gasp.

"Oh, I've been very, *very* bad, officer." The lights in the mask change color from blue to orange and then purple.

"What did you do?" I whisper.

"I haven't been taking care of my wife."

I can't stop myself from smiling. "Now, that is a crime." My shoulders dropping, I begin to relax.

"It's the worst crime of all. I deserve to be punished."

Feeling more confident, I ask, "Do you want to know what they do to bad boys like you?" I stand to all five feet four inches of me, feeling taller in my heels.

"Tell me." His mask continues to slowly change color as

he leans closer to my face, surrounding me in his familiar cologne.

He groans when I lay my hand over his pants and give his cock a squeeze. "They need to be strip-searched." I proceed to unbuckle his belt, but he grabs my wrist, stopping me.

"I'm afraid I can't let you do that, officer."

"Do you know I can arrest you for trying to assault an officer of the law? Take your hands off me," I bark, pretending to be angry, shaking him off my wrist. "Bedroom. Now."

His mask lights the way into the enormous bedroom and I poke him in the back with my plastic baton, urging him to move faster.

"Everything from the waist up, take it off. Leave the pants on."

He does as he's told, stripping for me, exposing his body, painted in lilies.

The neon mask highlights the deep divots of his abs and sculpted muscles. I'd almost forgotten what he looked like.

He takes off the black dress shoes he had on at dinner and loses his socks too.

Standing in front of me, a wall of muscles and oozing sex, in nothing but his dress pants, tattoos, and a mask, I think this is the sexiest thing we've ever done. Desire burns in my brain, unable to think of anything but touching him.

"What now?" he asks, head tilted again, and I find oddly disturbing how wet I am from him doing that.

"Do you like what you see?" I tease, running my baton down between my cleavage and then between my legs. I moan when it touches my swollen lips, my navy string panties of my bodysuit doing nothing to cover me.

"Fuck," he mutters beneath the mask. "You are so sexy."

"I'm an officer of the law and you're mine to do with what I please. I'm not yours to touch. And if you do, I might have to rough you up a little." He watches me intently as I push the baton back and forth between my pussy lips.

Unable to control himself, he launches forward. "Fuck it." He wraps his strong arms around my waist and lifts me into the air.

"What are you doing?" I squeal.

"I'm not playing anymore. I want you."

Oh, thank God. I want him too.

With me in his arms, he haphazardly lands on the bed.

"You're a very bad boy, and if you don't comply with my orders, I'm going to have to do a cavity search." I start giggling.

He flips us around.

My back now on the mattress, he pushes his mask off, revealing his gorgeous face. "Cavity searching is my job." He crashes his lips against mine and pushes my legs apart with his knees.

I can't wait a moment longer.

Desperately fumbling with his pants, I undo his button and zipper, then shuffle them along with his boxers down his hips. Frantically, he helps me to push them off, and in one smooth motion, he slips the slither of string from my thong bodysuit to the side and pushes his thick, hard cock inside of me.

Throwing my head back, I cry out in pleasure.

"Fuck me, baby, you're soaked." He drops his head to my nipple and sucks it through the mesh fabric of my bodysuit.

"I'm so wet for you, Ash." I have no control over my body when he's around.

"Fuck." He lifts his head and looks me straight in the eyes. He pounds into me as if he can't stop himself.

"Harder." I grab his ass, spreading my legs wider. The handcuffs I still have on clinking as they get rattled about.

The bright light from his abandoned face mask illuminates the room.

He groans loudly. "Why don't we do this all the fucking time? You are so fucking beautiful, and sexy, and holy fucking shit." His eyes roll back and I moan when the head of his thick cock rubs my G-spot.

"You swear too much."

"And don't fuck you enough." His hips piston in and out of me, driving himself deeper, and I never want him to stop. "I love you, Lily," he pants.

"I love you more."

"Not possible." He sucks my neck, and I know it will leave a mark, but I don't care as we ride each other at a fast, almost punishing pace. "You feel so fucking good. So wet."

"Always wet for you, Ash."

"Oh, baby." He licks my neck, then bites it.

My nails digging in his ass, I beg him to go deeper as an earth-shattering orgasm builds in my wet core.

Widening his knees, he pulls a pillow under my hips to tilt them to give me the ultimate orgasm. "Come for me, baby, come." Perspiration covers our bodies as we reach our climax, his hands pulling desperately at the suspender straps around my thighs.

And we come.

Together.

Hard.

Moaning, groaning, and crying out together in synchronicity. The emotion running through me as we connect again in a way I've wanted to for so long. Without inhibition or uncertainty.

Spilling himself inside of me, Ash lays his open mouth over mine.

I love the sensation of his heavy body above me, the feeling of us skin to skin, our bodies so in tune with one another, our hearts beating as one.

Resting his forehead on mine, we pant, gasping for breath, desperately trying to catch it.

We lay together, relaxed, enjoying the feel of each other again.

"I'm too old for this." He's still semi-hard inside of me.

"Yes, you are," I tease.

Out of breath, he leans back on his rested elbows, pleasure dancing in his eyes. "Are you telling me I'm an old man?"

I nod my head, my blond hair more than likely a matted mess and looks like a bird's nest. "What are you going to do about that?" I suck my bottom lip into my mouth. I can feel him growing hard inside of me again. He may be getting older, but Ash still has stamina.

"Make you come again." He sits upright, then rests on his haunches. Looking down at where we are joined together, he licks his fingers, then spreads me open. I moan when he softly pinches my swollen clit between his finger and thumb.

He moves his cock slowly in and out of me in a dream-like motion.

Knowing how my body will respond, he flicks my clit, then rolls it between his fingertips, causing me to arch my back in approval.

My body is burning for him again. He circles my swollen bud, then draws his fingers down either side of it in a *V* shape, rubbing it slowly, as his cock fills me languidly again and again, the overwhelming sensations making me lose my mind.

Hands on his thighs, I dig my fingertips into his solid flesh.

"Take everything off," he commands. "And the handcuffs."

I remove the detachable stirrup style suspenders from my bodysuit, then he helps me to slide them off my legs one after the other.

I push the handcuff off my wrist, then awkwardly undo the bodysuit poppers and peel my body suit up and off, arching my back to pull it over my head. My movement causes me to push his cock further into my body and I moan. Every nerve ending quivering at his touch.

"You look beautiful."

It never ceases to amaze me how many women Ash has been surrounded by throughout his career; female fans, broadcasters and journalists, celebrities, bikini models, and yet, he thinks I am beautiful. I've never fully understood it.

His fingers move quicker over my clit, rubbing it faster than before, and I feel my orgasm grow deep inside. I feel him everywhere.

"You're the only woman for me, Lily Johansson." His cock grows harder. "You're the most beautiful and sexiest woman I have ever seen. From your dimples to your smart mouth and super clever brain. You're the perfect woman. My heart belongs to you."

"I'm not perfect," I groan as he strums my clit to the brink of climax.

"You are fucking perfection. Don't ever let me hear you say different."

"Oh, Ash, I'm gonna come." I gasp.

"Then come." He moves his hips faster, spitting on my clit to make it wetter. He flicks it in such a way that I feel like I'm going to explode.

"Ash." My cries are so loud, I'm certain the other guests will hear. Then something happens that's never happened before. The pressure that's been building feels full to the point of bursting. Suddenly it releases, and like a volcano erupting, I squirt. All over his naked stomach, as he continues to pound into me.

Almost dizzying, I think I pass out for a moment as the feeling of what felt like fireworks burst inside of my body.

I reach down to stop him touching my sensitive flesh. It's too much.

Lacing our fingers together, he pushes my arms above my head while he continues to fuck me. "Well, that was new," he grunts, sounding really pleased with himself.

"That was—" I can't talk.

"Fucking amazing. You're gonna sit on my face and do that. You're a goddess." Kissing me, he tilts my hips in a way that I know he wants me to come for him again. He loves nothing more than giving me pleasure.

Every inch of him is savage tonight. There was never any chance of us not tearing our clothes off and then screwing each other's brains out.

Thrills run up and down my body as he kisses me roughly, his punishing hip thrusts begging me to come again. "I'm coming, Ash. Come with me."

Rock hard, my words are his undoing, "Fill me with your cum," I whisper in his ear.

Arms still above my head, his left hand entwined with my left hand, our wedding rings graze against each other, a small reminder of what we are. A husband and wife, who, after fifteen years, may have lost our way but found each other again before it was too late.

Eyes locked; I squeeze his hand. He squeezes mine in response and in a frenzy, our bodies fused, the power of our orgasms sends us into a pleasure bomb of ecstasy, exploding in shuddering waves as we take each other to the edge and beyond.

The simmering glow that was between us, now a full-on bonfire of love and desire.

His strokes slow down, my inner walls rippling around him as we come down from our high. Exhausted and feeling boneless, he's still semi-hard inside of me as we lie panting together.

"We're doing this every day. Sex with you is mind-blowing." Eyes half shut, he looks at me dreamily, as if he's punch drunk.

I'm a disheveled mess like him. "I need a shower."

"Yes, you do, Officer Johansson. You're a very dirty police officer."

I giggle when he calls me that. "That was fun."

"We're definitely doing that again."

"I feel like you made me yours again," I confess, something I haven't felt in a while.

He draws a line with his fingertip down my nose and across my top lip. "I'm sorry if I ever made you feel like you weren't, Lily."

"I love it when you do that." It's a gesture he used to do every day, then stopped because he always left for work before I woke up or came back late, so I was already asleep.

"I'm going to make up for all the time we've lost. I promise."

I believe he will. "Me too."

He looks mischievous when he says, "I've loved you since the day you hit me with that door."

A loud giggle shakes my chest because it's what he said to me the first time I ever told him I was in love with him. "Liar." I pinch his ass playfully the same way I did all those years ago.

"Ouch, okay, okay." He surrenders, reenacting and repeating what he said to me. "Maybe not, but definitely when I saw you in the coffeehouse. I knew then." Rubbing the tip of his nose against mine, he says, "Your smile, you make great coffee. Those big eyes I saw myself in, your runaway mouth." Impressing me, he remembers what he said to me word for word. Then he spoils it by saying, "Which I'm going to stuff full of my cock."

"Don't ever change, Ash." I roll my head side to side.

"You are so confusing, first you tell me I need to change, now you're telling me not to."

"Oh, stop." I wrap my arms around his neck, feeling content and happy.

"You are an exceedingly difficult woman to please, Lily Johansson. Although, I did make you squirt. Best. Moment. Ever."

And that's how the evening continued, teasing each other, laughing together, making love, and, more importantly, rekindling the deep love we have.

It's still there.

It never left.

CHAPTER THIRTY-FIVE

Lily

Sitting next to Ash's mom, her new partner, John, and my dad and Diana, we've just watched Ash coach his last winning game for the next two months.

Erika taps on my shoulder from the seats behind. "Can you tell Ash I'll call him next week about Christmas? It's getting late and I need to let Oscar out."

"Yeah, of course. Text me when you get home." I know she lives in a safe part of the city, near my old apartment with her dog, Oscar. Still, I always like to make sure she's okay.

She kisses everyone goodbye and disappears into the sea of fans filing out of the arena in streams.

"We are going to leave, too," Judy says.

"All of you?" I ask her, knowing how much they love each other's company.

"Yes. We are going to grab something quick to eat and try out the new wine bar around the corner." I adore how well Ash's mom and John, and my dad and Diana get along. It makes family events fun and stress free.

Our families are awesome.

Judy leans in and gives me the biggest hug. "Everything will work out; I know it will. He loves you, Lily."

"I love him more."

"I know you do." She chuckles. "Tell Ash I'll text him later about Christmas."

"What about Christmas? Erika said the same thing." Judy hosts Christmas every year. What's different about this one?

"Oh, he just asked about what to bring."

"Okay." I frown, realizing I'm being left alone. "Why are you not staying?" I lean out of our warm embrace.

"You two need time. Take this all in." She looks up to the ceiling of the arena and then all around.

My eyes fall on Ash over on the far side of the rink. He smiles and waves me down onto the ice. "Go, have fun, and remember what this felt like."

I think she means because it could be Ash's last time coaching the team.

Waving our parents and their partners off, I venture down the steps and round the perimeter of the rink.

With the arena almost empty, it's so quiet in comparison to the fanfare from earlier when the Eagles won 3-1 against Vancouver.

Shaking hands with his players and well-wishers, as well as a few fans, he spots me and excuses himself instantly.

His arms are around my waist and he's spinning me around. "I missed you."

"I saw you before the game."

"I still missed you." Kissing my lips, which he seems to have become obsessed with, he carefully places me back on the ground. "Skate with me." He sounds excited, as he pulls me by the hand along to the opening of the rink.

"What about the media? And postgame talk down and analysis?"

"I've asked the assistant coaches to do it all."

"Delegation." My response amuses him.

"Never been good at that. Neither have you." He pokes me in my ribs, making me yelp.

My relaxed, loving, playful Ash is back.

Loving Ash Johansson has never been so easy.

Spending the last week together, although hard at times, has been incredible. We've talked and talked. Man, have we talked. We've made love, tore each other's clothes off, shared baths, mealtimes, and enjoyed just being us.

Everything in the world feels right again with him in my life.

I make small talk with some of the team and the players before they slowly filter out of the arena until it's just Ash and I left.

"I forgot how huge this place is when it's empty."

The arena clean-up team gets to work, picking up discarded paper cups and disposable food cartons.

"Skates." Ash places my skates by my feet.

"Did you bring these with you?"

"Yeah." He toes off his dress shoes and pulls on the old skates he wore on our first date.

"You're going to look silly in a suit and skates." Fitting him perfectly, he wears that suit well and looks every bit the professional hockey coach.

"I think I can pull it off." He's right, he could wear a burlap sack and make it look sexy.

Ready to hit the ice, I step onto it and smoothly skate into the middle.

"You still remember?" Speeding past me, he does some fancy footwork my brain can't comprehend. I've never been able to understand how he can move that quick, almost elegantly on ice, and yet can still stub his toe on the edge of our bed.

"Skating is like riding a bike, you never forget," I counter.

"We won tonight because you wore your scarf." He points at the cream scarf I still wear to every game, facing me while skating backward.

"You won because you are an incredible hockey coach." I pause and stop in the middle of the rink.

He frowns, knowing I have a question. "Spit it out. What are you thinking?"

"I still have my doubts about you giving this all up." I throw my hands out on either side of me. "I know you said it's only for two months, but I think you've already decided you're quitting."

"Do you really want to know what I want to do?"

"Yes."

Skating over to me, he takes both of my hands in his. "I want to spend the next eight weeks with my wife. Quality time. Restructuring your business together. Spending Christmas with our family, before, during, and after. Not just for the day. And then we'll see what the New Year will bring."

I tilt my face closer to his and look up at him. "You're up to something," I say with a note of suspicion in my voice.

"I am. But I'm not telling you until everything is finalized. Just trust me."

I narrow my eyes and draw my lips into a thin line, pretending to be mad at him. "It had better be magnificent."

"It will be." His megawatt smile is brighter than a neon

light, illuminating his entire face. He changes the subject. "We are standing in the spot where we had our first date."

I look down at my skates and back up again. "So, we are."

"It's where I gave you my jersey with my name and number on it."

"I have twenty-three now." At my last count.

"I like you in my shirt." He looks down at my yellow and blue jersey with his name and old player number on it.

It's faded, but it's still my favorite.

"The first time I met you, I thought it would look much better on my bedroom floor." Moving his lips closer to mine, I wrap my arms around his neck.

"Oh, yeah?" My mouth dusts against his.

"I'd very much like to take you home and fuck you in it." He leans back. "If that's okay with you?"

"You seem happier tonight." It's not just the win, he seems lighter. Freer. And the players weren't sad to see him go either because they think he's only taking an eight-week break.

"I feel like I am doing the right thing. It feels good. Great, in fact."

Satisfying me with his reply because I know he's telling the truth; I answer his previous question. "I'm okay with you taking me home."

"Yeah?" He smiles against my lips.

"But—" I smack a kiss to his lips and before he knows what's happening, I'm skating away as fast as I can and yelling over my shoulder, "—you gotta catch me first."

"You need to skate faster. I'm coming to get you, Mrs. Johansson."

As I race across the rink, the fresh wind blowing through my hair laughing, as my husband chases after me.

Life is good.
Really. Really. Good.

CHAPTER THIRTY-SIX

Lily

Following the Eagles win on Saturday night, Sunday's press release went out. As predicted, and although Ash had asked for privacy, the Eagles' front office was inundated with press inquiries, and reporters still hounded him.

Of course, the speculation grew. Is he unwell? Am I unwell? Is he transferring to another hockey team? So many questions Ash refused to answer.

Overwhelmed with messages, I told him to turn off his phone and go out with his friends last night. Something he very rarely does.

We've spent almost every hour together finalizing the restructure of Tiger Lily Events, making love, eating, and watching *Game of Thrones* on the sofa, which led to more sex.

We can't get enough of one another.

Now Wednesday, a week away from Christmas, I'm dashing back to the house to grab my Santa's little helper costume for Brayden and Candy's Christmas party this Saturday. The last event I will personally coordinate because I've delegated all other ones to my newly appointed team leaders while Janice is taking over ninety percent of my role.

It feels great and I can see the New Year through a much clearer lens with a bigger, brighter vision for the business and my life. It's balanced and more harmonious. The two things I was craving the most.

I have interrogated Ash several times, trying to get him to spill the beans on his plans for the New Year, but he's keeping mum, which I find oddly annoying.

Clicking the button on my key fob, I drive through the security gates leading up the long drive to the house. Pulling up outside, I jump out of the car and draw my brows together. Ash's black truck is parked in the drive, which means he's here.

Running up the sandstone steps leading to the entrance, I push my key in the door to unlock it.

I take a moment to look around at the palatial home I haven't lived in for almost two weeks and feel bad because I don't miss it.

A feminine giggle snaps my neck in the direction of the living room.

What the hell?

I stand for a minute to listen, making sure I wasn't hearing things. Then, sure enough, I hear it again.

Sweaty palms, tight throat, my eyes pop out of their sockets.

Is Ash here with another woman?

Never.

That's impossible.

He'd never do that to me.

Would he?

I've never doubted him.

Although he was vague about his whereabouts this morning and it is his truck sitting outside.

Following the trail of soft feminine pants and masculine grunts that sound like people having sex, it drifts through the house, growing louder as I push open the door.

I cover my mouth with my hand when I see Britney sitting upright, having sex on my sofa. The back of the sofa hides whoever is lying down on it and I can only assume it's Ash, because she's wearing one of his old shirts. My shirt. While fucking him.

My lips trembling, I clutch my hands to my heart as it aches like never before in my chest. I step back and inhale a sharp breath. Then let out a stifled whimper, making Britney jolt her neck in my direction. Seeing me, her lips curve into a sinister smile. She continues to fuck him, throwing her head back and laughing as she shouts, "Harder, baby, harder."

And I'm done.

Tears running down my face, my heart breaking in my chest, I run out the front door and sprint down the steps.

Looking back over my shoulder at the house, I run into something solid, almost knocking me backward, but I'm surrounded by giant warm arms to stop me falling. The ones I know so well.

Ash.

I'm so confused. How did he get here so quickly?

I push him away. "Don't touch me."

Out of breath, I clutch my hand to my chest and look back at the house and then at him.

"Lily, why are you crying? What's going on? Who upset you? Did Wade say something?"

I tap my forehead in confusion. "Wade? What no, why? Why Wade?" I wipe my face and point back at the house then look at Ash. "Where did you come from..." I stop asking my question when I see Ash's truck parked next to my white Range Rover. I turn my attention to the truck on the other side of the drive that I now notice has flame decals along the sides, which Ash's does not. The lightbulb goes on, and I realize I've made a huge assumption.

"Oh, my God," I mutter, feeling stupid. "I thought..." I drift off.

"You thought what? What's happened, Lily?" Voice raised, he sounds angry as it booms around the bowl of our circular shaped drive. Ash holds me by the shoulders and rubs the top of my arms.

Hanging my head in shame, I whisper, "Is Wade living in our house?"

"Yes. Because he got kicked out of his apartment and had nowhere else to go. The team are through with giving him chances, and none of them would help him out. I'm not living here, so it made sense."

"You're not living here?"

"I'm living in the apartment above Home & Away. That's where I stayed last night. I moved there right after you moved out of here. This house doesn't feel right without you in it."

"Right." How did I not know this?

"I texted you to let you know that's where I was last night."

"I misread your text. I thought you said you were at Home & Away drinking in the bar. I thought you stayed here last night." Half asleep, I skimmed his text late last night.

"Leon, Buster, me, Troy, and even Brayden stayed at the apartment above the bar last night. Candy probably kicked his ass this morning for staying out. But it's the first time any of us couldn't see straight." Much calmer now, he chuckles. "I don't feel so good today."

"I'm sorry," I apologize, and bite my bottom lip with worry.

"What the hell is going on? I hate seeing you cry, Tiger. Why are you crying?" Placing a knuckle under my chin, he tilts it up.

I can't look him in the eye. "Britney is in there."

My eyes flit up.

Jaw clenched; Ash is seething. He hates that girl as much as I do. He looks up at the house. "In our fucking house? I will kill him." He pauses. "Wait, did you think?"

"I'm sorry." I cover my face with my hands. "I've never doubted your loyalty to me. But she... she... it looked like she was having sex with you on the sofa. I couldn't see your face, and she's wearing your jersey. But now I know it wasn't you. It was Wade. She's been through my things and the wicked way she looked at me like she'd won you. I... I..." I can't get my words out as I hyperventilate.

"Hey." I'm smothered by his strong body. Running his hand up and down my back to soothe me, he coos, "Hey, c'mon now, baby. No more crying. It's okay."

"It's not okay." My words are muffled against his firm chest.

"If I found a strange man in my place and I couldn't see your face, I would have made the same assumption." He tries justifying my stupidity.

"You would have chopped off his dick with your skates." I sniff, feeling better.

"Also that." His chest shakes with laughter as he kisses the top of my head. "I have never and would never cheat on you. I've been faithful to you since the day we met."

I lean back and look up at him. "Ditto."

Bowing down, he kisses me on the lips. "I quite like how jealous you were for a moment there but also—" He starts gagging. "Fucking Britney."

"She's vile."

"I want her out of our house." He wipes my tear-stained face, running his thumb under my eyes. I don't have any makeup on today as we are setting up at Candy's house in preparation for Saturday's party. I'm dressed to work in white sneakers, gray joggers, and one of Ash's hockey jerseys. "Let's kick her ass out. And remember, your house, your rules, Tiger."

I push my shoulders back. "Okay. Do I look like I've been crying?"

"You look beautiful. Go get her." He points in the direction of the still open front door.

Storming through the house, with Ash close on my heels, I push open the living room door and shout at the top of my lungs. "Get the hell out of my house." Britney lets out a yelp and scrambles off Wade when she sees Ash standing behind me.

"Oh, my God." Wade catapults upright.

"You too." I thumb over my shoulder.

"But I've got nowhere else to go." Hair ruffled, thick beard, Wade looks genuinely concerned.

"You should have thought about that before you brought the top puck slut that ever walked this earth back to my house," I rage, spitting venom in Britney's direction. "You're thirty-five, when are you going to grow up?"

Gasping in horror, she pulls the hem of my Eagles jersey down to cover herself. "I'm only thirty-four," she protests.

"You said you were twenty-five; the same age as me," Wade jumps in, looking horrified.

"I'm reporting you to management," Ash firmly informs her from behind me.

"No." Britney holds her hands up. "Don't do that. Please, Ash."

He stands his ground. "It's done."

"Now get the hell out of my house and leave the shirt," I yell. I'm going to have a ritualistic burning ceremony with Bree and Candy. They despise this girl as much as I do.

"Wade said neither of you are living here?" Britney finds her confidence. "Why is that?" Pointing at Ash, shocks me when she says, "And one of my friends saw you leaving the apartment above Home & Away." She then drives the knife in deeper. "And why are you on personal leave, Ash?"

"None of your business, Britney," Ash growls.

I push my shoulders back and stand taller, to cover how much of a freak out I am having internally. The last person on Earth I would ever want to know that Ash and I had separated momentarily is Britney.

I am not one for swearing, but *fuck.*

I raise a brow and pop a hip, feigning confidence. "We're here, aren't we? Standing in our home, together."

"Right." Britney's mouth twitches at the sides. She can see right through my bravado.

"Both of you get your stuff, and get out of my house, or I am calling the police." Turning sharply, I pat Ash on the chest. "I'm just going to grab my Santa's little helper costume for Candy's party."

He smacks me on the ass as I leave.

Suck on that Britney. In my head, I give her the bird.

"Where the hell am I going to go now, Ash?" I hear Wade's desperate voice as I climb the stairs leading to my bedroom.

"You're not my problem for the next eight weeks, Wade.

I was trying to help you, but you threw that in my face. You should never have brought Britney into my home," Ash replies. "Now do as my wife asked. Get the fuck out of our house. You could maybe stay with Britney." I laugh at the sarcasm dripping from his suggestion. "You'll be allowed to continue your relationship with her once management fires her for having sexual relations with a player." It's prohibited. She knew that when she signed her contract.

"Ash, please don't do that," she begs in her whining tone.

"You've been a thorn in the Eagles' side since the day you arrived on the hockey scene."

That's the last of the conversation I hear as I sit on the end of the bed listening to Ash's muffled barked orders at both Wade and Britney.

The front door slams, alerting me to their exit, and I wait in the bedroom for Ash to come and find me.

"Fucking hockey players," Ash mutters, making me laugh, as he walks through the bedroom door.

"Fucking puck bunnies," I counter.

Ash roars with laughter and it's so contagious I join in. "What's so funny?"

"Unless we are having sex, you never swear. It took a puck slut for you to stoop to my level."

I throw myself back on the mattress. "She makes me mad." I grit through my teeth. "She had sex on our sofa."

The bed dips by my side. "And Wade's sweaty ass," he groans.

I roll my head against the comforter. "Let's burn it."

"I think we should sell the house." Knowing Ash, he probably knew all along that I wasn't as in love with this house as I hoped I would be.

"Me too," I finally confess. Finding Britney here

tarnished it even further. It was the final nail in the coffin to push me and make my decision. "New Year, fresh start."

"Let's make love in our bed before we sell that too." His fingers move under my jersey, tickling the skin of my waist with his touch. "And you and I are moving back into the apartment together. I don't want to spend another night apart." He climbs on top of me and pushes my arms up over my head.

"I have a life sized, plastic gingerbread house to erect by four o'clock this afternoon," I protest.

"Well, I'm erect now, and you need to help me with it." He rubs his impressive length against my hip.

Giggling, we are naked within seconds. "You had better be quick," I gasp when he pushes himself inside of me.

But with Ash, it never is.

For the rest of the afternoon and the entire week leading up to Christmas, we spend the time between the sheets, in a rumbled mess, where I'm sure he's trying to kill me with orgasms.

Or make a baby.

The latter would be a dream come true.

CHAPTER THIRTY-SEVEN

Ash

Unbuttoning my suit jacket, I make myself comfortable around the boardroom table.

Somewhere I didn't see myself sitting again so soon.

Next to me, Elizabeth, the Eagles' senior recruiting and engagement manager, lays out paperwork in front of her. She tilts her head sideways to hear what Savanna, the people operations director for the team, has to say, as she mumbles something in her ear.

The boardroom door opens wide and in walks an unusually sheepish looking Britney.

Her eyes flit over to me, then away again, and her nostrils flair.

She knows what this is about and she's not too happy about it either.

"Thank you for joining us, Britney." Elizabeth threads her hands together and places them on top of the paperwork in front of her as Britney sits down in the chair on the opposite side of the table.

"I know what this is about. He's out to get me." She

points at me, looking like she's about to burst into tears and, at the same time, wanting to rip my head off.

Calmly, Savanna takes over. "That is a serious accusation, Britney. Not one I would be throwing around, given the circumstances."

Britney's jaw twitches as she tries to hold her tongue.

Savanna continues, "Britney, we have talked multiple times about inappropriate behavior and violation of rules. Today, specifically, we are referring to clause seventeen of your employment contract regarding having romantic and sexual relationships with colleagues. It has come to our attention that you have not once, but on several occasions conducted yourself in an inappropriate manner choosing to have sexual relations with members of the team."

An Eagles' contract of employment states all employees are to stay away from the players at all times. Romancing or dating a hockey player is a huge no-no.

She's slimier than a snake. How she got a job on the marketing team is also a huge sticking point for most of us. We have all questioned who she slept with to get that position. Regardless of her business degree, she's a liability and not suitable for the role; her professionalism is somewhat lacking.

Savanna adds, "Not only is it unethical, but violates the rules you agreed to." She pulls a copy of Britney's signed contract out and slides it across the table. "In addition, you were caught performing a sexual act with Wade Collins, a current player for the Eagles, in our head coach's home yesterday. As a result, we've made the decision to end your employment here, and today will be your last day."

"But—" Britney jumps in.

"Let me finish, Britney." Savanna holds her hand up. "You will receive your final paycheck on the last day of this month. This will include any extra hours you have worked, vacation time, and as an act of gratitude for your time, we will pay you until the end of the month."

"I can't believe you're letting me go. What about Wade's part in this?" Agitated, Britney tries staring me down.

Elizabeth told me to remain quiet at all times, and only to speak if Wade's behavior was mentioned. "We are not here to discuss Wade, just you," I tell her calmly. "However, Wade has been dealt with and has a four-game suspension." I broke the news to him this morning.

Dustin begged me to be the one to do it. I'm the only one Wade trusts, and he knows I have his best interests at heart. However, I thought after this debacle, he may change his mind about me, but he was pleasant to us during our meeting and didn't lash out like I thought he might. He knows he fucked up, promising to do better. I pray he does. He's an incredibly talented defenseman and I would hate for him to throw it all away.

Britney's skin flushes red hot up her neck and into her cheeks. "I hate you. You're just jealous because it wasn't you I fucked in your house. Wade was probably much better in the sack than you anyway."

I have to hold in my laughter at how delusional she sounds.

Slicing off my own dick with a blunt object sounds far more enjoyable than having sex with Britney.

"I would like us to part on good terms, Britney," Elizabeth says, sounding firm. "However, you need to lower your voice and refrain from saying anything that could further tarnish your name."

Spitting venom in Elizabeth's direction, she yells, "Fuck you."

"I'm calling security," Savanna drawls, as cool as a

cucumber. She's the perfect person for the role of people operations; efficient, kind, and no matter what the circumstances, she doesn't mind facing difficult employees. Which is just as well, because Britney launches herself at me across the boardroom table.

"You'll pay for this." Veins bulging in her neck, she yells at me, her spittle flying across the surface of the table she's clambering across.

I push my chair away from her clawing hands, just as the security team bursts into the boardroom.

She's out of the door kicking and screaming, making a scene, destroying any chance of working for another hockey team ever again. Not that she would. She's a die-hard Eagles fan and puck bunny through and through. Still, word will get around ruining her chances of finding employment anywhere in Edmonton.

In a way, I feel sorry for her. She landed her dream job and ruined it for herself. However, I have kept quiet for long enough about her involvement with several of the players. It happens, I know it does from time to time, but being in my house with Wade, she took it a step too far. She's been desperately trying to slither her way into our friendship circle for years.

Enough is enough.

"I hate you, Ash Johansson. This isn't over." Screaming at the top of her lungs, her words travel along the corridor.

I say a silent prayer that I never see that girl again.

CHAPTER THIRTY-EIGHT

Ash

"Where are we?" Lily holds her hands out in front of her as if she is a zombie, trying to feel anything to give her a clue as to her surroundings.

"It's a surprise." I move to her side. "You have three steps to climb. Careful." Unable to see because of the blindfold, I hold on tight to her waist from behind, as she tentatively takes the first step, then the second and third.

"A little more." I guide her to the open door that holds her surprise just beyond it.

Eager and alive with happiness, delight written all over her face, her mouth is spread wide in a smile.

"Take off your blindfold." I look through the doorway of the log cabin I've booked for the next three days.

Adjusting to the bright light in front of her, she blinks once, then twice just as everyone shouts in harmony, "Happy Holidays."

Lily throws her hands in the air. "You're all here. Wherever here is." Forehead wrinkling, she looks around at her surroundings.

"Farewells Pine Cabins," I tell her. "Merry Christmas, Tiger." My hand on her lower back, I usher her into the warmth and out of the bitter cold.

Candy, Bree, Troy, and Brayden greet Lily first, their kids in tow wrapping themselves around Auntie Lily's legs. They love her and she's grown close to them again since Bree and Candy are playing a more active role in her life. Lily is so good with them, promising them she'll read them their bedtime stories and bake cookies with them.

My mom, sister, and her dog, Oscar, are here as well as mom's new partner, John, who I am still unsure of, because, well, he's not my dad, but mom seems to have fallen in love with him and ultimately, I want her to be happy. Lily's dad, George, and his new wife, Diana, seem to love him too, and they all can't be bad judges of character. And of course, no Christmas would be complete without Leon and Buster.

"This is such a wonderful surprise. We're all spending Christmas Day together tomorrow?" She claps her hands together excitedly, overacting for the kids. "We have to go to sleep soon, because if we don't, Santa won't come. When do you think he'll arrive?" she asks the little beaming faces gazing up at her, getting them hyped up.

This is exactly what she needed. Her friends, family, and us reunited. I never want her to feel like she is alone. She's part of something incredible and without her, our friendship circle is incomplete. As is my heart.

Settled in, eventually we managed to get Troy and Brayden's excitable kids to sleep. It's great being part of their special day. If I could be granted only one Christmas wish in a lifetime, it would be a little family for Lily and me. We need a Christmas miracle.

Snacks out, mulled wine in hand, and hot chocolate for

Candy, we all make ourselves comfortable on the multiple sofas in the ten-bedroom log cabin.

"So, what film are we watching?" Erika plonks herself down on one of the comfortable armchairs in front of the open log fire.

A knock at the front door alerts us to another guest. "Lily, could you get that?" I tap her knee.

"Just because you are off for the next few weeks does not make you exempt from other duties." Using my knee to push herself to her feet, she walks across to the front door. "I hope I'm not preparing dinner for everyone tomorrow, too."

No way. I have outside caterers organized for that. No one is lifting a finger tomorrow.

All eyes on her back, every one of us eagerly watches the next few minutes unfold as she twists the handle on the front door of the log cabin, then swings it open.

She takes a minute to comprehend who it is.

"Gemma," she exclaims, completely taken aback. Then she leaps forward, wrapping herself around her sister tightly.

"Merry Christmas, Lily." Gemma snuggles into her, a few of us welling up as the closest sisters I know are reunited once again. "Ash flew me home," she explains, her eyes watery with emotion.

"I've missed you," Lily confesses. "More than anything, I've missed you." She leans out of their embrace and grabs the sides of her face, squashing her cheeks. "You're really here?" Lily questions it as if it's too good to be true.

Still holding on to Gemma's face, she looks over her shoulder to find me. "You did this?"

I nod, and she looks back at her sister.

"You're the best Christmas present I've ever had."

Gemma laughs between her squished cheeks.

"Oh my God, Dad, Gemma's here," Lily says again, pulling her sister inside.

Buster pats me on the shoulder. "You did good, Ash."

"Thanks." I look up at him standing behind the sofa.

"I might want her back for selfish reasons," he says in a stage voice, for my ears only. I thought he might.

At Candy and Brayden's Christmas party last weekend, Buster confessed to me that he has a thing for Gemma. Which I always suspected. As far as I'm concerned, anyone is better than Chris, her ex-husband. He was a fucktard for breaking her heart the way he did. Gemma isn't just my sister-in-law; I class her as my blood sister. Just like Erika. Although, no one is good enough for Erika, in my opinion. Maybe I'm the reason she's never settled down with anyone.

I side eye Leon, who is checking Erika's ass out, yet again, as she bends over the arm of the chair to pat Oscar.

"Leon," I bark in warning.

He rolls his eyes at me, waving me off. "It's all in your imagination." He taps his temple.

It's really fucking not. I've seen that look hundreds of times.

From behind, Lily tilts my head back, kissing me upside down, the same way Spiderman kisses Mary Jane. "Thank you for bringing her home."

"I love you," I tell her.

"I love you more."

"Impossible."

Best Christmas ever.

Although wait until she finds out what we're doing for New Year.

CHAPTER THIRTY-NINE

Lily

It's the morning of New Year's Eve.

"I can't believe I'm back in New York." I look out of our hotel room window overlooking Central Park and the hustle and bustle down below.

Full of endless surprises, Ash shocked me, yet again, with a trip to New York to bring in the New Year.

To top it off, I'm meeting Zoey, my old college friend, for lunch today. We keep in touch, but I haven't seen her since our wedding.

While I'm with Zoey, Ash is meeting with someone called Scott Cole in New Jersey. Apparently, he's a hockey legend and Stanley Cup winner.

He's been less than forthcoming with information about the details of the meeting, which is a two-hour drive away and back again. But I trust him, and he knows that whatever he decides to do moving forward with his career, I will be there to support him. Unless it takes up all of his time again, which he assures me, it won't.

I now have my business under control. Janice is pretty

much running the place and I have to admit, Ash was right. Delegation and a shuffle of staff, a few interns and managers, was all it needed to make things more manageable.

I don't know how Janice did it, but she had everything in place before we broke off for the holidays. She's absolute magic and I don't know why I didn't make use of her skills and expertise more before. I was too busy being busy to see what was in front of me all along.

Ash's phone buzzes on the nightstand.

He lifts his phone to read the screen. "My driver has arrived. They're at the front desk waiting for me." He pushes it into the pocket of his jeans.

"You're dressed too casually for a meeting, Ash." I frown, checking him out in his jeans, immaculate white sneakers, sweatshirt, and black puffer jacket.

"I'm going to his house. It's not really a meeting. It's more of a pick your brains sort of thing."

Oh-kay. That's vague.

"Say hello to Zoey for me." Ash kisses my cheek. "And wrap up. It's freezing out there today."

I'd forgotten how harsh the wind in New York is. "We should move to Hawaii. It's much warmer than here and Canada." I shiver just thinking about stepping out into the cold later. Our hotel room is spectacular. From the views across the city to the hot tub, and I'd happily stay wrapped up inside with Ash tonight.

"You find a holiday home for us in Hawaii."

I pull a face. "Are you being serious?"

"Try me." He winks as he pulls open the door to leave. "Behave. Not too many Cosmopolitans."

"Two at most, I promise." It will be five at the very least.

"Yeah, that's never going to happen. Don't worry, baby.

I'll hold your hair back when you're vomiting it all back up later."

"My hero." I hold my hands to my chest, pretending to swoon.

"Have fun."

"I will," I call out to him.

"Oh." His head appears through the gap in the door before it shuts. "It's supposed to snow later. I plan on returning before it starts."

"If that happens, we're staying in the hotel tonight."

"Wrapped up with you sounds like the perfect way to bring in the New Year." He looks at his watch. "Right, gotta go."

"Love you," I shout, just as he's closing the door, but he doesn't seem to hear me.

I walk into the bathroom, my hands on my hips, and look down at the whirlpool with dozens of water jets that's big enough to fit four people. "So how do you work, then?"

"We should do this more often." Zoey takes a sip of her cocktail.

We're on our fourth already.

I'm in total agreement. "We should." I place my empty glass down on the table and dig into my pepperoni pizza. There is no doubt about it, New York beats Canada hands down for pizza. "How's business?" I mumble around my food.

Zoey, who still works for *Majestic* magazine, has worked her way up through the ranks and is now the Editor for the largest women's magazine in the world. She knows every celeb, musician, and influencer in New York and beyond.

Famous in her own right, I'm a little in awe that she still wants to be my friend.

"Work is busy." She signals to the server to get me another drink. "I have an interview with someone very interesting in the New Year. She's incredibly talented and wants to move to New York." She smooths her fingers down her jet-black bobbed hair.

"Where is she moving from?" I wipe the side of my mouth with my napkin.

"Scotland."

"Wow. Big move." I grab another slice of the heavenly pizza.

"If I offer her the right salary, I think she would move tomorrow by the sounds of it. I think she'd be great on our executive team."

"What does she do?" She's piqued my interest.

"She's currently the CEO of The Scotland Golf Association."

"Wow. Sounds boring."

"Golf is huge, darling," she drawls. Zoey has developed a weird transatlantic accent in the last fifteen years. I guess, traveling all over the world to fashion shows and movie premiers, you become a hybrid of sorts.

"I'm a hockey girl."

We both laugh when I say that.

For the next half hour, we catch up on everything that has been going on in our lives. While I love Zoey, she's made me realize how much busier her life is than mine was previously. Systematic, repetitive even. Her demanding job allows no spare time whatsoever. She's even attending a fashion show where the catwalk begins at the stroke of midnight tonight. How dull.

With no partner or family around to bring in the New Year, she immerses herself in work.

Exactly what Ash and I used to do.

My phone rings and I get excited when I see Ash's name lit up on my screen.

I hit accept on my screen and lift it to my ear. "Hi. How did it go?" Although I'm clueless what *it* is.

"Really well. I'm already back at the hotel." Oops, I check the time. Four o'clock. Our lunch has almost turned into dinner.

He continues, "I thought I would book dinner in the hotel restaurant and have champagne delivered to the room for midnight. The snow has already started."

I look out of the restaurant window then down at the table, realizing we've eaten a twenty-inch pizza between us, and Ash wants to do dinner soon.

"Book it for eight o'clock, maybe nine." I correct myself, looking at Zoey, and fill my cheeks with air signifying I'm so full my stomach might burst.

"Big lunch?" Ash asks, knowing how excited I was about coming to Baker's Pizza.

"Huge."

He chuckles down the phone at my reply.

"You'll have to roll me into the restaurant this evening." I finish my drink, getting ready to leave.

"I'll make it for ten o'clock instead."

"Much better. See you soon. I'm just leaving."

"Say hi to Zoey from me."

"Will do. Love you."

"Love you more."

"That's impossible, Ash."

We hang up at the same time.

"You two are still so in love, Lily." Elbows rested on the table. Zoey stares at me with her chin rested in her hands.

"It's not all been smooth sailing." I don't want to go into the ugly details of our relationship. Only our closest friends know we've been through the wringer this year.

"But you made it work."

"Yes. We did."

CHAPTER FORTY

Ash

"What is this place?" Lily asks, looking up at the discreet sign above the clinic door. "Lorna Fitzgerald." She reads the name slowly as I close the door of the yellow cab.

"Let's get out of the cold." Winter jackets pulled up and around our necks, we huddle in together, through to the waiting area of Lorna's office.

Lily and I have had the best four days in New York.

It's exactly what we needed.

We spent New Year's in the whirlpool hot tub, submerged in the bubbling water. Through the circular window of the bathroom, when the clock struck midnight, we watched the snow fall and fireworks explode across the New York skyline.

It was the best way to bring in the New Year, promising each other to be open to new things and to never give up on each other.

We fly home tomorrow, and this is an appointment I booked at the last minute. One I hope she is okay with. If she's not, we can leave.

Shaking off the snow from our winter jackets, I stand facing her in the reception area of the clinic.

"It's a holistic fertility clinic," I say tentatively, worried she might leave immediately.

The world moves in slow motion as she stands in front of me.

"It's a non-surgical fertility treatment center, Lily. Noninvasive. We're here just to talk things through. See if there is anything we are missing. Lorna is the top holistic fertility specialist in the US and Canada."

"Ash." She sounds brokenhearted, almost hopeless.

"Three doctors have now told us there is nothing wrong with my sperm, and there is nothing wrong with your eggs. When they mix, the embryos are healthy in the lab, but when they are implanted into your uterus, they fail. And that's not on you, or me. It's something else." I let my words sink in. "I believe in us, Lily."

Her grin catches me off guard and then blows me away when she says, "Be open to new things and to never give up on each other." She repeats the resolution we made, then places her hand in mine. "You're an incredible man, Ash Johansson. I feel like the luckiest girl in the world, and I get to call you mine."

It's the other way around. I'm the luckiest man in the world.

"Ah, you must be Lily and Ash." The friendly woman, who I'm guessing is Lorna, breaks our moment, approaching us from down a narrow corridor. "You two are like complete contrasts of each other with names like that. Lily, as white as snow and Ash, made from fire." She's overly dramatic in her delivery, spreading her fingers out as if they are flames rising into the air.

We laugh at her analogy. It's perfect; ice and fire.

She shakes my hand, then surprises Lily as she gives her a warm hug.

"I'm going to lock the door. I opened especially for you two today. I'm officially out of office." She drops her voice, although there is no one else around to hear her.

When we spoke on the phone, she was more than accommodating, suggesting we meet the day before we fly home to save us another journey to New York.

"We're very grateful." I thank her.

"This way." Lorna beckons us to walk down a small hallway leading to a door at the end. "Gosh, you are very pretty, Lily," she says, walking past us, leading the way.

I've always thought that. Her heart of gold also makes her extra special.

In front of me, Lily turns around to look at me with a cheeky grin on her face. She likes Lorna. We're off to a good start.

We follow Lorna into a large open spaced area that looks more like a yoga studio than the fertility clinics we've sat in previously.

"Coats off, shoes off. Make yourself at home." She points to the sofa.

It's where we sit for the next hour recounting the last three rounds of IVF treatment we went through in detail, taking time when Lily gets upset.

It was hard on her, physically and emotionally. I never want to put her through that again. And according to Lorna, we won't have to.

"Let's move down to the floor." Lorna sits down on one of the yoga mats. "Cross your legs and face each other. You on one side of me, Lily, and Ash, you on my other side."

She urges us to move closer together as we get settled on the mats.

Lorna talks us through a guided visualization to reinforce how incredible our bodies are, having us repeat positive fertility affirmations.

It's an out of body trance-like experience I've never felt before, making me feel like I'm flying through a vortex of colors. As a pro athlete, I've read every book on positive mental imagery and how to reprogram your mind for success. Having a busy mind that's constantly wired, I found meditation difficult. Today's session with Lorna has changed my mind. I feel like every nerve ending is switched on and yet chilled out.

This is unlike anything Lily and I have ever tried before. Lorna's complementary therapy focuses on our mind and body, rather than pumping more hormones into Lily's system.

"5... 4... 3... 2... 1... Slowly, open your eyes and look at each other." She pauses to let us find our bearings. "Now, tell me the first thing that comes into your mind, Lily."

"I failed," she replies, the shock of her words pierces my heart.

"Why do you think you failed?" Lorna's calm voice pushes her to be more specific.

"Get married, have kids. Like most of our friends. I feel like I failed to make that happen."

"Ash. Do you agree with Lily?"

"No." I shake my head. "I feel like I failed you."

"You didn't fail me, Ash." With sadness in her eyes, she reaches over and places her hand in mine. "I feel like we waited too long to try for a family because my hockey career blew up. I was never around, and you immersed yourself in your business to keep yourself busy. I feel responsible," I say the words I've bottled up for years.

Lily's shoulders begin to shake. "It's nothing like that,

Ash. I think my body is faulty." Her voice cracks. "I'm broken. My body didn't do what it's biologically supposed to." The tears she's been holding in begin to choke her.

Desperate to give her comfort, I pull her toward me. Within seconds, her legs are wrapped around my waist and her arms hold my neck as if I'm her lifeline.

Cross legged on the floor, Lily sobs as I hold her tightly in my lap and rock her gently back and forth.

"Let it all out, Lily." Lorna encourages her to release the emotion that's been building for years.

Saying the words we have never said out in the open to each other has been more harrowing than I was prepared for. I didn't know she felt like this.

"I know there is more to us than having a family, Ash. Your hockey legacy will live on forever." Struggling to catch a breath, Lily trembles in my arms. "I've just always wanted a family."

"I know." I run my hand up and down her back as she nuzzles into my neck, soaking my skin with her tears.

"Lily, could you look at Ash for me, sweetheart?" I almost forgot Lorna was here.

My throat closes with despair when she does. Her pain matches mine and I would do anything to take it all away. No amount of fame or fortune can do that.

"Repeat after me, both of you." Lorna's steady voice instructs us with quiet emphasis.

I kiss Lily's forehead, then the tip of her nose.

"Our bodies work in harmony," Lorna says.

We repeat every mantra.

"We trust our bodies."

"We are a team."

"We are in this together."

"Our bodies are magical."

"We are worthy of a family."

We repeat dozens of affirmations, our confidence and smiles growing wider with each one.

I feel an unexpected shift between us, bringing us closer together.

Our mood raised; it feels like we created our own brand of atmosphere that's swirling around us. It's almost magical.

"How do you feel?" Lorna asks.

"I feel different," Lily says, and I swear she's glowing.

Full of more love for her than ever before, I feel incredible.

"This is just the beginning." Lorna's soft tone gives me confidence.

And for the last hour of our three-hour consultation I booked, Lorna works through our holistic treatment plan. Her number one recommendation is a reduction of stress levels through couples' yoga, meditation, acupuncture, and reflexology. She also gives us a list of the top specialists for us to work with back home.

"We'll have your next appointment via video call next week," Lorna confirms. "In the meantime, I want you to keep repeating the list of affirmations together and the meditation. More importantly, I want you to have faith and belief in your bodies. They always know what to do."

Shoes and jackets back on at the end of our session, Lily and I can't stop smiling.

"Did you see the photos on the wall in reception?" Lorna asks, and we both shake our heads, not sure what she is referring to.

"Come." She waves us through the door and back along the corridor. "Look."

Holding Lily's hand in mine, we stare at the rows and

rows of tiny photos. I thought it was a giant mosaic when I first saw it.

"That is hope." She points at the wall. "Like most things in life, there are no guarantees. But..." She sucks in a deep breath in and casts her gaze over the hundreds of microdot photos. "My success rate is high, and the couples I have helped and have gone on to conceive are on this wall. There are dozens more."

I want us to be on that wall.

"Hope," Lily repeats and squeezes my hand. "We have to start somewhere."

For the first time, I believe we're on the right path.

We have hope.

And each other.

CHAPTER FORTY-ONE

Lily

In the back of the cab, we drove back in silence.

Both processing the intense, possibly life changing session Lorna guided us through today.

Now, back at the hotel, I feel an odd sense of peacefulness that's new to me.

It's as if all the emotional baggage I've been carrying around for years was unpacked, left on the floor of the clinic, and is no longer dragging me down.

I've been masking how I feel. Today I felt the urge to release them and say all the things I'd stopped myself from saying for years.

My body is not faulty. My body is magical.

Just saying that to myself gives me a feeling of slight relief.

I don't fully understand what Lorna did today, but her dynamic yet calm energy was invigorating.

"Are you hungry?" Ash's voice breaks my thoughts as he unties his sneakers and rests back in the armchair of the lounge area in our hotel suite.

I had a huge breakfast. A good decision on my part because the session with Lorna was three hours long. "I was thinking we should have a late lunch, early dinner."

He nods his head in acknowledgment and slides his phone on top of the coffee table. "Are you okay?"

"I am. Never better." I feel good. "Thank you for making the appointment." It was a shock at first, but it turned into something special today. As if there is an invisible cord linking our hearts. I feel closer to him than I ever have. Something I didn't think was possible.

I sit down on the edge of the bed as I slip off my furry lined, gray winter boots and talk to him through the open plan space.

He leans forward in the chair. Resting his elbows on his knees, his chin in his hands, he looks like *The Thinking Man* sculpture. His words sound pained when he speaks. "I didn't know you felt faulty."

"And I didn't know you thought you had failed me." With my mouth downturned, I tilt my head. "We have been keeping too many negative thoughts to ourselves."

"I also didn't know you hadn't gone back on the pill."

"Like I told Lorna, after the IVF, there didn't seem any point. I couldn't get pregnant naturally or with treatment. I had been on the pill for years and pumped my body full of hormones. I just decided to let my body do its own natural thing. Regulate itself." Although my body seems anything but regular, my periods are sporadic and appear whenever they want.

My body is magical. I am deserving of a family.

Yup, that's going to take some getting used to.

"New rule, we tell each other everything," he says.

I agree, confirming with a nod of my head.

"Your body is not broken or faulty, Lily. You're exactly

as you should be. I've never seen you as anything other than my Lily. I love you. I love us. I love our life now that we are finally getting back on track. I love spending time with you." He rises to his feet and walks to me. His blue eyes meet my brown ones. Dusting his finger down my nose, he bows his head, and kisses me. His lips slowly work mine before he wraps a hand around my neck. Tracing his thumb over my rising pulse, he pushes the seam of my mouth open with his tongue, and in a trance-like state, he swirls his tongue around mine.

Breaking our kiss for a beat, he pulls my cream woolen jumper up over my head, then removes his sweatshirt, and his lips are on mine again.

With expert fingers I unbuckle his belt and slide his jeans and boxers down his legs.

Undoing my cream lace bra, and sliding the silk straps down my arms to remove it, I lay back against the mattress as he steps out of his jeans and climbs on top of me.

He takes his time, tracing my body with his fingertips, as if he's committing every one of my curves to memory.

My hands slide up his muscular back, then down his shoulders and strong arms. Moving them back up, he groans as I continue to explore his skin.

"I love the way you touch me," he mumbles, pushing his hard length between my pussy lips, my hips arching in response.

Sculpted from hours at the gym, painted in detailed tattoos, his body is a work of art.

He sucks my bottom lip into his mouth before he moves down my throat, covering my skin in kisses, branding me as his. He doesn't need to; I've always belonged to him.

Caressing every part of me, he moves south between my legs.

"Open yourself for me."

I spread the most intimate part of me. Exposing myself.

He covers his mouth over my pussy then sucks my clit, and gently flicks it with his tongue.

My body is burning for him when he slowly slides a thick finger inside of me and then another.

This is who Ash is, the ultimate pleasure giver.

With no desire to rush this, he savors each moment, taking his time licking and tasting me, then sucking my clit into his mouth, repeating the whole process over and over again until I'm begging him to fuck me. Sensual and loving, his hot breath warms my skin as he moves back up my body.

I wrap my hand around his hard cock, to let him fuck my hand while he continues to fill me with his fingers.

"As much as I love you doing that," he pants, our foreheads rested against one another. "I'm going to turn you around, and you're going to take me. I need to be inside of you." His words send a wave of goosebumps across my skin.

I instantly miss his touch when he slides his fingers out of me and eases me onto my side. Nuzzling into my neck, he whispers how much he loves me and I can't believe we almost lost each other. What was I thinking when I left him? It was a moment of madness and one I never want to repeat.

"I love you too, Ash." I moan as his hand shapes along my waist and he positions me with my back now to his front. Surrounded by his hard body, I feel safe in his arms as he lifts my leg up and holds it in the air carefully, while dusting kisses down my neck and shoulder. He slides his hard cock inside my wet center, making me moan. Hooking my leg behind his, he pants against the shell of my ear. The feeling of his hot breath on the sweet spot there sends shivers down my spine.

"Ash," I cry out as we rock together in harmony.

Addicted to everything I do with Ash, I twist my neck around, desperate to kiss him. He grabs my chin firmly, keeping it in place so we can fuck each other's mouths with our tongues. It's messy and wet and spurs him on to move his hips a little faster.

"Touch yourself," he commands, panting and groaning. His words make the ache between my thighs heavy with need, sending a shock wave of pleasure vibrating through me.

My left hand drops between my legs. I rub my clit, circling it faster, chasing my release.

Ash places his hand over mine and pushes harder, making my arousal flood his cock.

The sensation of him kissing my mouth, his cock moving in and out of me, and with his hand over mine, I can't take anymore. "You're the only one for me, Lily. You're perfect." His whispered words are my undoing.

Our wedding bands rub together as I come. My body feels like it bursts into a million stars across the galaxy. He increases his pace and fucks me harder.

Skin to skin, hand in hand, his heart pounds against my back. He growls and roars my name as he comes, holding himself deep, shooting hot ropes of cum inside of me.

Jerking, he slowly moves in and out of my body, my pussy milking him of every last drop.

"I could stay like this forever with you," he pants, trying to catch his breath.

Moving our hands away from between my legs, he links our fingers together and rests our hands on top of the comforter.

"We could, but we have a flight to catch tomorrow." I sigh, content as his hot, heavy body surrounds me.

Unwrapping our conjoined fingers, I run my fingertips over his lily tattoo on the back of his hand. "I love your tattoos."

"I'll be getting another one soon." He spreads his fingers out and I play with his wedding band.

"Sixteen years married this year." When I first met Ash, he always said he wasn't romantic, but he's the most romantic man I know.

"I have loved you for longer."

I remember the words he wrote on my card when he sent my flowers. "I will love you for a lifetime."

CHAPTER FORTY-TWO

Ash

Pointing up at the house we planned to sell, I ask Lily, "What do you see?"

Hands on hips, she looks at me with a wrinkled brow. "A house neither of us like?"

"What else?"

"A *huge* house neither of us like?"

She's not wrong.

We found the perfect house three weeks after our trip to New York. With four bedrooms and smaller spaces, it's much more welcoming and felt like home as soon as we stepped through the front door. It's also closer to our friends in a safe and friendly part of town. With a wraparound porch and a quaint yard with a small pool for the summer months, it's perfect for us. I don't know where our heads were at when we bought this monster. I look up at the beast.

"What if I told you I am going to turn it into a sports facility? Specifically, for hockey players?"

"Are you crazy?" she shrills, looking at me and then back at the house.

She's going to think I am even crazier when I tell her the next part of my plan. "And I'm building a private indoor ice rink over there." I point to the barren area on the right-hand side of the house we never did anything with.

She bursts out laughing. It's so loud you could probably hear it at the end of our long driveway.

When she sees how serious my face is, her laugh stops dead. "Oh my God, you're not joking?"

I shake my head and pull my lips into my mouth.

She points in the direction of where I plan to build the rink. "You're going to build an indoor ice rink over there?"

"Hear me out."

"This had better be good." She crosses her arms in front of her and pops her hip.

She looks cute when she's mad.

"We have money." Lots of money. Millions, in fact. "The last thing we invested in was this house. And that was ten years ago. We both worked our asses off to restore this monstrosity." It was financially and physically draining. "I figured we can make use of it in other ways." I pause. "I've decided I'm not going to coach the Eagles anymore. I handed in my resignation this morning." I only had a couple more days to decide if I was returning. Deep down in my gut, going back felt wrong.

I know this is what I want to do.

Lily's mouth drops open. I reach out and place my finger under her chin to close it.

"Don't be shocked. I am opening a training facility for hockey players. It won't be a full-size rink; it will be much smaller." It makes sense, after all, most games are played in the end zone. Smaller is better. "Hockey players often work with specialists and private coaches to improve their skills, specifically how to avoid contact and be safe. I plan to work with them on elite skills, like edge work. I can show them how to turn on a dime because when their edge work is on point, it means they can evade being checked when they're heading into corners to get the puck. It helps to stop the other team's player boarding you as you both battle for the biscuit." Fuck me, I'm excited and will be working with the best of the best from every team across the NHL. As a former pro and coach, it won't be hard to get clients. "They will work one on one with a private coach looking at ways to reduce their vulnerability on the rink."

"You never did that," Lily questions my reasoning, her brows dipping in the middle.

"I didn't need to. I learned from the best." Her knowing smile mirrors mine because she knows I'm referring to my dad. He was the best.

"Working with a private coach between seasons or when injured, is huge in the US, but nobody does it here in Canada. I want to be the first. I want to work with local NHL players as well as Division One athletes who are about to be drafted. And I can even do that between games if they are local." My voice rises in excitement. "They will train there." I widen my hands as if I am holding a box and point in the direction of the space where the ice rink will go. "And accommodate and feed them here." I point at the house. "I'm going to hire a nutritionist, a physical therapist." One who I think should incorporate meditation and yoga into the training plan. Since we started working with Lorna on a weekly basis, it's helped Lily and me mentally, training us to relax, and physically, my hip is less painful than it was before. "In addition, I would hire a sports psychologist to target any confidence issues they encounter following an injury or to conquer their fear of getting hit by a huge hockey player when playing." Contact is a huge part of hockey. The last thing you want is to get hit by someone much bigger than you. Escaping contact will be the biggest part of my private training.

I continue to stare at the house.

Fuck, it's a big dream.

I turn to look at Lily, scared about what she's going to say. Only I discover she's grinning at me. "You're excited about this?"

"Yes, I am." I can't wait to start.

"This is what you want to do?"

"Yes. I want to tutor hockey pros and work with them on their skills."

"Is this what you went to see Scott Cole in New Jersey about? Is that what he does?"

"Yes. He's so busy, he's already got a waiting list and pros who want to work with me."

She covers her mouth. "Oh my God, Ash. This is huge."

"I don't want to be away from you. Traveling, overnighters, being at everyone's beck and call. This will be my business on my terms. Dinner with you every night, home at traditional hours. And between training NHL and Division One players, I thought I would open this place up as a training camp for juniors. As well as offering the facilities for free for underprivileged kids." I love coaching that peewee team. I've already spotted a few talented players who have potential and I know the right people in the world of hockey to help them.

Jumping on board, Lily becomes animated, waving her hands around. "We could convert the four rooms in the east wing into six-man rooms with bunk beds for the kids." Lily sounds excited about that. "Tiger Lily Events could manage all your bookings. You wouldn't need to do any of the admin. We'd handle it all. From the pros to the charities. Cleaners and housemaids."

I fucking love this woman. "So, you're in?"

"I'm in." She beams up at me.

I fling my arms around her waist and spin her around, making her scream with joy. I plant her feet carefully back down on the ground. "I didn't think it was possible, but I think I fell in love with you all over again these last two months."

"Impossible," she counters.

"Because you love me more?"

"Absolutely."

CHAPTER FORTY-THREE

Lily

It's been a couple of weeks since Ash revealed his future career plans. As always, and like everything with Ash, it was genius, and he already has contractors in place to start building the new rink in the next few months.

His dream of becoming a private coach is moving fast, and I couldn't be happier for him.

Following Ash's resignation, an announcement was made and the outpouring of love Ash received from fans, fellow hockey players, and coaches alike was overwhelming. He's had several NHL job offers, but Ash has never wavered. He said he was ready for the change. The huge sums of money he's been offered didn't entice him to return, either.

He will always be a die-hard Eagles fan, player and coach.

And we were both willing to give up control to give us our second chance.

It all begins with a fresh start. We will be moving into our new house in a few weeks. Ash is currently back at the big house, placing sticky notes on the furniture we are taking with us. He's already started freaking out about the moving company and how carefully they will handle his arcade games collection. To be honest, I am more concerned with my vinyl collection, which has grown substantially since we moved into that house. I must have at least five thousand records now. I need to tell Ash to inform the moving company to stack them upright to prevent them from warping.

Almost midday, Ash and I spent the morning having breakfast together at Casper's. The best restaurant in the city, in my opinion. They serve amazing food all day, but breakfast is by far my favorite. Their bacon, eggs and pancakes are delicious and that's why Ash always has two portions.

I pull my chair in behind my desk to check my emails for the first time today; something I limit myself to twice a day instead of every hour, which is what I did before. It was difficult at first, but Janice has everything under control in operations, allowing me to focus on finance and marketing. I don't know why I held on to the reins so tightly for so long.

Since I promoted her, my inbox has reduced by more than half, which I am delighted about.

Life has become so much easier. More relaxed, more everything.

I never stay late; I don't start early.

I did, however, make the decision to work exclusively with one client every couple of months. Ash laughed at me when I told him. But he understood it was a way for me to keep my toes dipped in the water.

Since our trip to New York, Ash and I have had four sessions with Lorna. I'm also seeing a reflexologist and acupuncturist who specializes in fertility. After every session, I feel blissed out, but the next day I have so much bounce in my step that I could run a marathon. Not that I would want to do that. I've discovered yoga is the upper limit of the exercise ceiling for me. While Ash is strong and toned, and yummy, I'm still *curvy and soft in all the right places*, according to Ash.

I have no idea if any of what we are doing is working, but I feel better. I feel more balanced and harmonious. And Zen. Super Zen.

My eyes fall on an email with a red flag symbol next to it, signifying its importance. I check the time. It dropped into my inbox a minute ago.

Confused by the subject line, I click it open.

In a heartbeat, my Zen goes out the window.

Subject: URGENT: By the end of today

Dear Perfect Lily,

Pay attention.

I'm going to share the attached photo and video with the press if you do not electronically transfer $200,000 to the account number, which I will text you the details of by midnight tonight.

I have lost everything since I was fired from the Eagles, and I will never forgive your husband for what he did to me. He will pay me back for the things I have lost, including my home.

Transfer the money, I will delete the files, and you will never hear from me again.

This is non-negotiable.

The clock is ticking.

Nerves flutter in my belly and not in a good way as shock gnaws down my spine.

"Britney, you stupid girl," I mutter under my breath and click open the video file.

On screen, the video automatically plays, showing Britney prancing about our home in my silk dressing gown. She waves in the bedroom mirror, moving over to framed pictures of us on our wedding day and one of Ash in his hockey kit and me in his arms, my legs wrapped around his waist, wearing his shirt from his player days.

I cover my mouth. *Shit.* She's trying to make out she's his mistress, and he's invited her back to our home.

What a bitch.

Moving to the answering machine on the nightstand, she presses play. My voice pours out through the speaker. It's the message I left Ash the night I moved into the apartment, begging for him to call me and apologizing. I'm crying and asking for his forgiveness, telling him I never wanted to move out.

I sound sad. It doesn't resemble how I feel now.

A male voice shouts her name from outside of the room and that's where the video cuts off. I know for a fact that wasn't Ash's voice. It sounds nothing like him.

I know it's Wade.

Closing the video, I open the photo.

It's of Britney, and she's wearing Ash's hockey jersey; the jersey he gave me, and she's lying next to a bare-chested man whose face is blurred.

She's clearly never seen Ash naked before because his chest is covered in tattoos. What a pathetic attempt at blackmail. "There is no place for little girls in the women's playground, Britney," I mutter under my breath.

On the day we caught her with Wade, she questioned

why we weren't living in the house, but she already knew. She's been holding on to this for a while, waiting to strike.

Forwarding the email to Ash, I call him immediately.

Ash and I were right about Britney. She's a goddamn looney tune.

He picks up on the third ring as I storm across the office. "Hey, baby."

"Look at the email I've just sent you." I hit the elevator call button and wave back at Janice, making a phone shape using my thumb and pinky finger to tell her I'll call her later.

She frowns and mouths, *Everything okay?*

I shake my head, and she waves her hand, pointing at the elevator, telling me to go.

"What the fuck?" Ash roars down the phone. "That's not me."

I roll my eyes. "Of course, it's not. It's Wade. She's clearly never seen you naked." I lower my voice so none of my employees can hear.

"I may have just vomited in my mouth."

Even in a crisis, he makes me laugh. "I'm about to go into the elevator. I'll lose reception, but I'll call you when I get into my car. Can you check the house security footage from the day we found her in the house?"

"On it."

"Then call the police." I shoot off my instructions.

"That too."

"And Ash?" What is taking so long? I hit the call button on the wall again.

"Yeah?"

"Burn my dressing gown." I'm so happy to be moving out of the house. She's tainted it. "Oh, my God," I exclaim as a thought drops into my head.

"What is it, Lily?" Ash rushes in with his question.

"Check the safe. It has a dvd of us... you know?" I can't say having sex because I'm still within earshot of my staff.

"Fuck. I'll check that first, but it has three codes you have to bypass to get into it. It's impossible."

He's right. I'm overthinking everything.

I hear him running down the stairs of the house. "Just get here as fast as you can," he pants.

"On it."

Several *beeps* drift down the phone. It's the sound of Ash opening the safe. "It's still there."

My shoulders sag with relief as I step inside the elevator when it arrives. "She won't get away with this." I push the basement button on the panel to take me to my car.

"Oh, I'm not letting her get away with anything." He's firm with his reply. "We're unbreakable. You know that, baby?"

"I do."

She messed with the wrong tiger and bear; we're ferocious together.

Now hear us roar.

CHAPTER FORTY-FOUR

Lily – Four Months Later

It's the Stanley Cup Final, and the Eagles made it without Ash.

He knew they could do it. After all, with Brayden as one of the assistant coaches, they were always going to make it.

They still haven't replaced Ash yet, but they will before the new season begins. No one is indispensable.

Named after his father, the Theodore Johansson Hockey Training Facility is fully up and running. Almost full, there are only two slots available to work with Ash next season.

And the best thing about him opening the facility? When he has press and media interviews, they come to him instead of the other way around. Sports broadcasters and hockey journalists, including ex-hockey players, are fascinated with his new venture.

He maintains it's the best thing he's ever done besides marrying me, and I have to agree with him. Our lives have changed in so many positive ways in such a short time.

And it's about to get even better.

Following Britney's lame attempt at blackmail, where we discovered we weren't the only hockey couple she had tried it with, she was charged with several counts of extortion and is awaiting trial. While Ash and I are not pressing charges, many others are. We both agreed she didn't deserve our energy. Instead, we took out an injunction, which means she can't come within one hundred yards of either of us and no contact whatsoever. However, we won't need it if she ends up in prison, which is most likely, given the scale of her extortion demands.

Regardless of her efforts, Ash was right, she couldn't break the unbreakable.

Enjoying watching the opening fanfare, the screaming and shouting of all the fans as each of the players gets announced onto the ice takes me back to the evening he asked me to marry him.

Much like that night, when I stood around the edge of the rink with Bree and Candy, Ash and I are down by the boards, waiting to be called on to the rink. They are presenting him with an honorary member of the Eagles hockey team. Alongside his father, he will go down in history.

Finally, the red carpet is laid out for Ash and as we step into the rink, the fans go crazy, shouting and screaming his name. Squeezing my hand as we walk into the middle of the rink, with his other he's waving and grinning his face off.

Over the course of his twenty-year NHL career, and sitting just below his father, Ash holds firmly in second place for scoring the most goals, points, and assists in the league.

Regardless, in my eyes, he's my number one.

Approaching the players, Ash works his way down the

line, shaking each and every one of their hands, wishing them well and good luck for the game.

I make myself busy chatting to Dustin, Ash's former boss, and make small talk with the other members of the management team. They've all come out for him tonight.

Overhead, the commentator draws our attention to the giant television screens lit up overhead.

Arm around my shoulder, Ash and I look up to watch a beautifully curated video spanning Ash's career. Photos of him signing his contract, hugging his father when he played his first game with the Eagles, Stanley Cup wins, video footage, a full timeline of his career, including him asking me to marry him, along with dozens and dozens of funny moments and snippets in time move across the screens to "Best Day of My Life" by American Authors. It captures all the brilliant moments of his career as a player and coach, photos with the fans, the players, his old teammates. It's so emotional, I can't stop the happy tears from flowing.

I know I will be in pieces when they do the speeches after this and when they raise his giant jersey with his name and number on to retire his number. Ash's number eleven will be retired not just from the team, but from the league. He's a huge deal in the NHL.

My husband is a star. A beautiful, bright, shining supernova.

Scratch that, he's the entire galaxy.

In giant yellow and blue letters, his name appears across the screen, then a G, an O, an A, and lastly, a T, flash one after the other in time to the music. But then everyone laughs when the words, *Although his father still holds that record...* scrolls across the screen.

The music seamlessly mixes into the uplifting beat of "On Top of the World" by Imagine Dragons, which I helped to choose for this moment, and the words *...so, instead we'll call you the daddy...*

He frowns as the words disappear and change to an ultrasound photo of a baby.

You're going to be a daddy, Ash... congratulations Ash & Lily!

The loudness of the wild clapping and whopping from the fans almost shakes the arena, and it takes a few minutes for Ash to comprehend what he's reading.

Eyes popping out of his head, he looks down at me and gasps. "Are you?"

I hold up a newborn baby sized jersey with his number and name on the back. With a huge smile that reaches my heart, I nod my head fast. "Yes." I have to shout over the noise to be heard.

I only found out two days ago, so I'm still processing it myself. Never been one to have regular periods, I didn't think anything of it when I hadn't had one for three months.

For weeks, I've felt odd, and a little dizzy. At first, I thought I had a stomach flu, however, after days of it not getting any better, I visited the doctor. And after a few tests, she said the words I thought I would never hear. *"Congratulations, you're pregnant."*

I have been bursting to tell Ash and could barely contain myself.

Just as I was walking out of the doctor's office, Carter, the Eagles' videographer, called to ask for some behind the scenes footage of Ash and me together. I've known Carter for over ten years; I trust him implicitly and I couldn't resist sharing our news.

I asked him to keep it a secret. That's when we both came up with the idea to break the news this way. It seemed fitting. The Eagles have played a huge part in both of our lives and sharing it with fans seemed right, as if we've come full circle.

Ash opens his mouth to say something, then closes it again.

He spins around to face me and points at his chest. "I'm going to be a dad? And you a mom?" Emotion makes his eyes fill with tears.

"Yes." I throw my arms around his neck and kiss him.

Excitedly, he lifts me up and wraps my legs around his waist, the same way he did all those years ago, just like my favorite photo of us that sits next to my bedside.

The flame between us never went out.

It was there all along.

We took big swings to get us here.

And the love between us burns hotter than a raging inferno.

"This is the best day of my life," he shouts in my ear, almost bursting my ear drum.

"We're only getting started, Ash."

The End… It's really their beginning…

PART 3

THE FUTURE

FIVE YEARS LATER

"We are so blessed."

EPILOGUE

Ash

"This is not exactly how I imagined our first vacation in Hawaii." Lily lays back on her chaise lounge, enjoying the sunshine around the edge of the pool.

"No, it's even better." Buster throws our son, Theo, now four, into the air, and then down into the aqua blue water, making him squeal with delight. Our adorable two-year-old daughter, Grace, tweets in her little voice, "Me, me. Uncle Buster, me, now." She claps her little hands together with excitement.

Named after my father, we thought Theo was a miracle, but when Lily fell pregnant again with Grace, who is named after Lily's mom, we were in complete shock.

We are so blessed.

Lorna, the fertility specialist, didn't just work her magic once, or twice but—

"I think this little one is playing hockey with my kidneys." Lily rubs her swollen belly.

—three times.

Reducing Lily's stress levels, focusing on her nutrition

and overall well-being was the key we needed to conceive. The anxiety of falling pregnant was consuming her before and taking the holistic approach supported Lily completely; it was magic. All of it.

Smiling, I push my sunglasses up my nose. "It might be another girl."

"Nope, it's a boy," she says confidently.

She's probably right. She was on the money with both Theo and Grace.

Sun-kissed and looking more beautiful with each year that passes, I reach over and rest my hand on her moving stomach. "That's his butt." Lily laughs, laying her hand over mine.

"Or a foot," I suggest. Whatever it is, it's incredible and always makes me feel like a first-time dad all over again.

Gemma jumps into the pool, swims over to Buster, and jumps onto his back.

"When do you think those two will finally get together?" I ask Lily.

"As soon as your other friend, Leon, confesses that he's in love with your sister." Doing nothing to hide her amusement, her lips pull to the side.

"Erika isn't interested in Leon," I scoff. "And Leon isn't *in love* with Erika."

Lily pushes her sunglasses onto the top of her head and quirks a brow. "Are you sure about that?"

"Erika has a boyfriend, she's not interested in Leon," I state. He's a fucking douche canoe and she could do so much better than Mr. I'm Getting a Record Deal soon. Although, I can't see that happening. Not ever. Trust me, we were invited to his open mic night, and I cringed through every note he couldn't hit.

Lily swivels around to face me and sits upright, cross

legged. Her belly sticking out in front of her, she looks like she swallowed a beach ball. "Admit it. Had it not been for you, Leon and Erika would be together."

"That's not true." I lift my cold bottle of water to my lips and take a glug.

"Ash, you warn Leon away from Erika at every opportunity. Have you ever wondered why Leon hasn't had a girlfriend in, what is it, eight years?"

"It's not because of me." I feel oddly sweaty, and it's not from the heat of the scorching sun.

Her brows shoot up into her hairline. "It has everything to do with you. What if Leon is the love of Erika's life?"

I snort. "Impossible."

Lily grabs her tummy, alluding to the miracle she is carrying. "Nothing is impossible."

Shit, she's never wrong about anything.

As if reading my mind, she says, "What if I am right, Ash?"

I hold my hands up in mock surrender. "Okay, I won't say anything anymore." Otherwise, Lily will bust my balls.

Changing the subject, I ask, "We can stay on for another week if you would like?" Having flexible work schedules means there is no pressure to be home for a specific date.

"I would love that." Lily stretches her arms up over her head. "Let's make it two weeks."

Our life has changed beyond all recognition. But more than anything, it's full of love and joy and every day I fall deeper and deeper in love with Lily.

"Swim with me?" She holds out her hand for me to pull her up.

I place my feet flat on the ground and push myself to my full height. "I'd rather skate with you."

"That's a little difficult, given the climate." She giggles.

I look down at her. "It's hotter than fire here."

"And you much prefer the freezing temperatures of an ice rink." She moves up onto her tiptoes and kisses my lips. At the age of four, the same age I started skating, Theo's already incredibly talented on the ice.

"Which reminds me." She arches her back, trying to ease her back pain. "How do you like the name Blaze?" Lily runs her pointer finger down between my pecs. "I thought it was a nice mix of your name, Ash, and my nickname. Flaming orange like the color of a tiger lily."

"I much prefer Wynter for ice." I trace my finger down her nose and across her top lip.

"Blaze Wynter Johansson." She joins our suggested names together.

"Now, that's a good hockey name player if ever I heard one."

"Like fire and ice," she says, laughing.

"The best combination, Tiger."

Want more of Ash and Lily? Then download their short and spicy extended epilogue when Ash takes Lily by surprise and treats her to a special date night: https://dl.bookfunnel.com/5dmwbvlqsp

The Series Continues... Dive into Wade's story...
Wild Blades, Book 2 in the Elite Eagles Series
mybook.to/wildblades

ALSO BY VH NICOLSON

The Triple Trouble Series

Hunting Eden (Book 1):

mybook.to/huntingeden_VHNicolson

Inevitable Ella (Book 2):

mybook.to/inevitableella_VHN

Unexpected Eva (Book 3):

mybook.to/unexpectedeva

The Boys of Castleview Cove

Lincoln (Book 1):

mybook.to/LincolnVHNicolson

Jacob (Book 2):

mybook.to/Jacob_VHNicolson

Owen (Book 3):

mybook.to/OwenVHNicolson

Elite Eagles

Frozen Flames (Book 1):

mybook.to/FrozenFlames_VHN

Wild Blades (Book 2):

mybook.to/wildblades

ACKNOWLEDGMENTS

Firstly, I'm going to start by giving my beta readers the biggest shout out... Nicki (for your incredible hockey knowledge and never-ending support), Lizzy (for making my words less complicated and endless love for my work), Rita (for ensuring I get all the Canadian words right and loving Ash and Lily - HARD), Casey (for your incredible edits and freaking beautiful messages), Lynn (for your beautiful and impactful developmental suggestions), and Carolann (for all your enthusiastic WhatsApp messages), thank you for reading every chapter, in every detail. I appreciate the time you all took out of your busy days to read Ash and Lily's story. I will forever be grateful for your notes, voice messages and emails. Even when I asked question after question, adding and tweaking chapters, you girls had my back, and I know I have the best beta team on the planet. You girls rock!

To my husband, Paul, who was, and always is, a powerhouse of daily positivity and encouragement, thank you. I couldn't do this without you, babes.

A huge THANK YOU to Sarah, (AKA Sidenote Sarah, that's not her official title, it's what I call her) my editor at The Word Emporium. Your sidenotes always fill me with joy, often laughter, and I love how much you push me to be a better writer. Also the sidenotes like... *"I don't understand what you mean here, Vicki"* always make me chuckle because half the time, when I read it back, neither do I

Sarah! So thank you for your patience and knowledge. You really are a star.

To all of the book bloggers, my review team, and street team, the bookstagrammers and booktokers, a huge thank you for all of your support and the beautiful graphics and videos you create, every day you blow me away.

And to you, the spicy book reader, I write because you keep me going and I can not thank you enough for taking a leap of faith on a new-ish indie author, and continuing to support my author journey. You have no idea how much that means to me, I am eternally grateful and without you, I wouldn't be doing the job I love. THANK YOU! Mwah x

ABOUT THE AUTHOR

Since writing her first contemporary romance novel over lockdown, Vicki is now completely smitten with writing love stories with happily ever afters. VH Nicolson was born and raised along the breathtaking coastline in North East Fife in Scotland. For more than two decades she's worked throughout the UK and abroad within the creative marketing and design industry, as a branding strategist and stylist, editor of a magazine and sub-editor of a newspaper. Married to her soul mate, they have one son. She has a weakness for buying too many quirky sparkly jumpers, eating Belgium buns, and walking the endless beaches that surround her beautiful Scottish hometown she's now moved back to.

Website: vhnicolsonauthor.com
Facebook Group:
bit.ly/VHNicolsonFacebookReaderGroup

www.ingramcontent.com/pod-product-compliance
Lightning Source LLC
Chambersburg PA
CBHW052211160425
25271CB00014B/97

* 9 7 9 8 8 6 8 4 5 0 2 4 2 *